an addicted novel

KRISTA & BECCA RITCHIE

2020 Paperback Edition

This book is a work of fiction. Names, characters, places, and incidents either are products of the authors' imagination or are used fictitiously. Any resemblance to actual persons, living or dead, events, or locales is entirely coincidental.

Cover Design by Twin Cove Designs

ISBN: 978-1-950165-98-8

Addicted Series

Recommended Reading Order

Addicted to You (Addicted #1)

Ricochet (Addicted #2)

Addicted for Now (Addicted #3)

Kiss the Sky (Spin-Off: Calloway Sisters #1)

Hothouse Flower (Calloway Sisters #2)

Thrive (Addicted #4)

Addicted After All (Addicted #5)

Fuel the Fire (Calloway Sisters #3)

Long Way Down (Calloway Sisters #4)

Some Kind of Perfect (Epilogue Novel)

Prologue

2 Years : 05 Months

LILY CALLOWAY

Life moves too slowly.

Loren Hale told me that once. When we were sixteen, lying on his bed with comic books spread around us. He clutched a bottle of Maker's Mark to his chest and took a long swig.

For Lo—one minute on this Earth was a century. He was waiting for someone to end the pain of living.

Today he told me: Life moves too quickly.

After these two years, I have to agree.

Life does move too quickly. And I can't predict a second of it.

Part One

"You know I am not good with words.

Or anything else."

– Laura Kinney, X-23 Vol 3 #1

LILY CALLOWAY

Whenever I envisioned my twenty-first birthday, it included lots of booze, maybe some drugs, and a giant pack of male strippers. A *giant* pack. Possibly even the kind of strippers that give you a little something special at the end. That imagination belonged to a different Lily. From a different time. Possibly a different cosmic universe. At least that's what it feels like.

My twenty-first birthday, in actuality, is far less toxic. And the only men I'm celebrating with happen to be my boyfriend and his brother—as far from male strippers as I can get.

In fact, I had proposed a nice birthday in front of the television, but Lo dragged me out of the house, seducing me with my favorite place in Philly: Lucky's Diner. I previously told my sisters that I would not be having a party, and this impromptu event resulted after Lo found out. Now I kinda wish I invited Rose or Daisy or even my eldest sister Poppy.

A long wave of awkward silence passes between Ryke and me, and I silently beg Lo to return to the table. But he stands by the hostess podium, still talking to the manager about closing the blinds.

Ten cameramen are stationed outside of the diner, some heftier cameras perched on their shoulders, the lenses pressed to the glass window. A week ago we learned that Ryke's mom leaked my sex addiction to the press, the reason I am now on the front page of tabloids and discussed across social media.

Ryke keeps blaming himself, even when we tell him not to. If anything, this is all *my* fault. I'm the one who went down this path. If it wasn't true, it'd be a different story, right? But I'm a sex addict. Everyone knows it. And now we have to figure out how to deal with this spotlight.

The quiet grates on me, and I instantly break it without thinking. "You know what's funny, I always thought today would consist of a pack of male strippers," I blurt out. *Why, Lily, why?* I look anywhere but his face, already feeling my cheeks heat.

"A pack?" Ryke says in disbelief. "Men are fucking people too, Lily. Can you not talk about them like you're ordering a case of beer? And… what the fuck?"

I think he should have started with *what the fuck*. But I let that go.

He adds, "Don't tell me you used to look at men and only saw another dick to ride."

I flush but manage to reply despite my embarrassment. "*Used* to. Key word. Past tense," I say quickly. "Now I see all the other anatomy." I wave my hands towards him and then realize what I'm doing. "Not that I *ever* thought about you as just a dick. I mean, I thought you were a dick, but the metaphorical kind. Not the kind I would ride." Holy shit. I just need to shut up.

"You have some serious fucking issues, Calloway," Ryke snaps.

"So says you and the rest of world," I mutter and tear open a packet of sugar. I try hard to avoid the cameras that *click click click* behind the giant glass window.

His eyes soften and he shakes his head before letting out a gnarled groan. "Look," he says, "it's your birthday. I didn't get you anything—"

"I didn't expect you to."

"Let me fucking finish."

I roast again.

And he shakes his head. "You have to stop, Lily. Everything I say isn't sexual."

"Sorry," I mumble.

"I was going to say, I didn't get you anything *yet*. What would you like?"

What would I like? There are too many things I want, but most of them have to be acquired by supernatural forces.

"Are you a warlock?" I end up asking him.

"What?" His eyebrows knot.

"Never mind," I mumble quickly. The cameras suddenly flash in quick succession. I slouch further in the booth, so low that I'm practically hiding underneath the table.

"Get a fucking grip." Ryke glares.

"You shouldn't even be here," I hiss. I don't know why I'm hissing. The diner isn't even half-full, but I'm sure it'll be packed within the hour now that we're here.

"I was invited," Ryke retorts.

"By Lo," I whisper, "who somehow forgot that the press thinks you and I are hooking up. We don't need to give them another reason."

"So because I'm having lunch with my brother and his fiancée, we're obviously fucking." He gives me a hard look. "Makes complete sense."

"Don't say the f-word," I reply. "It gives me hives."

He glowers. "You're getting married in less than a year. That isn't fucking changing, Lily. You're going to have to accept it."

"I accept *nothing*," I say lamely.

He rolls his eyes. "You've stopped making sense ten minutes ago."

I'm about to refute, but Lo walks back to our booth, his cheekbones sharpened in aggravation. Shit. As he slides in next to me, he swiftly grabs my arm to lift me from my slouched position, as if it was the most natural course of action for him, as though he's done this a thousand times with me.

Has he?

All I know for certain is that my hiding place is gone.

Damn.

"He won't close the blinds," Lo tells us. "He says that it's good publicity for the diner." At least they were honest and upfront about it.

"Maybe we should leave." I throw it out there. Just like that. *Wow that feels better.* I wait for one of them to catch it. I spring up from the table, already expecting them to agree.

"No," Lo says, his hand on my shoulder, forcing my butt back to the seat. *Double damn.* "Today's your birthday, and you haven't been out of the house in a week." His arm fits around my waist, and I take a deep breath and lean into his warm body. I would like to admit that all my thoughts are chaste in this moment, but a brief flicker of a naked Lo fills my mind.

Of his muscles, his lean body…Naked Lo has a nice ass and a very large—

"Again," Ryke says roughly, eyes on me, crushing my dirty thoughts. "What do you want for your birthday?"

Cock.

I have to close my eyes while I curse my brain from automatically jumping to *that*.

"She wants something that you can't give her," Lo answers for me.

"Like telekinesis and teleportation," I blurt out, just in case Lo was thinking about the other thing Ryke can't give me.

"I was referring to sex, but that too, yeah," Lo says. Today isn't going so well. Nope.

I hide my face in my hands and I wait for the perfunctory *click click click* of the cameras. Any second now.

Click.

Click

Click

There it is.

I don't come out from my hand-fort.

"Lily…" Lo starts, concern in his voice.

"I don't want to talk about sex or cock," I blurt out.

A man clears his throat.

Shit.

I look over guiltily. The waiter stands at the end of the table with his notepad in hand. His gaze lands anywhere but on me. I might as well wear a walking road sign that says: Pervert and Sex Addict.

"What can I get you to drink?" he asks.

"Waters all around," Lo orders. The waiter leaves, and the diner door jingles as more young people enter: teenagers or college students. They gather in a nearby booth and whip out their cellphones, snapping photos.

Hibernating in our home sounds much more pleasant than this. Maybe the bears know something we don't.

Ryke unzips his leather jacket. "It's your twenty-first birthday; does that mean you're drinking tonight?" He sets the jacket aside, wearing a plain gray tee.

"No," I shake my head. "I'm going to forgo those traditions." My reasons extend beyond Lo being a recovering alcoholic. I want to remember tonight, especially if it involves sex.

"She lived vicariously through my twenty-first," Lo adds. I did. It wasn't pleasant.

Someone bangs on the window by my ear, and I jump so fast that I knock my water glass over. Ryke curses under his breath and mops up the spill with a napkin before I have the chance.

A cameraman raps the glass with his fist again, and my eyes gullibly follow the noise.

The flashes go off like busted light bulbs. And then the table of teenagers erupts in laughter, their gazes flitting to our booth and back away. My nerves spike, especially as more and more bells clink together, signaling a rush of people entering Lucky's.

We're going to suffocate in here or be attacked or worse. There's always a worse.

And I let Garth, my bodyguard, go home early. Mob mentality will overtake three people. Two's a company, three's a crowd, right? That makes four a mob. We're down a man.

"Lily, calm down," Lo whispers, his palm on my cheek, his thumb stroking my smooth skin. "Hey, what's going on in your head?"

Nonsense. Fear. All of the above.

I don't have a chance to answer him. The waiter returns with his notepad in hand, ready to take our orders. I haven't even looked at the words on the menu (even if I almost know it by heart).

The sad thing: I'm craving a hot dog. Literally. But I know photographs of me, mouth wide open with a wiener between my lips, will end up on the front page of every tabloid. Could I cut it up and eat it? Maybe, but it's not the same.

My eyes drift along the salad options, slowly jettisoning my stomach's cravings.

"And you?" the waiter asks me. I didn't even hear what Lo chose.

"I'll…just have the soup of the day." Safe. But I can't hide the disappointment from my face as I pass the plastic menu to the waiter.

Lo stares at me like I grew three horns. "You hate broccoli and cheddar soup." Oh. That's right.

"Maybe theirs is better." I shrug, avoiding his amber eyes.

Then Lo starts to climb out of the booth. The teenage girls squeal because he's about five feet from their table. He never breaks his focus from me. "I need to talk to you." He nods to the bathroom.

Ryke's brows rise. "That's not fucking suspicious at all."

Lo sets his hands on the table and leans closer to his brother. "I can talk in front of *you* but not the fifty other people in this place."

Just as he finishes his declaration, another group of people breezes into the diner and collects behind a growing line.

Now there are no free tables.

My thighs squeak against the cheap plastic seat as I scoot towards the end of the booth. Loren straightens up and waits for me. When I've successfully left my hiding spot behind, Lo rests a hand on the small of my back and guides me to the bathroom.

Chapter 2

0 Years : 00 Months

August

LILY CALLOWAY

We enter the unisex bathroom, the single kind without stalls. As soon as the door shuts, he flips the lock.

When he faces me, his eyes cloak with unmistakable concern. “What’s wrong?”

Great. I’m so transparent that he’s pulled me away for a powwow in the bathroom—over hot dogs. It’s slightly pathetic, which is why I blurt out, “Nothing.”

He grinds his teeth. “Lily.”

“Lo.”

“Don’t *Lo* me. You’re upset and not telling me why.” He crosses his arms over his chest and blocks the door, maybe realizing I’d be darting out of it right about now. “We’re not leaving until you explain.”

“You’re making a dramatic scene over nothing,” I whisper-hiss. “Seriously, you’re gonna feel awfully stupid.”

"Why are you whispering?" he asks. "And let me decide if it's stupid or not, Lil."

I let out a defeated sigh. "Hot dogs," I confess. "I wanted a hot dog for lunch." I wait for laughter and the *seriously, Lily?* but it never comes. He stares at me for a long moment, processing, and his brows begin to bunch together in this frustrated manner.

"I'm sorry," he says softly.

I shake my head. "Sorry should be saved for rejections to colleges, breakups and funerals. Not for a girl who can't eat phallic foods in public."

"You know this is more than that."

I suppose my life has been changing a lot these past few months. I was never normal, but the fact that this scandal has taken away the *option* of being normal—that hurts. I contemplate everything for a second.

Then I mutter, "I just don't want to feel sorry for myself anymore." I don't deserve to wallow in self-pity. Like my mom has said numerous times, this is my bed, and I'm going to have to sleep in it, dirty sheets and all.

He walks forward, closer, and my heart thumps with each inch squashed between us. When his arms wrap around my neck, it takes all of my energy to stay flat on my feet and not jump him right here.

I stay grounded and channel my inner-statue, probably the least sexy posture I can muster.

"I'm proud of you," he tells me. "As long as 'not feeling sorry for yourself' doesn't connote holing up at home."

"Maybe a little. Like half. Half-connotes," I admit.

He tries really hard not to smile, so I suppose I win. Or half-win. Or would that be a draw?

His heady amber eyes fall to my lips, and my heart bashes against my ribcage, as if telling me *now now now.* But I don't say a word.

His hand slowly rises up my neck, clutching the back of my head while his gaze devours me whole. Any chance to breathe has been thwarted by the desire fueled in his eyes, the one that I'm sure I share. My lips part, and he watches me closely, his chest rising and falling in sync with mine.

He teases me first, kissing my cheek so lightly.

I whimper, "Lo."

And then his lips meet mine with carnal desperation, stealing the oxygen from my lungs. He lifts me up around his waist, his hand lost in my hair, his other keeping me firm against him. My palms disappear beneath his black crew-neck, dying at the ridges of his abs, at his closeness. I don't unbutton him.

Not yet anyway.

But the spot between my legs pulses, and I tighten my thighs around his waist so hard that he groans in arousal. He stares at me while we both catch our breath for a second.

My lower back digs into the porcelain sink, and Lo never removes his narrowed, intense gaze from mine, the one that unravels me completely, that soaks my panties and leaves me bare.

He skillfully unbuttons my jean shorts and adjusts me so they slide off both legs. His slow pace speeds my heart, fearful that it'll end at any second.

"Don't stop," I whisper, practically panting for oxygen.

"I'm not going anywhere." And then he leans closer to me, one hand braced underneath my leg so I don't fall, the other gripping the porcelain sink behind me. He pulls my panties to the side. I didn't notice him unzipping his pants—not until his erection slowly (so, so slowly) eases into me.

I gasp, my eyes almost rolling back in my head. I clutch onto his biceps while he begins to thrust deep inside of me. I am so full of

Loren Hale, in a *public* bathroom, where his needs match mine. And he's feeding into them.

For us.

"Open your eyes," he murmurs, his breath shallow as he rocks into me. "Lil."

I didn't realize they were closed. I meet his gaze, and I nearly lose it at the way he's looking at me. Lo kisses me deeply while I struggle to hold onto him without coming right there. His parted lips brush my forehead while he quickens his pace, while the intensity in his gaze matches the one in our bodies. My nerves light on fire, and with one last thrust, we both come together.

I breathe heavily while I descend off this giant cliff of bliss.

"I love you," he whispers, his mouth near my ear.

My lips rise into a small smile. "I love you too." Everything right then felt too good for words. And as he stays inside of me a little too long, I wonder if it can happen again.

Don't go there, Lily.

A strangled sound latches in my throat. Like a dying hyena. *What the hell was that?* I think it's my body wanting something it can't have and being angry at my brain.

"Shh, it's okay," Lo says. "Lil." He pulls out of me and lifts up his boxer-briefs and jeans around his waist quickly. Then he holds me entirely, his hand cupping my face.

I shut my eyes. *You don't want anymore. You don't want anymore. You're done.* I try to repeat the mantra, but I already crave that climax again, one of equal intensity. The horrible thing: I know it won't match it. I know that the second time won't beat the first, so I'll keep wanting to try again and again to reach what I just had.

And it won't come. Not until I wait longer. Maybe tomorrow. Maybe the next day.

"Look at me," Lo says forcefully, his voice no longer as sweet-natured.

Just as I comply, someone knocks on the door.

"Someone's in here!" Lo yells. And then he whispers to me, "I want this to work because if it doesn't..." He shakes his head. "I don't want to have another Wednesday like that."

I remember back to the beginning of the week, where Lo proposed, where I declared how much I wanted to follow the blacklist—the perimeters my therapist created: no public sex, stick to morning and nights, no nooners in sight. I'd never seen the list.

Until Wednesday.

We had possibly one of the worst fights in the history of our fights. It was about our fears. Like a revolving door, we were slammed with the same exact issues we've been dealing with for months.

I worry *his* needs aren't being satiated.

He worries that I'll turn to another guy to obtain what he denies me.

I remember his words so clearly. "This isn't working, Lily," he said, his eyes bloodshot. We wanted all of each other, but we were purposefully distancing ourselves so I wouldn't become a crazy, compulsive beast.

The silent, excruciating statement clung to the air: *We should break up.*

We were both crying at that point, and I felt like it was the end, like someone gutted me. We were both on the carpet, and his arms were wrapped around me. Yet, neither of us could come up with a better solution.

Two hours later, sunken with this immeasurable grief that can't be justly explained, he whispered, "Be with me."

My heart clenched. "What?" My eyes burned all over again.

He held my cheeks with his two hands, his face full of pain and love, a twisted mix that reminded me of how wrong we are for each other but how right it felt. "No more rules. Fuck the list. You're strong enough to handle sex when I'm aroused and maybe even in public too." He wiped my silent tears that fell.

"How do you know that I'm strong enough?"

"Because you're better now," he said, almost convincing me. "And you have me—sober me. I'll make sure you don't spiral out of control." His voice lowered, and his forehead touched mine. "I don't want to live if you're not living with me."

I didn't either.

And since Wednesday, our new system has actually worked, despite me struggling a few times—which I think is to be expected. But Lo hasn't fed into my compulsions. Not once.

"I'm okay now," I say, more assuredly. *I can do this.* Sex starts to drift in the back of my mind. I hear the phrase: *I don't want to live if you're not living with me.*

I can't lose Lo. I just can't.

He scans my features and then kisses my forehead before helping me step into my shorts. Another knock beats against the door. This time, it's way angrier. "Someone's in here!" Lo yells back.

The person calls through the wood, the rough voice too familiar, "Your food is getting cold." I thought Ryke would say something like: *You better not be screwing in there.* But I remember that there are *hoards* of people outside, and he doesn't want to air our dirty laundry.

"I'm still talking to my girlfriend," Lo shoots back. "Start eating without us, *bro*."

I imagine Ryke rolling his eyes. "Is that all you're doing in there?"

"*Yes*," Lo growls. "Fucking Christ, leave us alone for a goddamn minute."

"I've left you alone for twenty minutes," Ryke retorts, jiggling the knob. "Are you going to let me in?"

"No," Lo snaps, now facing the door like he's battling with it and not Ryke on the other side. "I'll be out in a second."

I finish dressing, and then I comb my hands through my post-sex hair.

"You have thirty seconds," Ryke says. "And I'm actually fucking timing you."

Lo clenches his teeth so hard, restraining from spouting off a string of insults. His hands ball into fists by his side, and it looks painful for him to just slowly turn around and face me, trying to be a better person and leave a fight behind.

My cheeks start to heat with anxiety. "You think they'll ever find out?" I whisper.

With tension still constricting his muscles, he draws me to his body and wraps his arm around my bony shoulder. "We're good at keeping secrets," he murmurs. "How is this one any different?"

Right. I exhale deeply, wiping some of the wetness by my eyes. Curse Wednesday. That moment still feels fresh, even remembering brings waterworks.

"It helps that you look upset," Lo tells me under his breath. "He'll believe we were just talking."

Good.

No one knows we're having more sex.

Not my sisters.

Not his brother.

Not Connor or even our therapist.

We don't think they'll understand, and we're both exhausted from all the voices in our lives. For once, we just want to do this together. Alone.

Lily and Lo.

Like it was before.

Only better this time.

We're stronger now.

Lo unlocks the door, but Ryke is the one to open it. The chatter from the crowded diner almost blasts me backwards, but Lo keeps me close. I realize that they're both glaring at each other—that is until Ryke scrutinizes me, trying to spot the stain of debauchery on my clothes.

My jeans are zipped and my shirt is straight and wrinkle-free, thank you very much.

"We were just talking," Lo snaps.

Either Ryke trusts Lo enough to believe him or Ryke has very bad sleuthing skills. He could never be a private investigator. Maybe ditching journalism was a good idea.

His concern shifts off his younger brother and pins to me. "You okay?" He even takes a step closer, and at the nearness, the girls in the room shriek uncontrollably and start clapping.

Someone yells, "Love triangle!"

Oh my God. No, no, no. I push Ryke back with two firm palms, and he raises his hands in defense.

Ryke sighs heavily, almost growling, and agitation hardens his jaw. "So now I can't even be concerned about you?"

"I'm *not* cheating on Lo with you." I hope *everyone* in Lucky's heard that. I almost want to stand on a chair and scream it. That's something my little sister, Daisy, would definitely do. But while the idea sounds awesome, I can't bring myself to execute the task.

What if someone throws a hamburger patty at me? Oh my God—what if they chucked a hot dog at my face? That would be my luck.

"Lily!" Lo shouts. He shakes my shoulder. "Calm down."

"I…I am calm." Am I not calm?

"You're panting like you're being chased."

I glance between the two guys who've blocked my view of the diner with their bodies, literally creating a manly wall right in front of me. I'd find it sexy if I didn't know what was behind them.

And then someone else shouts, "Three-way!"

Oh my God. *No.* I start, "I am not having sex with—"

"Let it go," Lo tells me with a dark gaze, matching his brother's. "You can scream and shout but those tabloids are going to run a fake story tomorrow and the next day. I want to fucking eat." He turns to Ryke. "Do you?"

Ryke nods. "Yeah I'm fucking starved."

Lo looks to me again. "I'm not letting anyone run us out."

They've teamed up against me.

I think I like when they're united more than when they're against each other. It gives me the confidence I need to trek over to the booth, sit down, and order the food I want.

A hot dog.

Chapter 3

0 Years : 01 Month

September

LOREN HALE

Lying to everyone we love, it's not as difficult as it seems. Maybe because we've spent more time lying than we have telling the truth. Or because I love her more than anyone else in my life.

I'm tired of having third-party opinions about Lily's sex life. She's fucking me. The only opinions that should matter are mine and hers.

And so that's how it's going to be.

Fuck everyone who thinks I'm the same self-indulgent kid who begged her to date me without letting go of my booze.

That guy is dead.

I try to ignore the comics that litter my desk in unorganized piles. Connor Cobalt would shit his pants if he sauntered into my office right now. Last week, he spent an entire hour helping me file my work, but it arrives faster than I can manage.

Halway Comics, a small indie publishing company, exploded on the internet with the headline:

LOREN HALE STARTS A NEW BUSINESS VENTURE.

Now I'm flooded with proposals from aspiring artists—and no matter how hard I try, I can never keep up.

Maybe if I gave one-hundred percent of myself to the business it'd be easier. But I'm giving maybe forty percent. I happily give the rest to Lily.

"What kind of buckle is this?" Lily fumbles with my belt, her knees on the carpet in front of my desk. The leather chair squeaks as I roll back and push her hands away.

"You're out of practice," I tease.

She gasps. "Am not." She points to my belt buckle that I slowly undo. "You're either wearing a chastity belt or you put a spell on it so it won't open from outside forces...*Alohomora*."

I freeze and give her a look. Did she...she did. She just tried to unlock it with a fucking spell. Her cheeks redden.

"I was there when you *didn't* receive your Hogwarts letter," I remind her. She cried on her eleventh birthday, and to make her feel better I got her drunk off my dad's expensive scotch.

I was a fucking idiot.

"Oh whatever, I know you try out spells when no one's around."

I don't deny it.

I unhook my belt and she points. "Look, it worked," she says with a smile.

"Ha ha," I say dryly, but I'm staring at her grin. That happens so rarely now with the press bearing down on us.

She concentrates solely on my pants, making them her mission. She tugs the jeans to my thighs, and her eyes grow big at the sight of my erection, pressing against my dark red boxer-briefs. I watch her inhale more sporadically than before.

Even if this arouses her, she's learning how to be less compulsive and insatiable. She hasn't looked at porn, masturbated or gone off the deep end in a while. That's a fucking success, especially after her rapid decline when her addiction was first publicized.

I relax back against my leather chair, and she licks her lips. My blood heats when she reaches for my cock underneath the fabric. I brush her hair away from her face, bunching her brunette strands in my fist.

Her hand works my cock just right—not too hard, not too soft. I let out a harsh breath when it springs from my boxer-briefs and her tongue barely touches the head. I reach out on my desk with my free hand and turn up the music on my iPod dock, electronic, heavy bass. I think it's Skrillex, but my mind isn't focused enough to know for sure.

Her eyes glimmer with nothing but desire, and it takes my entire energy not to fit all of me inside her mouth. She lightly squeezes my shaft, and a groan penetrates my throat, even as I try to stifle the noise. Her lips rise, and she plants a delicate kiss on my dick before slowly taking it in her mouth. *Jesus Christ.* I grip the chair with one hand, my other still holding back her hair.

She begins skillfully sucking me off. "Right there, Lil," I encourage.

My nerves light up, and I clutch her hair harder. Before I can drown in this pleasure, my door swings open. No knock. No anything. I keep my hand on her head, alarm clenching my jaw, and she quickly stops giving me a grade-A blow job.

Her mouth is permanently open in panic, and she scuttles further underneath my desk.

I have just enough time to roll my chair closer to the desk, pull up my boxer-briefs, and prepare a verbal onslaught for whatever stupid fuck just barged in here.

"You need a goddamn assistant," my father tells me, walking straight into my office without pause.

I suddenly question the attack I'd planned. Jonathan Hale would swallow my insults like he does his bourbon. Unflinchingly. Always ready for more.

"I'm sorry, did we have an appointment?" I ask roughly, not able to hold back right now, even if I wanted to.

Lily punches my shin, silently telling me to be nice. But it's my father's scowl, the one hardened and cold, that does more damage.

"Don't be a little shit," he sneers. "How are you supposed to take meetings if you don't have a waiting room with an actual living, breathing soul outside these doors?" He scans my office, appraising my bookshelves with scorn. As if they're not organized correctly.

"Maybe I'm not planning on taking any meetings," I retort. "Therefore, I don't need a waiting room."

"Sometimes I wonder if one of my fucking nannies dropped you on your head when you were a kid," he says.

My childhood "nannies" that he claims he's banged. All *ten* of them. "No," I say, "I'm just this way because of you, Dad." I flash a bitter smile that my father matches quickly.

"I came here to discuss your business." He drags a chair from the wall over to my desk, positioning it in front of me.

I go rigid, and my eyes flicker to Lily who's hiding right below. Her eyes bug, and she holds her legs to her chest. She mouths, *he's right there?*

I don't affirm her suspicions because it'll freak her out more. Instead I watch my dad pick up a plastic *X-Men* action figure that sits beside an array of other characters. I could laugh at this moment, especially as he moves Sunspot's arm, but his curiosity is layered with a dark frown and narrowed eyes. I sense the biting disapproval even before he speaks.

"You're a little old for this shit, don't you think?" Surprisingly, he sets Sunspot back where he found him.

"I run a comic book business," I remind him. "I like this *shit*."

"That doesn't mean your office should look like an eleven-year-old's bedroom." He shakes his head at the rest of the superhero paraphernalia. "Your new assistant can redecorate for you."

"I don't have the energy to deal with an assistant," I refute. I can't handle interlopers. I'd shred them apart. According to Brian, my therapist, I drive people away before they have the chance to hurt me.

If I think about how many lies I've been fed in my life and the abandonment of *two* moms, I start believing he's right. I have trust issues. But I accepted Connor, a complete stranger. I welcomed a half-brother who had lied outright to me.

Isn't that enough?

Why do I need to add more people into my fucking circle?

"Is that it?" I ask my dad. "Because you're irritating me, if you haven't noticed."

Lily shifts uneasily and tugs my pants. She wants me to calm down. I'm not going to go drink after this. I may throw something at my dad on the way out, like a pen. Or at least imagine it. But I won't drink.

"The assistant is at the bottom of the list," he says, his breath smelling of bourbon. "What about this store downstairs?"

Shit. "Superheroes & Scones," I clarify. "Lily's running it."

"And I'm financing it," he reminds me. "When is it opening?" His gaze drifts to the pile of papers on my desk. He grabs the nearest manuscript, toppling over a mug that's branded with the *Halway Comics* logo. I lean forward and put it back.

My father's face literally hardens to fucking stone the longer he flips through the comic book.

My head spins, trying to think five steps ahead of where he's at. But this is a chess game that I'll always lose. "Lily wants to take things slow, so we'll probably open it after she graduates." Which could be in a few more years.

And I like that she can hang out downstairs without crowds. I'm afraid that once we open the store, it'll be too crazy for her. Like how it's been at Lucky's. Only worse.

Because it's ours.

My dad scoffs and tosses the comic back on the table. "That's a terrible fucking business plan. You're in the press *now.* You need to capitalize on the exposure as quickly as you can."

"She's a sex addict. It's not going to be good exposure," I say, frustrated. I glance down at Lily, who no longer tugs on my jeans. She stares faraway at the carpet, her neck red like anxiety is creeping in.

I'm about to tell my dad to get out, but his brutal glare silences me. "Loren." He says my name like I'm a complete fucking moron. "When you're making something out of nothing, bad press is good press. But when you've already established a reputation, bad press can kill you." He points at me. "You have nothing right now. Bad press is what you need. Use it. Don't be stupid."

I just don't want Lily to feel like she lost out on something else because of the media. We didn't expect the attention to last for this long and to just keep on escalating. At this point, I don't think it'll ever die down. There's just too much interest in my relationship with her and my half-brother.

It's like a tabloid's wet dream.

"I need more time," I tell him, trying to find a fucking excuse. "It's not ready yet. We still have inventory that needs to arrive—"

"I was just down there. If it's not already stocked, then you're overstocked." He stands up. "It opens by the end of this month, and if you don't set a date then I'll put an ad in the paper myself, and you'll just have to fucking deal with the line outside this building."

I grip the edge of the table, my teeth aching as I shut my mouth. *You're okay.* It's a dumb pep talk considering all I want to do is explode... and yeah, a bottle of Jameson sounds great.

He stops by the door to adjust his tie. "Also, word of advice. If you want to have blow jobs in your office, you really do need an assistant."

What the fuck?

My face falls.

My dad looks at the desk like he can see right through it. He can't. "Lily, try not to breathe so heavily next time. You give yourself away." With that, he saunters out of my office and out of fucking sight.

Just like my dad to have an exit as dramatic as his entrance.

"Oh my God," Lily says with wide eyes, not crawling out yet. I look down at her splotchy red face. She's way more embarrassed than me.

"Don't worry about it," I tell her. "We've both seen him come home after a one-night stand before." If a woman wasn't leaving with smudged makeup in the morning, then he was coming inside the house at 10 a.m.—fully clothed in his suit from the previous night.

No shame.

Ever.

My father doesn't work *that* late unless he's getting laid.

She doesn't say anything.

I roll my chair back and dip my head down to meet her gaze. "Come out."

She's immobile. I think I may have to pull her out. Which, oddly, wouldn't be the first time I've had to retrieve my girlfriend from under a desk.

I go to raise my jeans up to my waist, and this stirs her from her hiding place. "No, I'll finish you," she tells me, crawling towards my lap.

My stomach suddenly sinks. I know I have to reject her. She's too anxious—and sex shouldn't be used to demolish those hard-hitting feelings. She has to deal. When she places her palms on my knees, I say, "No, not this time, Lil." I scoop her hands and tuck them back to her chest. Then I pull up my jeans, zipped and buttoned to solidify my choice.

Still on her knees, her shoulders sag. She looks lost. I lift her onto my lap, and she places a leg on either side of the chair, straddling me. *Christ.* I don't want to keep rejecting her, but I also selfishly don't want to move my girlfriend.

Instead of bringing up sex, she surprisingly veers into another direction. "About Superheroes & Scones…" she trails off, not able to find the words. She places her hand on my chest, no happier than she was on the ground.

The store has been a safe place for Lily away from the house, and we both know if it opens, that safe place ends.

"We can wait," I offer. Her despondent gaze is really fucking scaring me. "I can convince—"

"No," she interrupts, but my muscles keep tightening. "He's right. We should open it soon." I know she doesn't believe that. "I'll hire a general manager and just keep in contact through phone and texts, so I know what's going on…"

"Lily," I say her name but I can't say anything else. My lungs constrict, and when I look at her, all I see is a girl trapped in her own world.

Hell, she's trapped in her own fucking body. She just needs time, but no one seems to be giving it to her.

She actually turns her head to look at the space underneath the desk, like she's contemplating returning. *Don't you fucking dare crawl back there, Lil.*

Slowly, she climbs off my lap. "I'm going to go count the inventory," she says in this really soft voice, all her humor gone. My biggest fear barrels into me. Losing her.

"No you're not," I snap. "You're going to stay here and help me with this pile of shit." I wave at my desk, motioning to the comics. She considers this like it's a suggestion. It's not. I don't trust her to be alone right now.

"Please, Lil," I add. "I'm getting bogged down here. I need your help. You can do the inventory another day." That does the trick.

She walks back to the desk and picks up a thick manuscript.

It's terrifying how the both of us can ride highs and lows so quickly. She slumps down on the chair and opens a comic, her lips slightly downturned. But I'd take a Lily at a low over no Lily at all.

That's the truth.

Chapter 4

0 Years: 01 Month

September

LOREN HALE

We opened Superheroes & Scones last week. Three hours before we unlocked the doors, we had to rope off the sidewalk to contain the lines and lines of people outside. The crowds haven't died down since. The shittiest thing: We barely sell any comics. People buy a cup of coffee and sit their asses in a booth, waiting to spot Lily or me.

We're the products on display.

Lily spent the last two weeks holed up at the Princeton house, hiding from the reenergized media. I invited her to lunch, and she threw out some excuse about studying. But I know she's binge-watching a TV show.

Right now, I ignore Ryke and Connor, the latter of which accepts our drinks from a waitress. She wears a multicolored Sombrero. Apparently it was some kid's twelfth birthday, so they sang in Spanish to him and shook maracas. The boy looked pretty happy.

I focus on my cellphone and text Lil.

I'm checking Netflix when I get home.

I press send, not clarifying. She'll understand where I'm going with this.

She replies quickly. Do it. I'm studying :P – Lily

Did you just stick your tongue out at me?

:P – Lily

While adorable, the emoticon is her way of being evasive. I wish she was here. It's easier to know where her head's at when I can actually see her.

"Are you joining us for lunch, Lo?" Connor asks me as the waitress leaves us with more chips and a bowl of guacamole.

I pocket my phone and attempt to clear the frustration from my features. It's like a permanent appendage, this pissed off *I fucking hate you* look. I can't get rid of it.

I don't know how.

My gaze drifts to that young kid in the center of the Mexican restaurant, at a table for ten, probably all family surrounding him.

While he opens a present, his mom collects the tissue paper and folds it neatly.

His dad snaps photos.

I hate everything about that kid. I hate that he's smiling. I hate that more than one person hugs him. And I hate that I hate him. Why does other people's happiness have to feel like someone punching me in the gut?

"Lo," Ryke snaps.

I face my half-brother and Connor. They can barely withstand each other sometimes, so I'm surprised they've chosen seats side-by-side. "I'm here, aren't I?" I say sharply.

I lean back against my wooden chair, trying to loosen my taut muscles. We sit in the back, away from lingering eyes and the glass windows.

No cameras. No paparazzi.

It's more freeing than I can explain.

"Physically, you're here," Connor replies. "But I prefer one-hundred percent attention from people."

Ryke lets out an unamused laugh. "You never change, do you? Still a narcissist."

I eat a chip and say, "I was going to call him an attention whore."

"I'm that too," Connor agrees with a burgeoning grin. "So I love myself. Not many people can say the same thing—which is a shame."

I wait for him to look at me.

But he stares off at the salsa bar, sipping his water.

I pop another chip in my mouth and try to relax. I don't question Connor's black button-down or his expensive watch or his wavy brown, perfectly styled, hair. The guy is put together, unlike my brother who seems to have rolled out of bed, disheveled dark brown hair, unshaven jaw and a University of Pennsylvania track T-shirt.

I think I fit somewhere in between.

At least I hope so.

"How's Lily?" Connor asks me.

"How's Rose?" I deflect and reach for my drink. A water.

"Busy. High-strung. You know she took over the wedding planning from Samantha?"

"Yeah." *I know.* "Lily and her mom aren't on speaking terms yet." I don't know if they'll ever patch things up. It's so complicated that I'm not sure if opening lines of communication is the right move. Lily was destroyed after her mom told her that she was a disappointment.

Samantha's whole life is about protecting her family's reputation, and her own daughter fucked with it.

Lily thinks our marriage will repair the shattered bond that she has with her mom—but I'm not holding my breath. I don't want to watch Lily's face crumble when she realizes that her mom still harbors deep-seated resentment.

So I'm counting down to our June wedding with nothing but dread.

Connor opens his mouth, and I cut him off. "Have you removed the wicked witch's chastity belt yet?" I ask, redirecting the conversation to his relationship. "Or is it still welded together?"

"Rose is still a virgin," he says like it doesn't bother him at all. He's almost been with her for an entire *year* and they've barely done anything, at least from what Lily and Connor have shared with me. Rose—she wouldn't tell me the barest detail of her relationship, even though she'd like mine advertised. Just to ensure I'm not screwing up her sister's recovery.

I'm not.

I grab a chip from the basket, waiting for the hot sauce to eat my chicken tacos. "Watch out for her nails. I wouldn't want her to mess up your pretty face."

"I'm not afraid of Rose, but thanks for the concern, darling." He winks.

I touch my heart. "Anytime, love."

Ryke rolls his eyes and slouches further in his chair, brooding. "How about save it when I'm not around?" he says.

"Homophobic?" I wonder, dunking a chip in salsa. I didn't really peg my half-brother to be like that.

"*No*," Ryke snaps like that's the furthest from the truth. "Just irritated."

I think he's just jealous of the relationship I have with Connor. It's simple. We're friends. But with Ryke—it just…it can't be like that. There's too much shit between us for it to be anything other than complicated.

Ryke takes out his phone and texts someone before setting his cell on the table near mine. When the waitress returns, we place our orders, and then three girls giggle loudly at the bar. They notice us in the back and smack each other's arms. I read their lips: *that's them.*

All wear themed sorority shirts like *Go Greek!* and *Tri and Beat Us* with running shorts. In their twenties—the kind of girls that go to the college I was expelled from.

University of Pennsylvania.

Ryke openly checks the girls out, and they nearly shriek, their eyes bulging.

"You'd think that you just gave them a ride in your Maserati," I say to my brother.

"I don't own a Maserati." *It was a figure of speech.* He stands up and tosses his napkin on the chair. "Give me five minutes."

Connor pockets his phone. "That long?"

"Fuck off," Ryke says easily before leaving to approach the girls.

I think the redhead on the end is going to faint.

They practically bounce on their bar stools, and Ryke slides in, using whatever game he has to pick them up. The short blonde with dark red lipstick speaks to Ryke, but she points right at Connor.

"Looks like one of them is into you," I tell Connor.

He waves to them in the most noncommittal way I've ever seen. Friendly, not like a brush off, but half-removed like he's silently disinterested.

"Cobalt," Ryke shouts. "They want to know your IQ."

"Higher than yours."

Ryke rolls his eyes and turns his back on us, still talking to them.

"What a pickup line," I say. "Damn, I missed the chance to use it on you." When I first met him, I was sure he was asexual. Lily suspected that he was gay. Now, I honestly don't even know what he is.

To me—he's just Connor.

Maybe that's the point.

"I wouldn't have turned you down." Connor leans back in his chair, checking his gold and black plated watch.

"Why is that?"

"You're good looking," he banters. "Not as good looking as me, but no one really is. So I wouldn't count that against you."

Before I was sober, I'd sit at a bar with Connor and people would fawn over him. Six-foot-four with those obnoxiously confident blue eyes.

Connor Cobalt is catnip for pussy and cock.

He knows it and he almost just doesn't care.

Turns out Connor *does* have a type, and she happens to be strutting through the restaurant right now. I let out an audible groan when I hear her five-inch heels and see her piercing yellow-green eyes. But Rose has zoned in on one person.

She raises her Chanel sunglasses to the top of her head, and then occupies Ryke's seat next to Connor. He greets her with a few words in French, and she replies back in the same language. His arm slides around the back of her chair, his body leaned towards her in possession.

If the girls at the bar didn't realize he was legitimately taken, they do now.

"Hey, Rose," I say unenthusiastically. "I thought you couldn't make it to lunch."

"I have ten minutes," she says, flagging down the waitress. "I thought I'd stop by just to piss you off. It's number three on my list of daily activities."

"Thought so," I say. "Is *filing your talons* number four?"

She shoots me a glare.

I shoot one back.

"Children," Connor says, "can you fight while Rose isn't near knives and Loren isn't near tables that he can flip? I find cafeteria brawls wildly amusing, but not when I'm in the crossfire."

"You've been saved," Rose tells me like a villain in a bad action flick. She's half-serious which is the stupid thing.

"Thank you, Darth Vader."

She flips me off, just as the waitress approaches and clears her throat. Rose is caught with her middle finger in the air.

I laugh—this is rich.

Rose looks hardly embarrassed. She lowers her finger and says, "I'd like a margarita, frozen, no salt."

"Can I see your ID?"

Rose pops open her clutch wallet and flashes her ID to the waitress.

"Thanks. I'll get that right out to you. Anything else?" She fixes her Sombrero.

"Yeah," I say, "a blow torch to defrost my girlfriend's sister." I smile dryly. "Thanks."

"And I'd like a fly swatter so I can smack my sister's boyfriend."

The waitress opens her mouth, partially, but no words escape.

"A margarita is all," Connor tells her with a warm smile.

She swallows. "I'll have that ready in a sec…"

When she leaves, my phone buzzes on the table. I collect it and open the text.

See you tomorrow. – Daisy

I go entirely rigid.

I flip the cell over and notice the dark green casing, unlike my black one. I accidentally picked up Ryke's phone.

Morality, ethics—I was taught to shit on them.

I don't even hesitate. I just scroll through the messages quickly, reaching the top of the conversation. My fingers rise to my lips in anxiety, my rapid thoughts drowning out Connor and Rose's French talk.

You left your shirt with me, you know. – Daisy

Keep it. – Ryke

What the fuck? I breathe heavily, dark emotions pooling into me from so many places. Some indistinguishable, others really clear. Daisy is only sixteen.

It's all I can think right now.

Back in Cancun, I made a promise—to trust Ryke, to lay off him about their growing friendship. I've been seriously *trying*.

My eyes flicker to my brother at the bar. He works the brunette girl, her figure curvy and her hand on his arm as she laughs at something he said.

She's working him just as hard too.

And I imagine Ryke messing with Daisy's head—just like that. Like she's another girl at a bar. Like he's trying to fuck her one night or for a week, maybe a month.

Nothing more.

I imagine the teasing.

The flirting.

I don't know what he's playing at with Lily's little sister, but it's not right. He can sleep with *any* girl—why does he have to go after her?

Or is he just leading her on, with no real plan to do anything more? Does he get off on that?

I'll ask him, I think. It's the only thing that stops my leg from jostling. I return to the texts.

I can just give the shirt back to you when we go riding. – Daisy

Whatever you want. Just make sure to wear fucking boots this time and not flip-flops. – Ryke

They were sandals. I also just found your shorts. I'll wear those the next time I see you too ;) – Daisy

Really?

Just wear the fucking boots, Calloway. – Ryke

You want me to ride naked? I usually don't do that until after second base. – Daisy

I'd rather you wore my shorts. – Ryke

Does it turn you on when girls wear your clothes? – Daisy

I'll see you tomorrow, Dais. – Ryke

See you tomorrow. – Daisy

That was the newest text.

"Are you okay, Lo?" Connor asks, off my volatile expression. Heat practically radiates from my muscles.

Rose twirls her straw in her margarita. I didn't even see the waitress come by again.

"I'm great," I say coldly.

Only a second or so later, Ryke returns to the table with a napkin. He sits right next to me in the free seat. "Got her number and her address." He pockets the napkin with the scribbled info. Then he reaches over and grabs his water that's near Rose.

"Does that girl know you just want to fuck her?" I ask, my voice coarse.

Tension spreads through the table, but remorse lies far off—in another realm of existence. In some good guy's body.

"Yeah," Ryke says, drawing out the word as he studies my expression. "I think she got the message when I said that I wasn't into anything serious." He pauses. "Did I do something…?"

I slide the phone across the mosaic-tiled table and set it right in front of him.

Since his chair is beside mine, he has to angle his body towards me. "You read my fucking texts?" He glowers.

"Why is she flirting with you?"

Ryke runs his hand anxiously through his thick brown hair. "It's innocent, Lo."

That's not what I wanted to hear. "Does she know that?"

"*Yes*," he forces.

"How? How does she fucking know that, Ryke? She's sixteen, and you're *leading her on*."

Rose stops sipping her margarita. "Are we talking about my little sister, here?"

"We should stay out of this, Rose," Connor tells her.

Rose snaps back at him in French, and they start arguing in the foreign language.

Ryke groans in distress and annoyance. "I'm not trying to lead her on."

I snatch the phone back from him.

"Come on, Lo," he complains.

I hold up a finger and scroll through the texts. Then I read: "*I'd rather you just wore my shorts.* What is that?"

"A joke."

I glare, two seconds from chucking his phone at his face.

"A dirty joke," he rephrases. "Okay, I know. It looks bad." He lets out a deep breath, almost growling. "You have to cut me some fucking slack. None of this is intentional. It's just how I am."

I hate that excuse. He *always* uses it. He blames his personality for everything—like it's a scapegoat. "I've never seen you talk to another girl like this."

"That's because other girls don't talk to *me* like this. She's fucking crazy and bold…" His mouth stays open like he's about to say something else, but then his lips press closed. Rethinking that last statement.

"Finish it," I snap. He's going to say she's hot. She's sexy. Whatever. It's written on his face.

He holds up his hands. "I'm done. I don't know what else to fucking tell you."

He absolutely *sucks* at relieving any sort of suspicion or anxiety that I have. "I'm trying to trust you," I retort.

"Yeah? You're not doing a good fucking job of it."

My insides twist. *You're not doing a good fucking job of it*—the words blare in the back of my head. It hurts that he'd even think that.

I lean closer to him, my heart pounding in my chest.

"You came into my life in a lie," I say. "You weren't honest about who you were, and when you came clean, I *still* let you take me to rehab. I still hang out with you, knowing that you could be lying about so much more. *That* is more blind trust than I've ever given anyone in my life. So don't tell me that I'm not doing a good job." My eyes burn. I'm giving everything I possibly can.

And it's still never enough.

"You're right," he nods a few times and rubs his jaw. "I'm sorry. You have a right to be cautious of me. I just…" He shrugs, not able to find the words. He turns away and takes a swig of water.

Sometimes I just want to shake Ryke so hard until he tells me things straight. No half-lies. No tiptoeing around me.

I just want the cold truth. All of it. Finding out later—that stings ten times worse.

Why does he have such an easy time speaking freely to other people but when it comes to *us* he hesitates? It's like our past is so dense that he refuses to crawl through it at times.

I'm stuck in it.

Like quicksand.

"Can you be honest with me?" I ask, remembering how no one told me that I was a bastard. Ryke had these answers for so long. And even when he finally met me, he kept them to himself for months. *To protect me from myself*, he basically said.

No one even gives me a chance.

They just assume I'm going to fuck up before I actually do.

I don't want to be blindsided anymore. Not by the people close to me.

Ryke stares at me for a long moment before saying, "I'd *never* sleep with Daisy." He's said as much before.

Rose suddenly rises from the table, her purse on her arm. "I have to go back to work, but next time you talk about my little sister in the context of *fucking*, be smart enough and don't do it in front of me." She drills a glare into Ryke. "She's reckless and impulsive, and despite those flaws, she's still my sister. I love her more than I will ever love any of you at this table." She pauses. "And you should know that I own a gun. I'm also a better shot than Connor." With this, she spins on her heels and walks confidently to the exit.

Connor never takes his eyes off Rose.

I'm so glad I'm not dating her.

I focus back on Ryke. "Why does Daisy have your shirt and shorts?"

"We rode to a quarry and went swimming," he explains. "My friend Sully was there. We ended up at her house…" he trails off, putting doubt in my head again.

"You mean her parent's house?"

"Yeah," he says. "Just to dry our clothes. It was closer than my apartment."

"This sounds so sketchy—"

"I know, but it's the fucking truth. I had to leave early, so I ended up just wearing an extra pair of shorts in Sully's Jeep. I left my clothes in her dryer." His Adam's apple bobs as he swallows. "I promise it wasn't anything like you're thinking." He sets an elbow on the table, angled back towards me. "I know you shouldn't trust me, but I need you to—I *want* you to. Please."

This is a moment that will define the rest of my relationship with him. I can sense it. "I'm going to ask you this one time, and I want you to be completely one-hundred percent honest with me."

Ryke nods. "Okay."

"Are you attracted to Daisy?"

He stares directly into my narrowed eyes. And he says, "No."

I try to breathe a sigh of relief, but this nagging devil on my shoulder says: *Don't believe him. Don't trust him. Don't love him.*

All he'll do is hurt you.

"Not one time? She's a model—"

"She's gorgeous," Ryke admits, "but she's sixteen, Lo. How many times do I have to say the same thing for you to fucking believe me?"

I don't know.

"And when she's eighteen?" I ask. I've never seen Ryke with a girl longer than a few weeks. I can't stomach the thought of my brother screwing over Daisy.

"No. Nothing'll change," he tells me. "I promise you that we'll always be just friends."

I nod a few times, letting this sink in, accepting it as the truth. "Okay." I pass him his phone. "I believe you."

Don't believe him.

I'm going to.

Because he's my brother, and he won't hurt me like that.

And if he betrays me—then it's my fault for letting him in.

Chapter 5

0 Years : 02 Months

October

LILY CALLOWAY

I lie on my stomach, my canopy net draped around my bed. *Too Cute! Puppies* on Animal Planet plays, and I try not to flip open the stack of tabloids beside me. Rose told me to burn the picture of me eating a hot dog, but it's still inside one of those magazines.

Burning one won't rid them all. Anyway, I think Rose just likes fire.

The door suddenly swings open, and I frantically swipe the tabloids off the mattress. They tangle in the net and hang midair. Uhh…

Lo hesitates in the door frame, his face sharpening as he looks from me to the magazines to the television puppies and back to me. "Okay, this has got to end." He slams the door and dials a number in his phone.

"What?" I kneel. "It's not porn!"

He walks further into the room and then slips his phone back in his pocket.

"Who'd you text? I thought we decided that we didn't need anyone else to deal with our problems."

"This isn't about sex," Lo says, climbing onto the bed and taking a seat beside me. He combs my hair out of my face. "This is about you, frightened to go outside, scared of the fucking paparazzi. You can't live like this. Christ, *I* can't live like this."

"It's getting worse," I tell Lo honestly. "I feel like every time I go outside with you, there's another article about how I'm a lying, cheating slut who's with Ryke." I shrug. "I figure it's easier for everyone else if I just stay here." My eyes flicker to the television. "And plus, the puppies…"

"You can watch your puppies in a park." Lo searches for the remote underneath decorative pillows.

"Hey," I say, tackling him to stop. "Baby sloths are coming on next."

"Then we can go to the zoo. *Anything* but staying cooped up here, Lil." He grabs my arms and pushes me back.

I climb on him, channeling my inner-monkey (it helps that *Chimps* was on prior to *Too Cute!*) "You can't…" I wrap my thighs around his waist, his back against the mattress now. And I try to press his arms above his head.

He rolls on top of me, basically pinning me much better than I pinned him. "Look at me," he says forcefully.

I do. I stare right into his amber eyes that seem to pull my very soul into his heart. It's so deep, so intoxicating, that I go utterly still and quiet.

"I won't lose you to anything."

"I'm not going anywhere," I whisper.

"Clearly," he says. "You can handle this. I know you can. You know you can. You just have to start believing in yourself."

I breathe in his words. "Okay." I pause. "But just after the sloths…"

Someone knocks on the door. "Is she in there?" I hear Poppy, my oldest sister.

Lo takes the time to reach above my head, grab the remote, and switch off the television.

"Don't knock," Rose says. "Just walk in." And that's when Rose barrels into our room as she normally does. She barely even acknowledges the fact that Lo is pinning me on the bed.

My cheeks start turning red. Even though we weren't even close to making out…I think. Who knows where this would've ended up after ten more minutes?

Poppy strolls in next but freezes a couple steps inside. "Oh sorry." She shields her eyes with her hand. To Rose, she says, "I told you we should have knocked again."

"Why? They're not screwing. They can't. It's the middle of the day. Right, Loren?" Rose asks. Lo slowly crawls off my body and lies next to me, propping himself on his elbows.

"Sure," he says with a sardonic smile. "You can drop your hand, Poppy. My dick isn't anywhere near your sister."

"Okay, but I still feel bad about barging into your room," Poppy says softly, lowering her hand. She gives me a warm smile. I haven't seen her much since the media crisis with the scandal. I can only imagine it's affecting her about as well as everyone else. Her brown hair is still long against her chest, her skin still sun-kissed and she still has that Monroe mole above her lip (not that she can really get rid of that).

At least these parts of her haven't changed. I can't imagine what else I've missed.

"Have you told her yet?" Rose asks Lo.

I perk up. "Told me what?" And since when do Lo and Rose conspire against me?

"We've been talking," Lo admits.

"What?" I frown and scrunch my nose. "What have you done with Loren Hale?" Although they do sort through the mail some mornings together.

"It hasn't been fun," Rose adds.

"For either of us," Lo chimes in.

Okaaay. "Someone better spill soon."

Rose stands in the center of the room, hands on her hips. Anyone can tell the difference between my older sisters by their wardrobe alone. Rose wears a black pleated dress while Poppy's in a bohemian maroon shirt and skinny jeans.

Poppy is probably easier to get along with, pretty laid-back, but I always gravitate towards my fiercest sister. She'd be a lioness on Animal Planet, for sure.

Lo slides off the bed and shuts the cracked door.

I scoot closer to Poppy, who stands by the mattress, and she actually starts braiding my hair.

"You need out of this house," Rose says.

I can't refute. I know I've been a hermit. Lucky's Diner was really my last real outing. It just got so crazy after that—and the magazines went wild with theories about Ryke and me and Lo.

As though I summoned the angel to Lo's devil—Ryke Meadows opens the door and enters the room, dressed in only track pants and what looks like a sweaty shirt thrown over his shoulder.

"What are you doing here?" I ask him, forcing my eyes to stay on his face and not his six-pack.

"I was invited to this meeting."

Meeting?

"I sent a mass text," Lo admits.

"Connor is in class," Rose tells me. "He can't come." And Daisy is in prep school. Okay…so that means: This is it.

"Does no one knock around here?" Poppy asks.

Ryke shrugs. "They shouldn't be fucking. It's the afternoon."

Rose pulls back her shoulders. "That's what I said."

Poppy stares between Lo and me with a little more concern and then she addresses Rose and Ryke. "You both realize that they have no privacy outside and *inside* their relationship, right?"

"You tell 'em, Poppy," Lo says, leaning against our dresser with crossed arms. He's smiling in amusement. Our other two siblings look like they could tear out his jugular.

"He's an addict," Rose says. "I don't trust him with our sister."

"And *she's* an addict," Ryke retorts. "I don't trust her with my brother."

Poppy raises her hands, coming in peace. I stay quiet. This is my role in my loud family. "It just seems, to me, that you both have trust issues…and maybe you need to have a little more faith in them."

"Just so everyone knows, I have a new favorite Calloway sister," Lo proclaims. He almost looks like he could high-five her.

I do like having someone completely on our side, champions for our relationship. It feels good.

"No offense," Ryke tells her. "You weren't there when they were fucking enabling each other."

"No offense," Poppy retorts, "but I've been here their whole lives. I've seen Lily when she's sad and I've seen Lo when he's angry."

Ryke just nods a few times, his shoulders relaxing. "I'm sorry then," he tells her. "I don't know you that well."

Poppy looks a little taken aback by his sudden kindness. She says quickly, "Me too."

I clap my hands. "So if that's it—"

"Not even close," Lo says.

"We're going out," Poppy explains, running her fingers through my hair as she gathers strands to braid.

"Like to a club?" My brows furrow. *That doesn't sound like a good idea.*

Rose stares at me like I've seriously lost some brain cells inside this room. "No, not to a club. There's a Comic-Con in Philly this weekend. We're all going."

My eyes light up. *Yes!* I almost bounce to my feet, but Poppy has my hair hostage.

Then my face falls as I seriously consider this. "Wait…I didn't hear about a convention." Are they lying to me? "Is this a trick?"

Lo already has his phone out and he passes it to me. I still only have a shitty flip phone without internet, which thwarts any temptations to look at porn, but it also keeps me bored. I cup his phone in my hands like it's a treasure. And then I quickly skim the advertisement for the small convention.

"Wait. Wait." My lips slowly rise in a big smile. "The director for the new *X-Men* movie is going to be there?"

Lo grins. "Yep."

"Okay, we're going." I pause. "Wait. Wait." My face falls.

"What is it?" Lo asks.

I hand him back his phone. "What about the crowds? If someone sees us, they'll stop us to take pictures or ask us questions…" I trail off. Conventions are already kind of crazy. But this craziness will surround *us.*

"That's where Lo and I have been talking," Rose says.

"We're going to dress up," Poppy cuts to the chase.

Rose glares at our oldest sister. "I was getting there."

"She seemed antsy," Poppy refutes, finishing tying my hair off. "Done."

Rose tilts her head at Poppy. "She looks five."

"She looks cute."

"Jesus Christ, she looks fine," Lo interjects. "Can we get back to the topic here?"

"Wait," I smile.

"If you say *wait* one more fucking time..." Ryke threatens, so irritated. I think my voice alone annoys him.

Whatever.

He can't burst this rare joy. "You're *all* going to dress up in costumes? For me?"

Poppy shares my smile. "I think we'd all do a lot more just to see you happy, Lily."

It's that kind of honesty that almost brings tears to my eyes. Poppy has her arm around my shoulder, a maternal force that I suddenly recognize in this moment. Even when my mother wasn't warm and kind to me, Poppy always was.

I wipe my cheek and bite my lip to keep the happy tears at bay. "I just have one question."

They wait for me to ask. The room calm and quiet, unlike before. When I talk, they all try to listen. That means...

A lot.

A whole lot.

"Who is everyone dressing up as?"

Chapter 6

0 Years : 02 Months

October

LOREN HALE

"So what's the deal with Sam?" Ryke asks, sitting on the hotel chair with an energy drink in hand, only wearing a pair of jeans.

"He's late," Connor declares as he unbuttons his white shirt. "So we all know you two will hit it off."

Ryke shoots him the middle finger.

I check my watch. "He's not that late." I almost never defend Samuel Stokes—because we don't get along.

Story of my life.

I pull my black shirt over my head, tossing it on my small duffel bag. My costume lies on the hotel bed along with Connor's. We each arrived at the convention in different cars, trying to throw off the paparazzi. Stepping out of the Princeton house wearing our costumes wasn't an option. We'd be all over the internet. The headline, **LILY CALLOWAY AND LOREN HALE GO TO PHILLY COMIC-CON**, would be enough to send Lily running back inside.

So we're changing here while Lily and her three sisters dress in another hotel room, and then we're meeting the girls downstairs at the convention floor.

"From the few handshakes we've had here and fucking there, I know absolutely nothing about the guy," Ryke says.

Connor takes off his button-down. "He's twenty-seven, the Chief Marketing and Commercial Officer of Fizzle, receiving the position purely by nepotism," he says without missing a beat. "His prior employment was Dairy Queen, and he has a four-year-old daughter with Poppy Cadence Calloway Stokes."

"Fucking fantastic," Ryke says dryly. "I asked what's his deal, not for his fucking resume, Cobalt." Ryke nods to me, looking for a better answer.

"I want to say that Sam's an asshole like the rest of us," I tell him. "But I don't think about him that much." Thinking about Sam means I have to dig through painful childhood memories. Where I threw back drinks to drown out the world. Where I vandalized houses. Where I screamed.

Where I ran.

Where I became a thing to be hated.

Samuel Stokes showed up in Poppy's life at fourteen.

I was only eight. I can't imagine that he sees me as anything more than a delinquent, rich kid.

And then, within maybe a second, a fist raps against the door.

Connor goes to greet the person on the other side, simultaneously unbuckling his belt. When Connor constantly wears collared shirts and preppy attire, it's hard to tell that he's ripped. He has better definition in his muscles than me, and I work out a lot to rid stress—but running cuts my muscle mass down.

"You're late," Connor says easily, swinging the door open. Without paying much attention to Sam, Connor returns to his wardrobe on the bed.

"Try having a four-year-old throw a tantrum over her Princess Peach costume." Sam walks further in the room, a travel-duffel slung over his shoulder. "I had to leave her at the Villanova house with Poppy's mom." Sam nods at Ryke and me in acknowledgement. "What are you two dressing as?"

I lean an arm on the television cabinet and swallow a smartass comment. "The Shirtless Wonder," I banter. "With my sidekick." I gesture to Ryke who hasn't moved his ass off the chair. My brother raises his brows and sips his drink, sizing up Sam with a long once-over.

Really Sam can be described in two words:

Pretty boy.

When he was younger, he had the whole nineties grunge look down, his hair hanging half in his eyes, like he was part of the Hansons. Now his brown hair is out of his slightly unshaven face, dressed in a plain shirt and jeans—he's the picture perfect representation of normality.

Without an ounce of humor, Sam says, "It looks like you're going as Cyclops." He motions to my navy and gold costume on the bed with a red visor: Cyclops circa 2010 comic book era. Before Bendis turned him into a villain. After he lost Jean Grey and had one of the strongest, most confident and beloved mutants by his side.

It's this Scott Summers that I love the most. Somewhere between good and bad. Somewhere between a stiff and a revolutionary.

"Caught me," I say with a half-smile.

He sets his duffel on the free bed and then glances back at Ryke. "What are you drinking?"

He shakes his energy drink can and then takes a large swig.

"Try this." Sam rummages in the pocket of his duffel before pulling out a slim black can with a lightning bolt insignia. He tosses it to Ryke, who easily catches it in one hand.

My brother reads the label. "Lightning Bolt…with an exclamation point. What is this shit?" He inspects it like Sam handed him arsenic. And then Ryke pops the fucking tab and takes a sip.

I just shake my head. How has he not died yet?

"You didn't know what it was, and yet you still drank it?" Connor says aloud. "Now I'm questioning our friendship."

"Good," Ryke says, "because I question it every fucking day."

"I remember now, why we're friends." Connor steps into his costume's black pants. "Every man needs a dog." He pauses. "*Lassie* taught me that."

I slow clap.

"Fuck you," Ryke says.

"I thought it was a compliment," Connor replies casually with a grin. "Everyone loves Lassie."

Sam sits on the edge of the bed. "You're holding an energy drink," he tells Ryke, circling back to the point. "Fizzle created it. We're unveiling the product in a few days."

"It's not bad," Ryke says, scrutinizing the Lightning Bolt! can.

"Good because if you're around Lily at all, you can't drink brands from Fizzle's competitors. It's bad marketing."

"No problem." Ryke stands and tosses his old energy drink in the wastebasket.

We all concentrate on changing clothes. Sam rises and tugs his shirt off before unzipping his duffel. I become acutely aware that he has four years on Connor and Ryke and six years on me with the way he begins commanding the room. Confident posture, assured stance—a build that would suit someone heading into the army. Not that he's ever going to enlist like his father and four brothers.

Sammy took another path in life to be with the rich and now the famous.

By the time I have the gold belt around my waist, along with tight navy pants and boots, Ryke lounges on the chair.

"You can't seriously be finished," I say, scanning his dark green leather jacket, a hood attached, and an identical colored crew-neck. Black jeans to top off his simple look.

Sam scrutinizes him. "Who are you supposed to be?"

"Green Arrow."

I shake my head in disapproval. He wore the same exact costume almost one year ago—when I first met him.

"It's the only thing I have," Ryke says to me. "And what does it fucking matter?"

"I can see your face." I point at him. "You can pretend your little hood will conceal your features, but the moment we hit the convention floor, people are going to swarm us."

"I'm going to shave," Ryke declares. "And I have black paint that I'm going to use for a mask."

"Where's your bow and arrow?" Sam asks, scanning the room for Ryke's props.

"I left them at my apartment—"

I groan.

Connor says, "Not surprised."

"Look, I already had one of the girls swing by my place and pick them up on their way. Problem solved." Probably Daisy...but I smother that suspicion. It shouldn't matter if she was the one—they're just friends. Like he said. I'd rather not put my doubts in Sam's head either.

Ryke zips up his leather jacket. "And worry about yourself, Cobalt."

"That's the thing," Connor says, "I don't have to worry about myself." He fits his black mask over his eyes and nose, shrouding half his face. "It's called confidence, in case you were confused."

"Sounds more like arrogance," Ryke says.

"Closely related," he says, not denying a thing.

Sam snaps his blue belt around his waist. "Poppy has my shield," he says to Ryke, "so do you want to stop by the girls' room with me?" He's being all buddy-buddy with my brother, which has me a bit on guard.

Connor checks his watch on the bed. "Rose already texted me that they're waiting on the ballroom level." Everyone is pretty much ready except my brother, who's been slacking. "Hurry up and shave, Ryke."

"I'll just meet you fucking down there." Ryke heads to the bathroom.

"No," Connor says. "A man never leaves his dog behind."

Ryke flips him off, not turning around as he does so. He disappears in the bathroom.

Connor grins. We end up waiting for Ryke in the doorway. Sam leans his shoulder on the wall, his arms crossed over his chest. The expression he wears—the faint humor mixed with seriousness as his lips rise—fits his character too well.

"Captain America," I say. "Aren't you glad you left your four-year-old at home? She'd learn words like *fuck off* and *fucking fuck* all within the span of thirty minutes."

"I guess I shouldn't be surprised," Sam says.

"What's that supposed to mean?" I snap back.

"He's your brother, right? Cut from the same cloth."

I don't curse as much as Ryke, not even close, but he's saying that he'd be hesitant to let his child around me. I can't do anything but glare.

Sam sighs, seeing that I'm taking offense to this. "I didn't mean anything by it other than you're both rough around the edges." I don't tear my gaze off him, and to throw up a white flag or maybe prove a point, he calls out to my brother, "Do you plan on procreating, Ryke?"

"Yeah," Ryke shouts back. "And I hope my kid is a horrible influence on yours."

Sam looks at me and outstretches his arms like *am I right?*

Yeah. My lips lift. Maybe he is.

Chapter 7

0 Years : 02 Months

October

LILY CALLOWAY

"Batman?" I stand beneath a towering figure with pink lips and broad shoulders. And I think: *Please let this be Connor Cobalt.* Within ten minutes, I lost my sisters among the costumed-clad masses. I was distracted by the best Ninja Turtle cosplay, of all things.

I'd search for the numerous Captain Americas and Black Widows, but it's easy to tell which ones aren't Sam and Poppy. Same goes for Cyclops—who'd be my first choice.

But the Batmans—I can't discern from faraway. So this is my fifth attempt at rejoining my group.

The guy lowers his head a little so his blue eyes meet mine. And then he says in a deep voice, "I am Batman."

Okaaay. "But do I know you?" I ask. I wish I could just be like: *Hey, Connor, are you messing with me?* I'd rather not shout his name too loudly.

Even though "Connor" isn't so original, people could put two and two together, right? And then they'll figure out that I'm Lily Calloway.

I straighten my blonde wig in anxiety, hoping that the glitter on my face is a good enough disguise. If it was up to me, I'd be a pink Power Ranger—totally hidden from head-to-toe. However, Rose and Lo said I need to be *partially* exposed to the world because I can't dress up all the time.

I feel *fully* exposed. I mean, these white spandex booty shorts are riding up and my top is nothing more than a boob corset with laces in the front.

And I think Batman may be checking out my cleavage, which is sparse. He can't be Connor—

"Should I know you?" Batman asks like he has gravel in his throat.

"Nope," I say. "I don't think we've crossed paths before." Off to find the next Batman. Or hopefully the right Scott Summers.

Just as I pass him, Batman sets a hand on my shoulder. "Wait, I do know you." He broke character, his voice no longer abnormally low.

My eyes bug. "No you don't." *I knew I should have been the Pink Ranger.*

"Yes I do." He smiles, which looks odd. Batman doesn't smile like that.

"I'm no one," I say stupidly and immediately blush. "Ihavetogo," I mumble that last bit out.

"I do know you," he says. "You're Emma Frost. The White Queen. Biggest bitch."

I glare.

"Hey and you kind of look like her too. Though your boobs need to be a lot bigger. It threw me off at first."

I purse my lips, feeling a little offended like Rose would. "Stop making Batman look like a pervert." As I pass, my shoulder shoves into his, and I stomp away. It's probably way more badass in my head than actuality.

Something about costumes—about being someone else—gives me a bit of confidence that I've lost since my addiction was publicized.

"You even sound like her too!" he calls out.

I turn around, walking backwards. I contemplate shooting him the middle finger, but my balls haven't grown to that size yet. Instead I squint, hoping all he sees is a fiery, narrowed gaze full of irritation.

He laughs.

Damn.

Suddenly, my back bumps into a hard chest.

I freeze.

This is a man-chest.

For sure.

"I lost something recently," he tells me.

My heart swells at the familiar voice, and I spin around to drop-dead-gorgeous cheekbones, a ruby-red visor, and lips that pull into a breathtaking smile.

"Found her," he says.

I don't know why those words almost bring tears to my eyes—but they do. They resonate deep within my soul, filling a part of me that only Loren Hale can reach.

I fling my arms around his neck, standing on the tips of my toes, and I kiss him. I feel safe in my costume and safe in his arms.

No one can stop me from loving him.

He kisses back, and he lifts me into a front piggy-back. In the middle of the ballroom floor, booths lining the walls, people milling around us.

I lose sense of everything, except the way his hands hold me close, the way his urgency, the degree of his love, matches mine.

"I missed you," I say between kisses.

He grips my ass, my legs wrapped securely around his waist, ankles crossed. All is well. "Me too, love."

We've been apart for three hours.

And then the surrounding noise escalates and breaches my happy place. Guys are whistling. Girls are clapping.

"Stick it in, Cyclops!" someone yells.

"There are kids here!" an angrier person rebuts.

"Emma Frost, looking hot!"

"Scott, stop cheating on Jean Grey!" Obviously that guy hasn't realized that Jean Grey is dead.

I break from Lo's lips for a second, the place between my legs throbbing for a harder entry, but I force the need away, shelving it as I concentrate on more important things.

Like being a spectacle *without* people even knowing our real names.

Camera flashes blind my eyes, and every fanboy and fangirl watch us like we're reenacting a scene from an *X-Men* comic.

We're not.

We're just…in love? Horny? Both. Definitely both.

"Letmedownletmedown," I slur together in haste (and fright), tapping Lo's arm.

He sets me on my feet but instantly grabs my hand, lacing his fingers with mine. "I'm not losing you again," he says. He scans our audience, and they start cheering.

"Encore! Encore!" about five people shout.

Nooooo. Well…I take it back. There will most certainly be an encore. Only no one will be watching it. Just Lo and me. Alone.

Lo draws me out of the crowds, giving them a stiff wave to say that the show is over. Now we're just part of the masses again.

"Should we go to the hotel room?" I whisper.

I can't see his eyes behind the visor, but he stares down at me with an intimidating scowl. He makes a good Scott Summers.

"Not to have sex," I amend.

"We have friends now, remember? No more fake Stacey and Charlie."

"Right," I say. *No more scapegoats.*

"And with great friends comes great responsibility," he tells me. "Like trying to listen to your sister talk without me referencing a demonic entity." He looks at me. "It's torture."

Before I can reply, someone shouts, "I see her!"

I only flinch into Lo because Daisy's voice emanates from seemingly nowhere. I whip my head around—how can she see me? And probably the least helpful thought pops up: *She'd be an awesome spy.*

"Emma!" Daisy shouts, using my character name to avoid attracting the wrong gazes. *Thank you, Daisy.*

I finally spot her...and she's sticking out of the crowd by a Cider Rose Comics booth—the indies where Lo would've put Halway if he wanted to promote. He didn't, and his father cut into him for that one.

"Is my little sister floating above people?" *What the...*I tilt my head. Her legs are as high as the heads. Is she standing on a table?

Oh.

No.

She's on someone's shoulders.

"Come on," Lo says, quickening his pace.

Daisy's short, bright orange wig molds her face. She wears a cropped white shirt and gold spandex. The giveaway of her costume happens to be orange foam suspenders that go beneath her crotch like a thong. I couldn't pull off Leeloo from *The Fifth Element* with the same vigor as Daisy.

We reach the line of indie booths, and I expect my sister to be on some stranger's body. She's way too trusting. The opposite of me, I realize.

I was wrong though.

She's on *Ryke's* shoulders. *Standing*. Not sitting.

His hands clutch her calves so firmly that I doubt she can even shift an inch. He has on the same Green Arrow outfit from last year's Halloween—oh my God, he shaved. I don't think I've ever seen Ryke completely shaven.

He looks more like Lo. I don't like it one bit.

"Hey, guys," Daisy says with a bright, beaming smile. She playfully twirls her plastic gun and aims it at no one in particular. "Have you seen any aliens that I need to kill?"

"Yeah," Lo says, "Connor should be around here somewhere with your sister."

I nudge Lo in the side. "Batman and Catwoman aren't aliens."

Lo tilts his head at me. "But Connor Cobalt and Rose Calloway might as well be."

I cover his lips, but it's too late. Those names have already drifted in the air and penetrated a few ears. I grimace. Penetrated. Ears. Ew… *bad one.*

"Fine, only Connor Cobalt then," he mumbles through my palm.

"Don't say 'you know whose' name." I drop my hand.

His brows harden. "Voldemort."

I punch him in the arm. Though I fell into that *Harry Potter* reference-trap too easily.

He mock winces. "Ow."

I take a deep breath and glance at my little sister. She now sits on Ryke's shoulders. He grabs her by the waist and lifts her off his body, dropping her on her feet—a lot less carefully than Lo usually does to me.

She lands perfectly fine, thankfully.

"She's a girl," Lo tells Ryke, motioning to Daisy who twirls her gun and searches the area for our older sisters.

"I didn't notice," Ryke says with thick sarcasm.

"Just don't be rough with her," Lo tells him, less defensively. He's trying not to jump down his brother's throat about Daisy.

"If she can't handle me, then I wouldn't have let her on my shoulders."

"I can't handle you, but you still hang around me. What do you call that?" Lo asks.

"Tough love."

Lo nods a few times, and that conversation is cut off by loud bickering.

"You can't just take my whip, Richard," she says. "It's part of my costume. You're breaking the convention's protocol."

"And you're making up rules. Are the fictional costume police going to jail me in their invisible prison?"

"Ugh! You are so…" She growls. They come into view, only about ten feet away. Rose stands with her hands perched on her hips, her black leather pants and leather jacket just as badass as her Catwoman eye-mask and ears. Her hair is sleeked back into a pony. Even in her stiletto boots, Connor stands four inches above her, appearing to have an advantage.

Batman and Catwoman are flirt-fighting.

The fangirl inside of me is singing right now.

"You love me," Connor tells her, still holding her black whip, the source of their argument.

"The more you say it, the more untrue it becomes."

"It's just the opposite." He takes a step nearer.

Rose raises her chin, not recoiling. She snaps, "So now it's Opposite Day?"

I'm fairly certain that beneath his Batman mask, a single brow arches. He has that arrogant look in his eyes, the one he wears a lot better than most people. "I didn't declare an unofficial, kind of pointless, holiday, but if you want to, go ahead. I doubt anyone will listen."

She smacks his chest. "Don't insult me, Richard."

Ryke asks, "Are we going to keep watching them?" He stands right beside me.

Lo and I nod at the same time, fixated on the couple who provide too much entertainment. No one on this planet are like these two. "Maybe you're right," I whisper to Lo. "Maybe they are extraterrestrials."

"It would explain a lot," Lo agrees.

"Like why Connor never stutters."

"Why Rose makes babies cry when she walks past them," Lo adds.

I nod. "And why Connor never has a bad hair day."

Lo laughs. "That'd be his hundred-dollar hair products."

"Oh." I pause. "Maybe his shampoo comes from space."

Ryke shakes his head at us. "You two are so fucking weird."

At that fact, Lo squeezes my hand. Today is definitely a good idea. I don't think I've felt like this since Cancun—before the media hoopla.

I don't want it to end.

I watch Rose point a threatening finger at Connor. "You're just bitter because *I* beat you at chess *four* times in a row last night. Now you're stealing my things out of spite."

Connor raises her whip, half of the black leather wrapped around his hand. "I only stole this because you were minutes from snapping it at that guy, which would have sent you to *real* jail."

"He smacked that girl's ass! Just because she was dressed in spandex—it didn't give him the right to touch her without her permission."

"I agree, but you can't whip every person that makes your blood boil."

They're only an inch or so apart now. "What if he did that to me?" she asks seriously.

He stares in her yellow-green piercing eyes for a long, long moment, reading her gaze. I still wish I had that superpower—or that smart person ability.

Finally he says, "I would've stepped in." So far, Connor hasn't really had the opportunity to protect Rose from a rude guy. Usually she does all the yelling and pushing herself before he even arrives.

"Even if you're not her boyfriend, you should have stepped in like I did."

"Clearly I'm not as moral as you, darling. You know this about me."

Rose's eyes narrow even more. Then she stomps forward, almost challengingly, and pauses for dramatic effect. With so much confidence, she grabs the back of his head and licks his face slowly, starting from his chin all the way to his nose—like a cat.

Connor stands poised, unmoving and unblinking. But his grin could shatter the world.

My smile grows. "Did she just…"

"Yeah," Lo confirms, sounding impressed. She recreated a scene from *Batman Returns* where Michelle Pfieffer licks Michael Keaton's face. I'm not sure if Rose has seen the movie or if it's just a coincidence.

"Daisy?" Ryke suddenly glances around. "*Fuck.* She ran off…" He whips around to go find her, and as he rotates, a sharper piece of his bow hooks onto the strings of my corset. With Ryke's haste (and strength), my costume *rips* right down the middle.

I gasp, my hands flying to my chest. Ohmygod.

I am naked! Nearly naked. Half-naked. Topless.

Shit.

I try to hold the costume together with just my fingers. "Lo!"

"Hey, it's okay, Lil." He spins me towards his chest and hides my body from view. Why is this happening? What Leprechaun did I piss off?

"Fuck…" Ryke says again, his hands on his head. "I'm sorry…"

"Can you go find Daisy?" Lo asks.

Ryke frowns and rocks back with shock. "Seriously?"

"Yeah. I'm going to help Lily, so…" He can't go look for my sister himself. Neither can I now that I may have, sort of, flashed a crowd of superheroes.

"I'll catch up with you once I've found her," Ryke says before he disappears.

And then a couple Disney Princesses ask, "Hey…are you Lily Calloway?" *Noooo.*

I shake my head at Ariel, envious of her shell-bra that I could definitely use right about now.

"You called him Lo," one girl says with a giddy smile, gesturing to my boyfriend / best friend / fiancé.

This is not happening.

I turn to look at Rose for more confidence. She points somewhere and mouths, *Bathroom. Now.*

"Lo…"

"I saw," he says, already leading me to the bathroom. My knuckles whiten as I try to force this stupid corset together with just the strength of my fingers. The trek to the bathroom is surprisingly fast—maybe because I was thinking about side-boob the entire time.

The door breezes open, and Rose clears out the stalls with one shout: "Can you believe it?! Michael Fassbender is outside!"

I've never heard toilets flush that quickly in my life.

When the last girl exits, Connor and Lo enter.

I am praying upon every star in the universe and galactic, habitable planets that my genius sister has a plan.

Chapter 8

0 Years : 02 Months

October

LOREN HALE

"Stop moving, Lil," I order, trying to tie the strings together on her corset. Most of the hooks are torn apart, but I find one intact.

It barely closes her top.

"Let me see," Lily says to Poppy, who's checking the internet for photos of us while Sam guards the door. Captain America's greatest duty is standing outside a girl's restroom. It'd be hilarious if Lily's eyes weren't about to pop out of her head.

"It's just a couple photos," Poppy proclaims, about to show Lily her cell.

Rose snatches the phone out of her hand, censoring my girlfriend from the news. "It's fine, Lily. Don't freak out."

"How can I *not* freak out?" she asks. "People know we're here. They could be swarming the area, ready to attack."

I raise my brows at her. "This isn't Mortal Kombat. No one is going to attack you when we step through the doors." I whisper, "You're safe, Lil. I promise."

"Technically," Connor says to Lily—I straighten up with a glare—"they only know about you *and* Lo. No one thinks we're here."

"Even better," I chime in with a bitter smile.

"I have a plan," Rose proclaims, hands on her hips.

Connor stares Rose down, his blue eyes popping among his black Batman attire. "Care to consult me first, hun? Our two brains are better than yours alone."

"No," Rose snaps with finality. "*My* brain can solve this crisis just fine."

Connor leans his back against the sink counters and crosses his arms. "And if you add my brain to yours, we'd have a much higher IQ—"

"Our combined IQs wouldn't even be humanly possible," she cuts him off.

"Exactly. We defy the impossible," he says with a smartass grin.

We'll be here all day if they don't shut up. "Okay, we get it," I interject. "You're both equally intelligent."

"We're not completely equal," Connor says.

Rose huffs. "So what? You have a higher IQ than me. I don't even want to be that smart. You know why?"

"Here we go," I mutter under my breath. When I look down at Lily, she no longer concentrates on her wardrobe malfunction. She stops shifting and leans her weight into my body. I rest my arms on her shoulders, wanting her even closer, but this'll have to be enough right now.

Rose and Connor's fights definitely push away her worries—for a moment anyway.

I'll take it.

"Why?" Connor asks casually.

"Because you see the world in a way that no one can understand."

I don't know what she means. At all.

"Why is that so bad?" he asks.

"Because you can't explain yourself without confusing people," she says. "You have to keep all of your thoughts to yourself because there's *no one* smart enough to understand you. I wouldn't want that burden. I wouldn't want to be so put off by societies' constructs only to realize that, in the end, you *have* to follow them. I wouldn't want to live as something lesser than I am."

The silence deafens the bathroom. I wear a heavy frown like Lily. I can't imagine what Connor thinks about on a day-to-day basis. So contemplating his beliefs—it's out of my reach.

"You say there's no one smart enough to understand me," Connor breathes. "Maybe you should listen to your own words, Rose. You sound pretty understanding." He pauses. "What's the plan you had in mind for Lily? We don't have much time."

Rose takes a deep breath, her collarbones sharpening. She closes that argument and focuses on Lily. "You're going to the director's panel."

"Rose," I snap. I don't want to give Lily false hope. She can't go to a panel and have people bombard her the entire time. She'll crawl into herself.

Rose holds her hand at my face like *shut up*.

I could smack it away, but I'm not letting go of my girlfriend.

Her eyes fall to Lily's. "We're switching outfits."

"What?" Lily and I say in unison.

Connor doesn't look surprised, and Poppy is nodding like it's the best idea she's ever heard.

"No one has pictures of me," Rose reminds us.

"Your boobs are bigger than mine," Lily notes. "And so is your ass."

"I don't care." Rose already plucks Lily's blonde wig off her head. "You can leave the bathroom as Catwoman and go watch the panel."

I stare hard at Rose. She's gone insane. "They have photos of *me*."

"I never said you could go with Lily. I'd tell you and Connor to switch outfits, but he's too tall for your tights."

"Spandex pants," I correct her, though Lily looks down at my crotch. Her cheeks flush. The pants are form-fitting enough to show way more than what most guys are comfortable revealing.

"*Tights*," Rose retorts, just to aggravate me. "I think I know fashion better than you."

"Whatever."

Rose unzips her leather jacket and hands it to Lily. "So you'll go with Connor, and I'll stay with Loren."

"What?" I shake my head. "No. I'm not acting like *you're* Lily. This is beyond insane, even for you."

"I think it's a good idea," Poppy chimes in.

"Maybe that red wig is bleeding into your brain," I snap. She's out of her bohemian shirts and into a Black Widow costume.

"Come on, it's just pretend," she tells me.

"Just when I thought I liked you, Poppy."

She laughs. Poppy may be the hardest person to offend. Right up there with Connor Cobalt. And then she adds, "You're good at pretend, Loren. You did it for three years with Lily."

My face contorts. She doesn't even realize what we did to each other in those three years. I used to tease the hell out of Lily. I used to touch her—and there is no way in hell I'm groping Rose. I'd rather set my hands on fire.

"It's not like you have to kiss Rose," Poppy says, reading my features well.

I cringe again. "Don't even talk about that." I glance at Connor, who should reassure me about this stupid plot where we switch girlfriends.

But he stays quiet.

"So now you don't have anything to say?" I ask him.

"Rose and Lily aren't twins, so it's not like this'll work out perfectly," he tells me. "But it'll buy Lily the time she needs to go see the panel, and that's why we're here."

"I don't have to go—" Lily starts.

"No." Rose tosses her leather jacket to her younger sister. "You're going."

"Rose, seriously, you won't fit in my outfit," Lily says, though she inspects the leather jacket with longing. Maybe this isn't the worst idea.

"Don't worry about that." Rose fishes out her sewing kit from her clutch purse. "Connor, Loren, turn around or leave while we change."

I knew that was coming.

I kiss Lily on the lips, and she grips my belt, not letting me go. "What is it?" I ask.

"I'm scared," she whispers. "But I don't want to disappoint anyone by giving up."

Without the wig, her hair's in a messy bun. I tuck a flyaway strand behind her ear. "If anyone stares, it's because you're Catwoman, not because you're Lily Calloway." *Or a sex addict.* I kiss her forehead. "You can do this, Lil."

Her hand slides along my waist, and I snatch it before she clings to me. She can't drown her anxiety with her vice.

I know this better than anyone.

"Okay?" I ask.

"Yeah," she nods more resolutely.

I leave her side to go stand next to Connor by the sinks, our backs facing the girls while they change. I imagine Rose pretending to be my girlfriend the moment we exit the bathroom, and I just shake my head at the mayhem. "Rose and I are going to kill each other five feet out the door."

"On the bright side," Connor says, "Emma Frost doesn't have a weapon." He unfurls the whip and snaps it in the air. "That could've been your ass."

"You'd like that, wouldn't you?" I banter.

He grins widely, looking less like Batman and way more like Connor Cobalt. "So much it hurts," he replies. "Just make sure you walk next to Rose and not ahead of her when you leave. She hates that."

Are you shitting me? "Anything else? I'm trying to avoid my heart being ripped out and fed to baby demons."

"I heard that," Rose retorts.

I almost spin around.

But she shrieks, "Don't you dare look, Loren! I'll literally stab your eyeball with my needle!"

"She's topless," Lily clarifies with a grunt, like she's struggling to put on her boots or pants.

I glare at the ceiling. "I'm definitely going to die today."

"You won't," Connor says. "You've lasted this long."

"True." I let out a sigh and then nod to him. "I'm surprised you're not going to try and catch a peek." As far as I know, he's never even seen Rose naked. They get off by talking more than they do by fooling around—it's kind of nuts.

"I know better," he tells me, taking his mask off, his wavy brown hair still contained, not even close to being unkempt and out of control. I pull my red visor to the top of my head and think back to how Rose described him. He has more power in his eyes without the mask, I realize.

"We're finished," Rose declares.

We both turn towards the girls who stand beside the stalls. My gaze immediately falls on Lily, standing with way more confidence in her black leather jacket and pants, less revealing.

I smile at how cute she looks in cat ears and a simple black eye-mask.

"Is anyone going to say something?" Poppy wonders.

Lily and I break our gazes at the same time, and the moment I see Rose, my jaw just fucking drops. I laugh. "Damn, Rose." She sewed the strings back on the corset, but it's much smaller on her chest, pushing up her breasts, and the silver spandex shorts might as well be underwear, riding up her ass. "You'd make a perfect Cowboy's cheerleader."

"Shut up, Loren."

"You're a terrible blonde though."

She actually flips me off.

I probably deserved that one.

Connor hasn't said a word, but I read the expression on his face really well this time. His eyes graze every inch of her, full of lust, like he's saving the image for later. Might as well. Who knows when Rose will be comfortable enough to have sex?

"Do you have something to say?" Rose asks, raising her chin like she's ready to combat him.

"You look beautiful." The sincerity is clear in his voice.

Her shoulders drop, caught off guard.

Lily approaches me and holds my hand about the same time that Rose walks up to her boyfriend.

"You know what?" Lily says, her lips curving upward.

"What?" I ask, her smile making me smile.

"Catwoman is awesome."

I'm not sure if she means Rose or the costume. Most likely both.

Right now, I kind of have to agree. Rose is strong. But so is Lily. She possesses this rare courage. It's quiet and unassuming, but it still exists. It's still just as worthy.

I rub her back and realize that Rose has her arms wrapped around Connor's neck. One of his hands dips to her ass, and she lets it sit there.

One minute they're fighting. The next minute, they're like this. I can't keep up.

I strain my ears to catch their murmured words. "I want to move in with you," Connor whispers under his breath.

My first thought: *If he lives at the Princeton house, he's going to discover that I'm fucking Lily a lot more.* Not: *Thank God I won't be the only guy under that roof.*

The addicted side of me trumps every moral part.

I'm a fucking terrible friend.

"You can't," Rose replies. "Your commute to Penn is too far…and Lily and Lo…"

"The commute is manageable, and Lo and Lily love me." He pauses. "Do you?"

"Don't manipulate me," she whispers.

"I'm not trying to. I just want to be with you more than I am now. I'll wait a few months if that's what it takes."

She nods. "Okay."

Poppy clears her throat. "I hate to interrupt, but Sam just texted me and said the crowds are starting to gather around the bathroom." Her eyes meet mine. "They're waiting for you and Lily."

Great.

Rose disentangles from her boyfriend and goes back into commander mode. "Lily, go with Connor," she orders like she's preparing for war.

I just hope there's no friendly fire.

"For Christ's sake, give her space," I say, trying not to touch Rose. She's having a hard time shielding her face from cellphone cameras. She uses the blonde wig to hide, which helps some.

We just need to reach the elevator. Connor already texted me and said they're waiting in line for the panel with Poppy and Sam.

No one noticed Lily dressed as Catwoman.

"Are you in love with Loren or Ryke?" people keep asking. Through my visor, everyone and everything is tinted red.

Rose surprisingly keeps quiet. She must be literally biting her tongue to stop from lashing out.

"Are you in a fight?" someone asks. "Why aren't you holding Lily?"

"Yeah. You always hold Lily!"

Shit.

Rose glares at me out of the corner of her eye. This is a girl who I've never even *hugged* before. Fuck, besides Connor, I've only ever seen her hug someone maybe three times in my entire life.

"She's sick," I say sharply, my voice like fucking knives right now. "So you should all back up in case you catch it."

The crowds start rocketing backwards like I said she had the bubonic plague. Jesus Christ.

"Does she have herpes?" someone asks.

Anger twists my face, my jaw clenching. "*No*," I sneer, trying to find the source of that voice. My heart beats rapidly.

"You sound awfully defensive."

I stop dead in my tracks, the cameras clicking, and now the real press shows up, pushing through glass double doors, padding along the ugly hotel carpet. About to bombard us.

"Come on, Loren," Rose says under her breath. She grips my forearm tightly and literally pulls me into the elevator. Before the doors shut, two people sprint towards us, a girl cradled in a guy's arms. I repeatedly push the button to close the metal doors. But I stop the moment they slip inside, when I recognize the girl with the bright orange wig and the guy with the green leather jacket.

"Finally we fucking found you," Ryke says, his arm underneath Daisy's legs and against her back. At first I think they're playing around, but Daisy wears a faint, pained expression.

I frown. "What happened?"

Ryke very carefully places her feet on the ground, and she leans her weight against him. "She popped her knee out of the socket doing a fucking backflip," he explains.

"I was in character," she adds, bending down to massage her knee.

"Hey, stop, Dais." He moves her hand away. "Wait for some ice first." He looks up at me and then completely freezes when he sees Rose.

"Stop looking at me like that," she snaps.

"You're wearing Lily's costume," is all he can fucking say. He's staring at Rose like he wants to bang her.

I smack the back of his head.

He blinks a few times, as though it just now registers in his brain who she is, along with her boyfriend's identity. "I'm just fucking surprised. Give me a minute to process this."

Rose fixes the wig on her head. "Process it and then move on." She looks to a confused Daisy. "It's a long story. I'll tell you in the room." She asks, "Where'd you run off to anyway?"

"Outside," she tells her. "I just needed some fresh air." The elevator abruptly stops on our floor, and Daisy almost topples over, teetering on one leg. Without asking, Ryke swiftly lifts Daisy back in his arms. A smile spreads across her face.

I internally shake my head. Then my phone buzzes in my belt, distracting me. I take it out.

> This is the second best day of my life. The director just accidentally touched my pinky finger!!!! – Lily

I smile so goddamn much that I can hear my father yelling at me for it. He used to do that when I was a kid. *Be serious for once in your fucking life, Loren.*

My lips fall. I text back: What's the first best day? I press send in an instant.

She's quick to reply.

The day I fell in love with you. – Lily

I shut my eyes for a second, and I try to remember that day. I try to transport my mind back to that place. But for every warmth there is cold. For every ounce of light there is blackness.

And for every happy memory, there is grief and pain.

I can't remember that day without crawling through it all.

So I open my eyes, and I let it drift away.

It's okay.

I'm going to make new best days with Lily Calloway.

I can feel it.

Chapter 9

0 Years : 03 Months

November

LILY CALLOWAY

Our annual Thanksgiving tradition has been put to rest, buried with other normal things that I can no longer do. We usually have a pre-meal at Lucky's Diner before eating with our families, but I haven't been back in three months: my twenty-first birthday when the manager refused to close the blinds.

Last Thanksgiving, the only people who knew about my sex addiction were Rose, Connor, and Ryke. Before all of that, we used to just sit at a family dinner table, carrying a lie in our hearts. Now that my addiction is out in the open, the event has been more awkward and uncomfortable for every person involved.

My mom hasn't even looked at me, and the weight only slowly ascends off my chest when we take a break before coffee and dessert.

"Are we having a sister powwow?" Daisy asks as she jumps on our father's oak desk.

Rose said she had something important to tell us, so the four of us retreated to the study before our mom calls us back for pie.

I sit on the uglier paisley armchair, a spring hurting my butt. I silently wish for the Hale's leather couches that I can sink into.

"Did Connor propose?" Poppy asks, a smile already enveloping her face. She crosses her legs on the suede couch.

Rose flinches back in surprise. "Of course not."

I try to adjust on the chair. Nope, the spring is definitely going to bruise my ass after this.

Poppy says, "I thought you were scared of babies, not matrimony."

"First of all"—Rose paces in front of us—"I am *not* scared of babies. I hate babies. They scream for no reason and can't walk properly."

I shake my head.

Daisy laughs, swinging her legs and tossing a crystal paperweight in her hand.

"They're little—" Poppy tries to justify.

"Devils. They're little devils that only exist to annoy me."

She's too dramatic for her own good.

"And strangely," Poppy says, "Maria adores you out of every person in the family. Why is that?"

"I don't know. That's obviously a character flaw on your daughter's part. She can't tell who her enemies are."

I snort.

Poppy sighs heavily and then looks to me. "Is she afraid of marriage?" She wants a confirmation since I'm the closest to Rose.

I hold up my hands. "I know nothing." I wait for someone to mention Jon Snow and *Game of Thrones*, but I realize that Lo's the only one who'd understand the reference. Wrong audience. And he's in the den with Connor and Sam.

Ryke was invited, seeing as how he's not on speaking terms with his mom, but he refused to come. He said that he couldn't be in the same room as Jonathan Hale, his father. There's still bad blood there, but I wish he'd show up for Lo and for himself.

I picture Ryke all alone at his apartment, watching sports and eating a sandwich, no big fancy dinner. No family or companions, not even the loud, rowdy kind. There's something sad about Ryke Meadows that he won't let us see, but its quiet moments like this, where he's gone, that I feel it anyway.

"…we haven't even had sex." I catch the tail end of Rose's explanation.

"Yeah," Daisy says, "but I thought you were just waiting until marriage."

Rose pauses in the middle of the floor. "I'm waiting until I'm ready and with someone I love," she refutes. "I'm not even sure I *want* to be married. And Connor wouldn't propose just so he can have sex with me."

"How do you know?" Poppy asks.

Rose shoots her a scathing glare.

She's as used to them as the rest of us. "I'm just asking."

"It's like cheating at a game," she says. "It's too easy for him."

Their weird relationship deserves to be observed. By me. I love it too much not to be a spectator. My smile consumes my face the longer I think about Connor and Rose's back-and-forth nerd wars.

Rose rolls her eyes at me and starts pacing again.

"Why are we here then?" I wonder.

She pulls her shoulders back like she's layering on armor. "As you know, Calloway Couture has been doing less than average lately."

My stomach immediately plummets, my smile fading, and turkey starts rising to my throat. I swallow it back down. Apologies swim in my head.

It's my fault. My sex addiction ruined her fashion line. There is no forgiveness for me, and I don't want it.

She continues on, "I've been struggling with serious solutions, but recently, someone made an offer that might actually work. The only problem is that it involves the three of you." Her yellow-green eyes ping from me to Poppy and then to Daisy. "I don't want you to do anything you're uncomfortable with. I'll understand if you say no."

"Sounds dangerous," Daisy says with a mischievous smile. "Color me intrigued."

"Sounds like *nothing*," I correct her. "She hasn't said it yet."

"What is 'it' exactly?" Poppy asks with air quotes.

"A reality show."

My mouth immediately falls.

The room cakes in thick silence, but not the awkward kind. We're all processing. And if we were in an *X-Men* comic right now, Poppy, Daisy and I would be the cuckoo sisters—thinking the exact same thing with their creepy telepathic hive-mind. There is no other response to Rose's proclamation.

"You're insane," Poppy says first.

I mock gasp. "That's what I was thinking."

"Me too," Daisy agrees and gives me a side-eye. "And you stole my mock gasp."

Rose waves us off, as if commanding us to stop talking. "I'm not insane. Calloway Couture needs good exposure, and I may be rolling the dice with this show, but it's *something*." Her eyes travel to me. "And maybe the world can see you how we do. Funny, sweet, and not just a sex addict."

Can that really happen? Won't a reality show just place a bigger spotlight on our family? But…Rose is the genius…so she should know better, right? If it'll help my sister, I won't ever say no.

I put her in this position to begin with.

"Okay," I nod. "Let's do it."

Rose steps back like I exploded a bomb at her feet. Jeez, she must have been expecting a fight. "Really? You can take more time to think about it, Lily. It'll be a big change."

A big change. I hate those. But sometimes change can be good, right? That's what my therapist tells me. "No." I shake my head. "I don't need more time. If there's a chance this'll help Calloway Couture, then I want to be involved."

"I'm in," Daisy tells us. "It sounds like fun, and besides, I'm used to cameras. So it's not a big deal for me."

Cameras…

More of them.

Don't think about it, Lily.

We all turn to our oldest sister, who just sits on the couch in silent contemplation. She lets out a long sigh. "Why can't the show just be about you, Rose?" she asks.

"The production company pitched that idea to the network, and they didn't bite." She holds in a breath, her collarbones protruding. "They wanted Lily in the show." She takes a step towards me. "I don't want to lie to you. You should know that the show will try to focus more on you than any of us—even if they're calling it *Princesses of Philly.*"

Before I can assure her again, Poppy blazes ahead of me. "Is this really the only thing you can do?" she asks. "It seems drastic, and I'm concerned about Lily's safety."

"I would *never* intentionally put Lily in harm's way," Rose says. "I've tried everything, Poppy." Is Rose about to cry? "This is my only chance."

Poppy's maternal side has kicked in, and she won't back down yet. "So you're going to put the family under more scrutiny, all to save your fashion line?"

The loyal part of me almost comes to Rose's aid, who rarely ever cries. But she's ready with a quick response. I realize that she's prepared for this type of questioning. "I've talked with our parents. They both support the idea. They've consulted the publicists who believe we can't sink much further, and maybe the media attention will finally be positive." She pauses to take a much needed breath. "So *yes,* Poppy, I'm willing to put our family under more scrutiny. For Fizzle. For Lily. And selfishly, for my fashion line."

Poppy relaxes a little more, and she fixes her brown hair off her shoulder. "Honestly, I wish I could just say *yes.* I want to stand by your side and support you, Rose, but I have a four-year-old daughter. I don't want a camera in her face, and neither does Sam."

"I understand," Rose says. "I'll get the contracts to Daisy and Lily to look over. The show can go on without you."

I add, "But you will be missed."

Rose rolls her eyes. "That was implied."

The sex scandal has rocked my family in so many ways, but I just now realize that I'm not completely aware of the degree that it's affected Poppy. I just kinda hoped, all along, that it didn't.

"Is she okay?" I ask Poppy, changing the subject again. "Maria, I mean. Paparazzi aren't following her around or anything, right?"

"No, nothing like that," Poppy says. "I think her last name saved her from the press. Stokes isn't as volatile as Calloway right now."

Good. At least one person in my family dodged the speeding bullet. I just wonder how many bullets a reality show will release, and who will be caught in the crossfire this time.

Chapter 10

0 Years : 04 Months

December

LOREN HALE

"Stop calling," I say with edge into the flip phone. Lily sits on the kitchen counter, eating peanut butter from a jar. My gaze lingers on her, especially as she sucks her index finger and lifts her thin legs to her chest.

My breathing deepens for a second, honing in on the way she licks the peanut butter off. She hasn't realized how sexual it looks, and I bask in this moment—the one before she blushes in embarrassment.

I grab two glasses in the cabinet beside her head, my arm brushing her cheek. My cock says to walk forward and fit right up against her. I wait, only to watch her longer. She pops her finger out of her mouth, her eyes radiating with eagerness when they meet mine. It's a *come hither* that I return, edging closer. But instead of acting on her feelings, she tries to focus on the peanut butter.

I set the glasses on the counter and run my hand through the side of her hair. *Christ, I want inside of her. Now.* But she ignores the motion and squints at the label on the jar.

Through the phone's speaker, Rose's cold voice disrupts my thoughts. "You shouldn't answer Lily's cellphone. She has two hands."

"Yeah? Well one is occupied," I retort.

Lily rests the jar between her knees and lets out an audible moan with her second scoop of peanut butter. *Goddamn.* My dick screams at me to respond to that noise. I resist, only because one of the biggest pains in my ass is still on the phone.

"You better not be—"

"She's eating," I clarify, though that's going to change once I hang up.

"Loren," Rose snaps.

"She's not blowing me. For Christ's sake."

Lily's brows jump and her eyes bug. She mouths, *what?* Her gaze falls to the zipper on my jeans, and she blushes on cue.

I press the speaker button so she can hear her sister. And then I fish my button through my jeans, Lily's mouth drops like I performed a fuckin' circus trick.

I can't help but smile. My girlfriend is beyond adorable.

Rose says, "I just want to know—"

"Privacy," I state the one word that no one seems to understand, not even our friends and family. *Maybe* Poppy and Sam have their heads screwed on tight, since they both refused to sign their rights away to television producers.

"We asked to be alone on New Year's Eve, and you've called us a record-breaking twenty times."

"And Lily didn't answer eighteen of those," Rose notes.

"Are you dying?" I ask. "Please tell me you're dying or suffering from a life-threatening affliction and not calling to check up on us."

Lily mouths, *be nice.* But she's ditched the peanut butter, her fingers hooked in my belt loops, drawing me nearer.

I cup my hand over the speaker. "I'm being *very* nice right now," I whisper. "I could have easily hung up on her after I said my piece." I wait for Rose to launch a grenade over the speaker, but she stays quiet, inadvertently answering me.

I groan in agitation. "Rose." *We're fine.*

Lily grabs the phone out of my hand and interjects, "You're at a party. Shouldn't you be having fun?"

"I'm at the Cobalt's *business* party," Rose reminds her. "Having fun at these events is never on the agenda." She pauses. "The food isn't terrible." She hesitates like she has more to say. Maybe she wasn't calling to nag us like a worried parent.

Now I feel like an asshole.

"What is it?" Lily asks, sensing the same thing.

I rest my palms on the counter, on either side of Lily. I'm still a head taller than her, and she stares up at me while she waits for her sister to reply.

I watch her chest collapse, desire blanketing her face. I just want to fuck my best friend. *Hurry up, Rose.*

"Connor booked the suite tonight," Rose whispers, as though to keep the people around her from hearing. "I found out when we arrived."

I run my hands up Lily's thighs, her jeans soft underneath my palms. I step closer so my cock is right against that spot, the one I know is already soaked. *Christ.* I begin to harden, just ready to push completely inside of her. We fucked twice already tonight—but this time is killing me more than the others.

I just want to hear Lily cry out.

Her lips part in a heavy breath.

"Lily?" Rose snaps, ice returning to her voice.

I remove my hands so she can talk to her sister, but I can't back up. I lick my lips and rest my palms on the cabinet beside her head, leaning into her.

"What's...so bad about that?" Lily asks. She forces her gaze to the ceiling so she can focus. I press my lips to her neck, lightly and then deeply. A noise catches in her throat just in time, so soft her sister can't hear.

Lily's hand tightens on my waist, and when I look up at her, she mouths, *do you want to get caught?*

No.

Rose and Ryke—they won't understand. All they'll see is a list of rules we've been given and tally off how many we've broken. Nothing else will matter.

I hear Rose inhale loudly. "Yesterday, I made this grand statement about how I'm ready to have sex with him—just to shut him up—and now I think he's calling out my bluff."

I can solve this problem. I glance at the phone in Lily's hand. "Just tell Connor that you changed your mind. He won't care."

"He'll *win*," Rose says like that's the stupidest idea.

"So what?"

Rose growls. "You wouldn't understand."

Lily mouths, *I got this.*

Great. Because I don't speak Rose's language.

Lily clears her throat. "Put him in a really uncomfortable position and then he'll freak out and you both will be off the hook."

I can practically feel Rose shaking her head. "Trust me, he's not uncomfortable in any position."

"How about just castrating him?" I chime in. "You threaten *my* balls every day."

"That's because they're hanging around my sister," Rose snaps. I hate that she makes a good point. "And you have full right to threaten my eggs or fallopian tubes. Have at them."

I grimace. "I'm not going anywhere near your vagina."

Rose says distantly, "I'm just trying to be fair."

Lily thinks hard, her brows pinched in this adorable way. "I don't know, Rose. You may lose this one. I mean…you can't go home with another guy…" Lily lets that terrible option drift in the air.

And her sister stays completely silent on the matter.

"Rose!" both Lily and I yell.

"I wouldn't cheat on him," Rose says. "That's disgusting. He's just staring at me right now." Her voice lowers. "I think he can read my expression."

"Your bitch face?"

"*No,*" Rose drags out the word. "…I'm scared."

I regret my words as soon as I hear her honesty. It doesn't come often, especially not around me. "Rose," I say, trying to soften my edged voice. "Sex is a big deal, and you shouldn't sleep with Connor if you're afraid."

"Why are you being nice to me?"

"I don't know," I admit. *It feels weird.*

"Well…I don't like it."

I glare at the phone. "Good because it's not happening again."

"Thanks," she says. I can't tell if it's for the advice or for my last statement. "He's walking over here…I'll call you later ton—"

"Tomorrow," I force.

"Right," she says distractedly. And then she hangs up first.

I slide Lily's flip phone down the counter, to the coffee pot, *away* from us. "No more sisterly or brotherly interruptions." I announce this as a fucking rule. Ryke has called three times tonight to ask how I'm doing. I spent last New Year's Eve in rehab. It's not like I'm going to grab a bottle of champagne because the day of the year tells me to.

"Do you remember before we were together?" Lily asks as I unbutton her jeans.

I freeze. "You mean when I was piss drunk?"

"No, I mean…yes, but that's not what I meant." Her skin blotches with dark red patches.

I lace my hand with hers. "I'm listening."

Her shoulders rise with confidence as she speaks. "You used to do this with me all the time," she says. "Pin me in the kitchen, toy with me…" She smiles at the memories. "I liked it, even when we weren't together. But this is rare now." Her eyes dance around our bodies. "I just wondered if you're afraid of teasing me."

I lift her chin so her gaze meets mine. "If I was afraid, I wouldn't be doing it tonight."

"But we're going to have sex," she says.

"Yeah?" I frown, not understanding what she's getting at.

"So you won't flirt with me unless we can have sex. Because you're afraid of me."

I glare. "Can you stop saying that? I'm not fucking scared of you, Lil."

"Then you're afraid of enabling me."

I shake my head. All I've wanted is to be with her completely, fully, without compromise. But maybe there's a signal in my brain that says: *Don't touch her like that. Don't make her hornier than she is. Don't tempt her.* Not unless she can have something more afterwards. "Can you handle me?" I ask lowly.

"I want to start trying," she says, her chest elevating at the proclamation. "I want to have everything we had without all the bad."

I've never been more in love with her. "I'm going to trust you to stop on your own then."

She nods repeatedly. "I will. I can. I know I can."

"Yeah?"

She smiles. I kiss her deeply, her body pulling towards mine with the embrace, and I pin our clasped hand to the cupboard above her head.

As she catches her breath, my forehead rests against hers. Softly, I whisper, "I believe in you, love." This is a goal I've never heard her make. It's one I'll entertain and help her reach.

But tonight—I want to fit perfectly against her with no room for hesitation or fears. I slip the jeans off her legs and step out of mine.

She slides her hands underneath my shirt with a heady gaze. "Can I take your shirt off?"

"You don't have to ask," I say.

Her lips curve up, and she hungrily raises the fabric over my head. Her fingers comb through my brown hair. "Closer," she whispers.

I grab her legs and yank her towards me, my cock between her legs. The fabric of our underwear is in the way. She holds onto my bare shoulders like I've already started driving into her. This is the only time that I'm glad she bites her nails. Otherwise, she would draw blood.

She clings to me so tightly that I have no chance of removing her V-neck shirt unless I ask. I'd rather keep her in my arms, like this, than have her completely naked.

Lily rests her cheek on my chest and whispers, "Closer."

I suck on the base of her neck, and she whimpers and gasps at once. Her ass barely rests on the counter. I support most of her weight with my body. If someone wanted to tear us apart, they'd have to claw her off of me.

I grin as I kiss her lips. Heat gathers between us. The nerve-splitting sensations start before I even push in.

"Closer," is all she can say.

Almost.

I take off my boxer-briefs and slip off her panties. Her need is apparent when I distance our bodies. She squirms like she hates the empty air.

Her arms hook underneath mine, and her beautiful green eyes remain fixed on my amber irises. Overwhelmed. Both of us.

"Closer," she breathes.

And I grab my shaft and slowly push my erection deep inside of her. *God.* My eyes almost roll back in my head.

She cries out, "Lo!"

I rest our clasped hand back on the cupboard. "Lil..." I thrust against her, so deep that a groan scratches my throat. With our bodies melded together, she stares straight into me. I rock, barely able to separate from her.

She kisses me first, and my smile disappears to carnal desire. I hold the back of her head, my tongue parting her lips and sliding against hers. Lily's confidence, during sex, has been lost for a while. It's nice to see it start to return.

I thrust hard again, and she breaks away to let out a sharp moan. No one else is listening in. When filming begins for the reality show—our audience will multiply unless we're careful. In this moment, it doesn't matter though.

We just let go.

After we both reach that peak, I keep her in my arms and comb her damp hair out of her face. The television plays a New Year's Eve concert in the living room, the faint sounds now audible in our silence.

"I love you," I tell her. Even though I say those words often after we have sex, she still glows when it reaches her ears.

"I love you too."

Just as I go to kiss her again, the front door creaks open.

Rose. It has to be Rose. She came home to avoid spending the night in the suite with Connor. It's a stupid decision, considering he now lives in this house with us. They even share a bedroom. What's so different about a hotel?

Lily's eyes widen with panic. "Oh my God."

I'm standing in the kitchen. Buck naked.

While Lily has a shirt on, her panties are littered on the floor with the rest of our clothes. I lift her off the counter and set her feet on the ground.

I don't know why I'm surprised. I have the shittiest luck in the whole universe. How many guys wake up one day and are told they're bastards? How many have their biological mom basically say: *hey, I didn't want you when you were born nor do I care about you now?*

I've been stampeded so many times already; I might as well brace myself before it happens again.

I zip my pants and turn to Lily and button her jeans. "We're fucked," she hisses.

"Not yet," I whisper. "Fix your hair."

She rapidly tries to flatten the messy strands.

The door slams closed, and as I bend down to grab my black crew-neck, I spot leather boots and long legs in the archway between the living room and the kitchen. My eyes travel up to her green army jacket and blonde hair.

"Daisy," I say hesitantly. I breathe out, just glad it's not Rose.

Her green eyes—swollen and reddened—dart between Lily and me. "Sorry…I didn't mean to…" She rotates and heads back into the living room.

"Wait," I say, rushing after Daisy with Lily by my side. I hurriedly put on my shirt and realize that Daisy's aimed for the door.

"What happened?" Lily asks, fear pitching her voice.

"Daisy, don't leave," I add, sprinting ahead and blocking her exit. I lean my back against the door and keep a hand on the knob.

Then I scan her features. But her insanely long hair drapes along her cheeks and brows, masking her expression. Her fingers brush beneath her eyes—wiping tears?

My face twists. "Are you crying?"

"I'm fine," she breathes. "I'm just going to go. I didn't mean to interrupt you."

My jaw locks. She knows we had sex.

Great.

And she's going to tell my brother—because he prods for information, and they're strangely friends.

Lily rests her hand on Daisy's shoulder. "What happened? I thought you were spending the night at Cleo's house?"

My brows furrow. "Cleo?" I try to wrack my brain for an image of Daisy's friend. I think she's blonde too. That's all I picture.

"She's my best friend," Daisy mutters and tucks a piece of hair behind her ear. "I just…the party was lame. I thought I could come back here and watch the countdown on GBA with you and then crash in the guest room."

"Then that's what we're going to do. You're staying here," Lily says adamantly, guiding Daisy over to the couch. They sit down together. I can't remember a time where Lily was this protective. Maybe when I was in rehab, she grew closer to Daisy, but I never saw this side of their relationship. Lily, being the big sister like Rose, except without all the ice.

"We can watch *Adventures in Babysitting*. That's one of your favorite movies, right?" Lily offers.

Daisy smiles. "You remembered?"

Lily nods. "Yeah. You told me…" She closes one eye as she recalls the date. I could kiss her again. "…last week, I think."

"That sounds good." Daisy takes off her jacket, settling in.

"Here, I'll hang that up," I tell her, grabbing the green fabric.

"Thanks." She gives me a weak smile and scoots closer to Lily. Both girls have their feet on the couch. "So…" Daisy pauses.

Don't say it. Don't bring it up. I liked thinking that she'd pretend it never happened. I open the hallway closet and take out an empty hanger.

"…I thought you weren't supposed to have sex in the kitchen or the living room—not that I'm judging. I just always thought it was a rule." I hear the curiosity in her voice. Still, I've never had the urge to discuss my sex life with my girlfriend's sixteen-year-old sister. In fact, it's as uncomfortable as it sounds.

"Uhhh…" Lily draws out the word. "Lo?" She peeks her head over the couch, waiting for me to return to handle this one. Her cheeks are tomato-red.

I hang up Daisy's jacket, shut the closet and take a seat on Rose's Queen Anne chair. "It's not a rule so much as a suggestion." I smile a bitter smile. Then I collect the remote, about to increase the volume to GBA's *Ballin' New Year's Eve.*

"Are you sure Ryke and Rose know that it's a suggestion and not a rule?" Daisy asks us. "I think they'd be really upset…" She licks her dried lips. "I mean…it's not considered relapsing, right?"

Guilt washes over Lily's face.

I go cold.

"No," I interject quickly. *We're at a good fucking place. She's confident, not compulsive. I won't let their fears fuck with her progress.* "Not that I really want to explain this to you," I add and then grimace. *Way to be a prick, Loren.* "Lily's therapist says that we can move things forward, depending on how well she's doing."

This is completely true, but even if Rose and Ryke had a sit down with Dr. Banning, they'd probably still believe that Lily needs more structure and limitations. Outwardly, she seems aloof and anxious, but most of that is because of the media.

It's complicated.

Daisy wears a pained expression. "And you're doing well?" she asks her sister.

Lily nods, but she has very little evidence to prove this, considering she hides under desks, dodges cameras, and isolates herself from people.

"Hey, Daisy?" I rub the back of my neck, my eyes narrowed. "Can you *never* tell my brother what you saw tonight? In fact, let's just keep this between us."

Lily says, "Please. We've been trying not to advertise our sex life as much."

Daisy's not stupid.

The gears click in her head—thinking we're on a dangerous road. We aren't. Not yet, at least.

Lily clasps Daisy's hand and then says, "Do you want ice cream? Rose stocked up on double fudge for you."

"I can't...I have a photo shoot next week."

"Oh," Lily says, more remorse filling her eyes.

"No, it's cool." Daisy hugs her sister back, and just like that, their relationship has been reversed. Daisy cheering up Lily, something that only makes Lily feel like shit. "Let's just watch the movie after the countdown. Who needs ice cream, right?"

Then the door swings open again.

And both Lily and I look to Daisy. Her loyalty to us is about to be tested.

Chapter 11

0 Years : 04 Months

December

LILY CALLOWAY

A six-foot-three brooding—mostly iritated— guy bounds through the door. “I fucking hate people,” he states, barely glancing at Lo on the chair. I have to crane my neck over the couch to catch sight of Ryke, as does Daisy.

He saunters into the kitchen with an angry stride, disappearing through the archway.

“Not that I don’t love you here,” Lo shouts from across the room, “but you said that you were spending New Year’s at that frat guy’s kiddie pool.”

Ryke returns from the kitchen with a bag of pre-popped popcorn and a water bottle. “It was his hot tub, and he graduated in May, same as me.”

Ryke must have had a not-so fun time at his friend’s party. His stormy expression says it all. The irony: Lo and I were having a pretty good night, all things considered. Usually we're on the other side of the fence.

"Can you imagine a hot tub full of frat guys?" Daisy asks me, nudging my elbow with hers, a smile playing at her lips. It sounds like one of my fantasies. Before Loren Hale. But then again, Ryke would not be a participant in my fantasy hot tub.

I don't answer her, but I do, however, catch Ryke's muscles flexing at the sound of Daisy's voice, surprised by her presence here.

Ryke steps around the couch to face us, and he gives Daisy a long once-over that seems friendly enough. "What are you doing here?"

"Lo asked you the same thing," she deflects.

Ryke sinks down in the open chair, his harsh gaze still on Daisy. "You want to know why I left my friend's fucking party?"

"Yeah," Daisy says.

"I was sick of people asking me how Lily is in bed."

*Whaaa...*My eyes pop out. I despise those rumors. "I hope you told them I never—"

"I told them to fuck off," Ryke says before I get worked up. "They're fucking assholes."

"We're assholes," Lo says. "They're dipshits."

"Are you really schooling me on curse words, little brother?"

Lo lets out a short laugh and grips the armrests too tightly, like he longs to stand up and grab a drink. "No. I don't run as fast as you. I'm not as smart as you. And I definitely don't curse as well as you." I hear what's beneath his words: *My life is pretty much a losing battle.* Cold washes over me. I glance at Ryke—his arms have chill bumps. "I'm just saying," Lo finishes, "that you're an asshole."

On instinct, I leave my seat beside Daisy, and I nestle on Lo's lap, hugging his tense body. His shoulders begin to loosen as soon as my legs tangle with his, and his large hands slip around my waist, pulling me even closer to his chest.

Ryke drinks a swig of water and wipes his mouth with his arm. "At least we have something in common then."

Lo lets out a laugh, his scowl completely vanished. He's happy that Ryke didn't convince him of things he knows are true. Lo spent his childhood running away from people. Ryke competed in track and field. I don't think either of them believes that Lo will gain the strength to beat his brother in a race.

I do though.

Lo has the will to speed right past the person who lifted him to his feet. I think, sometimes, we have more faith in each other than we do in ourselves.

Daisy shifts on the couch for the third or fourth time, restless. She starts braiding the fringe of a purple throw blanket. "Are you spending the night too?" she asks Ryke.

"If it's okay with my brother." Ryke turns his head towards Lo. "I can drive back to Philly if it's not."

"It's almost midnight, so you should stay," Lo says. "We can crack open a bottle of champagne, toast to the New Year, then switch to whiskey." He tops it off with that now *literally* famous dry smile. *Celebrity Crush* even ranked his bitter half-smiles from best to worst. My favorite was the one during Halloween (ranked only #6). I thought he'd want to stay at home for his twenty-second birthday, especially since last year's Halloween was so apocalyptic, but he drove everyone to a haunted house in northern Pennsylvania.

He was a pirate.

A *sarcastic* pirate.

A girl dressed as Pippi Longstocking took the picture of his half-smile when he wasn't looking and posted it to Instagram. I almost wish I could thank her.

It's one of my favorite photos of him—maybe also because he's carrying me on his back. I was a mouse. I thought it'd be ironic since

I've been so quiet, but Ryke thought I was a rat so…maybe it wasn't the best costume choice.

"That's fucking hilarious," Ryke says to Lo, unamused.

"Haven't you heard? I haven't had a sip of alcohol since rehab," Lo says. "*I'm cured.*" I don't think he even believes that.

"And Connor isn't a genius. Lily's not a sex addict. Daisy's not a supermodel. And I have fucking fantastic college buddies who ask me about *anything* other than three-ways."

"I don't know what world you're living in," Lo banters, "but that one sounds fucking weird."

Ryke laughs, his eyes lightening.

"You can stay here as long as you want," Lo professes, his voice filled with sincerity.

"Just the night," Ryke says. "I love you and Lily, but I just can't be around Connor for that long."

"I thought I wouldn't be able to withstand Rose for long either, but it's going on ten months, and she hasn't even killed me yet." His arms fall to my legs, lifting me higher on his lap so our chests touch. It just happened out of the blue.

Flirting should be full of fearless advances like this.

Somewhere in our timeline together, fear has snuck in and invaded our peace. Hopefully that'll change for good.

"Why don't you like Connor?" Daisy asks Ryke, tearing my attention away from Loren Hale.

"He's just annoying."

I think we all know there's more to the story.

"He's cool," Lo says easily. "I'm annoying, and somehow you like me more?"

"You're not that fucking annoying." He runs his hand through his hair, not explaining *why* Connor gets on his nerves so much.

"Is that it?" Lo wonders with pinched brows.

Ryke shakes his head. It takes him a moment to gather his thoughts. Then he says, "You let everyone see *every* part of you, and Connor offers a very small portion of himself. I don't like watching you stand vulnerable in front of someone who wears more armor than you can ever have. It's not fair, and it's a fucking shitty thing for Connor to do to you."

Lo lets his words sink in, and my stomach flips at the idea that Connor may hurt Lo. I never even considered it. Not once.

"I don't mind it as much as you," Lo tells his brother, though his forehead creases like Ryke has planted a seed. He's never thought of it like that before. Neither have I.

"And I don't fucking understand why that is."

"You said that he wears armor, and I'm what—naked? I don't think he'll turn around and stab me…so I'm happy with our friendship." Lo pauses and rubs his lips in contemplation, and he leaves it at that.

With the silence, I steal the remote from Lo and increase the volume of the New Year's broadcast. "We're here in Times Square…" the host announces cheerfully.

"Hey," Ryke says, pelting popcorn at Daisy. A kernel hits her square in the eyeball. He doesn't apologize. "What are you doing at your sister's house?"

Daisy picks the popcorn out of her hair and crosses her legs. "I just decided to crash here."

"It's more than that," Lo says, exchanging a concerned look with Ryke. As someone who's been on the receiving end of their united brotherly force, it's very hard *not* to succumb to their demands.

Daisy has no chance.

And while I should be all Girl Power, Team Calloway—I care about my sister too much to blindly side with her. I just hope that she won't use the only ammunition she has against us. Lo and I had sex in the kitchen. That's definitely something she can fling at Ryke to take the heat off her situation.

It scares me, but her wellbeing means more than sheltering our lie.

Daisy shakes her head. "I'm okay."

"You were crying," Lo says.

"What?" Ryke's dark frown casts a shadow over the room.

"It was just prep school people being rude, not my close friends," Daisy says vaguely. "The crying part was an accident…sorry."

Ryke's face contorts in confusion and agitation. He throws a handful of popcorn at her. I stretch across Lo to reach his brother's chair and snatch the bag from his hands. He barely even notices that I've taken his snack.

"Are you seriously fucking apologizing for *crying?*" he growls.

"I guess so."

Ryke shakes his head repeatedly while I munch on the popcorn and stare between them, my head whipping from side to side.

Lo digs his hand in the bag to eat some too.

"*Don't*," Ryke says.

"You didn't cry about *your* friends," Daisy states.

"I stormed in here cursing. You're allowed to show some human emotion, Dais. I did."

Daisy shifts again like she can't get comfortable. She smashes a pillow on her lap, and I hold my breath, expecting her to distract Ryke right about now with our issues. She says, "Is it okay if we don't talk about it?"

I exhale.

Ryke's muscles constrict. He clearly doesn't want to drop it. Daisy kicks off her boots, a little more fidgety than I've last seen her. She eyes the *door*. I imagine my fearless sister speeding down the dark roads on her motorcycle.

Death comes next.

"Daisy," I say in warning.

"You're not leaving," Lo tells her.

I nod in agreement. "We all want you here."

"I saw ice cream in the fridge," Ryke says as he stands. "I can make you a bowl."

"I have a photo shoot—"

"Run with me tomorrow morning."

Okaaayy...that sounded more like a proposition for a date, but everything about Ryke is kind of sexual. The way he stands, the way he moves. I bet he thinks about sex just as often as me too.

"Sounds like a date," Daisy says exactly what I was thinking. I can't tell if she's hoping it is. *She's sixteen. He's twenty-three.* She can have a crush on him, but it can't progress further than that.

I rest my palms on Lo's chest, his muscles hard as a rock, too rigid right now.

Ryke tenses. "It's not, Calloway. I run with Lo all the time, and we're just brothers."

"So I'm like your sister then?" she asks.

Good question, I think, shoveling more popcorn in my mouth.

His face darkens. "No."

"Then what am I?"

"My fucking friend." His eyebrows rise. "Any more questions?"

She smiles weakly. "That's it."

"I'm going to get you a bowl of ice cream," he says. "Okay?"

"Yeah." She bites her lip and he rounds the corner. When he disappears, both Lo and I glance back at Daisy who has moved on to twisting the button in the pillow.

"Thanks," Lo whispers to her, "for not ratting us out."

"Even though you ratted me out," she finishes. She's too smart for us.

His eyes narrow. "That's different."

"I hope it is," she whispers back.

"It is," he says adamantly. "You're doing the right thing."

She nods, and then Ryke returns with a bowl of double fudge ice cream. He places it in her hands and then brushes the popcorn off the cushion before sitting next to her.

Lo kisses my cheek, tearing my gaze off them and onto him. I like this view better.

I smile. "Do you think Rose is swiping her V-card tonight?"

"Most definitely."

We all stay quiet as we watch a few bands perform in Times Square. I rest my head on Lo's shoulder, and thirty minutes must past before noises escalate…from outside.

"He was *not* flirting with me. Your definition is wrong."

That is one-hundred percent Rose's fierce voice.

"What the hell?" Lo says. He finds the remote on my lap and mutes the television.

On cue, the door breezes open.

Dressed in an expensive tux, Connor holds open the door while Rose stomps ahead in five-inch winter booties, a black cocktail dress, and white fur coat. "To flirt," Connor recites, "to behave in a way that shows sexual attraction. You can take my definition or we can consult Merriam-Webster, though mine is more accurate."

I whisper under my breath to Lo, "I think Rose is still a virgin."

"Good call."

"I'm *so good* at picking up signs," Rose retorts, still in a verbal battle with Connor. "I know when someone is flirting with me, Richard."

He shuts the door, hardly upset by whatever happened. He wears only amusement in his deep blue eyes the longer Rose huffs and puffs like a wolf ready to blow down a pig's house. And then he speaks in fluent French, so effortlessly that the words sound like golden honey off his tongue.

She replies back in angry French.

It sounds violent.

They face each other like they're dueling. "All they need are some wands," I whisper to Lo.

"I'll never understand Ravenclaws," he tells me. Connor and Rose would belong to the smartest house in the wizarding world. No question. Before the sorting hat even touched their heads, it'd scream *Ravenclaw!*

"Luna Lovegood is pretty cool, and she's from Ravenclaw," I say as Rose arches her back and steps nearer.

Connor laughs at something she said in French, his million-dollar grin too bright to contain.

Lo says, "Only because Luna Lovegood likes the other houses just as much as her own."

I look between Rose and Connor. Even though they're so smart, they spend so much time in our realm of being.

They're my favorite Ravenclaws that ever were.

"Connor doesn't believe in magic," Lo reminds me.

"I think Rose could convince him."

"Maybe." Lo raises his voice so they can hear him. "Shouldn't you both be at a hotel right now?" He doesn't add *having sex* but the idea is silently stated. At least…to me it is.

Rose whips her head to us, just registering our presence. "The party was horrible."

"The party was boring. There's a difference," Connor says easily. He takes note of his surroundings, scanning us on the chair and then Ryke and Daisy on the couch.

Rose spots our little sister just as quickly and walks around the couch to approach, Connor by her side. "What are you two doing here?"

"Both of our parties fucking sucked," Ryke answers. And I realize how quickly he was able to move a spotlight off of Daisy. Exactly what she would want.

Lo holds up his hands. "I'm confused. Was the party *in* your hotel room?" Lo asks like he's the only one thinking logically. "Otherwise, you could have left the party without coming *here.*" He gives Connor a look like *what the fuck happened?*

"We're no longer welcome at that particular hotel...for eternity. Those were the manager's exact words." Connor loosens his bowtie. "I don't blame him for thinking we're immortal. In some preclassic civilizations, I'd be considered a god."

Rose's yellow-green eyes drill holes into him. "Congratulations, you are officially the cockiest human being on planet Earth." *That'd be Iron Man.* But I hold my tongue.

"That's Iron Man," Lo says. I literally rise like I'm floating. I kiss him on the lips, so suddenly that I think he's caught off guard too.

Rose holds her hand at him like *stay out of it.*

Lo doesn't care. His eyes fix on me with questioning and longing. Like he wants to kiss me again. But I stop. I show him I can.

I don't want sex.

Just a kiss.

Like back in Cancun. When I was on the road to truly recovering. I'm going to be there again. I can feel it.

Today is a very good day.

His lips rise, saying everything that needs to be said.

He's proud of me.

I glance back to my older sister. Connor still grins at her and speaks French. *Damn.* I flip open my cell and try to log into a translator, but he talks too quickly for me to type the words. This is when I wish I had my nicer, newer phone with app capabilities that translates by sound, no manual typing involved.

I consider snatching Lo's phone, but one of my hands is still in the popcorn bag.

Thankfully, Rose uses English. "The manager was exaggerating."

"Clearly," Connor says, "but it doesn't change the fact that we were kicked out tonight."

The gears in my brain start spinning. My eyes widen in realization, and I cough on a popcorn kernel. Lo pats my back. He hands me what used to be Ryke's water. It's grossly become communal. Survival instinct triggers and I drink it anyway.

Rose. She found a way to dodge Connor's suite without cheating on him or putting him in an uncomfortable position. She got the hotel to *kick them out.*

She's ballsy and slightly nuts. Wouldn't it have been easier to tell him that she didn't want to have sex?

"I broke *one* bottle of champagne in the lobby," Rose states. "The punishment was hardly warranted."

"You called the manager an oversized twat," Connor says with an arched brow. "And what you did was *hardly* an accident."

"So?" she retorts defensively.

"If you wanted to go home, darling, all you had to do was say so."

Ha! I suggested as much to her, didn't I? I hope I did. I can't remember that phone conversation that much. Lo's hands and lips were traveling to dangerous places during it.

"Then you would've won," she says.

He gives her a look. "I already did."

"But—"

"Sex isn't a prize to me. I don't know how many times I have to tell you for you to believe it."

They start speaking in French again, and Lo scoots me closer to his chest, resting his arm around my collar.

I pick up the remote and unmute the television, which hangs above the fireplace mantel.

"Thirty seconds," the host counts down.

I think back to last New Year's where Lo was in rehab, where I spent most of the night with Daisy, where we sat in Ryke's car—stuck in traffic—as the clock struck midnight.

"Twenty seconds."

Now I'm in Loren Hale's arms.

He's sober.

I'm in recovery.

I wasn't sure if we'd ever be at this place. I glance at Daisy who balances her spoon on her nose with a bright smile—the first genuine looking one I've seen from her tonight. Ryke stares at her for a long moment before messing her hair with his hand. The spoon falls to her lap.

Connor and Rose stand only inches apart by the coffee table, his hands on her hips. Her chest rises and falls faster than his, but his gaze is glued to Rose, entrapped, like she's beyond gorgeous—like he could take her right there without hesitation.

I turn back to Lo and rest my knees on either side of his waist, straddling him.

"Ten seconds," the host declares.

"I missed you last year," Lo murmurs, his hand on my cheek, his thumb stroking my skin.

I kiss his sharp jaw, and before I pull away, he kisses the outside of my lips, nerves singing at the touch. *Yes.*

"Remember how when we were little?" I whisper. "You'd chase me around before midnight."

"Eight!" the television blares. "Seven!"

Lo's fingers comb into my hair as he holds my face. "You always ran out of breath."

I smile. "I wanted you to catch me."

His amber eyes dance along my features, like he's engraining every detail. "I thought so."

"Five!"

"Catch me," I whisper.

"Four!"

"I already have," he murmurs.

Our bodies press together, as though they've never drifted apart, not for three months or years or any moment's time.

His lips touch mine, his hand gripping my hair. I pull even closer to his body, the kiss magnetizing me to him.

"One!"

In this moment, everything else is just background to our story.

It takes a few minutes to actually hear the cheers from the television, the people in Times Square celebrating with confetti and more kisses.

Connor and Rose are full-on making out. Like passionate, powerful kisses that would occur after pent-up emotions from a fight. He's in control, one hand on her ass, their lips never disconnecting as he walks her backwards. Her shoulders hit the wall.

"Whoa," I say. Before Lo covers my eyes, I shift my gaze. I don't want to be aroused by *that*. How embarrassing—on my part.

"Do you guys realize what this means?" Daisy asks, drawing my attention to the couch.

At first I think she's talking about Connor and Rose. To me, it means that their nerd love is in full orbit. Where it should be.

But her eyes aren't on them. She's staring at the TV screen, and Ryke has his hand on the couch behind her head. They don't look like they shared a New Year's kiss, but I wonder if they thought about it. Even for a second.

"What?" I ask.

She stares off in thought, neither excited nor scared. "In a few days, we're going to be filmed." She pauses. "For a reality show."

Oh.

Shit.

Part Two

"That's how I survived.

Time and time again. That's my secret.

I survived because I willed it to be …

How did I survive apocalyptic fire?

I simply refused to feel the flames."

— Emma Frost, Dark Reign:

The Cabal Vol 1 #1

Chapter 12

0 Years : 05 Months

January

LOREN HALE

"So you have to film everything we do?" I ask the short, pudgy camera guy. Brett can't be any older than twenty-five. When Lily explained the reality show, my first thought was *fuck no*. Why would we voluntarily participate in that kind of torture? And then she started stammering about how this might relieve the guilt and how people might see us as a real couple.

She only sold me when she said, "I'm doing this, Lo. With or without you. So if it's without you, then we're not going to be seeing each other all that much for six months."

Six months without her.

It's never happened before.

I try to wrack my brain for a memory that doesn't consist of Lily for that period of time, and I can't come up with a single one. The only future I want is the one that ends with her.

If it means participating in a reality show, I can do it. Easy. All the drama will be supplied by us.

I stand outside of our bedroom door. In the Princeton house. Staring down a Canon Rebel and the stubby cameraman behind it. Lily clings to the door frame, shielded by my body.

Exactly where I want her in this moment.

Brett remains quiet, but my glare must motivate him because he finally says, "I can't talk to you. You know…" He clears his throat. "The fourth wall."

I raise my brows. Interesting. "So you're just going to stand there *silently*—no matter what?"

He nods.

Maybe I overestimated how terrible this was going to be. No probing questions? No heckling from the cameramen? We can do whatever we want.

Huh.

I glance back at Lil, who wears a black romper and gold necklace. An outfit chosen by Rose. Apparently the girls have to wear clothes from the Calloway Couture line—for promotion.

Thankfully she doesn't *look* like Rose.

She still has that delicate round face, the gangly arms and legs. She's adorable. In every sense of the word. And she's all mine to take care of.

I take a step closer to Lily and rest my hand above her head. When I stare down at her, she parts her lips in questioning like *are you flirting with me?*

I force back a smile. *Yes, I'm flirting with you, Lil.* I shove any concerns towards the back of my head. She can handle this without having sex. She has to. Because we can't fuck every time I touch her *this* way.

With one hand over her head, my other falls to the hem of her romper. I slip my finger in the belt loop on her hip and pause.

Her breath hitches, her gaze flitting from my lips back to my eyes. And then her neck flushes. She glances at the goddamn camera.

Thing is—we have more free reign where PDA is concerned now that the cameras follow us. Instead of Rose thinking we're having more sex, we just blame it on hamming it up for the viewers at home. Rose rarely scolds me now.

As long as Lily can handle it, we should be fine.

I clutch her waist, still hooked to her belt loop. My fingers dip below her hipbone, the romper's fabric a lot softer than the jeans she normally wears.

Her back arches against the door frame, and her arms fly around my neck. I lean in to kiss her, and she tries to meet me halfway. I pull back a little and she catches air.

Her mouth falls, breathless. "No fair."

"Didn't you hear?" My lips curve upward. "I'm the biggest tease in Princeton." I pause, smiling wider. "And Philadelphia."

She lightly punches my arm.

My brows rise. "Is that a love tap?"

She hits me harder.

I rub my arm and mock wince. "Are you working out, Lil?"

She raises her arm and flexes her "muscle" which is a very tiny bulge. "Ryke gave me a five-pound weight for my birthday, remember? He said I needed to bulk up."

I remember. "That was a shitty birthday present."

"Yours was better," she declares with a warm smile. It was a belated present, on purpose. During Comic-Con, I managed to get some of the artists to sign Lily's favorite *X-Men* issues. It helped that we split up when she went to the director's panel. I returned to the convention floor just for their signatures.

The nearby camera fills the short silence, groaning as it zooms in on us. Lily freezes again.

Brett asks, "What did you get for Lily?"

I glare. *So much for not asking questions.* "You told us that we can't talk to you, but you can talk to us?" How the hell does this work?

"Yeah," he says evasively.

I grimace and scowl at the same time.

Brett takes one step back. "You don't have to answer," he mutters under his breath.

He's probably scared that I'm going to slap the camera out of his hands. Something Ryke has done to paparazzi before and been severely fined for it.

I stare right at Brett and ask, "You want to know how I satiate a sex addict?" When I shift my gaze to Lily, she already holds her breath. I tilt her chin up, forcing her eyes to mine.

And then I kiss her. Deeply. Passionately. Like we were born to share oxygen. I part her lips with my tongue, tasting her, and then focus on her bottom lip. I suck gently, and her leg instinctively rises up to my hip, silently craving for me to fit between her thighs. I almost harden, especially as she clings tighter to me, blanketed with strong, feverish need.

She wears her insatiability with every breached moan and grind against me. I feed into it with every coarse, rough movement that slams against her thin body. It's a hunger that only compulsives and addicts know well. It's why people look away when we kiss. The raw desire grips my cock, my lungs, my mind. My lips drift to her neck, and my hand perilously rides the edge between her waist and her abdomen.

When we kiss full-force again, my head just explodes and I lose sense of my surroundings. I don't care about anyone else but Lily. I raise her hand above her head, laced with mine like I've done so many times before.

She moans into a kiss, but we don't stop.

I'm going to love Lily how I want to love her.

Overwhelmingly, uncompromisingly.

Look away if you have to.

My one hand on her hip falls between her legs, and I squeeze. She tries to stifle the cry, but it escapes her lips. I grin into our next kiss while she moves her hands up to my chest and shoves me back.

Her eyes flit to the camera.

That may have been the first time she's rejected me—since we've been an official couple that is.

Jesus, maybe this reality show will actually do some good.

My lips sting. She breathes heavily.

I follow her gaze, and my grin stretches.

Brett's cheeks are flushed red, and he makes a concerted effort to avoid our eyes.

Lily said she missed the teasing. I didn't realize how much I did too, until now.

A thin sheen of sweat is gathered on my forehead. "You hot and bothered, Brett?" I ask him.

He makes an uncomfortable noise that sounds like a grunt. "You can't..."

"Talk to you? Right." I flash a half-smile.

Six months of a reality show—we can do this. Easy.

Lily's cell chimes. She takes her flip phone out of her pocket, and her mood clouds. "Rose is asking about cake tasting."

I try to suppress a cringe, but I'm sure it passes through my features. I'm not Connor Cobalt. I can't hide what I'm feeling. "What do you want at the wedding?" *Our* wedding. Now I really grimace. *Shit.* I train myself not to glance back at the cameras.

We're being married for appearance's sake, even though it'll be real. I love every single part of Lily, but I hate that this day is being dictated by her mom and my dad.

I'd rather just elope.

But that's not part of the "image rehabilitation" plan.

"I don't really care," she says in a small voice.

I shrug. "Me either. Just tell her to choose."

Lily nods, her shoulders drooped.

When she finishes texting back, I pull her close and wrap her in my arms. I don't say anything. I just hold her.

Six months until our wedding—yeah, shit just got real.

Chapter 13

0 Years : 05 Months

January

LILY CALLOWAY

In just three days, our world has warped. Whether this is a terrible change or a catastrophic one is to be seen.

"Have you checked out the bathrooms?" Daisy asks me, plopping on my bed.

"Not yet," I say. *I'm on another mission.*

Empty cardboard boxes litter the floorboards of my new bedroom in a Philadelphia townhouse. I still can't find my canopy net. Either the movers took it for themselves or Lo tossed it when we were unpacking. I didn't realize I'd grown an attachment to the thing until I lost it. Pretending to be in a jungle safari at night just won't be the same.

I cautiously eye the door in case Brett or Ben or Savannah (the camera trio) dart into my new room to film us.

I need to be incognito for a few minutes. I hoist my body on the dresser that the movers just heaved in here. With a broom in hand, I do a piss poor job, but I manage to stand on two feet.

Daisy collects her long blonde hair into a high, messy bun. "What are you doing?"

"Checking for bugs," I say. *The electrical, peeping Tom kind.* In the hallways, living room, kitchen and other common areas, rafters make up the ceiling, rigged with so many wires and cameras. Rose said we had to move to the townhouse for better sound, but the contracts say we can't be filmed in the bedrooms.

I'm not taking any chances.

The world already thinks I'm a sexual nutcase. I don't want them to have footage of *private* acts between Lo and me. With the end of my broom, I poke at the wires and a suspicious looking black box. I stand on the tips of my toes.

Oh my God.

There's so much space between the rafters that a whole body could crawl on top of them, army-man style, and then they can hang down like *Mission Impossible* and film us while we're sleeping.

"What's wrong?"

I spin at Lo's voice and the dresser wobbles underneath my bare feet. While I concentrate on *not* falling, Lo scoops me up in his arms and sets me safe on the floor.

"Are you cleaning?" Lo asks with raised brows. "Because I have *never* seen you pick up a broom."

"She was checking for bugs," Daisy tells him, legs crossed on the end of my bed.

Lo frowns. "I thought Rose already hired an exterminator." The townhouse is old, which made Rose upset more than anyone else. She likes clean areas, not musty, moldy creaks and crannies filled with spider webs and the occasional daddy-long-leg. I don't mind it so much. Maybe because I'm so focused on the cameras.

"Not those kind of bugs." I point at the black box. "That's a camera."

His frown morphs into a scowl and then he follows my finger. "That looks like a battery."

Really? My neck heats. "I just wanted to check." Now I'm a compulsive, *paranoid* freak. "Crawlers may be up there, too."

I realize that made absolutely no sense to anyone outside my brain.

Professor Xavier would have understood it.

Lo sets his hand on my waist and draws me to his body. "I'll check the rafters with Ryke."

"Crawlers are people," I say lamely.

He just smiles. "I figured."

I gasp. "You can read my mind now? Your superpower finally kicked in."

"No," he breathes, staring down at me. "I just know you too well."

Oh. "Will you let me know when you get your superpower?"

He nods, and his fingers slide across the base of my neck. I love that he touches me so much more. "I have to warn you though, I may not have one."

"That's okay," I say. "Sometimes I like the idea of just being mortal with you."

Lo leans in to kiss me, but a loud *clatter* tears us apart. Brett tripped over a lamp on the ground, landing on his knees.

"Nice catch," Lo says dryly. Brett didn't drop his camera, but it's strapped to his chest with some weird device that looks like a bulletproof vest, only plastic. I think Connor called it a steadicam.

Ryke passes by our room and stops when he notices Brett. He helps him to his feet and then enters. "Have you checked out the bathrooms?"

Daisy asked the same thing. They must know something that we don't.

"Not yet," Lo says, not as concerned as me now.

Daisy rises off my bed, and the four of us stand in more awkward silence.

We're all living together.

This has never ever happened.

It's new and weird and something the production company wanted so badly. It's a big reason why we moved to this townhouse. The six months filming *Princesses of Philly* just got a lot more interesting.

Daisy breaks the quiet. "I've never lived with a guy before," she exclaims, just putting it out there with more confidence than I would have. She'll be in the same house as Lo, Connor, and Ryke. I've spent most of my time living with Lo, so it's not so different for me.

Ryke and Lo share a look that I can't decipher, and then Ryke says, "It should be similar to what you're used to."

"I doubt that."

"Why?" he asks.

"I'm not used to six-foot-two guys sleeping two floors above me." Daisy chose the basement, of all rooms. She said something about coming home late from modeling shoots and not wanting to wake up everyone. The stairs are creaky. And she's nice. That combo led her to the darkest room.

I'd rather have her up here.

It smelled like cat pee in the basement, and since Sadie, Connor's feline, is now living with us too—she could have been the culprit and already chosen her first target.

Sadie is a born criminal.

"I'm six-foot-three," Ryke corrects with hardened brows.

Daisy shrugs. "Same thing."

"No," Ryke says a single word.

Daisy tries not to smile. "I've also never shared a shower with a guy before."

Lo and I frown together. He beats me to the question. "Don't you have your own shower downstairs?"

Daisy's smile fades, and she exchanges a look with Ryke. Okay, everyone is sharing looks without me. I feel like the kid picked last for dodge ball.

"You don't have a shower?" I say, trying to find the answer here.

"Um, maybe you both should come check out the bathrooms," Daisy says, having to step over a box and squeeze past Brett to reach the door.

We follow her.

"Is the shower gross?" I wonder.

Lo clutches my hand as we walk. "Maybe they found mold or something."

Good theory. "Maybe a turtle had babies in the bathtub."

Lo considers this and then says, "And the shower is definitely full of snakes."

"Monkeys," I add. "There's a monkey nest in the cabinet." I picture *Jumanji*, a full out zoo inside the bathroom with ivy and deadly plants. Killer bees come next.

"Monkeys don't have nests," Lo says. *Where do monkeys live then?*

"You two are fucking weird," Ryke says. Our imaginations are vast. It doesn't help that we love comic books more than reality.

Ryke and Daisy abruptly stop in the middle of the long narrow hallway. I almost bump into Ryke's chest, and when I take a step back, I knock into Brett's camera.

"Sorry," I mutter. I clearly don't do well in confined spaces.

Voices from the main level below trickle up the staircase.

"Traveling somewhere, Scott?" Rose snaps. "Hopefully to California where you're actually needed." Rose sounds more ticked off than usual.

"Who's Scott?" Daisy asks in a whisper.

I think she's the only one without this info. Someone should have told her sooner.

"The producer," Ryke says, "for the show."

I consider edging closer to the staircase to see if I can catch a glimpse of him. Rose has spent plenty of nights complaining about the misogynistic producer. She has to deal with him though, for the sake of the reality show.

My feet stay glued to the floorboards, too anxious about the bathrooms to move just yet.

"I'm needed here," Scott says. "It just takes people time to realize what's good for them."

Ryke crosses his arms over his chest, listening intently with Daisy and Lo. They're all eavesdropping while I internally freak about the bathrooms.

I don't actually think monkeys are in our cabinets.

I don't discount the turtles though.

Lo whispers, "I already hate this guy."

"Same," Ryke says. "If he fucks with one of the girls—"

"It's not going to happen," Lo cuts him off. "Connor already ran a background check on him."

"I don't have as much faith in Connor as you do," Ryke whispers.

Lo actually pats his brother's back and says, "Then have faith in me." He's known Daisy, Rose, and me almost all his life. Lo wouldn't let Scott harass us without a major fight.

Ryke lets out a tense breath and just nods.

I count five doors along this hallway. Daisy has her hand on a brass knob to one of them. Is that the hall bathroom then?

I catch the tail end of Scott's comment. "…showing your tits would increase the ratings."

My jaw unhinges. *What?!*

"So would shoving my foot up your ass," Rose refutes.

Lo clenches his teeth.

"I'm going down there," Ryke whispers.

"No," Daisy says, grabbing Ryke by the forearm. She stops him before he heads down the hallway. "We need to show Lo and Lily the bathrooms. And Rose won't appreciate you coming to her defense."

"Yeah," I agree. "Rose can handle anything."

Ryke reluctantly redirects his course of action, and he rests his hand on the small of Daisy's back, silently telling her to open the bathroom door.

This is it.

The old wood creaks as she opens it wide. We all slowly walk in, and my mouth just drops further. No turtles or monkeys or even mold.

The *two* showers are huge. Too large, in fact. As if they're made for communal purposes. Oh my God. What if they're made specifically for orgies? What if production believes that I'll hook up with *multiple* people in them?

"What is this?" Lo asks with a deep glare.

"We're all sharing one bathroom," Ryke announces, leaning against one of the four sinks.

"Rose would have said something…" I trail off.

Daisy says, "I don't think Rose knew before today."

"Lily…" Lo places a hand on my shoulder, concern cloaking his gorgeous face. I must look petrified. At least, that's exactly how I feel.

My privacy has been slowly stripped for months, and now it's almost all disappeared.

"I don't like this," I mutter under my breath.

My immediate thought isn't *damn, we can't fuck in the shower.* It's my third or fourth thought, which (I think) is progress. My first thought is how embarrassing it'll be if Ryke or Connor walks in on me showering. Oh no…what if a cameraman sees me naked? What if he catches it on film?

"They can't film in the bathrooms. It's in the contract," Lo reminds me.

"Are you sure you can't read my mind?" I whisper, the humor lost in my voice.

He hugs me close. There is nowhere safer than in Loren Hale's arms.

"Do you jack off in the shower?" Daisy asks casually to Ryke, a smile to her voice. It instantly causes Lo to tense. She's become almost too open around his brother.

Ryke doesn't miss a beat. "I don't have to jack off, sweetheart."

"Wow, the pent up frustration must hurt then," she says with sarcasm. "No wonder you're so moody."

"Fucking hilarious." And then he undoes her bun, sliding her hairband on his wrist and messing her long locks with a rough hand. Her blonde strands stick out wildly. When he finishes touching her, a small smile peeks on the corner of her lips.

"Out of curiosity," she says, not fixing her unkempt hair, "where do you pick up girls?"

Ryke glances at his brother, just recognizing that we're in the room with him. I know what it feels like to be so magnetized by someone that you forget about your surroundings.

My lips part at a sudden realization.

Ryke may be actually falling for my sister.

A girl who turns seventeen next month.

It's a feeling, but one I sense deep in my bones like I did Connor and Rose.

I can't tell Lo about my suspicions. Nothing good will come of that.

"You're always curious," Ryke answers vaguely. Still, he has trouble censoring himself. "I meet people at the gym or really anywhere I fucking go out."

"Have you dated a fan?" she asks.

Lo interjects, "Yeah he has. Twice so far. And they were his age."

Ryke stares at the ground, not saying a word. I can't read his dark expression either.

"Cool," Daisy says, nodding a couple times. "I bet they were sweet. I've considered dating a fan, but most of mine are too old."

"Like twenty-three?" Lo wonders, his voice biting. I wince. That's Ryke's age.

"No, more like thirty-five."

I'm pretty sure Daisy is picking up all the hints. She's just dismissing them with ease.

I hold onto Lo's arm. He's at such a good place with Ryke. I don't want that to change because of my little sister. Maybe, one day, it'll have to, but not now.

"You should consider dating someone around your age, Dais," Ryke says pointblank.

"I have," she says, heading towards the door. "It hasn't been anything special." With this, she leaves. My eyes meet the camera lens that remains pointed at *me*. Jeez.

"She likes you way too much," Lo says.

"Look, I'm trying to shut her down without hurting her fucking feelings," Ryke retorts. "But she's my friend. I'm not going to push her away completely."

"Here's a tip: maybe you shouldn't talk about jacking off in front of her." Lo crosses his arms. "Is it that fucking hard?"

"For me, it is."

Lo stares at him for a long minute. I anticipate something really nasty. He says, "I bet your teachers hated you in high school." That wasn't so bad.

Ryke lets out a laugh. "I got detention almost every day for saying *fuck*. So yeah, they weren't too fond of me."

I peek past Lo's shoulder to scrutinize the showers again. "They're huge."

"It'll be okay," Lo reassures me, his hands lowering to my hips.

I hope so, but everything the production company has setup feels like drama bait.

We're bound to feed into it.

Chapter 14

0 Years : 05 Months

January

LOREN HALE

"This is ridiculous." I flip through a five page *script* in disbelief. As soon as we arrived at the Philadelphia Museum of Art, Scott handed me what I thought was a museum pamphlet. Turns out production wants Lily to talk and act a certain way. Most of which is crude.

Lily leans over my arm and gasps as she reads a line. "I can't say that."

I skim the paper and see where she's concerned.

Lily stares into Loren's eyes with longing and carnal desire.

Lily: I remember how you tasted last night. I can't wait to taste you again.

"Jesus Christ," I curse. "This is like a bad porno." I scan the small crowd, hoping it won't grow into a larger one later today. Quickly, I find Scott speaking in hushed tones to Brett, who has a camera attached to his chest.

I take Lily's hand and lead her over to the twenty-eight-year-old dipshit. As soon as we approach, he turns and I chuck his five-page script at his body. It hits his chest with barely a sound and then flops to the floor. "We're not reading off a script," I snap.

Scott Van Wright has found every way to grate on me in the *shortest* amount of time. First off—he *lives* with us. No one fucking invited him to permanently crash upstairs. Secondly, I can't stand to look at his dirty blond hair, his smug face, and those douchebag tailored pants. He's like the anti-Connor. An arrogant prick who one-ups you and screams about it at the top of his lungs.

Thirdly (and most importantly) he antagonizes my girlfriend.

Yesterday he tried to corner Lily to ask her questions about her old hookups. We're not even a month in with the cameras. That's not fucking okay. I'm trying to stay positive, but shit like this is why I opt for a quiet bar and a bottle of Macallan.

"Then tell your girlfriend to speak up," Scott replies smoothly, not even breaking a sweat. "She's so quiet that she literally disappears in the background. We're making a show around a sex addict, not a wallflower."

"I'm standing right here," Lily says before I can chew him out. "You can talk *to* me."

His eyes never waver from mine. I could seriously deck him in the face, but I rarely fight with my fists.

"While the cameras are rolling, you both need to stop acting like I'm the producer of the show," he says, completely ignoring the issue.

"Right," I say. "You're Rose's ex-boyfriend." It's nothing but a lie. Just scripted drama. Scott's creating a fake love triangle between himself, Connor and Rose. His motives are all over the place.

"Exactly," he says, unbuttoning *one* button on his white shirt. So what—viewers can see his muscles? This guy—

"Do you think Rose and Connor will make it today?" Scott smiles, like we're friends. Lily instinctively checks the camera. The red light is on.

Scott already knows the answer to his question. GBA, the network airing *Princesses of Philly*, wanted more scenes with Lily and me, alone, so they planned a trip to the museum with just us. And apparently Scott. I have a strong suspicion he's just tagging along to piss us off.

My eyes narrow in contempt, and Lily squeezes my hand to help calm me.

Scott grins wider. "How's sobriety, Loren? Are you doing okay?"

My blood boils, my glare intensifying. "No, I'm not doing great. I just feel sorry for you, man. For six months, you're going to watch us drive our expensive cars, attend our exclusive parties, and fly our private jets. And when it's all over, you'll go home to your one-bedroom apartment in LA and realize that you'll never have our lifestyle. You'll *never* amount to anything other than a second-rate producer of a garbage reality show." I touch my chest. "That just makes me feel so fucking sad for you."

Scott's smile and pretenses vanish in an instant. "You're a dick."

"You're a slimy prick," I refute. "Don't ever ask me about my sobriety again."

Lily follows me as I storm off towards one of the exhibits in the back, as far away from Scott as I can get.

"He's trying to provoke us," she reminds me.

A pressure weighs on my chest. My left hand shakes. "Well it's working," I say under my breath. This rabid hate simmers underneath my skin. I just want a sip of alcohol. Anything. God, drinking is so much better than dealing with this bullshit.

"I love you," she says, her eyes tracing my features quickly.

I take a deep breath. *I love you too.* The words stick to my throat. Instead of speaking, I rest an arm along her back and hug her to my side.

She brings her hand up to her mouth, about to bite her fingernails. But she drops it before she gets that far.

"I can't stand here, Lil, and not fight back. He's making you nervous and he's pissing me off. I can't take that crap, not from anybody."

A sliver of silence stretches where my lie resides. I take shit from my dad all the time, but Lily chooses not to announce this fact. Thankfully.

"I just don't want you to come off as a villain when the show starts airing in February," she explains, "because you're not."

I've tried so hard not to be *that* guy—the one that terrorizes other people. The one that no one else but Lily can possibly understand. It's hard to walk away from this instinct. It's self-preservation. If I don't attack first, I'm going to be slaughtered by gut-wrenching pain.

I'm saving myself.

"Lo?" Lily says, her voice pitching in worry.

I turn to Lily and hold her delicate face between my hands. I notice Brett filming us from a distance. "We're going to be ourselves for this show," I say. "Fuck anyone who doesn't like us. It doesn't matter."

She nods confidently and gives me an encouraging smile. I drop my hands. Her eyes flit around the museum. "Out of all the places production could pick, they chose something more up Rose's alley."

"Yeah, I know." Paintings and sculptures sit against white walls. People wander around with headsets on, quiet like we're in a library. "How boring is this going to be?"

"Maybe we can just go around and try to guess the names of the paintings. Ohhh." She points to a portrait of a woman in an oversized Renaissance gown holding a cat. "Here's one. I think it's called *Lady with a Cat.*"

My lips rise. "Very creative."

"It's my best guess."

I approach the painting nearest us and read the small plaque underneath the frame. Jesus. "You were close. *Lady in the Blue Dress.*"

"Really?" She beams.

I'm about to reply when I spot Scott Van Wright sauntering towards us. Why can't he just stay the fuck away?

"I have to call my brother," I tell her in a low voice. The moment I say it, the moment I know it's the best plan I've had all day. That weight on my chest starts to lessen.

She whispers, "Are you okay?"

I don't want her to worry about my addiction. "We need someone to distract Scott from us." Or else I'm going to do something I regret.

Lily's face contorts in a multitude of emotions. She knows I'm not doing well, and I'd rather have him here. But she hates perpetuating tabloid rumors about three-ways and cheating.

"What about Rose or Daisy?" she asks.

"Rose is working in New York, and Daisy is at school right now." I omit Poppy since she wanted nothing to do with the reality show. "I'd call them before Ryke if I could." I add that, just for her. If I'm being honest, I'd prefer my brother over her sisters.

Lily opens her mouth to reply, but Scott steps closer. In hearing distance. He acts like he's appraising the *Lady in the Blue Dress.* "I'm thoroughly surprised you two haven't jumped on each other yet," he says, his gaze pinned to the painting. "It might be a new record."

"You don't know us," Lily combats.

"You're a sex addict," he says. "You want the short definition?" He licks his lips. "You like to ride dick."

I fume, my teeth aching from gritting them. Lily rests a hand on my chest. Her face is flushed, red patches dotting her neck and cheeks. I hate that he embarrassed her. I hate that he's shaming her.

More importantly, I hate that *nothing* I say does any fucking damage to him.

This is the point where I'd walk away and start fucking with his life.

I'd ruin him from the inside out.

His career. His money. I'd utilize the tools my father gave me to destroy a man. But I can't.

I can't do that this time.

We're *barely* into the reality show. What's the alternative though? Stand here and eat shit?

I can't.

My muscles burn. Each inhale is like trying to breathe through black smoke.

"Look at me," I sneer, so aggravated that Scott won't tear his eyes off the painting. He's pathetic.

Finally he turns his head, but I can see it's becoming harder for him to keep up his self-satisfied smile when he's facing me.

"Stay out of my goddamn face." These are my only words before I drag Lily to another side of the museum where antique furniture and silver flatware are on display. Scott stays behind for now.

I unpocket my phone and start texting Ryke.

Stop climbing fake rocks and come meet us at the museum.

"If he's this mean to us," Lily mutters, "I wonder what he's like to Rose and Connor." Her eyebrows knot together in confusion. "Do you think he says dirty things about her?" Concern plagues her face. I'm not used to Lily being protective of Rose.

"She can take care of herself," I remind her. "And if she can't, she has Connor."

"Yeah," Lily says softly, "you're right."

My phone vibrates in my palm. I read the text quickly.

I'm not invited. – Ryke

Really? That hasn't stopped him before.

Do I need to extend you a written invitation? Get your ass over here.

I hand Lily my phone and then say, "Want a ride around this place?"

She nods with a smile.

I bend down and then lift her onto my back, my arms underneath her legs. I can practically feel the heat of the camera on us. Paparazzi had to stay outdoors. But the *Princesses of Philly* cameras just go wherever we do.

I expected it, but it's different when it actually becomes your reality.

I carry Lily in a piggy-back over towards a painting of a watering can.

"It's criminal, you know," she says, her voice faraway in thought. "We didn't even have communal showers our freshman year of college." She pauses. "Do you think this is cosmic payback?"

"They're not bad." I don't want her to be afraid of them. I've called her sex therapist to talk about the issue, and she said that I need to find a way to motivate Lily.

I feel like I've tried everything. I repeat the same words over and over, and she's still scared shitless that someone will film us and put it online. She said she has a "bad feeling" about them.

"That's a nice watering can," she says, dodging the issue.

"You're not going to take a shower, are you?"

"That's a strong phrase," she breathes. "I'm going to *forgo* the shower for a bit and opt for an alternative choice."

I gently set her on her feet.

Her shoulders curve towards her thin body. She's disappointed.

But this is serious. "A bath?" I ask, hoping but disbelieving she'd choose that option.

She tucks a piece of her hair behind her ear, the strands already becoming greasy. "More like a washcloth bathing experience."

I don't blink. "Not for six months." It's not a question.

"People in the wilderness do it."

"People in the wilderness jump into a river when they smell. Are you going to jump into a river?"

She pales. "No."

"Then take a shower."

"Why are you being the hygiene police all of a sudden?" she questions, her eyes welling up with tears. My stomach drops. "You never used to care if I skipped for a week."

I hate that I have to be a hardass. I lower my voice so Brett's filming equipment can't pick up the sound. "This is six months, and we live with other people now. You smelling like sex is not the way to go, Lil. They may think we're fucking more than usual and then they'll be all over us." Her pleading, watery eyes try to sway me. "Skip tomorrow, fine, but I'm going to have to start being careful when I come on you."

She frowns. "You haven't done that in…"

"A long time, I know." Crazy sex has been out of the picture for a while.

She glances at her boobs like she's visualizing the event.

"Lily," I snap. "What's wrong?"

"I was just thinking…" She turns red all over. "…about your plans."

I hug her close and kiss her lips lightly.

"Your phone just buzzed," she tells me as we part. She hands me the cell, and I open the text.

Is everything okay? – Ryke

I don't know. I type the text and think of more to add, but so many phrases pop in my head. I realize I'm just overwhelmed.

Not all days are easy.

Most of them make no fucking sense. A good handful tears me apart, limb from limb. The best days are the ones I try to remember, but sometimes, even those are swallowed by the bad.

I send the text as it is. Three words.

I'm on my way. – Ryke

I'm about to pocket my phone, but it vibrates again.

Don't drink. – Ryke

He's told me that a million times before, but it's this one time that affects me the most. *Don't drink.* I won't turn this bad day into a terrible one. For me.

But really, for her.

Fear of failing Lily—it motivates me in ways that no one can understand.

Chapter 15

0 Years : 05 Months

January

LILY CALLOWAY

Lo and I walk around the museum in deadened silence, a camera shadowing us. Ryke arrived about ten minutes ago and pulled Scott outside while Savannah, a pretty redheaded girl, films them. When we passed the glass windows, I saw Ryke shouting at the producer, but his fists weren't raised.

The whole day, I sensed how distraught Lo was becoming. He has a lot to worry about. Halway Comics, Superheroes & Scones, his father breathing down his neck, alcohol…and me.

It hurts to realize that I can't take away his pain today and that in a small way, I may be contributing to it.

We sit on a bench, a mammoth painting hung on the wall before us. A white angel battles a dark-haired man in red silk; the man is most likely on the losing end.

Angels always win.

I don't know its true meaning. Or the context. But the longer I stare at the image, the sadder I become.

"I'm sorry," I breathe.

I feel him turn to look at me. "For what?" He edges closer, his thigh against mine. I stare right into those amber swirls, seeing his agony, his love and his vice. All at once.

"You have so much going on," I say softly. "I don't want you to constantly worry about me too."

He frowns. "I'll always worry about you," he tells me. "It's impossible not to."

"In a future," I whisper, "I'd like to think that you just know wherever I am, I'm smiling…and content." *No agonizing. No stress over my wellbeing.* "It's just whether that future is ours or someone else's." I focus on the bench again.

He presses his fingers underneath my chin, lifting my gaze once more. "You remember when we were in tenth grade and we decided to ditch comics in Earth-616 for all the alternate universes and realities?"

I nod. "It was fun for a few months." We read some of the most bizarre comics during that time, and months later, we preferred the main continuity in Marvel comics. Earth-616.

"And you know what we decided at the end of it all?" Lo asks me.

"That Magneto and Rogue should never be allowed to date—in any universe."

His lips rise. "Yeah, and that alternate universes usually have the worst endings with the unhappiest conclusions." His warm hand slides to my cheek, and his eyes bore into me, intense and unyielding. "But we're in Earth-616, love. We're going to have our happy ending. It just may take us awhile to get there."

My chest lifts at his rare optimism, stirring something powerful inside my heart.

It fills me with so, so much hope.

Chapter 16

0 Years : 05 Months

January

LOREN HALE

I check rat traps that Connor, Ryke and I set in the crawl space. Daisy found two dead ones in her room, not surprising since we saw droppings on the basement stairs when we first arrived.

"Your cat isn't doing her job," I tell Connor while I squat by the small door, a trash bag in hand. Ryke has already crawled through, and I wait for him to return with hopefully a dead rat or two.

"She's already killed three of them," Connor defends his pet. He leans his arm against the wall, staring down at me. "Anymore and I'd question her domestication."

"I hate to break it to you, Connor," I say, "but your cat is feral." In private, Lily calls her *the orange beast.* I mean, Sadie scratched the hell out of Rose when she tried to put a collar on her. I thought Rose was impenetrable to almost everything.

"I found Sadie, you know." He cups a mug of steaming coffee. "She was in the rain outside my boarding school. The mother was dead. So were the three other kittens."

I don't know how many other people he's told this to. "I never pegged you as the nurturing type."

"I'm not," he says honestly. "It wasn't like she tugged at my heart in that moment." *Of course not.* "I just knew I had the power to save her life, so I did."

That was fairly conceited, but I try to dig around that. "And now that she's older and angrier?"

"I raised her exactly how I wanted," Connor says. "She doesn't need me to survive anymore. Though she loves me most."

Huh. I scrutinize the way he rests against the wall, tired. His body isn't stiff and straight like usual. Dark rings lie beneath his eyes. "You look like shit," I say. *Seriously.* I've never seen him so worn down before.

He sips his coffee. "I'm a grad student trying to take over a multi-billion dollar company. If I didn't look like shit, I'd be on drugs."

I forgot that he's been trying to take the reins of Cobalt Inc. I almost mention Scott, but even the thought of him irritates every nerve in my body.

I look back through the crawl space just as Ryke hits his head on one of the pipes. "*Fuck me,*" he curses.

"Fornicating with the rats already?" Connor asks with a grin.

"Fuck you, Cobalt." He's on his stomach, using his forearms and legs to army-crawl through the small area. "The shortest one of us should have crawled through here."

That was directed at me. "If I knew you were going to bitch, I would have done it myself, and I'm only one inch shorter than you, *bro.*"

Ryke bangs his forehead this time. He makes an animalistic noise. "I'm still six fucking three."

I watch him move at a snail's pace. "Besides being a giant, what's taking you so long? You set the trap. You should know where it is."

"It must have carried the trap with it."

"Just use your nose," Connor says. "Dogs have the best sense of smell."

I actually laugh.

"Fuck off," Ryke retorts.

I'm pretty sure that Ryke can handle Connor's digs. Even when Connor pisses him off, it seems like the comments never really eat at him. Ryke is the strongest person I've ever met. Stronger than me.

It's why Connor taunts Ryke and praises me.

I don't know if Ryke realizes it or if Connor recognizes how well I understand his relationship with me. But I see how Connor spends his time trying to build me up—so I believe that I'm just as worthy as my brother.

I'm not. I won't ever be as *good* as him, but it's nice to have a friend try to remind me of it.

Connor pulls his phone out of his pocket and starts texting. Less than a minute later, he asks, "Is Lily having more sex than usual?"

I stiffen. Keeping a secret from a guy ten times more intelligent than me is hard. But not impossible. I spent three years pretending to be in a relationship with Lily. I've got this.

"She's not having it, but she wants it." I fist the black trash bag and rise, my legs aching in this position. "This whole fucking reality show puts her on edge." It's the truth, but we're fucking a lot more than people would like. Most of the time, we screw in her car, away from cameras and thin walls where people can overhear. I layer on everything he'll expect, "And she medicates her anxiety with sex, which means I'm not getting laid for the next week, and she only gets my fingers."

I find the nearest camera, hanging on a ceiling rafter, and I wave my fingers. And wink, just for further effect. Maybe it'll distract Connor.

The cameramen are on lunch break, so fixed cameras are the only thing shooting us.

"So you're not having sex?" he asks.

I can't read the tone of his voice at all. I fucking hope I'm selling this well enough.

The longer he stares at me, the more I realize I may have overestimated my ability to lie to him.

Heat gathers on my forehead. I rub the back of my neck as I weigh the options in my head. I have to partially come clean. "No, I mean…" *Just go with it.* "We fucked the other day. She was a little compulsive afterwards, so I want her to abstain for three or four days and see how she does with that."

She wasn't that compulsive. She stopped herself from continuing past her limits, and there's absolutely no goddamn way we're abstaining. But I think it'll appease him to hear a plan.

Not too long ago, I even asked him to keep an eye on us—to make sure we were keeping to a twenty-four-hour schedule. Sex every night, nowhere in between.

"And you used condoms?" he asks.

My lips part in shock, not expecting this. My stomach flips, and I slam my fist on the wall. "Ryke, hurry the fuck up." I *don't* want to share all the details of my sex life. Connor barely shares his. I need to keep *something* private, for fuck's sake.

"Lo," he says.

I spin to him, my eyes flashing hot. "This conversation is over."

"I'm trying to imagine what Lily will look like pregnant." His tone is conversational, not spiteful. "Would her entire body swell or just her belly?"

My chest rises with irritation and with something so dark. I'm selfish. But I don't ever want to be *that* kind of selfish—to have a kid, knowing he or she could be plagued with this lifelong struggle.

"At least I'm getting laid," I say, my voice like razors that physically pains me. But I keep going. "How long have you been *fucking* your hand?"

"My hand and I go way back," he says easily, a warm smile attached.

My muscles loosen. It's a mystery why people keep me as a friend.

"I'm not your brother." Connor nods to the crawl space. Ryke is still searching for the traps. "I'm not going to curse you out for doing something stupid. But I am dating your girlfriend's older sister, so my own balls are on the line here."

Right. I nod. "The repercussions of getting into bed with a she-devil."

"And I fucking like her," he says, "so make my life easier and use a condom."

I completely relax. I can imagine how annoying it must be having Rose in his ear all day. I contemplate whether or not Lily and I have been safe. I think we have. She's on birth control. I mutter, "I'll be better about it."

Ryke crashes into more pipes, cursing and then shouting back, "There's so much fucking mold down here. No one should be fucking living on this floor until we hire someone to clean it."

I read in between the lines.

Daisy lives on the lowest level.

I saw the way he looked at her in the bathroom when we first arrived at the townhouse. For so many reasons, I can barely stomach the possibility that he could like her more than just a friend.

I squat again and see Ryke heading to the door. "If this is your way of getting Daisy to room with you, you can *forget* it. I'm just barely tolerating your friendship."

"Are you fucking kidding me?" Ryke retorts. "There were rats in *her* bedroom, she's living near mold, and your first assumption is that I want to fuck her?"

I glower, trying not to picture that. "I didn't say anything about fucking her."

Ryke groans. "I'll fucking room with Scott," he shouts. "Daisy can take my room. Or I'll stay down here and switch with her. I don't give a shit. None of the girls should be around this."

"And what if she hears Lily and me fucking through the walls? There's a reason she's on the lowest level." It's hard to believe that Daisy is the one protecting our secret—a girl who jumps off cliffs, rides a motorcycle and runs headfirst into life.

I wish I could keep her ten-thousand feet from all of this. The basement is safe from Scott. From most of the leering cameras. From us.

Maybe she can grow up normal, have a real, peaceful adolescence that none of us really had.

Ryke gives me one of the darkest looks I've seen in a while.

I frown and crane my neck over my shoulder, looking at Connor for his opinion.

"You can't censor a girl who's nearly seventeen, especially not a high fashion model," he says to me. "She's heard and seen everything you have, if not more." *So it's too late for her then.*

She's all grown up.

"I'll call someone to look at the crawl space," Connor continues, "but until it happens, Rose would want her sister somewhere clean."

I let out a breath. "Ryke, you'll room with Scott?"

"I said I would."

"Fine. More eyes on that prick, the better, right?" *Especially if Daisy is moving upstairs.*

Ryke mumbles a *yes*, and his arm thumps into a hanging piece of wood. "Fucking A," he curses, reaching the door. I grab underneath his arms and help pull him through the small exit.

We both stand on our feet. He clutches the trap, a dead rat attached, the tail nastily caught in the silver metal.

Connor grins. "Have we found you a new profession?"

"At least I can get my hands dirty, princess." He swings the rat trap in Connor's face.

Connor remains completely stoic, his grin only spreading wider.

Ryke rolls his eyes and reaches for the trash bag.

"Wait," I say, putting my hand on Ryke's arm. My chest thrums, blackness stirring inside of me. "Maybe we can do something with this thing." Scott needs more than just a few words to back off. He hasn't stopped getting in my face, or Lily's.

"No," Ryke and Connor say in unison.

I narrow my eyes at them. "You didn't even let me finish."

"You want to use it against Scott," Connor says.

Haven't they seen what he's like? Aren't they worried at *all* about what he could do to us, to the girls?

We have to stop him *now.*

"He's the fucking producer," Ryke explains off my anger. "You start a war with Scott and he could turn you into a psycho on the show. Just fucking relax."

"He made Lily bawl!" I scream. *Don't they get it?* He shames Lily every time he nears her. I hate Scott more than I've ever hated another person. Because I did *nothing* to him. And he's still coming at me. "I'm not going to sit here for six months and ignore all the shit he says. This is different than social media and gossip blogs. We're *living* with this bastard."

I breathe heavily and both guys stare at me like *I'm* the crazy one.

Because I'm the addict.

Because I think irrationally.

But I'm a person. I can *feel.*

And there's only so much I can put up with before I begin to drown.

LILY CALLOWAY

I tuck my shower caddy under my arm and use my free hand to keep the towel above my boobs. My wet flip flops slap against the tiled floor as I waddle to my bedroom. The only upside to this situation: I'm not naked underneath my towel.

Lo and I devised a strategy for bathing in the communal showers.

Swim suits.

My one-piece keeps me covered and lessens the risk of flashing anyone who accidentally walks into the bathroom. The first couple of times, Lo showered with me. He even wore his swim trunks in solidarity.

But today, I wanted to take a step and be by myself. I fall into my codependent ways far too easily. Another item added to my *Needs to Work On* list.

I kick the bedroom door closed with my foot and set the shower caddy on my desk. When I plop down on the leather chair, it lets out a farting noise from my wet bottom. My eyes bug and I check over my shoulder, making sure I'm alone.

No lurkers.

No ghosts (that I know of).

Good. I return to my laptop and log onto the internet. If I don't check my calendar every day, I'll forget about some random homework deadline—or worse—a quiz.

The joys of online classes. The upside is that my internet privileges have been restored. Lo trusts me more, and I'm beginning to find the same trust in myself. I need to navigate the internet without "stumbling" on porn.

Before I pop up my calendar, an alert pings.

5 new articles featuring Lily+Calloway+sex

This isn't porn.

Just so we have that clear.

I've set my computer to track the articles that talk about me. It's a little obsessive, sure.

I scroll through a few of the articles, most featuring a variation of the same headline.

LILY CALLOWAY TO STAR IN REALITY SHOW THIS FEBRUARY. WATCH THE PROMO VIDEO HERE!

I've seen it ten times already, but it doesn't stop me from clicking on the link.

The screen turns white and starts playing "Animal" by Miike Snow. I don't know what the production company was trying to say. We're not all animals. Okay, I may be a *sexual* animal, and I think Ryke is a literal animal, but the others aren't beasts.

We filmed the footage in a studio; all seven of us (Scott included) stand in front of a white backdrop. I waited for someone to hand me a script, but the director told us to act normal, that the video would be candid.

The promo begins by panning down the seven of us, and then it cuts to close-ups, starting with Daisy on the end. She does a handstand, her white T-shirt bunches up at her neck and reveals her green lacy bra and bare stomach. She sticks out her tongue and smiles goofily. A caption pops up over her boobs.

Daredevil.

And then Ryke shoves her legs, and she crumples to the floor with a laugh. On his chest, the caption scrolls: ***Jackass.***

The first time I saw the promo, it was like a hurricane tore through the house. No one anticipated being labeled. And it didn't take long for me to deduce mine.

Lo and me are next in line. His arms hold me closely, our chests mashed together, and our lips devour each other in an intense kiss.

Even though it's my eleventh time watching it, I still have to look away at this part. I never thought that watching him kiss *me* would turn me on. But it does. It stirs places that should not be stirred when he's not around. I don't trust myself *that much* now that I have access to the internet again.

My eyes flit up to the computer.

The words ***Sex Addict*** *and* ***Alcoholic*** *appear across our bodies.*

And then Rose, Connor, and Scott fill the screen. Rose's yellow-green eyes are practically radiating heat, and her body is shifted towards Connor. He stares at her like she invented the sun, a look I've seen a million times when they have their epic nerd battles. Connor leans over to whisper in her ear, and it sets her off, her cheeks concaving in anger.

She shoves his arm and he grins.

The word ***Smartass*** *flashes on his body.*

Then the screen pans to Scott, who looks down (very quickly) at Rose's boobs. And then my sister gives Scott a quick glance. The editing makes it seem like they were a couple, or had some sort of relationship. Scott tilts his head and gives pretty good bedroom eyes.

When his caption appears, it just makes me hate him more.

Heartthrob.

Seriously. He's a douchebag. I find it insulting that out of all the guys, he gets the only decent label.

And finally the promo shows Rose, wedged in between Scott and Connor, further exploiting the fake love triangle. Both guys stare down at her with longing and desire.

Her caption pops up just as she looks directly at the screen.

Virgin.

Now everyone knows about her sexual status, but she didn't much care about that. Rose isn't ashamed of being a virgin. I think she'd shout it from the rooftops if she could—just to prove a point.

The promo ends with the Princesses of Philly logo and title, and then the tagline flashes on the bottom.

Get inside the Calloway sisters this February.

Dirty. That was dirty, and I don't have to be a sex addict to know it.

Plus, I got confirmation from Daisy that she thought it was a sexual innuendo too. So there's that.

I scroll down and read some comments underneath the video.

Havana33: Are they going to show LiLo f*cking on this show? I feel like it needs to be NC-17.

NoelMarch: +Havana33 No way. GBA would be sued big time. So curious to see how crude it's going to be tho.

JamesGGG: How old is the Daredevil? She's hot as fuck.

James. Your GGG must stand for *gross, gross, gross*. I have to click out of the video and clear my head. It's not his fault, I remind myself. Daisy isn't his sister. He doesn't know her. But it's hard to convince myself that he isn't some creep in his parent's basement.

I log onto the last alert, an article from *Celebrity Crush*. Just great. This magazine has been nothing but nasty to me.

The headline alone makes my stomach turn.

POLL: WHICH BROTHER SHOULD LILY CALLOWAY CHOOSE?

A poll? There's a freakin' poll now.

My disbelief and masochistic curiosity compels me to read Wendy Collins' article from the top.

POLL: WHICH BROTHER SHOULD LILY CALLOWAY CHOOSE? LOREN HALE OR RYKE MEADOWS?

By Wendy Collins

With only a few days left before the premiere of "Princesses of Philly", we have one huge question left to be answered. Does Lily have more chemistry with Loren or Ryke? While we have strong suspicions that she's been dating both at the same time, one of these men is bound to have more fire on-screen than the other.

Let's break it down:

Loren Hale is her "long time" boyfriend, now fiancé, and a recovering alcoholic. Just click through our photo reel of him and you'll realize he has a panty-dropping body but it's the face that seals the deal. "Gorgeous" just doesn't even cut it. Oh, and he has a nicely-sized inheritance of a rumored $2 billion dollars, the direct heir to Hale Co. baby products.

Ryke Meadows is Loren's half-brother, routinely spotted riding his Ducati and climbing at a local Philadelphia rock wall. He's notorious for his fights with the paparazzi, shoving cameras away from Lily and his brother. Despite Lily's "proposed" engagement to Loren, we believe Ryke brings a certain heat in bed that Lily craves.

> Now remember, Lily is a "recovering" sex addict, so her needs have to be satiated by her man (or men). Since we don't know their...ahem, full packages, we're going to base their chemistry between each other from recent candid photos.

I quickly scroll through the photos, none of which make me seem too chummy with Ryke. I'm literally kissing Loren in most of them. The poll resides just below the pictures and before I click into the results, I read a disclaimer at the bottom.

> Note: While it's my firm belief that Lily may very well be sleeping with both men, we know, in the very end, that she can only be with one. And while she may choose Loren for publicity, this poll is for you to choose who she should be with despite whatever happens.

I hate her.

I click into the results and my heart drops.

22% Loren Hale
78% Ryke Meadows

...no.

I do not accept this. How could she even have a poll? It's rude. No one is polling to see if Kate Middleton would be a better match with Prince Harry than Prince William. I realize that I may have just compared myself to royalty. Not my intention.

I'm just freaking out.

A lot.

A lot, a lot.

Fuck it. Wendy Collins can't just write biased articles and not have consequences. I pop up my email and start pounding the keys in frustration. I've never written a nasty letter, but as long as it's legible, I'm fine with it.

Dear Ms. Collins,

I don't know you personally, and you don't know me personally, which is why I'm writing to you today. This is your fifth or so article about me and the supposed Ryke/Loren rumors floating around the media. These rumors are NOT TRUE. I would gladly appreciate you focusing on another topic. Hell, I wouldn't even care if you still have to write about me (though, I would prefer you not). But just stop claiming that I'm sleeping with my boyfriend's brother.

Thank you,

Lily Calloway

I reread it a couple of times, checking for grammar. It sounds more professional than I thought it would. And then I hit send.

As soon as my finger touches the button, and the email dashes off into cyberspace, my anxiety rockets up about ten levels.

Chapter 18

0 Years : 05 Months

January

LILY CALLOWAY

Its been thirty minutes since I sent the email, and I haven't heard a response. Not that I assumed Wendy Collins would reply. I just thought *maybe* she'd email back with an "okay, I understand, thanks for letting me know. I won't post anything else." Wishful thinking.

I sit on the couch, my mind reeling. I know exactly what would calm me down and clear my thoughts. My fingers inch towards my shorts.

No.

I can't.

I stand up quickly and pace back and forth. When I catch myself biting my nails, I drop my hand. Food. I can distract myself with food. The kitchen has been stocked with necessities and junk food. Perfect.

I open a cabinet and find a tub of icing in the top of the shelf. Standing on my tiptoes, I have to reach up to grab it. All the while, my pelvis "accidentally" grinds against the edge of the counter. It was an accident.

I think.

I don't know anything anymore.

I let out a strained breath and back away from the counter, taking the icing with me. After I open the lid, I dip a spoon into the container and let out a relaxed breath.

The chair looms close to me and a sudden image bursts into my head. Me. Rubbing up against it. Just like the counter. Only maybe this would be better. I step closer, changing my mind just as my crotch brushes against the wood. I suddenly back away, my face burning. I whip around. There aren't any camera*men* but there are still cameras in the rafters. Shit.

Shit.

Shit.

Shit.

Maybe they won't use that footage. I have to believe that.

And what's worse, my anxiety is so high that I'm grinding on inanimate objects to relieve it. That's a little extreme…and weird, even for me.

I walk into the middle of the kitchen, my icing in hand.

What do I do? Nowhere is safe. If there are bad days for sex addicts, this is a *very* bad one for me. Should I call Lo? No. I don't want to burden him with this. He'll be overly concerned, and I need to figure it out myself.

The front door opens before I have a chance to make a proper decision. And the townhouse's living room and kitchen are all in one visible space, nowhere to hide.

"What the fuck did you do?" Ryke growls.

Uh-oh. Did he see me grind on the chair? No. That's impossible. He doesn't have X-ray vision, and the world isn't so unjust that it'd grant him a superpower before Lo or me.

"I'm…I don't…" I end up stuttering.

"You wrote to *Celebrity Crush*," he tells me, storming further into the kitchen.

"How do you know that?" I pull out my phone as soon as I say the words. But I remember I don't have internet on it, so I slide it back in my shorts.

"They posted your email online." He hands me his smart phone and my stomach does handstands and acrobatics worthy of gold medals.

LILY CALLOWAY RESPONDS TO CELEBRITY CRUSH AND REFERS TO LOREN HALE AS HER BOYFRIEND, NOT HER FIANCÉ. IS THE MARRIAGE A HOAX?

Oh….no.

They have my original email underneath the title with a few choice words from Wendy Collins. Mostly, her calling me dramatic and sensitive.

The sad thing: I am a little dramatic and a lot sensitive.

I look back up at Ryke and his eyes have darkened considerably. "I had to do something. They had a poll, Ryke, a poll! And you freaking won it over Lo. That's not okay!"

His eyebrows knot in confusion. I guess I'm not explaining it very well. "How many times do I have to tell you to forget about the fucking rumors?" he snaps. "Not only have you given the media a reason to believe they're true, but my dad is fuming."

My heart stops. "What?" I whisper.

"Lo's back in the car on the phone with him," Ryke explains. That's why he's so upset. It's not about the rumors, not really. It's because I put Lo in a position where he had to confront their father, the man that pushes him to drink.

I'm fucking things up.

My body goes cold and chills rake my arms. A pressure sets on my chest, so heavy that breathing takes work.

The door swings open again, and I expect to see Lo gracing the room next. Instead, I hear my sister's edged voice.

"I'm walking in the house right now, Mother," Rose says, her hand tight on her cell. My stomach thrashes in another beating. My mom's pissed too?

"Hold on, I'll ask her." Rose cups the speaker and meets my gaze. "Mom would like to know why you didn't use the family publicist before making a statement."

"That's a good question," I say softly. My eyes trail away, looking for the answer, as if it's on another side of the room.

Rose lets out a sigh and returns to her phone. "She didn't have Cynthia's number," Rose says, which isn't a complete lie. I have the number to Jonathan's publicist, but not our family's. Acquiring Cynthia's number means communicating with my mother, something I haven't done for a while.

Brett walks backwards into the house, filming Connor as he passes through the open doorway. Did they all come home early for this? I know I screwed up, but I didn't expect to ruin everyone's Saturday.

Connor talks through his own phone. "Don't worry about it, Greg. Rose and I will remind everyone how to address the media."

I take out my cell and check for missed calls.

Zero.

Which is also how I rank to my parents. Or at least, they still don't know how to talk to me. Not before the sex scandal and definitely not after. Though, I am a little disappointed in my dad. I thought we were making progress. He's called me a few times to discuss Superheroes & Scones and school, but I suppose those were safe topics.

I take a couple steps back, aware that Brett's camera is whipping around the room, trying to determine who's the most interesting person right now.

He lands on Rose, who starts arguing into the phone.

I tune her out and turn around completely. There's not much I can do here. No one will trust me to do damage control. There's only one place I should go. To my bat cave! (my room). I need to check the internet for more alerts or wallow or both.

Someone grabs my arm, stopping me.

When I spin around, I sink into Lo's amber eyes. Anger doesn't invade them. Only concern. The kitchen, I realize now, is silent. All phone calls finished and pocketed.

"I'm sorry," I whisper, my throat swelling. "I didn't mean for this to blow up." *Don't cry. Channel your inner Rose. Tears are for babies and losers.*

I wipe my eyes.

I suck at being Rose.

"It's not you, Lil. Our parents are blowing this out of proportion," Lo says, his hand sliding up my arm to my bare shoulder. I'm so scared of myself that I take a step back, away from his touch, no matter how good it feels.

Wrinkles crease his forehead in more concern. It hurts to be away from him, but it's dangerous to be near him.

Rose walks forward, her heels making an aggressive noise against the hardwood. "As much as it pains me to agree with Loren, he's right—" she rolls her eyes at the word "—they're being dramatic and trying to make you feel bad."

"It's working," I mutter.

"Well, get thicker skin, Lily."

Ouch. But true. So true.

Lo glares at her though. "Not everyone has iron balls."

"I don't need *balls* to be resilient," she says curtly before turning back to me. "Next time a reporter gets on your nerves, you can write a nasty email but send it to me instead. I'll even pretend to be the reporter and reply to you."

I have the best sister in the world.

Hands down.

As much as her words soothe me, they don't erase what happened. It's not so easy to move on from something that just happened five minutes ago.

"Maybe we should watch a movie," Connor says, typing on his cell.

"No," I speak up. "You all were out doing things. Just, go back to them." I don't want to interrupt their lives with my stupid mistake.

"We were just having lunch, Lily," Rose says, her hand presses against my back, guiding me towards the living room couch. "We have those every day."

Yeah, but I ache to spring in Lo's arms, for a little bit of his hardness. Okay, a lot more than a little. The rubbing up on furniture thing I did before—it actually sounds more desirable now, even if it's weird. My neck heats the longer I contemplate sex in the company of other people.

Lo and Ryke follow close behind. When we reach the couch, I pause for a moment, watching Lo take a seat on the oversized, plush chair. I picture myself straddling his waist, legs tucked tight around him, and he'll buck up into me—

I can't lounge on top of him. I force my rusted, unoiled joints to bend and sit next to Rose on the couch. Connor uses the remote to scroll through movies on the television, silence thickening, especially as I sit straight up.

And Lo is stiff as well, his eyes flickering to me every so often.

Everyone, not just us, assesses the weirdness. Aware how strange it is for Lo to be over *there.* While I'm right *here.* A large chunk of space between us. We're not together. Physically.

That rarely happens nowadays.

It would be fine, but everyone knows why I'm separating myself from him. I can feel their judgy thoughts in my own head. *I can't believe she wants to have sex right now.*

Ryke's glare says it enough.

Before Connor switches on the film, the front door opens. I crane my head over the couch to see Daisy strutting in with a can of Fizz Life in hand, head down, texting on her cell.

When she steps into the room, she looks up and freezes. "Um…" She frowns. "Was there a meeting or something?" Her face suddenly falls, thinking she wasn't invited to our group gathering.

"Or something," Ryke replies first.

Daisy scans the area. Her eyes ping from Lo to me, noticing how we're not sitting together. "Did you two…" She motions between us.

Shit. She thinks we spilled our secret.

"I fucked up," I explain swiftly. "I replied to a reporter without going through the publicist."

Her green eyes turn into saucers. "Mom has to be pissed."

"She's venting," Rose corrects her. "She just needs to cool off."

Daisy sets her soda can on the end table and plops down on the other side of me. "What are we watching?"

Connor starts listing off names of movies, and I tune him out. I appreciate that they're all trying to avoid the *Celebrity Crush* topic, but it still weighs on me.

The point of having a publicized wedding is to appease my parents. But if I do something small and anger them anyway, how much will the marriage even matter?

My eyes flit to Lo, and I realize that he's watching me. I want to touch him—not for sex. Just to let him comfort me without needing anything else. How do I know if I'm strong enough for that?

He slowly pulls his gaze away and forces his eyes to the TV screen. My heart tears apart in a million different ways, conflicted beyond terms.

I follow his moves and redirect my attention to the movie. But my head revolves around him, and I find myself trying to watch him through my peripheral vision. Maybe I can catch him looking at me. I notice everything. How rigid he sits. When he squirms or adjusts himself on the chair. How he keeps his hand on his mouth, resting it there and hiding the definition in his jaw. I notice the way he glances at me every few seconds, the same clandestine looks I give him.

And I realize that I won't ever know if I'm strong enough if I don't try. The one thought propels me to my feet and cuts the thick, silent tension in one move. Everyone looks to me, but I focus only on Loren Hale.

His chest rises in a strong inhale as I near. Without hesitation, I crawl onto his lap, and his hands instinctively pull me higher and closer, meshing our bodies together. Our limbs entangle until I can't tell where one begins and the other ends.

I release a staggered breath and rest my head on his chest, his heart beating so fast. His fingers tightly intertwine with mine, and the rhythm of his pulse slows when I close my eyes.

Any craving for sex is drowned out by my conscience, not nearly as bad as I thought it'd be.

He kisses me on my head, and I pray for a temperate sleep, tears creasing my eyes whenever I start thinking about what happened.

People make mistakes every day, some small and some big, but I just wonder when I'll stop making them. Or is this a lifelong thing? Do we all just wander through life, fucking up and trying to put ourselves back together only to continue on again?

Are we the accumulation of our mistakes?

A part of me regrettably thinks so.

My failures have defined me more than my triumphs.

But I don't want to live in that hopeless reality. Not anymore. I want to be the accumulation of my failures, my successes, of all the people I've ever met, of the man I love, and the life I want. I want to be defined by so many factors that it's too complicated for any mathematician to piece apart.

That would be the perfect life.

Not good or bad.

Just complex.

Chapter 19

0 Years : 06 Months

February

LILY CALLOWAY

The premiere of *Princesses of Philly* couldn't just be a quiet event at the townhouse. I counted over ten cameras swarming the ballroom of a five-star hotel. Servers meander with champagne and snacks, adding to the masses of bodies and general hoopla.

My mom is here.

With my dad.

And all of their socialite friends.

In a few minutes, the big screen televisions along the walls will air all of our antics. And we don't have *any* idea what will be shown. "So this is live television from here on out?" I ask Lo, his arm around my shoulder.

We stand close to a potted plant, which shields half of our bodies from the narrowed lenses.

"Not exactly," Lo says. "Connor tried to explain it to me. I think we're just going to be filmed every day, and they'll play footage from the previous week." Oh. There'll be a small delay then, *almost* live. Most shows are filmed months in advance, and the shooting wraps before the first episode ever airs.

But we're still filming while the show plays on television.

I think it's just going to make everything crazier.

"Hiding out?" Ryke asks, nearing us from the bar with a can of Fizz Life and a plate of Swedish meatballs.

"Maybe," I say. My stomach grumbles at the sight of the meatballs. I've been so nervous all day about the viewing party that I forgot to eat.

"Come to join us?" Lo asks with a half-smile.

"Yeah," Ryke says, giving Lo the Fizz Life can and then he hands me the meatballs. *For me?* I smile so much. Before I can thank him, he adds, "If I have to listen to Sam Stokes talk about Fizzle's product placement for another minute, I'm going to fucking shoot myself."

Lo's lips rise, and he laughs. "Maybe you should take notes."

In the center of the room, Poppy's husband converses with my dad, a handsome smile on Sam's face, his hands gesticulating as he speaks. My oldest sister stayed home with Maria, just to shelter her from the cameras.

"What do you mean?" Ryke asks, running a hand through his hair. He wears an expensive suit jacket with a regular shirt underneath like Lo, tailored perfectly for their bodies.

I kind of want to take the shirt off Lo though and slide my hands across his abs. *Maybe later,* I think as I chew my meatball.

"I know I don't fit into this." Lo motions towards the ballroom and the fancy decorations: gold-leafed lilies, daisies and roses as high-table centerpieces. "But you stick out even worse than me."

"It's true," I nod.

Ryke extends his arms. "I've been to events like this one before. I've told you both that." Plus he attended Fizzle's soda unveiling with me about a year ago. It was just as glamorous.

"You look kind of angry," I add and scrunch my nose to illustrate.

Ryke frowns. "Are you constipated?"

"No." I relax my face.

"Then what the fuck are you doing?"

He's so mean. "Exactly," I say, not making much sense. But he demonstrated how rough around the edges he really is.

I don't think anyone has approached him this whole time.

"People don't have to like me," Ryke tells us. "I am who I fucking am."

Lo takes a swig of his drink and pats Ryke's back with more affection than dry humor. "I guess we'll find out *how* well people like you after the show airs." Then he turns and snatches one of my meatballs by the toothpick.

"How was that thievery for you?" I ask him.

He washes the food down with his soda. "Illicit," he says with the wag of his brows. I punch his arm and he actually winces. For real this time. "Jesus Christ."

"I've been lifting weights, remember?" I flex to show him my bicep muscle (still tiny, but a bigger tiny than before). The cameras go wild behind me, flashing crazily, and I immediately drop my arm and roast.

"You mean that dinky weight that Ryke bought you?" Lo asks.

Ryke no longer pays attention to us. He focuses on Daisy across the room, who's being chatted to death by our mom. I should go rescue her…but a run-in with my mom—who acts like I'm a daughter, twice removed—is not high on my list of things I want to do.

Lo waves his hand in both of our faces and we sufficiently face him instead of the gathering crowds. "Maybe we should just bail?" Lo tugs at his collar. He has a point. We're standing in the loser's corner with slightly sullen faces, despite a good laugh here or there. And I've only thought about bathroom sex *once*.

Definitely a success on that count.

"Fine with me," Ryke says.

"No," I end up declaring, surprising even myself.

Both Ryke and Lo stare down at me like I've grown a unicorn horn.

"Rose needs us," I explain. Across the ballroom, my sister stands next to Connor while he schmoozes some business people. This show is for her, mostly. A little for Fizzle's reputation. But we're all here and participating so Calloway Couture will survive the blowback of my sex scandal.

Lo hugs me to his chest like I said some magic words. My dirty plate almost smashes between our bodies, but Ryke swiftly steals it from my hands.

He has quick reflexes.

And then the countdown appears on all the television screens. The boisterous talk dies to soft murmurs.

"I can't look," I whisper, my hands flying to my face. Lo keeps his arm around my shoulders. *Five seconds.*

"No matter what happens," Lo says, his lips brushing my ear, "I'll always be here, Lil."

I'll always be here.

I inhale.

I think I'm ready to watch myself. Even if I turn out to be one insatiable fool.

Chapter 20

0 Years : 06 Months

February

LOREN HALE

As the reality show continues, I'm more and more surprised that they're focusing on the romance aspect of my relationship with Lily, not just making out, but real stuff where I talk about how she's never cheated on me. Where she says that she loves me more than anyone.

Next to us, Ryke, Rose, Connor and even Daisy didn't seem that shocked by the good light we've been put in. I'm not counting on it to last the whole hour.

"You sure you want to stay for the rest?" I ask Lily who holds my hand.

"Positive," she says, taking a deep breath.

"Okay."

Not long after, a montage airs. It takes me a few seconds to discern that they're all moments where Lily was at the townhouse.

Alone.

Lily squirms on the leather couch. And then her hand lowers towards her jeans. She retracts quickly and then checks over her shoulder.

She looks straight into the lens, at the viewers, and stuffs a pillow in her face.

The bottom of my stomach falls.

I didn't realize…it's been that hard for her while I'm at my office during the day. "Lil," I whisper. She drops my hand, her palms pressed to her face. I'm not sure if she's even watching through her fingers anymore.

Lily lies on the couch, her laptop on her legs. She looks around and then shuts her computer. Her hand descends towards her jeans but remains on top of the fabric.

She reaches the place between her thighs.

Lily almost crumbles in front of me. Christ. I lean down and whisper in her ear. "It's okay."

She shakes her head, trembling.

My whole body tightens—my muscles on fire. I speak quickly, words gushing out of me. "You did fine, Lil. You didn't break any rules. You didn't do anything that we haven't done together. You stopped yourself." I hope that this'll relieve the pain in her chest, the nearly unbearable kind that slams into me like a thirty-foot wave.

I wait for it to drag us beneath the current. As I hold her from behind, her tears drip onto my arms. The footage airs just as rapidly as my voice meets her ear.

Lily rubs up against a kitchen chair. She flushes when she notices what she's doing.

Lily rubs her pelvis against the counter.

I feel so fucking sick.

Not because she failed herself. She didn't. But because she believes that she did. She knows that everyone will see this and think she's a head case.

Lily spins into my chest and clutches my black crew-neck. Before I can grab her, she ducks underneath the shirt, hiding inside. I feel her wet tears on my bare chest, and her arms wrap tightly around my waist.

"I'm not coming out," she murmurs, her voice cracking. "Don't make me come out, Lo."

I place my hand on her head and stare down at her through my collar. "Stay there as long as you want, love." She knew the show would humiliate her in some way, but it's different when it actually happens.

When you feel the unrelenting judgment from every goddamn person in the room.

I get it.

Any eyeball that pins on her—I meet with the hatred that turns me cold and dark. I could kill right now. It's not a lie or an exaggeration. It's a feeling.

It's a hurt so deep that *the worst* seems possible.

I want to hurt people the way they hurt us.

"Hey," Ryke says looking between me and my shirt, where Lily has hid away from the party. He mouths, *you okay?*

I can barely shrug.

He takes a step nearer. "She's alright," Ryke says under his breath. "Lily, you hear me?"

Lily sniffs loudly but she can't form words. She hiccups, and I rub her back. Her body relaxes into mine.

"Stay strong," Ryke says, patting my shirt. He looks up at me. "Tell me that was her head."

I let out a weak laugh. *God, how the hell am I laughing right now?* The noise ends up fading quickly. "Yeah, it was."

I barely watch the rest of the premiere, mostly disinterested in what Scott edited. Lily stays buried beneath my shirt, and she clings tighter when they switch to a series of interview questions cut together.

> *"Do you think Daisy is as sexually active as Lily?" Savannah asks me, Ryke, and Connor the same question but at different times.*

I clench my teeth. They keep trying to paint her sister as a sex addict too—or at least a girl that could become one. Lily's breath catches like she's trying not to cry again.

This sucks. This whole fucking thing. Shame. Guilt. What more do they want to throw at her?

> *I stand up, the leather chair rolling backwards. "I'm done with this sh*t."*
>
> *"What the f**k kind of question is that?" Ryke asks. He rises and throws a pillow.*
>
> *"No, she's not," Connor says, with more force than usual. He stands and buttons his suit jacket. "That's enough for the day."*

Daisy, who was texting on the ground, slowly rises to her feet. She avoids my gaze.

My brother's.

Connor's.

"You okay?" I ask her. I realize we've all been checking each other throughout the show. If something can rip friendships and family apart, it's airing dirty laundry.

"Perfect," she murmurs, eyeing the emergency exit door.

My brother leans close to me and whispers, "She's going to bolt."

I tilt my head towards him. "You wanna go after her?" Daisy terrifies me. But so does the idea of my brother being with her.

Ryke frowns and turns to look at me, studying my expression. "No. I want to stay with you."

I've been too paranoid about his intentions with Daisy. And I've been an ass to him all night. He's just looking out for that girl. That's it. "You can go if you—"

"No," he says forcefully. "I'm not leaving you."

His weighted words hit me hard. He stares at me like they mean more than just this single moment. I've been abandoned by family before. A birth mother—who didn't want to acknowledge me as a kid or an adult. By his mother, someone I believed was mine for too long.

It'd be easy for him to just leave. At any second. I'm not the nicest person to be around. I'd have given up on me within a few minutes.

But Ryke is still here.

This guy…he's too good for me. I don't deserve someone like that in my life.

After some minutes with the cameras creeping up on us, Daisy is gone. Disappeared within the masses of people.

We're in the last portion of the show, where it focuses on the fake love triangle between Scott, Rose, and Connor. When Lily unburies herself from her hiding place—my shirt—I wipe away her remaining tears.

She sniffs and holds onto my belt loops. "That was bad."

"Yeah," I agree. "They didn't even show me flipping off the camera. Not once. Those assholes."

She laughs and rubs her cheeks with the back of her hand. "I'm sorry."

"Don't be," I say. "You didn't pull me into the bathroom or the car, Lil." *You stayed strong.* I kiss her lightly on the lips, but it turns into something more desperate. Her body curves into mine, and my hand clutches the back of her head.

"I think about her all the time."

Scott's voice echoes through the ballroom, causing us to break apart and turn to the screens.

Scott wears a longing smile. "She's a firestorm that I won't ever smother. I'm the one who inflames her, who riles her to a new confounding degree. She's my perfect match."

That sounds like something Connor would say. Right beside Rose, Connor actually pales, his lips parted in shock.

"I hate this guy," Ryke says softly.

"You want to do something about it?" I hope he's reached the point I have—ready to fight back, something more than just saying *fuck off.*

Ryke inhales deeply. "What can we do? We signed a fucking contract."

"Plenty," I retort.

"Don't go down that road again, Lo. You need to bury those demons."

I thought I'd never attack a guy after I apologized to Aaron Wells and shut the door on that feud. But isn't this different?

Scott is waiting for us to explode. For ratings. He won't stop until the show does. And Lily and I care too much about Rose to do that to her company. So *Princesses of Philly* has to continue.

Ending it isn't an option.

"I'm still in love with her," Scott says. "And I can't help what I feel, but it's there. I love Rose the way she deserves to be loved. I just...I just don't see Connor being the best thing for her. He's too self-absorbed to care for that girl the way I do. And I hope, over the course of living with her again, she'll realize that we're meant to be."

My blood boils at each word. I shake my head and look to my brother. "The things we bury," I say under my breath, "have a way of coming back to haunt us."

Ryke can try to bury his problems.

I'm going to face mine.

Connor sits in the study room for an interview.

"What do you think of Scott?" Savannah asks.

"I find him comparable to a little teenager jimmying the lock of my house. He's nothing more than a petty thief, trying to take what's mine. Is that honest enough for you?"

"And what about Rose?"

"What about Rose?"

I frown. He said her name like she means nothing to him.

"Do you love her?" Savannah asks.

"Love is irrelative to some."

"And is it to you?"

His fingers rest on his jaw in mock contemplation, and he smiles self-confidently.

For the first time, his smile really rubs me wrong.

"Yes," he says. "Love holds no meaning in my life."

What…the fuck.

The screens fade to black.

That was it.

So many thoughts toss around my head while everyone claps. People start talking and heading to the bar for more drinks.

Ryke and I face Connor. I never thought production would've turned the seemingly nicest guy into the evilest. But they definitely did.

Rose plucks another champagne glass from a server's tray and relaxes her back against Connor's chest. He holds her in place since she's buzzed. I can't believe she's okay with everything he just said in the show.

"So was that the real Connor Cobalt?" I ask, sliding my arm around Lily's shoulders. Some of the scenes could've been fabricated by editing, but how much?

I hear my brother's warning, about Connor not being open enough with me. I never thought he had a similar relationship with Rose, but she puts herself out there and he's not even *willing* to admit that he loves her.

"I spoke honestly," he says. "And that wasn't the first time I've done so."

"So you've never loved anyone?" I question. "Not another girlfriend, your mom, your dad or a friend?" I don't want our relationship to be a game. I knew, in the beginning, that he was just collecting me like he did everyone else. He was upfront about it, which was why I liked him. I had money and connections, so that's why he befriended me. But I thought we'd grown beyond that. Hadn't we?

"No," he says. "I've never loved anyone, Lo. I'm sorry."

Rose points at me, her glass of champagne in hand. "Let it go, Loren. I have."

"Why?" I snap. "Because you're both cold androids?"

Her glare is softened by the booze. "It's just how he is. If you even understood half of Connor Cobalt's beliefs, your head would spin."

"Rose," Connor says, as though telling her to drop it.

I've never seen her give so much of herself to one person, and I fear, *badly*, that she's being manipulated by him. Maybe, all this time, I have been too.

Rose still defends her boyfriend. "No, Connor has done nothing wrong."

"He doesn't *love* you," I sneer. "He's been with you for over a year, Rose." He's going to hurt her. A girl who *never* lets anyone get that far is letting the wrong person in. Why am I the only one who sees this?

"Lo," Lily warns.

"No," I say, "she needs to fucking hear this." I point at Connor but speak to Rose. "What the hell kind of guy stays with a girl for that amount of time without anything in return? If he doesn't love you, then he's just waiting to fuck you."

Connor stays calm. And this time, it really fucking irritates me. "She doesn't need your protection," he tells me. Rose sways in his arms, tipsy. "She knows who I am."

"So you're okay with that then?" I ask Rose. "He's going to fuck you, and then he's going to be out of here. Does that make you feel good, Rose? You've waited twenty-three goddamn years to lose it, and you're going to give it to a guy who can't even fucking *admit* that he loves you."

He's a coward. A guy that I thought was the best goddamn person in the world—is nothing but a fake.

Connor says, "I'm not going to admit something that I don't feel." I have a retort ready, but he beats me to it. "Would you like me to sit you down and fill your head with numbers and facts and relativities? You can't stomach what I have to say because you won't understand it, and I know that hurts you. But there's nothing I can do to change the way things are. I am a product of a mother as brick-walled as me, and trust me when I say that you won't ever see more than I give you. In order to be my friend, that has to be enough, Lo."

I process each heavy word. I wish that he felt like I could handle all of him. I wish that I didn't idolize him so much from the beginning. "And what about you, Rose?" I ask, turning to her. "Is that enough for you?"

Lily sidles next to Rose and holds her hand. The fact that Lily can even comfort someone after what's happened to her tonight—it builds something pure inside of me.

Rose nods, her neck straightened and shoulders pulled back. But I catch her squeezing Lily's hand. "I'm going to the bathroom. You guys can meet us at the car." Lily braces Rose around the waist, and they weave between the scattering crowds.

I watch how Connor keeps his blue eyes locked on Rose. With more and more concern.

He *is* in love with her.

For once, in his life, Connor is blind.

When he meets my gaze, I say, "I just want you to know that I lost some respect for you tonight. And you're not going to get it back so fucking easily." I don't want to play his games. I'm not an investor he needs to slip in his back pocket. I'm his *friend.* I just want him to be real with me.

"Sure," he says softly. "I understand."

His gaze drifts to the carpet in deep thought. A faraway look that I don't often see from him. My stomach is in knots. I already want to forgive him, to say *don't worry about it.* He has that power over people. It's insane, and I realize how much I love the guy.

That's the funny thing right:

He'll probably never love me.

LILY CALLOWAY

"LILY! LOREN!"

The paparazzi swarm us like ants crawling out of a hill. Only now they're willfully rushing between cars in the street, just to film us on the sidewalk as we try to push our way into a New York City building.

A camera lens accidentally knocks into my head. *Ouch.* I shut my eyes as the pain swells.

"Back up!" Lo yells at the paparazzi. He guides me forward and protects my head by tugging me closer to his chest.

Ryke physically restrains cameramen with the length of his strong arms, using them as barriers. He's like my replacement Garth since I had to sadly put him on hiatus. The production team wouldn't let Daisy and me keep our bodyguards, something about "getting in the way."

I miss Garth's brutal, intimidating stares that shrank any pedestrians who gave me stink eyes.

And I miss the way he smells like bagels in the morning. No matter if he's a man of few words. He was brawn that I severely lacked.

I try to hold out my leopard-print canister of pepper spray for self-protection, but I practically have a T-Rex claw hand, not able to outstretch my arm very far.

"Who's better in bed, Lily?!" a cameraman shouts. "Loren or Ryke?!"

Fire burns my belly. I wish I was a T-Rex. I'd eat him.

In a *non-sexual* way. Just to be clear.

My neck heats.

"Lily," Lo says, his lips right beside my ear. "*Breathe*."

I realize that I'm taking slow, shallow breaths. My forehead sweats, and my upper lip is probably perspiring. How sexy. "Lo," I whisper over the shouting paparazzi and Ryke who hollers to *move back!* "Are we going to make it?"

I meant to the building. We're here to support Daisy, who's in a runway show for a popular designer. But my words seem to encompass more than this time and place. *Princesses of Philly* was the most viewed reality show on GBA *ever*. We didn't have this amount of fame before. It's a whole new level of crazy.

Lo answers by lifting me up in his arms, front piggy-back style which is intimate and safe. I wrap my arms around his neck, pressing my forehead to his shoulder. I block out the noise. It's just Lo and me. Like old times.

He says, "We can make it."

I believe him.

My legs tighten around his waist, and a bad part of me starts to ache...for something harder. Sex is on the brain today.

Just go into the building. Everything will be quiet.

It's a wishful thought.

As soon as Ryke pushes through the doors ahead of us, Lo enters with a string of five or six cameramen trailing him. Only two belong to the reality show.

More flashes and clicking.

There is no escape.

We sit on plastic white chairs that line the runway. I lean closer to Lo, gripping his bicep while his hand remains on my knee. "Can you put your hand higher," I whisper, my heart racing in my chest. I need something.

Wait. My eyes bug.

I take in the setting. Front row seats to a runway show. Press snap photos of the audience before the models begin to walk. I'm wedged between Lo and Ryke. For some reason, production separated us from Rose, Connor and Scott, who sit across the white runway.

I can't be *fingered* right now. On this chair. In front of *other* people.

Some logical part of my brain died outside.

Lo gives me a worried look.

"Nevermind," I slur together. "Keep your hand, right here." I pat the top of his hand on my knee for further emphasis. But I wonder if I can just pull it up a little higher.

No.

I cross my legs to put some pressure between my thighs.

It doesn't help. I think I'm sweating through a Calloway Couture blouse. I'm going to ruin one of Rose's garments. *Shit.* I waft the silky fabric away from my chest to avoid boob sweat.

Lo rubs my shoulder. "Look at me, Lil."

I do. His amber eyes almost melt me beyond recognition. My heart is speeding so fast. Everything will feel better if we just…I just want him to thrust…*no Lily.*

He scrutinizes my state of mind, his scotch-colored eyes dancing over me. Then he holds my head to whisper in my ear, "I can't have sex with you today." His voice is very stern.

I exhale a tight pain in my chest. "I know." It'd be the bad sex that only medicates my anxiety. The compulsive, beastly side of me that comes out with stress and loneliness.

"Why are you here, Lily?"

I frown. "What do you mean…?"

"In this chair," he says, "in this building. What are we doing here?"

I glance around. Oh. The cameras. The runway. I look across it. Rose and Connor are talking so quickly, probably in French, and their eyes keep flickering to me. Concern coats their faces.

Even a few famous actors line the front row. Some even former models themselves.

I turn to Ryke on my right. He stares down at me with those hardened brows. "You look like hell."

Déjà vu. I abandoned Rose's fashion show for sex once upon a time. *Never again.* I don't want to keep repeating the same mistakes. This time will be different.

"I'm here for my sister," I tell Lo.

He nods again, seeing that I understand.

I take a deep breath, uncross my legs and lace my fingers with Lo's. *Don't think about sex.*

Good plan, Lily.

And then the music fires up—an electronic beat that I wholeheartedly approve of. People still brush elbows with their friends, whispering as the models prepare to do their thing, but the overall chatter is drowned out by the song.

I squirm and sit taller, straighter in my chair, inflated with this temporary confidence. *Don't think about sex.*

"Lily," Lo winces. I'm gripping his hand so hard that his fingers purple.

"Sorry," I mumble.

"It's okay," he says, resting his hand on my knee.

I stiffen, and he retracts almost instantly.

"Wait," I say hurriedly, "don't be afraid of me…"

Lo stares at me for a long second with confusion. "I'm not, Lil." He rubs my *thigh* just to show me.

I nod. This is good. The spot between my legs pulses. *Shut up vagina.*

Now I'm speaking to my vagina. Great.

I can leave.

But that means I let my addiction rule my life. I only win if I stay put. Lo's hand drifts to the back of my neck, his thumb making melodic, calm circles that slow my heart.

His amber eyes never leave mine, and I find myself scooting closer, my leg pressed up against his, my hand on his waistband.

"Lily…" he breathes shallowly. It's a warning but why does he sound so sexy?

His *concern* is turning me on? Dear God.

I focus on the runway for uglier scenery. Loren Hale is too gorgeous to stare at right now. But as soon as I turn my head, I realize the models have already started strutting along the white lane.

Half of them are *male.*

Who did I smite this past week?

I train my gaze on their feet. They're the non-sexiest part of a human being, in my opinion. I've never been into the whole foot fetish thing.

Ryke slouches beside me, his grumpiness strangely helping keep my anxieties at bay.

Lo says to us, "Rose thinks Daisy's boyfriend is one of these models she's been working with."

I still can't believe none of us have met him, and apparently they've been dating since *January.*

"I know," Ryke says tensely. "It's a stupid theory."

"Why?" I ask, the conversation the perfect distraction. But my hand has yet to leave the band of Lo's black jeans.

"Do you not see these fucking guys?" Ryke says to me.

I flush. "I'm not staring…why, did you think I was?" I squint one eye at him.

Ryke shakes his head at me like *I can't even*… "Are these models really turning you on right now?" I grow even hotter than before. Technically Loren Hale is turning me on the most.

"Hey," Lo cuts in. "You don't know what she's going through."

Ryke raises his hands in defense. "I just don't see how these guys wearing sweater vests and checkered shirts could arouse *any* girl, not just her."

Lo thinks about it and nods. "Point taken."

Whaaa…I pinch his arm.

He smiles, not even pretending that it hurt.

"Just tell me what they look like," I say, focusing on Lo's kneecaps. If he could just move a little closer, I could swing my leg around his—

No.

"Twenties," Lo explains. "Nice hair."

I wait for more, but that's it. "Horrible description."

"If I paint a vivid picture, you might as well just look at them."

And fantasize about someone else besides Lo? Not gonna happen. My mind is in DEFCON mode. I have to take precautions, lock it down, before it betrays me.

Lo motions to the runway and says to Ryke, "What if that's her boyfriend?"

"The blond shirtless one?" Ryke's face completely darkens, and his jaw hardens to stone.

"Don't look so upset about it."

"He's probably twenty-eight," Ryke retorts.

"No way, he's most likely seventeen. Models usually look older than they are."

"Example A," I chime in, "my sister." Daisy has been mistaken for a twenty-something college student as much as I've been mistaken for a teenager.

"Exactly," Lo adds.

"It's probably that guy," Ryke says, briefly pointing to someone.

Curiosity compels my gaze that-a-way. The models aren't nearly as attractive as Lo, so I take a relaxed breath. I find the guy Ryke picked out. He's tall, lanky with large ears and a shaved head. I cannot see him with Daisy. At all. It'd be so mismatched. Maybe that's why Lo and I start laughing at the same time.

From across the runway, I catch Rose rolling her eyes at us, but her lips rise as she whispers to Connor again. Despite her usual cold glare, she radiates happiness. Maybe because Lo and I are exuding some bright sentiments rather than stormy ones.

And Scott has seemed to only push Rose and Connor closer rather than tear them apart. For a brief second, the producer locks eyes with me. He combs back his dirty blond locks, his smile just as greasy as his hair.

He winks at me.

I shiver. My sex cravings begin to nosedive, and I gladly focus back on my boyfriend.

"Right," Lo says to his brother. "Out of all the models here, Daisy is going to choose the oddest looking one."

"I don't have anything to go off of," he growls, practically sulking. "It's not like I've met her old boyfriends."

I look up at Lo. "Have you met her ex? His name was...Josh, I think." I hone in on Lo's pink lips.

He thinks hard, and I watch his forehead wrinkle in contemplation.

Kiss him.

Later. "He had an average build, brown hair," Lo recalls. He leans into us as he speaks to avoid disrupting the runway show.

Seriously though, everyone is talking.

That description doesn't ring any bells for me. "Why haven't we even seen a picture of her new boyfriend?" I ask them. "Shouldn't he be in the tabloids?" I check them daily still, and nothing. No headlines with: **DAISY HAS A HOT MODEL BOYFRIEND!**

"I'm with her when she's around town," Ryke explains, "and she refuses to bring him for some reason. It's fucking weird."

"Maybe he doesn't exist," Lo theorizes.

"I thought about that," Ryke says, "but she had..." He cringes and gestures to his neck.

Lo groans. "God. Stop...she's still thirteen to me."

"What?" I perk up. *Hickies. Must be hickies.* But I don't want to be called a pervert in public, even jokingly by Ryke, so I don't offer my guess.

"Hickies," he says. *Knew it.* "You'll probably see them on next week's episode."

Lo groans even more and pinches the bridge of his nose. "Why does she even have a boyfriend?"

"The sex," I blurt out.

They both stare down at me like *what the fuck?* Their angered, dark scowls could kill, looking like brothers. I realize that *sex* was the wrong thing to say.

Now *I* raise my hands in defense. Daisy has been trying to find the "right one" for a while. But she's always all over the place: picking up scuba diving, parkour, skateboarding, etc. On occasion when the topic surrounds guys, she always shares the same, unsatisfactory story.

"It's a logical guess," I whisper-hiss. "She's trying to…you know."

"No, I don't *know*." Ryke stares at me like I'm talking in another language. I know I'm speaking English here.

I whisper really, really softly. "She's trying to have…an O."

Lo covers his face with his hand. "This is more than I ever wanted to hear."

Ryke crosses his arms over his chest. "In Cancun, she said that she had an orgasm during sex, remember?"

How can he say all of that without flinching? I'm in awe. "Rose doesn't think she did," I whisper. I see Lo out of my peripheral, and a naughty image flashes in my head: my lips around his cock. It's like a memory and a prospective future.

"Lily," Lo says, grabbing my hand.

What'd I do? My heart lurches to my throat. He caught my fingers sneaking to his zipper. Oh my God. Cameras *click, click*, this time, some of the lenses pointed more towards me than the models.

Lo tries to distract me with more talk and less silence. The quiet lets my mind wander, especially if it's fueled with upbeat music and fantasy-inducing backdrops (aka Loren Hale).

"Say she really does have a boyfriend," Lo whispers between us, "how the hell is *he* going to feel about the reality show?" He pats Ryke's back. "You're in *every* scene with Daisy, you realize that?" I wonder if her boyfriend already feels threatened by Ryke.

"The asshole couldn't even show up to her seventeenth birthday party," Ryke retorts. "You really think he cares about *Princesses of Philly*? At this point, I don't even think he fucking cares about *her*."

Sadly, I think I agree.

The men's collection ends with the designer walking halfway and bowing. He clasps his hands together in thanks, his polka-dot bowtie preppy and eccentric like the rest of his clothes. Once he leaves, the whole room softens, the music dying down.

Some women and men flip open notebooks and click pens to jot down their thoughts. Most likely press for magazines or department store owners. My importance as "Daisy's sister" shrinks, and the intensity of this fashion show dawns on me.

The lights dim on either side of the runway, the audience cloaked in blackness while the long, wide lane glows white. Every lamp and flash is directed to the middle of the modest-sized room. Black fabric rises against the glass windows, encasing us, even darker and more intimate.

Rose has never had a fashion show of this caliber for Calloway Couture.

This is the major leagues.

I recognize the song that starts the show: "Sacrilege" by Yeah Yeah Yeahs.

The first model starts strutting down the runway in black platform heels. How is she not face planting? She wears a thigh-length khaki dress with a salmon-colored belt. Her brunette hair is perfectly straightened and delicately curled at the ends.

Before the model reaches the end, another girl is sent out onto the runway, keeping pace with the tempo of the music. I count one, two, three, four models before my sister emerges.

Daisy. I smile—the kind of smile that I can't restrain, that hurts my cheeks a little bit. She's outfitted in a gray dress with expensive, elegant fabric and a yellow belt, more high fashion than commercial. Her long, long blonde hair hangs to her waist, the ends wavy.

At seventeen, she walks like a mature, powerful woman with poise beyond my capabilities. Her hips sway; each towering high heel steps in front of the other.

Her gaze is dead-locked ahead of her, seduction blazing in her red lips and focused eyes. The flashbulbs don't cause her to blink or to falter. My young sister moves like the world is being created beneath her feet.

The moment just steals my breath away. I'm filled with pride for her.

She possesses the audience, even as she passes the other model and briefly poses at the edge. On her way back, she's closer to our seats. I take a peek at Ryke beside me, and his tense muscles never loosen, his hard jaw stays put like usual. But his breathing is heavier than it should be.

He watches her head down the runway, the song near its end.

And the corners of Daisy's lips just subtly rise, as though she can feel him, right there. When she moves along, I elbow Ryke in the side.

He glares at me. "What?" he whispers defensively.

"She has a boyfriend." My sister deserves romance, the red roses kind with chocolates and epic orgasms. Ryke will give her the best one-night stand of her life and leave her with a broken heart. It's one thing that Lo and I mutually fear.

We're around Ryke more than Connor and Rose. We know his habits better, and screwing in the bathroom of the Lincoln Field isn't that romantic. I've done it four times, I should know.

"Lily," he whispers, "she's *seventeen*."

We shouldn't be talking, not during this particular show. Everyone pays attention to the clothes the models wear, and I should too. I just nod and let it go.

Only fifteen minutes later, the girls disappear off the runway, gearing up for the final walk. And then the first body emerges.

Daisy leads the models, a coveted position. Her pale pink baby doll dress blows with each sway of her hips, practically gliding in her silver gladiator heels. About twenty women behind Daisy wear the same garment in a different hue.

The audience begins to clap. I happily join in, but even as we do, I start to see this normally-contained sadness eke out of Daisy's eyes. A numbness that padlocks her bright, erratic personality.

Lo whispers in my ear, "She seems upset."

Clapping should cheer someone up. It's basically like shouting *I do believe in fairies!* but it does the opposite for Daisy, her light flickering out like a withering Tinker Bell.

When she turns, heading back down the runway and looping the models to create two lanes of bodies, she passes us again.

This time, Ryke speaks.

"Just run, Calloway," he tells her as she walks past.

She almost falters, nearly stopping dead in her tracks. I swear it was like Ryke chiseled at something deep in her core, something hurting her. I can't make sense of it, and the fact that he can...everything just becomes more complicated.

Ryke clenches the side of the chair like he's restraining himself from *not* standing up and storming the runway. I imagine him walking backwards as he talks to her, desperately trying to convince my sister to do something she loves and not what our mom tells her to.

Modeling has never been her passion.

Even if she's great at it.

Instead, Daisy keeps her course, staying as professional as she can.

"You can't force her to quit," I remind him in a soft whisper. "Her job means something to our mom."

"She hates it," Ryke says back to me. "Can't you fucking see that?"

"We're supposed to do things we don't like sometimes," I say, thinking about the reality show, my impending June wedding.

"What for?" Ryke asks.

"Our family."

Maybe one day he'll realize how far we're all willing to go. For the people we love most.

Chapter 22

0 Years : 07 Months

March

LOREN HALE

"I'm not asking you to help me." Snow falls on the back patio of my dad's mansion. In a wealthy Philadelphia suburb. I brace the cold with him, heaters blazing from silver machines. We both drink coffee. Only difference: his has Irish liqueur.

"You don't have to ask," he reminds me, sitting back on an Adirondack chair. "I'm your father—it's in my job description to help you." Before I refute with *I'm not struggling* or *where were you when I was drowning in alcohol and needed rehab*, he adds, "You'll understand when you have kids."

I clench my teeth. No matter how many times I tell him that I won't ever have children, he just doesn't hear it. "I guess I won't ever understand then," I snap.

He sips his coffee, watching me closely while I stare out at the frozen duck pond. The grass is blanketed in snow, all white. "Ryke says that I shouldn't go after Scott."

"Is Scott attacking Ryke?"

"Not really."

"Then he has no fucking say in it." He scowls, his face unshaven. He looks more like Ryke right now, but I won't tell him that. Their relationship is still fractured, maybe even beyond repair.

"Yesterday," I say, "Scott handed Lily a script that told her to hump a pillow." It hurts to breathe fully, emotions barreling into me. "Who does that?"

"Men will do *anything* for money, Loren. He's just trying to profit off the two of you, and so far, he's doing well." Right, the show is a success.

My stomach tightens. "Yeah?" I lean forward, my arms on my legs, cupping the mug between my hands. I'm scared of Scott Van Wright.

I'm terrified of how far he'll push us.

I try to bottle this fear, smothering it so low that I can't feel an ounce of it. I didn't come here to plead for my father's help. I don't want him involved. I just needed to hear someone agree with me.

"Hey," he says forcefully.

I turn my head to meet his hard gaze.

"Don't let any motherfucker come into your life and destroy what belongs to you. Not your women, not your home, not your money or your career. You protect all of that, you hear me?" He sets a firm hand on my shoulder. He may offer backwards advice for me, but he's always been there.

That's more than any mother of mine can say.

"I only have *one* woman," I tell him with the raise of my brows.

"Don't be a smartass."

I digest *all* of his words, even if I shouldn't. "I never wanted to attack someone again." *But I know I'm going to have to.* I admit this to him, of all people. Not Connor, not Ryke or Lily.

"If you don't want to ruin the reality show, like you told me, then you've got to do something to *him*. He'll bulldoze you, son. And if you won't stick your fucking neck out, *I* will. I don't want him near Lily. She's like a daughter to me." He takes a large gulp of his coffee.

It's like there's a war inside my body with no signs of surrender. I attack Scott, I feel like shit. I do nothing, I feel like shit. What the fuck is left for me?

"*Don't* help me," I suddenly say to my dad. "I need to do this on my own."

He nods. "Just make sure you fucking hit him where it hurts most."

I don't even know where that is.

The worst part about being the underdog: I never win until the last minute. So I dig and claw and scrape, struggling in hope that in the final act, I'll rise above.

But what happens if I never do?

Chapter 23

0 Years : 07 Months

March

LILY CALLOWAY

The middle of the afternoon in the middle of the week has to be the most depressing time. Stuck directly in the center where no one wants it. Lonely. When the house has emptied. People at work. People at lunch. No one *here*. Not with me at least.

I'm A. L. O. N. E.

Even the cameramen have all but scattered.

Right now would be the moment I'd beat myself up over procrastinating on schoolwork. But I finished my online assignments two hours ago.

Go me.

I thought I'd feel more accomplished, but celebrating by myself isn't nearly as fun as doing other things by myself. *Things* I'm no longer allowed to do.

Carefully, I crawl onto the bed with the latest edition of *Uncanny X-Men*. It's not my comic, and Lo has a strict "don't read my comics before me" rule. Something about me creasing the pages or smudging the pictures. But boredom calls for risks, and I'm willing to risk his anger for Cyclops.

Five panels. That's how long I make it before my mind drifts. I picture Lo. His abs. His dimpled smile and sharp jawline. I have to stop myself before my imagination leads to more nefarious places, ones with nudity and gyrating bodies.

My bedroom door opens just as I look back at the comic. Lo stands in the doorway like an apparition from my mind. Maybe he is.

I pinch myself.

Ouch...

Lo gives me a look. "I'm real, Lil." He closes the door behind him and sets his leather briefcase on the desk. A gift from his father. It's hard to pull my eyes from it. A year ago, that briefcase didn't belong in our picture. Now it has a specific spot it rests.

It doesn't feel out of place. Not like I once thought it would.

When I return my gaze to Lo, I realize he hasn't moved. He carefully watches me the way one would a lightning storm. With curiosity, concern, and rapt attention.

"If you're real," I say, narrowing my eyes. "Then why aren't you at work?"

"That's the funny thing about working for yourself," he says with a wry smile. "I can set my own hours, take my work home, and spend the afternoon making love to a girl."

Oh...

Middle of the days and middle of the weeks don't seem so lonely anymore. He doesn't move closer and my breathing has already betrayed me. At least my body isn't doing anything spastic...yet.

"Just *a* girl?" I ask. "Not a specific one?"

His eyes flit from my head slowly down the length of my body. I become so wet in response. Damn him.

He licks his lip and I have to grip the sheets not to jump off the bed and rush him. I'm so not used to horny Loren Hale coming to seduce *me*. I'm always the overly aroused, emotionally corrupt one. It's a nice change, even if my body is screaming to *go go go*.

"I have a girl in mind," he tells me. "But here's the thing…" He begins to unbutton his shirt, and I start a mantra in my head. *Focus on his words, Lily, not his abs. Words. Not abs. Words. Not abs. Definitely not his cock.* "Last time I made love to her, she ended up crying when we finished."

My head whips up. "I didn't cry," I defend. "I had salt sweat in my eye. That's a thing, you know."

"She cried," he continues without missing a beat, his lips curving. "She had these big tears in her eyes and she turned into this sappy love monster, blubbering about how much she loved me."

He starts moving this time, and I try hard not to smile.

"I did not." I bite my lip and then give up, my grin spreading. "If I remember correctly, I told you that I could feel your soul. It was poetic."

His knees knock into mine and his shirt slides open, revealing his bare chest. But I don't have to chant my mantra any longer. His amber eyes and sharpened words have my undivided attention. The humor floats away and his hand glides to my cheek. "It was beautiful," he breathes.

Thoughts creep into my head, and I can't stop my mouth. "Did you come home just for a nooner?"

I internally groan. *Way to go, Lily. Ruin the moment.*

He reads my embarrassment and breaks into a smile. "I'm not being clear enough?"

"Ummm…" My mind has blanked. Flat-lined. I am brain dead.

He stirs me back to life by grabbing my hand and placing it right over his pants. On his erection. "Do we have an understanding now?"

Oh yeah.

We're fucking.

Or making love.

Both. Maybe both.

I'm dancing and hoola-hooping on the inside. He throws his shirt on the floor and my eyes meet his. I'm not removing my hand. It's just going to stay right there. "You know what this means?" I ask.

He narrows his eyes and leans forward, causing me to lie back on the bed. His fingers find my jean's buttons, not waiting any longer. "You're going to have to help me out with this one, Lil."

I frown. "They're normal buttons."

He smiles again. I could get used to that. "Not the buttons. Help me with your question."

I flush. Right. "Well, you came to *me* for sex. You're the one undressing me. You're practically *begging* me to fuck you."

"Am I?" Even with his lips together and flat, he's still smiling. I see it in his eyes.

I nod wildly. "Oh yeah. The tables have turned, Loren Hale. This is a monumental day. You are aroused *before* me." I grin.

He shimmies my jeans to the ground, and I'm too elated to realize that my panties have gone with them. When his fingers enter me, I gasp and drop my hand off his pants. His fingers pulse just slightly, and my head collapses back on the mattress. "You feel aroused to me," he says softly.

Fuck.

"Key word: *Before,*" I reply in a staggered breath.

I'm about to lift myself on my elbows, but I don't have time. He doesn't give me warning before he replaces his fingers with his erection, entering me fully. I cry out in euphoric pleasure. Every inch of me thrums, like an instrument vibrating in blistering joy.

He hikes my leg over his hip, deepening himself. He doesn't pull away, not yet. His lips find mine and he kisses me fervently, without pause or hesitation. Ever since I started recovery, I could see the reluctance in Lo's eyes. Like a nightly passenger to our passion. I never thought he'd gain enough confidence in himself, enough trust in me, and enough hope in our relationship to let all those hesitations go. To make love to me so unrestrained that every movement is an impulse and nothing takes a second thought.

It's just natural.

He thrusts and lets me move my hips to meet his. I moan deeply, the noise catching in the back of my throat. He smiles and his movements become harder, more aggressive. I no longer attempt to rock my body into his, not when I'm white-knuckling his biceps and holding on for dear fucking life.

His low grunts fill my ears and send my body over the edge. I feel myself riding the steep mountain to my peak. "Lo," I choke. "I can't… hold on…"

He stops moving all together and I let out an involuntary whimper. At least, I think it's involuntary. I would never make that noise on a *voluntary* basis.

Lo rubs the sweat off my forehead with his hand. "Come now," he tells me. He presses feather-light kisses to my neck.

Now?

"You stopped moving," I remind him. I squirm underneath him, and he pulls his lips away, his jaw clenched.

Oh. He's having some trouble.

His hands brace my hips, settling me. "Please come now," he tells me, "because when I start moving and you have an orgasm, I'm finished."

"So?" I frown. "We can do it again after. I'll blow—" His hand rises to my mouth, silencing my words.

"We won't have time. Ry…" he pauses to catch himself. "*People* are coming home from the gym in a half hour."

He removes his hand. I'm grimacing. I can't help it. "You almost said his name. And now you want me to come?"

He moves his hips just slightly and the pressure of his cock numbs my body and clears my head. "Ahhhhh…." I moan into my arm.

"*Come*," Lo commands, kind of meanly.

"You're mean," I mutter into my pillow, my cheek smashed into it.

His lips brush my ear. "I said please first. You just didn't listen." He combs my hair back out of my face, and my legs stay tightly wrapped around his waist. And then his hands descend to my shirt. It's ripped open before I have any say in the matter.

Still no reluctance in his movements.

He stares at my bra like it accosted him.

"Looks like you're not the Hulk," I say into a smile.

His eyes flit to mine, humorless, and then he pulls the bra up to my chin, my breasts popping out. Shit. I go to restrain them, partly just to rile him, but he beats me to it. He grabs my wrists and hoists them over my head, and as he does so, his pelvis moves and I crumble underneath him.

My moans are soft and sound more like whining than actual noises of pleasure. Lo lets out a heavy breath and clenches his teeth like he's struggling to control himself.

Coming sounds very blissful right now. I'm not sure I could do it without his help though. I think he knows this. His tongue grazes my hardened nipple and I try to jerk forward, but his large, heavy body holds me still to the bed.

It doesn't take much to get me off.

He sucks gently on the small bud and then lifts his head. "Just think about my cock, love," he says. "It's waiting, very fucking impatiently, for you. Can't you feel it?"

Yes. I feel very, very full.

I repeat his words in my head and focus on his thickness. My heat spasms, and I clench tightly. He takes one hand off my wrists and lowers it to my clit, rubbing me so quickly that I cry out. The whole world rotates, and I lie back, barely hanging onto his motionless body as I ride the waves of pleasure that pound into me. One after the other. Over and over again. Until my clit is too tender to the touch, causing me to shake when he brushes against it.

He pulls his hand away and leans in to kiss my neck, my breathing too ragged for him to kiss my lips. He sucks gently, then forcibly, and he begins to rock into me again, building up my arousal once more.

When I catch my breath, he presses his forehead to mine and he thrusts. Strong, rhythmic movements that steal my oxygen every few seconds. His lips are so close that we could kiss, but he keeps them apart. I can feel his breath entering mine and mine his.

His hands cup the top of my head and he starts to pump faster and harder, until we're both on the same high, trying to reach the same blistering climax together.

Chapter 24

0 Years : 07 Months

March

LOREN HALE

I pull my pants up and watch Lily tuck a pillow underneath her chin. Her eyes follow my movements as much as mine follow hers. I'm not sure if it's fear or love that keeps our gazes matched. Maybe a mixture of both.

I tug at a tangled throw blanket on the bed, about to fold it, and a comic book suddenly tumbles to the floor. When I bend to pick it up, Lily springs off the mattress and snatches the comic first. My black button-down hangs on her body like a dress, stopping mid-thigh, but her breasts are exposed when she shifts certain ways.

My eyes flash from her nipple to her hands, shielding the comic behind her back.

"That's my comic." I don't ask.

Her red face answers my question before her words do. "Do you remember that time we had sex and it was so good that I didn't ask for anymore?"

"You mean five minutes ago?"

She nods. "Yeah, well, um…turns out we may have been doing it *on* one of your comics. Whichjustmakesitmoreawesome!" She slurs the last part together, and I have to piece it apart slowly.

"Which one?" I can already feel my glare. I try, pretty poorly, to suppress it.

She lets out a puff of breath, like she's thinking hard. "You know, I'm not sure."

"It's behind your back," I deadpan.

"Oh…right." Lily steps forward and offers the comic to me. Before I even read the title, I notice the large creases and wrinkled pages. We really did fuck on it. *Jesus.*

And then I skim the title: *Uncanny X-Men.* The latest edition. The one I haven't read yet. Irritation flares for a second, but it's gone before I can even bottle it.

"I'm so sorry," she says, her eyes big and round. "I'll buy you a new one."

The smallest slights usually grate on me enough to open a bottle of Macallan. Not today. "It's fine, Lil. It's just a comic book." I can always buy another.

The surprise in her face almost makes me smile.

I step forward to wrap her in my arms, but our bedroom door opens abruptly, no knock, no warning. I expect Ryke to come barging in. For our secret to catch up to us.

But it's so much fucking worse.

Scott Van Wright stands in the doorway, chest pumping with livid intensity. He clutches a bottle wrapped in a brown paper bag. I try not to concentrate on it.

"Get the fuck out of our room," I sneer, my veins turning to liquid fire. I block Lily's body from view. I'm used to our siblings invading our privacy, but not this guy. That's something that I will never be okay with.

Instead of leaving, he shuts the door closed with a loud *thunk*. "We need to talk." No humor in his voice. He pulls his cell out of his pocket, and his dirty blond eyebrows rise like *you know what I'm talking about.*

Oh yeah.

My lips curve in a bitter smile. "Sure. Talk all you want. I'll listen." I mockingly wave him on. Lily plops down on the edge of the bed, a pillow pressed to her lap.

"You deleted *all* of my contacts."

"Did I?" I feign confusion. "I don't remember picking up your phone." I scratch my head. "But now that I think about it…I may have touched it once. With gloves. I was scared of catching whatever disease you have that turns you into such a fucking prick."

"*Loren*, I had contacts stored from executives that I *can't* get back without making a billion phone calls of numbers that I now don't have. You see the problem here?"

"Yep," I say. "Sounds like a real fucking problem. Sucks for you, man." I shrug.

"I'm *not* acting," Scott snarls. "There aren't cameras rigged in here. This is serious."

I glare. "As serious as you approaching my girlfriend every *goddamn* day and calling her a slut?" I take a step towards him. "You've been making our lives miserable for the past three months. And you just walk around here—*smiling*." Another step closer. "You think I'm the weakest person in the house, so you've been going after me and Lily. But get this straight, Scott. I'm the *last* person you wanted to fuck over. You try to pull my arms like I'm a fucking marionette, and I'll yank yours out of the socket."

His nose flares.

And before he has a chance to say a word, I ask, "So how's texting going for you? Has it *sucked?*" I reprogrammed his auto-correct. Every time he types in *yes,* it reformats to say *cocksucker. No* is now *blow me.* And the phrase, *I'm on my way* is retranslated to *I want to smell your asshole.* It's as unpoetic as I could get. And I fucked with probably fifty common phrases and words.

His skin reddens the longer he fumes. "The cat shit was you too?" The litter box was in the laundry room. Decided to give him a surprise in his expensive loafers.

"That was Sadie," I say. "Congratulations, you're the first guy she's ever hated." I clap, watching his face morph into pure rage. *Good.* He looks how I've felt.

He closes the gap between us quickly, and I drop my hands.

I threaten, "You make our lives hell; I make yours hell. That's how this works, Scott. You leave me alone, we have no problems. Your choice."

Scott tries to break me by simply staring into my goddamn eyes. That's not going to work. I've stared down Jonathan Hale many times before—Scott is sweet in comparison.

"Did you come here to cry?" I ask him. I could have easily accepted my father's help and fucked over his life, emptied his bank account, totaled his car. What I did was small but still significant—or else he wouldn't be so upset.

"Fine," he finally says. His eyes flicker to Lily, but I sidestep so he can't see her. "I'll play nice from now on." He slips his cell in his pocket and then he shoves the bagged bottle in my chest. "Cheers."

He backs up, waiting for me to unwrap the paper bag.

I don't have to. I've opened enough Maker's Mark to recognize the red waxy seal on the neck. He handed me bourbon whiskey.

He wants me to drink and break my sobriety. It's not going to—

Lily darts beside me with a high-pitched scream, steals the bottle out of my hands and chucks it at Scott. The bottle, still in the bag, makes a loud impact on the wall beside his head. He jumps back in surprise, the glass shattering and whiskey dripping down the wallpaper.

I'm so stunned that I can hardly move. Did Lily just…*yeah, she did.*

"Don't you dare give him alcohol like it's nothing," Lily says.

Scott grinds his teeth and flashes a pained smile, his lips twitching. Then he slams the door on his way out.

It takes me a moment to speak. "Lily Calloway," I say, shocked beyond belief. I turn my head towards her. "Did you just defend *me* by throwing perfectly good booze at a douchebag's head?"

"Yes," she says with a nod and then tilts her chin up for further effect.

I touch my heart. "I'd propose to you, but I already did that."

She smiles but tries to stay serious, pressing her lips tightly together. "He can't screw with your addiction."

"He's not." I draw her to my body.

Lily shakes her head, more worked up than me. "He's like Draco Malfoy," she says, resting her hands on my arms. "Slimy and evil and a complete narcissistic buffoon."

"Plus he has blond hair," I add.

She catches the humor in my eyes. "It's not funny. The whole thing is so *not* funny."

"Lil…" I cup her cheeks between my hands. "*No one* is going to mess with us or make our lives harder just for shits and giggles. Okay?"

After a short moment, she nods in agreement.

My hands fall to her ass that peeks out of the button-down, but she walks out of my grasp. I watch her bend down to the wet paper bag. "I'll clean this up," she says. "You shouldn't touch the alcohol since you're taking Antabuse."

I grimace, but she can't see my expression, her back turned to me. I haven't exactly told her that I stopped taking the meds. After the premiere of *Princesses of Philly*, everything got crazy. Superheroes & Scones has been packed, more and more manuscripts are sent to my office, Rose bugs *me* to bug *Lily* about the wedding, and then Scott—I started running on empty.

The last thing I wanted to do was take Antabuse, accidentally eat something cooked with alcohol and puke. I don't have the energy to check the ingredients of all the restaurant dishes. So yeah, I flushed the pills that physically make me ill if I relapse.

At the time, it felt like I unstrapped a fifty-pound weight from my ankles. Now I'm just terrified to see the disappointment in Lily's face if she finds out—or worse, she'll blame herself. Like it was her fault for not motivating me more or not realizing it sooner.

I'll tell her.

Not today.

Maybe when the reality show ends, when everything slows down and I can stomach the thought of popping those pills. I'll come clean, then.

I pass her a waste basket. "Be careful," I warn.

She pinches the ends of the paper bag like a dirty diaper, the glass shattered inside, and dumps it into the trash.

"This stuff with Scott stays between us," I remind Lily. "The moment Rose knows that he's fucking with us, she'll want to end the show." Connor will probably convince her otherwise though. Rose's fashion line has seen a major boost in sales since *Princesses of Philly* aired. But we don't want to be the ones who ruin her success or cause her trouble.

"I know," Lily says, standing up next to me. "We can't tell anyone."

Chapter 25

0 Years : 07 Months

March

LOREN HALE

I wake up at 5 a.m. with a massive headache and nonstop, rambling thoughts. I sit on the edge of my bed, careful not to disturb Lily who lies on her stomach while she sleeps, arms outstretched to embrace her pillow.

I pull the blankets up to her shoulders, and she lets out a quiet sigh, her eyes still closed. I wish I could fall back to sleep next to her, but I can't turn off my brain this morning.

I leave the room, gently shutting the door behind me. Shower. Coffee. Office. It's like I'm a full-fledged adult. Most days, I feel like I'm still pretending.

When I aim my sights on the bathroom door, Connor suddenly steps out of his room and into the narrow hallway.

I freeze in place, scanning his navy blue, cotton pants, shirtless with abs that make mine look like child's play. He's going to take a shower in the communal bathroom. And I've been more or less avoiding him since the premiere, when he confessed to not loving Rose.

"Morning, beautiful," he banters like nothing has changed between us. He saunters to the bathroom and holds open the door for me. "After you."

Screw the shower.

I walk to the stairs with flexed arms and rigid shoulders.

"Lo," he calls out, sounding conflicted.

I stop on the first step and look back. He stands in the bathroom door, but he offers not a single extra word for me, not *I'm sorry* or *you were right* or *I do love her.*

I shake my head at him and then descend the staircase. Only after I enter the kitchen and start the coffee pot do I finally hear the pipes groan through the walls, the shower starting.

"What are you doing up?"

I jump at Rose's cold voice, the blue coffee mug almost tumbling out of my hands. I take a deep breath. "Jesus Christ, don't sneak up on me like that," I whisper, leaning my back against the counters.

"Please, if I announced my entrance in the room, you'd call me the Queen Bitch. If anything, I'm doing you a favor. You need new material." She retrieves a red mug out of the cabinet beside my head, already showered and wearing a black dress with a gold necklace.

"Great," I say, too early to have a verbal battle with her.

She waits impatiently for the coffee to brew, her high-heeled foot tapping the floorboards. "He's not perfect, you know," she says.

My jaw hurts from clenching, I realize. Now I really want this stupid machine to hurry up. "You don't say," I mutter, both our gazes glued to the coffee that drips too slowly.

"Connor feels horribly," she adds.

My stomach tightens. "Wow, Connor Cobalt can feel?" I quip. "I thought his insides were all IP addresses and router cables." I cringe; the insult stings me worse than I thought it would.

For some reason, Rose doesn't feed into my dry sarcasm today. "You're his best friend," she emphasizes, now staring at me while I avoid her piercing eyes.

"I thought his best friend is his therapist."

"He was," Rose says, "before he met you. And what Connor sees in you, I have *no* idea. Hanging out with you for more than five minutes is like lying on a bed of nails."

"Likewise," I tell her. I finally rotate, actually seeing the way her face has softened, not as severe, defensive or on guard. She's *trying* to be real with me. "Did Connor ask you to come patch things up for him? He got you to do his dirty work?"

She glares. "I'm not Connor's bitch," she snaps. "I do what I want to do. You want to know the truth? He told me to stay out of his relationship with you because he's afraid I'll do more harm than good. He's so scared to lose you, and you can't see it because Connor won't let you."

I process everything she says. "Why is that?"

"He enjoys acting like he's invincible. It's infuriating, but we all have our faults, even him."

I put him on a pedestal above everyone, above my own brother. I thought there was *no fucking* way Connor Cobalt would hurt me. He was designed to be there for all of us. He made me feel worthy of love even if he never truly loved me.

"Our whole friendship feels like a lie," I tell her.

"It's not," she says. "I've known him since I was fourteen, Loren. I've seen his superficial friendships and the ones he creates to further himself in life. You're *not* one of those. He's more himself with you than he usually is. You have to believe that."

"Why are you sticking up for him?" I ask. "He doesn't even love you, Rose." This time, I think she'll have a different reaction to the words, no longer drunk off champagne.

But her expression remains exactly the same. "He's incredibly intelligent," she says, "but that comes with a few quirks. This is one of those that I'm okay with. I don't need him to love me because it's not as though he'll ever love another woman. Not if he doesn't believe in it."

My headache pounds. "Sometimes I'm glad I'm not as smart as you two." I open a nearby drawer and pull out a bottle of Advil and swallow a couple pills without water. They lodge in my throat before sliding down.

"Loren," she says, her voice still icy, "just give me a sign that you understand *anything* I'm saying." She really wants me to make up with Connor. This is coming from a girl who dislikes me the most out of everyone in our group of six.

Everything Rose said makes more and more sense to me. Connor won't apologize or say he's wrong, not if he believes he's right. But the fact that I frazzled him in some way—that means he cares about something other than just himself.

It has to mean that our friendship is real.

I give her a weak thumbs-up, practically sideways, like a half-assed affirmative answer.

"Always juvenile." She gives me a look like *I'll take it* and approaches the quarter-filled coffee pot, too impatient to wait any longer.

I set my mug on the counter and open the pantry door.

Footsteps sound on the floorboards. "Rose, have you…" Connor trails off only when he sees me. I don't pay him that much attention. He swallows and then regains his focus. "…my passport, have you seen it? I thought I left it in our drawer."

"I organized it with our itinerary."

I grab a bag of bagels and set them on the island. Connor's eyes flicker to me again, tension mounting in the air. He's already dressed in a white button-down and black slacks.

I put a bagel in my mouth, take out an extra, and twirl the bag closed.

Connor speaks to Rose in French, and she snaps back in the same language.

I'm too used to the French to be bothered by it. I just fill my coffee and slip the extra bagel in the toaster.

Then Connor says, "Lo…"

I don't spin around as I head to the living room. I just point to the toaster. "I'm not going to butter it for you." I take a bite of my bagel and only glance back once. Yeah, I made the guy breakfast, a small, *small* sign of peace between us.

I watch as his lips pull into one of those genuine smiles—one that holds no trace of arrogance.

I add, "It doesn't mean that I'm not still mad at you." I won't let him off the hook that easily, but I doubt this fight will last much longer.

"I prefer my friends angry," Connor says. "It makes me look better."

"Too soon," I tell him, eating my bagel and walking back to the living room.

I can practically feel his grin widen behind me. And it takes me a minute to realize that I'm smiling too.

Chapter 26

0 Years : 07 Months

March

LILY CALLOWAY

I underestimated the amount of people that watch *Princesses of Philly.* A couple teenagers sip lattes and peek around a tall bookshelf, whispering as they spy on Lo and me. It's impossible to be invisible with Brett's camera pointed at us.

I keep asking myself why we left the townhouse. My brows crinkle. I don't have an answer, so I turn to Lo who peruses the Sci-Fi/Fantasy aisle in the local bookstore.

"Why did we leave the townhouse?" I ask

"Fresh air." He pulls out a small trade paperback and scans the summary. He mostly reads comics, but on occasion, he'll branch out into these genres. He devoured *Game of Thrones* before watching the television show. I told him that I finished the first book, but really, I just skipped around and read Arya's parts.

She's the best.

Laughter emanates from one shelf behind us. My shoulders curve forward, hoping that it's not something I did. "The air was pretty fresh back home."

He gives me a look, one that says: *I don't want you becoming a scared, little hermit.* His looks say more than his words. That's a fact.

I inhale strongly and try to follow Lo's lead. *Just relax, Lily. Be casual.* I shake out my arms and scan the row of books. Then I freeze, sensing beady eyes bore down on me.

Slowly, I look up and spot someone with a mop of brown hair, watching us from *above* a shelf. He ducks quickly when our eyes meet.

Holy shit.

I can't do this.

I can't.

I grab Lo's hand, my chest constricting in a paranoid, freakazoid way. Swiftly, I drag him into the nearest bathroom, ignoring the fact that Brett trails us. I shut the door on the cameraman before he enters.

He pounds on the door in protest.

"I'm peeing!" I shout.

His fist must fall because everything grows silent outside.

My eyes dance over the door like someone is going to intrude any second. "Everyone is staring," I whisper to Lo. I shiver, like eyes have attached onto me. Like they can see me *in here.*

When I turn to Lo, his gaze softens for me. I prepare myself for an epic pep talk. He holds my biceps. "You're a sex addict and I'm an alcoholic," he says, "and the whole fucking world knows it. We have to get used to people staring, love."

He's right of course. My mind seems to calm, but my body doesn't follow just yet. My legs feel gooey, and my shoulders shake a little, on edge.

The words leave my lips before I can stop them, "Can I give you a blow job?"

"No," he deadpans.

I raise my hands. "You're right. You're *so* right. Blow jobs are so '89."

"Let's not go that far." He smiles softly, and I don't know why, but tears prick my eyes. I'm such a sap. And there goes that smile, fading away. "Lil…"

"I'm sorry," I blurt out. "I shouldn't have asked. Can we do take-backs?"

"Sure," he says. "And how about we wait in here for a while, see if we piss off Brett enough that he'll ditch us for Ryke or Rose?"

"I like that idea."

"Yeah?"

I nod. "And maybe a virus will infect everyone, turning them into zombies, and when we leave the bathroom, the bookstore will be completely deserted."

"Nice," he says, "but I'd rather not be inserted into the plot of *28 Days Later*."

Damn. He's good.

"I love you," I suddenly say. I mean it. Because who else would stay in a bookstore bathroom with me, just to hide out for a little while.

Definitely not Rose. Maybe Daisy. Ryke would rather die, I'm sure. And Connor can never be added into any equation without hurting my head.

So that leaves Lo. Just Lo.

Chapter 27

0 Years: 08 Months

April

LILY CALLOWAY

"Did it hurt? Did you like it? Have you done it again?" My questions pour forth like a broken dam. This isn't the first time I've asked Rose, but she never provides details, so I've waited until we could talk alone. But we haven't had much of a chance since the Alps vacation, a trip planned by production. I thought I'd squeeze some conversations in on the plane ride home, but she sat with Connor.

The biggest event of the trip, in my opinion, was Rose losing her virginity.

Rose hisses at me, "Lower your voice."

Okay, so we're technically *not* alone. Production wanted another group segment, so we've gathered everyone together for an evening of bowling. When Rose went to pick her bowling ball, I followed her to the rack.

The others congregate behind our lane in the plastic swivel chairs, out of earshot. But Savannah hovers beside the rack, pointing her camera right at us. Even so, Scott has refused to air anything about Rose and Connor sleeping together. At first I thought he didn't want to come across like the loser on television, but Rose said that they just want to perpetuate her "virgin" label for marketing.

"Do you not want to talk to me about it?" I ask.

"It's not that." Her lips purse while she scans the colorful bowling balls. "I just hate that Scott is taking advantage of a throwaway comment I made in an interview about being repulsed by bowling."

Germs. Rose grew out of the obsessive compulsive trait when we were little, but the intensity of the cameras and lack of privacy has reignited some of her old habits. She has a strict policy on hygiene, and sticking her fingers in three holes that were once occupied by sweaty, unidentified hands kind of breaks it.

"Daisy will probably roll the ball granny-style," I say. "Just copy her technique."

She ponders this for a second, and her expression softens a fraction. "Connor and I have had sex again."

I grin, and I swear she tries so hard not to. "Was it everything you thought it would be?" I ask.

"Better…different, but better." She stares faraway, a smile playing at her lips. I try to imprint the image. My sister—swooning. Her glow flashes away all at once, replaced by ice. "Since when do *you* want to talk about sex?"

True. I'm usually tight-lipped and rosy red about the subject. "I'm trying to be better about it," I admit, "and shockingly, it's easier talking about someone else's sex life."

"Not shocking," she refutes and squats like a lady to grab the bowling ball on the middle rack. Her blouse shifts, and I notice a red bite mark on her shoulder.

"Ohmygod," I slur.

"What?" She straightens up quickly in alarm. "What is it?"

"He *bites* you," I whisper, my surprise filling my face. She immediately presses her hand to my mouth, silencing me. I never pegged Connor to be rough. I thought he was the sweet, gentle type. Like a friendly giant.

"Don't be so overdramatic." As though she's never dramatic? She pauses and then blurts out in curiosity, "Has Lo never bitten you?"

I frown and recall the times we've had sex. Uhh, there are too many to remember the *exact* details of each one, that's for sure. He's probably nipped my neck before.

She drops her hand so I can speak.

"It's not the biting that I'm surprised by," I whisper. "It's the *Connor* biting that weirds me out."

"Then don't think about it," she snaps. Good point. "In fact, while I love this newfound confidence in talking about sex, I'm not sure you should be thinking about it so much."

She's right. I need to relax.

"I'm just excited for you," I tell her. "It's like a milestone in your relationship." The orbiting nerd stars have finally collided.

Out of my peripheral, I spot Daisy slipping on her bowling shoes while simultaneously sprinting across the carpet towards our lane.

"Babe, what the hell?" That comes from the guy behind her. Twenty-three. Dark hair. Tanned skin. A model. And also her boyfriend. "Be cool."

She spins around and walks backwards with a lopsided smile. "I'm totally cool." The moment she steps onto the slick bowling surface, her feet slide beneath her and she falls straight on her butt.

Ryke, slouched in a chair, turns his head to assess the situation and then glances back at the lane. "How's that ground, Calloway?"

"Hard," she banters with a mischievous smile. "It'll probably leave a mark."

"That's usually what happens when your ass meets something hard, sweetheart."

Okay, this is sexual. I *know* for a fact because Julian looks ticked, glowering at the back of Ryke's head. Daisy picks herself off the ground, and Julian suddenly kisses her out of nowhere, one roaming hand gripping her butt.

Uh. This is why I don't like him.

Ryke and my boyfriend see their spontaneous make out session, and they both end up glowering, mildly disgusted and definitely infuriated.

Everyone met Julian in the Alps, and things did not pan out so nicely. Lo doesn't like him. Ryke doesn't like him. Even Connor, who can find a morsel of decency in *anyone*, claimed that Julian was nothing short of an ape.

"You gave a speech to the guys, right?" I ask Rose. She places a teal ball back on the rack and heaves a bright pink one into her hands, cringing at having to touch it.

"Yes," she says, "I told them if they're rude to Daisy's boyfriend that we'd have serious problems." She lets out a harsh breath. "And then Connor had the audacity to tell me that the same rule applies to me."

I don't mention that I agree with him.

Rose has bitched Julian out far more than Lo or Ryke. But my little sister wants everyone to get along, and production wants her boyfriend in the show for more drama, so we're all going to put on a happy face.

For her.

And so we can have one sane day.

Chapter 28

0 Years : 08 Months

April

LOREN HALE

I struggle with the frayed shoe string, forcing me to take an extra minute to tie them. Ryke sits beside me, his dark scowl plastered to Julian, who continues to stick his tongue down Daisy's throat only ten feet behind us.

"I can't be nice to him," Ryke says, finally removing his gaze off them. "I'm not fucking created that way."

"By using the word 'created' you imply that someone else made you into a barbarian," Connor replies, almost absentmindedly as he types our names into the computer. I smile, amused by him but my brother doesn't take the same route.

Ryke shakes his head. "I sincerely thought your personality was the product of jerking off one too many times this past year." He touches his chest. "For fuck's sake, *I'd* be a dick if I didn't get laid for twelve months. But obviously, being a prick is just programmed into you."

"You're still not understanding," Connor says casually, "being a prick is a choice. The same way you being rude to Julian is a choice. It's not that hard to take responsibility for your actions."

Ryke groans. "Just fucking shut up."

"Hey," I cut in and nod to Connor's computer screen. "You know we're bowling, right? We're not signing up for Model UN. You're supposed to make nicknames."

Connor stares at the screen like I told him that he answered a quiz question wrong.

Ryke almost laughs. "Cobalt, is this your first time bowling?"

"In a public bowling alley, yes." He begins to delete all of our names. "All the bowling I've done has been at someone's house."

Ryke's grin transforms into a glare. "Fucking prick," he mutters under his breath. Connor just smiles wider like he's enjoying being called one.

When I finally finish tying my shoes, I sit up and my elbow knocks into Brett's camera. "Can you give me some room?" I snap, on edge.

Connor and Ryke exchange a long look. *Yeah, I get it.* I haven't been too kind to production this past week. On the ride here, Brett wanted the passenger seat so he could film me driving, and I told him that he either rides in the back or I'd throw him out of the car halfway down the road.

All the nice sentiments I had towards the camera crew died on the plane ride home three days ago. Scott played nasty in the Alps. He fucked with Lily again, handing her a *Magic Mike* DVD like it was an innocent gesture, but his actions had a clear motive. It was the same as him shoving Maker's Mark into my chest.

And then later, Lily and I caught Ben leaving *actual* porn in our room.

We didn't tell anyone. Lily threw the magazines in the trash on her own accord, overcoming a huge hurdle. And although Scott tried to make her relapse, we both considered the trip a success. We skied down the slopes. We laughed. We felt normal, even under the hot gaze of the camera lens.

I try not to let my frustration and anger towards Scott surface. Not when he's back at the townhouse, editing footage from the trip. Which is fine by me. The less I see his goddamn face, the less I feel like ripping it off.

"Enough," Rose snaps, physically pushing her way between Daisy and Julian, separating them. "I'm not rushing my sister off to the hospital for oxygen deprivation, thank you."

Daisy tucks a strand of her blonde hair behind her ear, shifting out of Julian's arms, embarrassed. She claps her hands, acting more lighthearted than I think she truly is in this moment. "So who's going first?" She plops down on an empty chair.

"Why don't we let Julian go first?" I say with a half-smile. Just saying his full name out loud makes me grimace. He shouldn't be allowed to share it with my favorite X-Men: Julian Keller. It's fucking sacrilege.

"Works for me," Julian says, standing next to Daisy's chair. He motions for her to stand up so he can take the seat.

I'm pissed, but Ryke's narrowed eyes flash hot, unquestionably murderous.

In France, Julian blatantly admitted to us that he was only with Daisy for the sex, but he's waiting until she turns eighteen, legal. It was both moral and despicable all at once.

Daisy reluctantly rises to her feet and then hesitates, swaying on her heels as she realizes there aren't any other open chairs left.

Julian ignores her as he speaks. "I hate to break it to all of you, but I'm an amazing bowler." Awesome.

Ryke clears his throat like he's trying to swallow an insult. "Excuse me," he coughs into his hand. "I'm going to get something to drink. Dais, you can take my chair." He rises, and Daisy walks towards his open seat.

"Thanks," she whispers.

He nods stiffly, and she slumps down onto the chair.

"Make it a double," I call out to him.

He gives me a sharp glare and the middle finger before leaving, passing Lily and Rose as they approach our lane.

Rose places the bowling ball in the return machine and holds out her hands like they've been infected with H1N1.

"Why didn't you just buy a brand new ball?" Daisy asks as she swivels in the chair. "You already bought new shoes."

"She tried," Lily answers for Rose. "None of them fit her fingers."

"This is just confirmation of what we already know," I say, "Rose is a witch. Witch fingers are supposedly very skinny."

Rose rakes me with a long yellow-green-eyed glare. "I hope you get athlete's foot."

Lily's eyes widen. "Don't curse him, Rose."

I break out into a grin. There aren't many times Lily sides with me over her sister. She likes to stay neutral for the most part. Rose, offended, turns on her sister, hands on her hips and her glare focused.

"I'm. Not. A. Witch," Rose says slowly and distinctly.

Lily shakes her head and cringes. "Sorry. It slipped." Funny thing is, I think if Rose were really a witch, Lily would love her even more.

Rose still has her hands out like she's trying not to infect her clothes.

"Here, darling…" Connor swivels in his chair and squirts some hand sanitizer on her palms.

"That only kills 99.99% of the germs, Richard. What about the .01%?"

"It's called an immune system, Rose."

Her eyes flash angrily, and his grin overpowers all of his other features. They start talking in French, the moment Lily plops onto my lap.

I groan from the impact of her bottom, and she gasps. "I didn't hurt it, did I?" she whispers with fear flickering in her eyes.

God, I love her.

"My dick is fine," I say and scoot her over just a little so that the bony part of her bottom isn't digging into my cock. "How's your ass?"

She squints at me and then looks around, checking to see if anyone pays attention to us. They're all busy fixing their laces. Rose removes the lid off a box, neatly folding the tissue paper after she picks out the brand new pair of shoes.

When Lily realizes we're in our own world, she rotates back and cups her hands around my ear. "Are you making sexual innuendos for later?"

I rest my hand on her lower back, my thumb dipping below the band of her jeans. She inhales sharply, but she leans away to examine my expression, truly curious about my motives.

I motion for her with two fingers to come closer. Her lips immediately part, dead-locked on those fingers. *Yes, Lily, I'm teasing you for later.*

Sometimes I think I have to spell it out for her. I probably should have when we were pretending to be in a relationship…that time feels like ages ago.

She finally scoots closer, and my lips brush the soft skin of her earlobe. Her breath hitches. "I'm going to slide deep into your ass tonight, love." Subtly, my other hand slips between her legs, her jeans of course still there.

She almost trembles.

I would have never done this right when I returned from rehab, too afraid she couldn't handle it. Now I trust her a thousand times more.

"Lo…" she whispers. "Maybe…"

I wait for her to collect her thoughts.

"Maybe…we should do it both ways tonight," she says, watching my lips. She kisses me suddenly. I hold the back of her head, deepening it before we pull apart.

"You're that wet?" I whisper, forcing myself not to harden at the thought.

She nods quickly. "Yes." She squirms. "Or do you think it's too much to do both?"

"We'll see." I kiss her again, and then Ryke returns to our lane, handing me a bottle of water. Daisy is about to stand up, offering him the seat back, but Ryke waves her to stay there.

"Can we start this fucking game?" he asks.

Lily frowns, eyeing the alley. "Where are the bumpers?"

"We're not playing with bumpers," Rose tells her, squirting more sanitizer on her palms, even though she just touched *brand new* bowling shoes.

"Bumpers are the best," Daisy concurs. "You can throw the ball really hard and try to ziz-zag it into the pins."

"Yeah," Lily agrees.

"Then you two go play on that lane." Rose points to the empty one beside us.

Lily springs to her feet. "Fine. We'll be having more fun anyway."

Daisy hesitates for a second before rising, and then she nudges her douchebag boyfriend's leg, who's texting. "Do you want to come?"

"What?"

"Bumpers or no bumpers," she briefly explains.

"I'm not playing with the kid bumpers. They're dumb."

"Hey, they're grownup bumpers," Lily says, "for grownups who don't like gutter balls."

Julian looks at Lily like she's a complete idiot.

"Julius…" I start with what should be his *rightful* name, but I stop myself, remembering our promise to Rose. *Be civil.* Whatever. My lips close, but I grind my teeth harder than I like.

"It's *Julian*," he says for the thousandth time to me.

"How about we team up against Rose and Connor?" I flash Rose a look like *is that civil enough for you?*

She nods in approval while Julian shrugs, seeming a bit skeptical about the olive branch I've extended. It's not a trick. Then he says, "Sure, man."

"Great."

Lily kisses me quickly on the lips, and I pat her on the bottom. When she leaves to her lane, her entire face is bright red, and she tries hard to avoid the cameras.

Ryke watches my girlfriend depart with her sister, and I can see his choice even before he takes a step in that direction. Julian being the same age as Daisy is ten times worse than Ryke. I can't even trust Julian for a second. I have no reason to.

"I'll be—" he starts.

"Whatever, go play on your bumpers, *bro*." I can't help but give him a hard time. It's like a busted function in my brain.

He rolls his eyes, wavers for a moment, and then follows Daisy to the other lane.

Connor deletes some of the names, leaving just four. I laugh when I notice he took my tip to heart. He's nicknamed all of us after Greek gods.

I scan the remaining list:

Zeus/Athena

Hades/Dionysus

Julian picks up a light blue ball from the carousel. "Who am I?" he asks. "Zeus?" He's not the brightest anything.

"You would be Hades. God of the underworld," Connor says.

"All around fantastic guy," I add dryly.

"Sweet."

Jesus.

Ryke notices the screen from afar and glares at Connor. "You're a real douche, you know that?"

I don't get it.

Rose puts her hand on Connor's shoulder. "Oh please, Loren would be Dionysus regardless if he drank or not."

Ryke just keeps shaking his head until Daisy distracts him, holding up two giant green bowling balls to her boobs.

I internally grimace. *Do not think about that part of her anatomy.* "Who is Dionysus?" I ask.

Rose clarifies, "the god of wine, parties, and basically hedonism."

"He's a man of chaos and pleasure," Connor adds.

"Sounds about right," I reply. "Thanks, love."

He winks and motions for Julian to start us off.

Daisy's boyfriend steps up to the alley with his ball in hand, and my stomach constricts the longer I have to watch him. How do you withstand a guy you just don't like? He knocks down all the pins but two and then pumps his arm.

"That's what I'm talking about."

We continue to play a few rounds, with Connor and Rose clearly in the lead. Connor forgot to mention that his *boarding school* had a bowling alley, and they'd bet on games with money and favors. So basically, he hustled us.

I don't mind at all. The more we lose, the more Julian's competitive nature rises—glaring, huffing, a poor sport all around. Whenever I look to the other lane, Lily and Daisy are in fits of giggles, sitting on their knees and trying to spin the bowling ball before rolling it down the alley.

Daisy even covers Ryke's eyes so he has to bowl blind. He's actually grinning. My gaze shifts to Lily. She practices her bowling stance by the swivel chairs and every time she goes to mock throw, the weight of the ball causes her to careen unsteadily on her feet. Her brown hair hangs in her eyes and she brushes it away before trying again.

I love her.

The world seems empty whenever I watch her. It's a peaceful existence. But I know a life with just the two of us, alone, is a future better as a fantasy. Friends. Family. They're not easy to leave behind anymore.

Laughter beside her lane breaks my focus. Ryke lifts Daisy by the legs, hanging her upside down, and she can't catch her breath, her laughs echoing through the bowling alley.

"Hey!" Julian shouts. Shit. He storms over to my older brother. "I'm sick of you always hanging around my girlfriend, man."

Ryke only drops one palm, holding Daisy perfectly upside down with one hand, clutching her calf. She swings in the air, blood rushing to her head, but her smile is huge.

"Then maybe," Ryke says, "you shouldn't leave your girlfriend with another fucking guy."

Julian is about to shove him, but Lily intervenes. *Shit.* I shoot to my feet, sprinting to the lane while she blocks Julian with two hands. He swats them away.

"Back off," I sneer at Julian.

He takes a couple steps in a safe direction. "Daisy…" Julian says. "Play with me." It sounds like an order.

Ryke grips Daisy by the waist and flips her right-side-up, her body meshes with his, sliding down his chest slowly before her feet touch the ground. She breathes heavily, her lips parted. Ryke has a way with women. There's no denying that.

He fixes her shirt that rides up her stomach. "What do you want?"

She swallows hard like she's never been asked that before. And then she shrugs.

Ryke looks around at all of us as we watch him. I don't know what to make of anything anymore. I'd wish for people to be simple—just so I can understand everyone—but then they wouldn't be real.

"I think it'd be better if I just went home," Daisy says. "I'll see you all tomorrow?"

"Daisy—" Ryke starts.

"No, it's cool."

"I'll drive you home," Julian says.

"No, I will." Lily steps up from behind me.

And then Rose rises from her seat. "You guys can finish up." She tosses her empty bottle of sanitizer in the trash on her way towards the door. Daisy skips to keep up with her older sister and Lily is right there with them in a quick second.

After the girls are gone, Julian says to Ryke, "You want to fuck her, that's fine. Just stop getting in my way."

Ryke charges forward, "You motherfucking…" And then Connor steps between them.

"We're in public," he announces.

"Let's go outside then," Julian says. "He wants a fight—"

"You're not fighting my brother, *Julius*. Leave it alone." I grab Ryke by the arm. "We're going." I drag him towards the exit.

"How can you put up with him?" he growls at me, turning his back on them with rigid joints.

"I can't," I say. "That's why I'm heading out this door. I walk away from fights all the time. You should try it once in a while." I push open the door and squint at the bright sun.

"Yeah?" he says, shielding his eyes with his hand.

"Yeah."

Between Scott and Julian, I've reached my limit on dealing with people I don't like.

That's Connor's game, not mine.

Chapter 29

0 Years : 08 Months

April

LILY CALLOWAY

Lo and I curl on the couch, rereading *Avengers: The Children's Crusade* together. Even though this is our fifth read-through, Lo flips the pages so slowly, allowing my mind to take mental detours.

Not the sexual kind.

The wedding infiltrates my brain, especially since Rose asked me what color bridesmaids dresses I preferred this morning. Like always, I told her to choose.

I can't believe I'm just twenty-one, on the path to marriage when all I really wished was to walk down the aisle with my head on straight. Emotionally ready for something so serious.

My wishes have not come true.

Everyone fears I'll become the runaway bride. No one says it, but I see it in their eyes. But it could just be my own fears, my own reflection staring back at me.

The front door blows open, and dressed in his usual button-down and slacks, Connor shuts it behind him. At the same time he sets his sights on the staircase, Rose's heels clap down it. She latches onto his wrist, her eyes pulsing with hot fury.

I thought if Rose lost her virginity to Connor, their relationship would be less volatile, filled with even *less* verbal sparring and wit that tosses my brains. Wrong. They still fight in French, and she still looks at him like she could rip off his balls.

I crane my neck over the couch to watch them, too curious.

Connor pries her gingerly off his wrist. "I think I know where the bedroom is."

"We're not having sex right now." She doesn't even attempt to lower her voice.

So the fight is about sex?

"All I meant was that I can lead myself upstairs. I said nothing about sex."

Oh. Never mind.

Connor slides past Rose mid-stair and disappears out of my view. Shit.

Rose huffs and says, "We don't have time to accommodate your ego." She stomps upstairs behind him, out of earshot.

I sit up, untangling myself from Lo while he continues to read the comic. I check the internet on his phone, popping up Twitter, and Lo watches me out of the corner of his eye. When I search #LilyCalloway, brutal messages appear.

@NorthGuy77: Do you know how many diseases #LilyCalloway must have? I wouldn't go near that twat.

@DaniellaESP: #LilyCalloway's vagina has to be huge.

A lump rises to my throat. I have to switch to a different hashtag.

@RealityTV89: Lily and Lo are the absolute cutest AND sexiest couple on TV. If you're not watching #PoPhilly, you suck.

It's a bit disheartening that people don't like me, by myself, but when they talk about me with Lo, they gush. But I'll take the good with the bad. I'm not that choosy.

"Lil," Lo says, closing his paperback comic. "Stop going on Twitter. It's not healthy."

"That's the first time I checked it all day," I defend before logging off. I pull up *Celebrity Crush* and my heart does an extra pump at the headline:

RE-POLL: WHO SHOULD LILY
CALLOWAY BE WITH?
LOREN HALE OR RYKE MEADOWS?
by Wendy Collins.

Great.

Of course I remember the poll months ago where Lo lost to his brother. Wendy Collins most likely wants to see if opinions differ after the show aired. I swallow the lodged pebble in my throat and click into the article.

I scroll down to the poll and vote for Loren. The minute I click his name, the current results fill the screen.

Ryke Meadows: 12%
Loren Hale: 88%

"Ohmygod!" I flinch back, nearly jumping on the cushions, and hit Lo's arm repeatedly. "You're eighty-eight percent!"

Confused wrinkles crease his forehead. "Eighty-eight percent what?"

I frown, not sure how to phrase it. "Eighty-eight percent of a winner against your brother…"

He tosses his paperback comic onto the coffee table and leans into me to read the article. He laughs and meets my eyes. "I guess those rumors will start ending now."

I didn't even realize…but yeah, they will. If people are starting to believe that Lo and I are an actual, real couple, not for appearance or for publicity but because we're *in love*, then they'll forget about Ryke as a three-way option.

Today is a good day.

"Lily, Lo!" Rose calls from the bottom of the stairs. We both turn our heads. Her expression flips between concern and pure rage.

Any momentary smile just vanishes in an instant.

"Can you come up here for a minute? We need to talk to you both."

We?

Lo and I exchange looks. We're both clueless what this could be about. For all I know, they're calling us upstairs for a surprise party…

Fat chance.

Chapter 30

0 Years : 08 Months

April

LOREN HALE

What the fuck is happening?

The thought plays on repeat while Lily and I sit on Connor and Rose's bed. The longer he spills these details, the more darkness spreads over my face, clinging to my emotions like tar. My leg jostles in irritation and anxiety while Lily shakes her head, as if their words are nothing but wrong.

Connor and Rose locked up their alcohol—a bottle of wine and tequila—and it went missing.

I sense where this is headed, even before Connor says, "We found the empty bottle at the bottom of your closet."

Their eyes, along with my brother's, drill into me. Questioningly. Accusingly.

It's not true, but I have no fucking evidence. Why would my word hold up? I'm the addict. I'm untrustworthy. Anything I do or say won't matter because it could all be a lie.

It's why I remain quiet. It's why my heated gaze stays fixed on the wall. Through my silence, Lily begins to defend me. "He would have thrown up if he drank!" she yells. "He's on Antabuse."

I rub my lips to hide a grimace. I should have told her that I quit taking the pills. *Christ.* I should have *fucking* told her.

I bury my anguish beneath confusion, trying to piece together who put the alcohol in my closet. But it's not a difficult problem to solve. Scott wants drama. He's received plenty from us, despite his declaration to *play nice.*

"Are you still taking it?" Ryke asks me.

His words push the wrong button. Hate sears my lungs. "Shouldn't you know that? You count my pills." My harsh voice hurts my ears. I hate this.

I hate that I'm going on the defensive, but it's the easiest mode to be in.

Rose almost steps forward in retaliation, but Connor places his hands on her waist to keep her calm.

Ryke scratches the back of his neck. "I stopped because I was trying to trust you."

Why are you such a fuck up, Loren? My eyes start to burn. "I don't even know why you ask me," I say. "You already think I drank."

"Honestly, I don't know what to think."

Connor cuts in to ease the situation. "We can squash this really easily. We haven't seen you sick these past couple weeks. All you have to do is show us your pills so we know that you're taking them."

I can't. They'll hate me. I don't need to see their disappointment. "It's not your fucking body, Connor," I sneer. Why can't they just leave me alone? It'd be so much easier. "This doesn't affect *anyone* in the room but me and maybe Lil. I don't have to tell *you* shit." I stand, about to leave this all behind me.

I can't look back at Lily. I just storm towards the exit, but Rose steps in my path, stretching her arms on the door frame to physically block me. I don't need this right now, not from her.

"Your addiction affects *everyone* in this room," she nearly yells. "If you can't see that—"

"I see just fine," I say coldly. *Don't push me, Rose.* My jaw throbs. My muscles strain. I just want to escape *this.* Doesn't she get it?

"Don't be an idiot."

Don't be such a fucking idiot, Loren. I let out a short laugh. "That's so fucking easy for you, isn't it?" I say with malice. I am being swallowed by blackness. I can't see a way out besides hurting her as much as she's torturing me. "Being *smart.*" I step forward in her face. "Miss Perfect. What do you have to worry about? Does my hair look good today? Do my shoes match my dress?"

"Lo," Connor warns.

His voice is so soft behind me. I drown it out. I watch Rose's ribcage fall and rise heavily, venom seeping out of her eyes.

I begin to numb.

I rotate and spot her organized bookshelf, too meticulous, nothing out of place. I walk over to the shelves. "Let's see, Rose..." I pick up a hardback and flip through the pages before throttling the book, the spine ungluing. "How does this feel?"

She inhales severely, her collarbones jutted out.

Her pain slices my insides, and I just keep moving, being cut open with each soulless action. I open a stack of manila folders and shake the papers loose.

"Stop it!" Rose shouts, dropping to her knees to collect each page.

"This doesn't bother you, right?" I say, agony clenching my stomach, gripping my bones. I wish she would hit me. Deck me right in the gut. I just want this pain to go away. "Nothing's fucking wrong with Rose

Calloway? I'm the idiot. I'm the fucking moron in your world who's so stupid and selfish that he would drink again and again." I'm the fuck up. The degenerate. The loser.

Just leave me alone.

Let me go.

"No…" she says, eyes wide in horror at her scattered papers.

My throat almost closes at how crazy she's become. I stare dazedly as she breathes sharply, hyperventalting. Connor approaches quickly and bends down to her, whispering in her ear. Then he lifts her by the waist.

She screams manically, "No!" Rose kicks out to try to reach the papers.

I'm going to throw up. Sickness rises from my stomach.

"Stop," Connor says in the pit of her ear.

She screams shrilly, a desperation that I've never heard from her. While Connor holds her back, Rose's eyes meet mine.

And my mouth moves before I can stop it. "It took you twenty-three goddamn years to finally lose your virginity," I say, finding a chink in her armor. "And you lost it to a guy that's just fucking you for your last name."

"LOREN!" Connor shouts.

I almost stagger back by the force of my name from *his* lips, his face blanketed with rage. Cold washes over my body, guilt squeezing my lungs. *Why can't you just hit me? I deserve that.* I open my mouth to ask, but he says, "*Don't.*" The room silences. My full name off his tongue still rings in my ears. "Give me a minute."

While he takes care of Rose, I concentrate on the rafters up above, my legs weak from that outburst. This could have gone another way… *any* other way would've been better.

Ryke sets his hand on my shoulder. I can't look at him.

"Hey, it's all right."

It's not.

"Look at me."

I can't. I choke on a breath, tears welling. What the fuck is wrong with me?

He cups my face between his hands, forcing my gaze on his. "We're on your side, Lo. We're not against you."

I barely glance over at Rose, who sits on the vanity bench, Connor wiping her tears with his thumb. She almost never cries.

"*Lo*," Ryke says, turning my head again so I focus on him. "You're okay."

"Yeah?" I breathe. "You all look at me like I'm a dog that needs to be put out of his misery. I'm just waiting for one of you to finally do it."

His expression just breaks. "That's not going to happen." He doesn't deny that it's the case.

"Right," I whisper. And then I make the mistake of finally looking to Lily, who's on the edge of the bed. She is frozen in confusion, which is why she never intervened. She wears a haunted expression, like I betrayed her.

I guess I did. I swallow hard.

"Are you going to puke?" Ryke asks.

"I don't know..." I scan the room, searching for a way out again. But I can't really escape myself. I have to break away from my brother. The tension between Lily and me is what's tearing me apart.

In order to resolve *something*, I have to talk to her.

So I head over to the bed while Ryke crosses his arms. The longer I stare at her features, the more this hurts. "What?" I say.

"Did you drink?" she questions.

I stagger back. She actually thinks I drank?

"I just...I don't understand why you wouldn't get your pills to prove it," she says in a small voice.

"So you're going to take their side over mine?" I choke. *Stop being defensive.* It's one of the very few positive voices in my head.

"I'm not taking sides." She stares at her hands while she thinks hard. "I just want the truth, Lo."

"I didn't drink." I shake my head over and over, my eyes clouding. "But I can't prove it. I stopped taking Antabuse months ago." The truth doesn't free me—doesn't lift a weight off my chest. I am strapped with baggage so heavy that there's no hope to reach the surface.

"You did what?!" Ryke shouts.

"They were driving me nuts!" I yell. I hate this, but it's a conversation that I can't avoid anymore. "I'm paranoid about everything I eat—if it's accidentally cooked in alcohol. I picture myself puking from a shitty fucking meal. I can't do that for the rest of my goddamn life." I turn back to Lily. "You *have* to believe me." I don't know what I'll do if she doesn't believe me. I can't handle this—

"I do," she says without any doubt.

I exhale deeply and walk to the bed. I reach in for a hug.

Then she pushes me in the chest and points a finger at me. "But it's not okay. It's not." I should have told her. Her chin trembles, and she pulls her shoulders back with more confidence. I love her for it. "You can't stop taking them just because it drives you nuts. And it's not okay that you kept this from me…from *us*…"

Her tears match mine. "I know," I tell her in a whisper. "I'm sorry." I sit next to her, and she scoots closer to me. Then our arms sort of meet each other at the same time. I don't want to let her go.

"We're in a fight, just so you know," she whispers. "I'll sleep in Daisy's bedroom."

Pain contorts my face. "You haven't had sex in three days." It's the truth. She's been cramming for an exam in May, and she falls asleep before we ever get that far. It's been good, but she won't be able to keep the routine up for long. It's just not how her brain works. "I was going to…" I trail off as she shakes her head.

"I don't care about sex. I care about you being healthy and not drinking."

I'm suddenly overwhelmed with pride. For her. But also fear for me. I'm falling behind. I can feel myself regressing while she's barreling ahead. I have to get my shit together.

"We have another issue," Ryke suddenly says, pulling our attention to the room.

"We don't have to bring that up now," Rose snaps.

Connor and Rose stand together, hand-in-hand, and I try to string some apologies together, but when I open my mouth, nothing comes out.

Rose raises her chin, poised again. Like nothing happened. She just gives me a single nod like *it's done, let's move past this.*

I don't think I'll forget it though. I'll have this guilt within me forever.

Ryke grabs a camera that belongs to the crew. I frown, and Lily and I both stand up, coming to his side. "Watch this," he says.

My stomach overturns.

This isn't good.

Chapter 31

0 Years : 08 Months

April

LILY CALLOWAY

Nononono.

I peer at the camera in Ryke's hands, already emotionally drained with Lo. I wish we could rewind, go back to the couch with our comic books and pretend like this was all a nightmare.

Instead, Ryke hits the "play" button on the camera. *Oh my God.* My eyes widen. Lo and I are in the bookstore—the day that people, in general, started to freak me out. I watch myself drag Lo into the bathroom and then shut the door closed on the camera.

Anxious heat builds across my skin. In the video, I say, "Can I give you a blow job?"

I can explain. My hand shoots in the air, about to gush forth all the excuses that are surprisingly truths. "I was having a bad day," I start.

"Shhh," Lo says, frowning and really *glaring* at the camera. I'm sure that look is meant for Scott. And as we just watch the door in the video, sound effects start playing...of *moaning* and male groaning. They never showed how Lo rejected my request? Or how I took it back too? My frown deepens.

"What is this?" Lo asks, his hand slipping in mine before I have a chance to bite my fingernails. "Is this some kind of fucked up joke?"

"You tell us," Ryke refutes. "You're fucking in a public bathroom in the middle of the afternoon."

My stomach sinks. Is this how they'd react if they knew we've done *that* many times before the cameras started invading our personal space?

"N*ooo*," Lo says the word slowly. "We didn't fuck in the bathroom. We don't fuck anywhere but our bedroom." I shut up because I'm a worse liar than him. This is fact. "Someone must have tampered with the video."

"So you didn't ask to give Loren a blow job?" Rose questions me, her hands set on her hips.

"I..." My elbows are roasting. "I did do that..." I mutter.

"And then I told her no," Lo adds. We're not lying about this—that's the weird thing.

"What were you actually doing for thirty minutes in the bathroom?" Connor asks casually.

I relax a little, not feeling as defensive with him.

Lo says, "I was giving Lily a pep talk."

"I needed one," I say. I smile at Lo, and he rubs my back. Then I remember my earlier declaration. I never believed that he could start lying to me after rehab. And I take one step away from him, his hand falling from mine. "We're still in a fight."

His throat bobs. "I'm going to start taking Antabuse again, Lil."

"Good," I say with a nod. I ache to step into his arms, for him to hold me and for me to hold him. Nowhere feels better than in his embrace. But I have to do what's best for him. No enabling. So I can hold out for a day or so. I turn to Ryke. "Fast-forward to the end. When we come out of the bathroom, I know I'll look disappointed."

Ryke speeds up the footage, and when he presses play, I watch myself exit the bathroom, my fingers laced with Lo's. My hair is perfectly flattened, but my lips are just slightly curved downwards. "Ah-ha!" I point at the camera. "I look *so* upset."

Rose nears the screen with disbelief. I expect her expression to flood with realization. It doesn't change.

"That's you disappointed?" Ryke asks. "You're sweating and your face is red."

"It was hot in the bathroom," I defend.

"It was," Lo agrees but his voice is soft. He knows that we have no evidence in our favor. They just have to trust us. Maybe they shouldn't. We are lying to them on one account.

"Are they going to air this?" I ask.

"Probably," Connor says, "but it helps promote your wedding." *The wedding.* I internally shrink. "The bad edit would be you slipping into the bathroom with another guy."

"We're just concerned about your health," Rose says.

I wish, so badly, they could just believe I'm doing okay. But only Lo truly sees my progress. He's the one wrapped so closely with my sex addiction. The others just see glimpses here and there, and the bad times seem to stick out far more than the good.

"I didn't have sex, Rose," I tell her, desperately hoping she accepts this truth. "I'm doing better. I mean, I shouldn't have asked Lo that… that question. But besides that, I'm doing better."

I can go a day without sex, no crippling anxiety or fear attached. Sure, sometimes I cling onto Lo more than I should. But it's an everyday fight.

I don't know how to show them what I feel.

Lo reaches down and his fingers brush against mine, silently asking if he can hold my hand.

I stare into his amber eyes that express a thousand regrets. He's beating himself up about the pills more than I ever could. This video is no one's fault…but maybe Scott Van Wright's.

I squeeze his fingers, and he laces them with mine.

"I thought you were in a fight," Ryke says to us.

"We are," I say softly, not taking my eyes off his. *No one is going to hurt us:* I read in his gaze. *No one is going to pull us apart.*

Not Scott.

Not my sister.

Not his brother.

If someone sinks us, it'll be ourselves. That, I'm sure of.

Chapter 32

0 Years : 08 Months

April

LOREN HALE

I stand rigid like marble at the base of the staircase. The living room television is turned on, playing a rerun of *Princesses of Philly*. The episode revolves around the Alps trip where we all played party games and had to endure Julian as well as Scott.

Rose sits on the couch, her computer on her lap and her eyes flitting to the television. She doesn't notice me lingering.

"Haven't you already seen this episode?" I ask. She doesn't turn around to acknowledge my presence, which pounds another ounce of remorse into me. I haven't confronted her about what I did after they accused me of drinking. Apologies infiltrate my head. But I always relate "sorry" to a plea for forgiveness. And I don't know if I want her to forgive me.

Silence hangs in the air and I let out a long breath. Maybe I should just say it anyway. Because I am sorry. I do mean the words.

Before I can open my mouth once more, she finally answers my earlier question, "I'm making a list of how much screen time each Calloway Couture piece has, who wears the garment, and then I'm cross-matching the numbers with sales."

"How's it going?" I wonder.

"Surprisingly, the clothes that Lily wears have the most sales, but she also has the most air time, so that's probably a factor," Rose tells me.

My eyes lift to the TV, and I see Julian rolling his eyes and taking a sip of beer. Even his virtual presence causes my nerves to fire and my skin to crawl. And yet, I still tolerate him. Is that something we do for the people we care about?

"How can you stand to be around me?" I suddenly ask what's been plaguing my mind.

Rose shifts in her seat to look over the couch, her gaze meeting mine.

"What do you mean?"

"You hate me," I say, "but you put up with me for Lily. It must be hard, right?" I'm no easier to be around than this guy. That's the sad truth that tears at me.

She reads between all the lines, her eyes flitting to the screen and then back to me. "You're not Julian," she says like I'm an idiot. "You don't even come close."

"I made you cry," I say, my voice hollow. In her bedroom. I pushed all of her buttons on purpose.

"I forgive you," she says easily.

"How?"

She's not soft. She sits up straight with barriers hundreds of feet tall. "Because I know you'll never forgive yourself," she says. "Your guilt is punishment enough, don't you think?"

Maybe. I don't know. But I do think she knows me too well.

"Anyway, Daisy doesn't even like Julian. She's only with him because she's too scared to dump him and hurt his feelings. We all have a right to dislike him if we collectively know the relationship is doomed." She pauses. "But you and Lily—you two love each other. It's not that difficult to put my feelings aside when I can see how happy you make her."

Her honesty surprises me, and I know, in this moment, I have to reciprocate it. She deserves that at least.

"Regardless…" I say. *I'm sorry, Rose.* The words stay trapped in the back of my throat.

Still, she nods in understanding. "As long as you keep my sister safe, we'll be even."

It's not even a fair price to pay because I'd do that no matter what. But I take it.

I'm about to turn around and head back up the stairs when she says, "I hope you know that I'm not mean to you because you're a guy…" She lets out a deep, strained breath.

I overheard Connor yesterday trying to console Rose about the comments online. The ones that call her a misandrist. She was crying. I never thought she would take offense to anything, but they chinked her iron wall. I figure the topic has been on her mind lately.

"It's just…" she tries again. "…I don't hate men." Her shoulders tighten, probably at the thought of all the ridicule.

Rose has always been dramatic—she threatens to castrate guys, to snip off their balls. It's a part of her humor, but on air, it's been taken the wrong way.

"I think you dislike types of people," I tell her, "both men and women. The TV just shows parts of us. I wouldn't worry about it."

She nods, and after a brief minute, she focuses back on the television. Our rare, honest moment ends just like that.

Chapter 33

0 Years : 08 Months

April

LILY CALLOWAY

Lo found the best way to stick it to production: barricading ourselves in our bedroom. Scott wants footage of us; well, now he has none.

Seven days into our protest and cabin fever starts setting in. I'm used to holing up in a *house*, but holing up in a *room* is quite different. For one, Lo and I have agreed that we'll only sneak out for bathroom breaks.

We're waiting for Scott to apologize for all the mean things he's said *plus* altering footage of us. It's different than handing me porn and passing Lo a bottle of alcohol. He's actively trying to turn our friends and family against us. That's a new low.

However, I think it's more likely that we'll die from starvation up here. Our only source of food comes from my youngest sister, who smuggles us bagels and cookies whenever she's home—which isn't often.

I'll be back in 10 minutes. Taxi got lost. – Daisy

I groan as Lo does pushups on the floor. He had to skip the gym a few times this week, which helps take his mind off drinking and alleviates stress. "We're going to starve," I tell him. "Maybe I can convince Connor to bring me a Pop-Tart."

"No chance," Lo says, his chest lowering to the ground. "I texted him to bring me a Fizz, and he started lecturing me about anatomy and how bipedal mobility works. All in a damn text. If I wasn't so irritated, I would have been impressed."

"Yeah, but Rose is my sister. He *has* to be nice to me."

I quickly compose a text. Connor, I need food. I'm dying. SOS! I hit send.

Too bad Rose and Ryke have bonded together to denounce our protest. They think hiding out in a room, isolating ourselves, will cause us to regress. But we're not having any more sex than we usually do. Mostly, we've spent our time bingeing on Netflix and reading comics online.

I flip open my laptop just as my phone pings.

The refrigerator is stocked. If you've lost mobility in your legs, Loren can carry you downstairs. And you know how I feel about hyperboles. – Connor

Ugh.

I close my phone. "He's on Team RoRy. Mission aborted." I sit on the edge of the bed, typing on my laptop, and Lo rolls onto his back to begin sit-ups.

"RoRy?" he questions with a grunt.

"Yeah, also known as evil siblings Rose and Ryke," I tell him. "They needed a name." I start scrolling through Tumblr's #PoPhilly feed. Most of the comments are essay-long paragraphs detailing how they love the show.

Secretly, I just like looking at the gifs. Many people have created them from videos of Lo kissing and flirting with me. We've been called OTP (one true pairing) so many times that I literally have to stop myself from producing happy tears.

I never thought *we'd* make it into a fandom. It's not something I sought, and now that it's happening it feels more surreal than anything. I have to admit, I love this side of pop culture much more than the paparazzi. Maybe because Lo and I have always been fans at heart.

I click the #Coballoway tag and find gifs of Connor's arched eyebrow and Rose's brutal stare in reply. I instantly smile.

"Are you on Twitter?" Lo asks as he blows out a heavy breath. He lowers his back to the ground and stops just before it touches the floor. When he rises, he gives me a look like *we talked about Twitter*. We did. It's not a healthy place for me.

"Tumblr," I reply, my voice small.

He freezes mid-sit-up. "*Lily*," he says my name in warning. Tumblr is worse for me.

"I'm looking at chaste gifs," I blurt out. "The kind with you and me kissing."

"You can't even watch us making out on TV without getting wet," he reminds me and resumes his workout. "You shouldn't be looking at gifs of it either."

"I'm getting better at it," I admit truthfully.

"Okay," he says, "but what happens if you stumble onto gifs of naked men and cocks. You've abstained from porn for so long, Lil. You don't want to ruin that by accident."

He's so right. But I glance back at the computer screen and see a gif of Connor wrapping his arms around Rose's waist, his eyes lighting up with desire, possession, and love. I'm so touched that we're all a part of a fandom. It's going to be so sad to abandon this. To never see it again.

"Lil." Lo sits up, his arm on his bent knee. "Give me ten minutes and I'll sit beside you and we can look at them together. I'll cover your eyes if I see any penises. How's that?"

I smile. "What if there are boobs? Can I cover your eyes?"

"Sure," he says into a laugh as he lowers back to the ground. I log onto the Marvel website, a safe place, while he continues his workout.

The door swings open a few minutes later, and Daisy stealthily glides inside on her skateboard...okay, not so stealthily, but it's a pretty cool entrance.

And her appearance triggers a bright feeling, like Christmas morning. I rush her before she gets far. "What'd you bring?"

She grins, setting a foot on the floor and leaving one on her board. "Your favorite." She shakes a paper brown Lucky's bag.

"You're the best." Between keeping our secret and smuggling in food, Daisy has shown her loyalty to Team LiLo (that's what they call us online now).

Lo jumps up from the ground and takes the bag from Daisy. "Thanks, Dais."

"Always happy to help," she says, standing back on her skateboard. She rolls around the room. "I have to warn you though, Rose is giving me these dirty looks. I think she's catching on that I'm sneaking in food."

"Stay strong," I encourage as Lo passes me a box of fries.

"She has those eyes, you know," Daisy tells us. "They're kind of scary."

"That's what it feels like to be turned to stone," Lo says. He sits at the desk and unwraps a burger.

"LILY! LO!" Ryke yells from downstairs. "I'm coming up! You both better be clothed!"

Shit. Fuck. Shit.

"Hide," I hiss to Daisy. I don't want her to get in real trouble from Rose or Ryke. We both glance at the bed at the same time, and Daisy lies on her skateboard and rolls underneath, out of sight.

I shove a fry in my mouth and find the Nerf gun by the nightstand.

Lo snaps his fingers at me. "Uh-uh." He shakes his head in disapproval.

I swallow my fry and then say, "He's the enemy, Lo."

The door pops open before he can reply, and I pelt the Nerf balls at Ryke's chest. He doesn't flinch, not even by the fifth one. "What the fuck, Lily?" he growls and storms over, tugging the plastic toy from my hands.

I look to Lo, and he has that expression like *told you so.*

Damage not inflicted. Point taken.

I slump down on the bed, stiffening a little as I remember Daisy hides beneath the mattress and box springs.

Ryke narrows his eyes at the Nerf gun. "Where did you get this?"

"We've had it," I lie briskly.

"If you've had this, you'd have shot me weeks ago."

So true.

"It apparated into our room."

His eyebrows knot. "*What?*" He turns to Lo. "Is she even speaking English."

Lo wipes his mouth with a napkin, still focused on his food. "It's a *Harry Potter* term."

"For fuck's sake, both of you are being ridiculous. Stop this silly fucking protest and come down…" His voice trails off when he catches sight of *what* Lo is eating. A Lucky's bag guiltily sitting beside the innocent lamp. And then Ryke's face darkens. "Calloway!"

"Yes?" I ask.

He rolls his eyes. "Not you." His head whips around the room. "Daisy!" He flings open the closet door, searching for her between my shirts and Lo's crew-necks.

"You should be directing your anger at Scott," Lo refutes, sipping from a fountain Fizz. "The moment he apologizes, we'll be back downstairs with the cameras."

Ryke doesn't listen. He concentrates on finding my sprightly blonde sister. "Daisy!" And then he rests a hand on the mattress, about to duck his head underneath the bed.

"Wait!" I shriek. But it's too late.

He grabs her ankle and rolls her out onto the floor.

She's smiling wide, her blonde hair tangled and hanging half in her face. "Hey there," she says, looking up at Ryke.

He gives her a long once-over that's hard to miss. "Stop giving them food and…*toys*." He tosses the Nerf gun on the bed.

Daisy turns over, her back against the skateboard. "They were getting bored," she refutes like it makes all the difference. It so does.

"Good."

She glides away from him with the push of her hands, like she's floating on the pool on her back.

Ryke puts his foot in between her legs, stopping the skateboard from rolling. My sister inhales a little deeper than before. This looks utterly sexual. Right? I glance to Lo, and his glare could burn a hole in his brother's forehead.

Ryke never backs down, waiting for Daisy to speak.

"I have this theory," Daisy says, "that if you leave two people who are *really, really* attracted to each other, alone in a room, without anything to do, they'll have sex. A lot, *a lot* of sex."

I blush, wondering if she's talking about us or about her and Ryke.

We wait in uncomfortable silence for Ryke to reply.

He says, "If that theory is right, you must really find your boyfriend fucking ugly."

"Who says I haven't had lots of sex with him?"

His glare could kill. "He's twenty-three, Dais. If you're fucking him, he's going to jail."

She raises her hand in defense and sits up on the skateboard. Ryke's leg is closer to her crotch in result, but she actually grabs onto his ankle so he doesn't move. "I'm not…I wouldn't do that to someone." She glances at me for back up.

"She's just being nice to us," I say. "Don't jump down her throat, Ryke." My eyes bug. "Notlikethat."

Lo groans behind me. "Appetite lost, Lil."

Yeah, I don't want to think about Ryke's *you know what* near Daisy's mouth either.

Daisy breathes heavily and says straight out, "I just thought that if they got bored, then they'd probably want to have sex."

Lo coughs hoarsely, and I walk over to pat his back. He takes a large sip of his soda before he says, "Please, don't talk about my sex life, Daisy."

She sighs and sets her forehead on Ryke's leg in frustration. He still towers above her. "I was just trying to be helpful."

"You're not fucking helping," Ryke says rudely, though his hand is on her head, closer physically than I've seen them before. Their friendship has made a few extra strides it seems. *Hopefully not too far.*

"Hey," I pipe in. "She is too helping. If I didn't have my Nerf gun, I probably would have jumped Lo. Sex crisis averted."

Ryke steps away from Daisy and turns on me. "If you're having problems controlling yourself, maybe you shouldn't be locked in a room with your boyfriend." He points at the toy gun on the bed. "But this is your fucking solution? Really?"

"Looks more fun than doggy style," Daisy chimes in with a lopsided smile.

"No," Ryke says one word to refute that.

I'd have to agree with him. Nerf guns are not as fun as doggy style.

Lo pinches the bridge of his nose and then rises from the desk. "Okay." He grabs the Nerf gun off the bed and shoves it in Ryke's chest. "Take the gun. Take Daisy." He clasps Daisy's wrist, pulls her to her feet and hands her the skateboard. Then he rejoins me in the middle of the room. "We're going to be protesting in *private*."

Ryke doesn't look happy.

"Told you," Daisy says under her breath, "I tried to keep them from—"

Ryke swiftly draws her to his chest and covers her mouth with his hand. I can tell she's smiling underneath his palm.

"You'll really come out if Scott apologizes?" he asks.

"Yep," Lo says.

"I'll have him in here within the hour," Ryke proclaims, a promise attached to the words. "This shit ends tonight." He releases Daisy, his eyes drifting along her features. "I don't know what kind of doggy style you're doing, but it's wrong." He pats her head before exiting.

Lo shouts back, "Inappropriate, *bro!*"

Daisy watches Ryke leave before she sidles next to me and nudges my hip. "Sorry."

I shake my head and give her a side hug. "You've been a valiant soldier. The best."

When she smiles, it's bright and beautiful, and I wonder how I spent so many years avoiding a relationship with her. Daisy is one of the most soulful people to be around, and maybe if I opened up a little sooner, I'd have felt this joy from the start.

Chapter 34

0 Years : 09 Months

May

LILY CALLOWAY

I rest my back against a shelf with an array of pill bottles for sale, trying not to engrain this mental image in my brain. Lo and Ryke, side-by-side, staring at a huge wall of condoms. Scott apologized after Ryke physically pushed him in our room. His "I'm sorry" wasn't very sincere, but we both were ready to move on. I just never thought that I'd be *here*. On our way home from lunch, the three of us made a pit stop at a local drug store to pick up the love gloves.

It's funny—before Lo, condoms were my staple. Now I hate them.

How things change.

"Why do you have to wear condoms?" I ask Lo for the third time.

He hasn't answered me yet. They've been making fun of the Magnum XL glow-in-the-dark condoms for the past minute, not because of the size though. I would partake in the jokes if I wasn't so confused.

"I understand why Ryke has to wear them," I continue like they're listening. "What if one of his conquests claims to have a Ryke baby? That's a scary thought, right?"

Ryke spins around to face me. Finally! "Can you not call the girls I sleep with *conquests*? You make it seem like my goal in life is to fuck women, and they're not trophies to me."

"Sure, can you ask Lo why he has to wear condoms?" I reply.

Ryke gives me a look like *are you really fucking serious?* "It's called protection from an unplanned pregnancy."

"I'm on birth control," I whisper-hiss, lowering my voice as people pass our aisle. They don't notice who we are though, or if they do, they don't care. Ryke and Lo chose an out-of-the-way drug store instead of one in town. To accommodate me and my paranoia. It was nice of them.

"Lil, it's just for a little while," Lo says, grabbing a box off the rack. He's been getting badgered by my sister and his brother about being more careful. They're worried that with the reality show stress and hamming it up for the cameras (aka excessive teasing), we're going to have a mistake.

"Wearing them doesn't feel as good." I pause. "For either party involved." And then I point my finger at Ryke. "Don't deny it."

He raises his hands. "I wasn't going to, but some things are worth sacrificing, Calloway."

Fine. "So how many boxes are you going to buy? Three? Five?" He needs like eleven. His one-night stands can almost compete with past-me.

"One," he replies. "And don't you have to buy tampons?"

It would have been a rude comment if he wasn't completely serious. "I don't need them. I delay my period on birth control," I say it all without blushing. Internally, I am patting myself on the back.

"Let me guess," he says, his eyes darkening. "So you can have more sex." My cheeks redden. *Damn.* But I have to give myself credit; I've been able to last this long talking about condoms and sex without my body revolting against me. When Ryke looks away, I give myself a literal quick tap on the shoulder. Go me.

"Hey," Lo cuts in and puts his hand on Ryke's shoulder. "Stop giving her a hard time."

I'm used to it, and I'm sure I irritate Ryke just as equally. He barely glances at the rack before he tugs a pack of condoms off, which basically means he has a particular brand and size that he always wears. I focus on the check-out, avoiding eye-contact with the condoms—because knowing the size will weird me out.

My brain does a tailspin the minute I notice the line of magazines and tabloids stacked beside the counter. The headline stops my heart:

LILY CALLOWAY, NYMPHOMANIAC AND REPORTEDLY SLEEPING WITH BROTHERS.

I've seen this many times before. But that's the problem.

I thought that after the *Celebrity Crush* re-poll and positive effect of the reality show, these rumors would be put to rest. Not only that—but I would've *never* taken a quick condom pit stop for both Lo and Ryke if I knew the media was still buying into the rumors.

"Is this for you?" the attendant asks, eyeing the condoms and then the two guys. And me. Holy shit. Out of all bad ideas, this is a *horrible* one.

"No," I cut in, wedging myself beside Lo. "We don't want those anymore. And we'd like to buy all of these." I start piling all the tabloids up on the counter.

"Not this again," Ryke groans.

"Lily—" Lo starts.

"You don't understand," I snap. "You were eighty-eight percent, Lo. This shouldn't be happening."

"So you don't want the condoms?" the attendant asks, confused.

"Yes, we want them," Ryke says.

"No, we don't," I refute. "Just the magazines." I empty the shelves and slide my card on the counter.

"For fuck's sake, Lily," Ryke snaps. "I'll let you buy your fucking tabloids, but at least let me buy my condoms. I don't want to have to go back out."

"Fine," I surrender. "The condoms too." My neck heats. "But just so you know, we're all three *not* sleeping together. These are wrong." I slap my hand on the stack of tabloids. "He needs the condoms for other girls."

"She gets it, love," Lo says.

The attendant swipes my card, looking freaked out by me. I don't care. All I want is for people to listen to the truth—is that too much to ask?

Lo sidles up behind me and wraps his arms around my shoulders. "She's very protective of me," he tells the attendant. "It's sweet actually, when she's not going bat-shit crazy, that is."

The attendant smiles warmly, and I punch Lo in the arm. "I'm not crazy."

His eyes soften in an apology. "I know."

I carry the large stack of magazines in my hands, Lo and Ryke refusing to help on principle. The drive home is layered in awkward tension. I start reading the articles, and my anger only escalates. The word *nymphomaniac* sets me on edge. I've always identified with being an *addict*, and calling me a nympho makes it harder to argue that sex addiction is real. So many people claim sex addiction is used to excuse people of their philandering ways. And that's not what this feels like at all.

By the time Lo pulls into the driveway, I'm fuming.

I jump out of the car only a second before it stops moving. "Wait up, Lily!" Lo yells at me. But I'm on a mission.

Brett and Savannah appear out of nowhere, but I'm sure they were waiting for us to come home. Their cameras zip to me and flash to Lo and Ryke. I walk past in a hurry.

"You're being overdramatic!" Ryke screams at me.

I open the door. "I'm not being overdramatic!" I yell back. Okay, that was a *little* dramatic. I storm into the kitchen, shifting the magazines so they don't fall over.

I make it to the sink and toss them right in. Perfect. Then I bend down to a bottom cupboard where Lo keeps the lighter fluid for the grill outside. I take it out and start squirting the pile of magazines.

"Whoa!" Lo and Ryke yell together. They rush me all at once, and then I feel someone else pry the plastic squirt bottle from my hand.

Connor.

Where the hell did he come from?

Lo draws me to his chest, his hands snug around my waist in comfort, but I hardly calm down. I just want to destroy the *thing* that has hurt me. If I can't reply to the reporters or the comments, I might as well take it out on the actual magazines.

My older sister suddenly appears, tossing the soiled magazines in a large trash bag. Dammit. I struggle in Lo's arms, hoping to reach at least a single tabloid and set it on fire.

It's clear by his firm grip that he's not letting me go.

"What's going on?" Connor asks. His calm voice hardly instills tranquility. Tears threaten to rise, so helpless and angry, a toxic mixture that burrows nasty emotions inside of me.

"People suck!" I scream.

Connor reaches for a tabloid before Rose adds it to the others in the trash bag. He doesn't even flip it open, not that he could. The soaked pages cling together.

"I don't fucking care about the rumors." Ryke extends his arms. "How many times do I have to say that?"

"I'm not a cheater! I don't even like being an alleged cheater," I say, my heart racing. It'll fly out of my chest any minute now. It's not fair to me or to Lo. He doesn't deserve to be with "the girl who can't close her legs."

I point a finger at the magazines. "And I *hate* being called a nympho!"

"What do you want to do about it, Lil?" Lo asks, his lips near my ear. "Throw a tantrum in front of the cameras. Done. They've got your reaction on film."

I go utterly still. That's not what I wanted.

Connor clears his throat. "Or you could light this on fire." He tosses the magazine into Rose's trash bag. "It might be cathartic."

My shoulders lift at the thought.

Rose gives Connor a disapproving look. "Don't encourage her." She drops the bag and keeps her lighter-fluid soaked hands away from her clothes. I didn't mean for her to clean up my mess. I would have done it. Guilt bears down on me, and before I can apologize, a voice rings out from the living room.

"Are you fucking serious?!" Julian yells.

Daisy's boyfriend has her up against the wall, his nose in her face, and his hands on either side of her head. He's pinning her. My heart does fly out of my chest, but it's not even because of the tabloids. *Daisy…*

"Do you know the *hell* that I went through for you?!"

Oh my god.

"HEY!" Ryke shouts. Before I can blink, he's running, his whole demeanor changing to a furious, dark Ryke Meadows in a split second. Brett sprints beside him, keeping his camera angled to the living room in case of a fight. I try to take a step forward, but Lo won't release me, not even for this.

"I have to help," I whisper.

"I don't want you to get hurt."

Connor follows Ryke with a hurried, determined stride. Rose is in a rush to wash her hands, and I think if it wasn't lighter fluid, she'd say *fuck it* and go help Daisy on instinct.

"What's going on?" I ask Rose.

She squirts a huge glob of soap onto her palm and talks rapidly, "We were in the middle of breaking up with Julian for Daisy." Her eyes flicker back to the scene. "*Fuck*."

"Come again?" Lo snaps.

"Yeah, what?" I ask, my pulse speeding. I flinch as Julian slams his fist into the wall beside Daisy's head. Fear bubbles in my chest. With Connor and Ryke helping, I know she'll be okay.

Rose's alarmed gaze stays fixed on the fight while she scrubs harder, faster. "Daisy wanted to dump him, but she didn't want to hurt his feelings. I thought that if Connor and I did it for her and embarrassed her a little bit, she'd have enough sense to do it herself next time." She adds coldly, "If I'd known you were going to have a mini-meltdown during the middle of it, I would have rescheduled."

Ouch. "I'm sorry."

"It could have gone bad regardless."

At least she called my meltdown *mini*.

We watch Ryke grab Julian by the shoulder. He throws a well-deserved punch into Julian's jaw, the force knocking him back a couple steps. Then Julian regains his balance and careens into Ryke, attempting to pummel him to the floor. But Connor grips Ryke's shoulder, keeping him upright.

Rose turns off the faucet in haste, just as Ryke slams his fist into Julian's face again.

Daisy stands petrified by the wall, and I wish I could run over to her and bring her to safety—far, far away from her *ex*-boyfriend.

Rose is by my side. "Get her out of there," she says under her breath. I don't think she's talking to me though.

Julian cusses and stops to touch his swollen eye. His chest rises and falls heavily. I wish Ryke would knee him in the nuts.

Julian sets his sights on Daisy, his face hardened in anger. Both Rose and I start forward on instinct, and Lo reaches out, clutching our arms. I think Rose would curse him out if she wasn't so hypnotized by the ongoing fight.

"You're just going to fucking stand there?!" Julian yells at our sister.

"What do you want from me?" Daisy questions.

"For you to give me back *months* of my life that I wasted with you, you stupid cunt."

Whoa. Everything moves so fast. Connor holds Ryke by the shoulders while he shouts a series of expletives, some I've never heard before. And then Lo releases Rose and me, only so he can step in to help too.

But I want him in the fight just as much as he wants me in it.

I climb onto his back so he'll stay put.

"Go fuck someone who actually likes you, Julius!" Lo yells. "Oh *wait*, that leaves *no one* on this planet. Better go find someone who can take you to Mars, you motherfucker!"

I award him extra points for creativity.

Without Lo restraining Rose from attack, she disappears into the kitchen, retrieving a can of pepper spray in a drawer. Oh *yes.* She charges the living room like a warrior queen, directing the can right at Julian's bruised face.

"Get out," she sneers, shoving his arm. "Or I will burn more than just your eyes."

I wrap my arms around Lo's neck, and his hands slide to my legs as he settles down. My sister has this under control.

Julian raises his hands, sending the room one long, useless glare before he exits the townhouse.

"One douchebag down," Lo says under his breath.

One more to go.

Chapter 35

0 Years : 09 Months

May

LOREN HALE

"Can I ask you both something?" Connor says, leaning against the dresser in our room. The clock blinks 4 a.m., but he stands there, fully clothed like he just returned from a business meeting.

Lily and I have had a few minutes to rub our eyes and sit up against the headboard. Her body rests against mine, basically using me as a pillow. My lethargic brain has trouble processing what topic this could be about.

"If it has to do with Scott or production, I'm going back to bed." I just don't have the energy to deal with that at four in the morning.

Lily lets out a small yawn, her eyes partially closed. We had sex for over an hour. She was a little compulsive…I think because Rose made her try on the wedding dress to see if it needed any alterations.

"It's not about him," Connor says, his voice quiet in the dead of night. "I want to know your feelings on your wedding in a month."

I rub my eyes again. "You know, this is one of those things I *really* don't want to talk about this late, Connor."

"Me…either," Lily yawns and begins to scoot underneath the covers.

"Wait," Connor says, stepping forward. "I need you to answer me, please."

I only hesitate because of the *please.* Connor rarely pleads for things, not like that. I shake my head as I try to pick through my emotions on the matter. "I don't know…" *I do know.* "I mean, we're not looking forward to it."

"Why?" Connor wonders.

"You know why," I snap, frustrated and tired. "Connor, I don't know if this is the time when you do your best thinking, but the rest of us—the average people—sleep now."

Connor stuffs his hands in his pockets. "I needed a time where Rose wouldn't be awake to hear us."

"Is this a riddle?" Lily asks sleepily.

I don't even know.

"What if I told you that you don't have to get married?"

Now he has our attention. Lily's eyes snap open fully, and my back straightens like a board. "What?" we both say in unison.

"You don't have to get married," Connor repeats. "Not in one month. Not in six months or seven. You choose the time, the date, the place, everything on *your* terms, no one else's."

"This is a dream," Lily says under her breath.

He shakes his head like *it's not.*

When I look at her, I see tears just streaming down her cheeks. "This is a dream…" she repeats as though to convince herself that it can't be real.

I feel something wet slide down my face. Good things don't happen to bad people. Lily used to tell me that all the time. This does seem too good to be meant for us.

"My father…" I start, not able to finish. I lift my knees and rest my elbow on one, pinching my eyes to dam the waterworks.

"I talked with Lily's parents and briefly with Jonathan. Everyone agrees that the reality show helped improve your reputations. It's hard for any media outlet to deny that you're in love, and so the wedding, at this point, isn't as important as it once was." He continues, "Lily will regain her inheritance since the wedding won't be a stipulation anymore."

Neither of us really cares about the money. I drop my hand. "Won't it seem suspicious if we suddenly cancel the wedding?"

He takes a deep breath. "I want to marry Rose on that day, if you'll let me."

My mouth opens in surprise. "What?" I breathe.

Lily is nodding repeatedly, overwhelmed with so much emotion that she begins to sob in her hands. I hug her to my side.

It's like someone finally gave us a break, and then went one step further, clearing a dark storm into a bright blue sky.

I am about to ask if he loves Rose, but the expression that washes over his face—it says it all. Connor is smiling, his gaze far off as he's picturing that future already, glowing with something innately human.

Hopefully one day he'll accept how much love has actually overcome him.

And then he looks back to me, and I nod at him. "If you're serious—"

"I've never been more serious in my life," he says. Connor rarely exaggerates, so I'm flooded, once again, with the power of his words.

"Yes," I say. "Marry Rose." I let out a short, stunned laugh and shake my head. I can't believe this is real. "If you survive your wedding day, that is." Rose not in control...how is that going to blow over? "She's going to be pissed that she only has one month to fix everything."

Lily calms a little and wipes her eyes with the blanket. "She's so particular," she says.

"That's why I'm not going to tell Rose. It'll be a surprise to her." He adds, "And I know her well enough to plan a wedding that she'll love." He walks to the door, solidifying this as a night that I'll remember for the rest of my life. And it had nothing to do with our addictions.

"And darling," he says to me, his grin lifting his lips, "you'll be a great best man." He taps the wooden frame and shuts the door gently behind him.

Lily sniffs and says, "When did Connor Cobalt become the tooth fairy, granting wishes in the middle of the night?" We've known for a long time that Connor Cobalt possesses some form of magic.

I smile, tackling and pinning her on the bed. I plant kisses all over her face, and she laughs into more tears. I realize I'm crying again too.

We're starting to feel in control of our own lives.

It comes with sentiments so strong that the only response is to laugh, cry, and finally, fall into a peaceful, quiet sleep.

Chapter 36

0 Years : 10 Months

June

LILY CALLOWAY

"You passed all your classes?" Ryke asks for the third time on the couch, the disbelief a little insulting.

"Yeah, I mean, I was only taking three this semester, but I passed." Granted, they were *pass* or *fail* online courses from Princeton, but still it's *Princeton* so I deserve a tiny pat on the shoulder, back, arm, I'll even take the ankle.

"I never even saw you crack open a textbook." His lack of confidence in me is nothing special.

"You wouldn't. I did most of my homework in my room."

Lo snacks on sour gummies beside me. "And weren't you busy climbing rocks?" he snaps at his brother. We're barely into our movie marathon with Ryke and Daisy, and we've already had to pause *The Fellowship of the Ring* five times for unnecessary interjections that don't pertain to hobbits or hot elves. When we learned that both of them hadn't seen *The Lord of the Rings* trilogy, Lo and I wanted to correct that immediately. At this rate, we'll finish all three movies by next summer.

"Not all the time," Ryke refutes, shaking his bag of popcorn beneath Daisy's chin. She's squished beside me and him.

She absentmindedly scoops a handful, eating more now, especially since one of her giant modeling campaigns wrapped up.

"Let's watch," I say, pressing a button on the remote. When Frodo arrives at the elven kingdom, my mind wanders to celebrations. The nearest one for all of us is only in four days. We'll be in France for Connor and Rose's wedding. We've all kept the secret about the switch from her, and despite Connor's proclamations that he has it under control, I'm a little worried she's going to have a mental breakdown from the surprise.

Rose isn't the type who fantasized and planned every detail of her wedding when she was a little girl. On the contrary, Rose never thought she'd tie the knot. But she's also a touch OCD, and having someone else control the biggest day of her life might upset her.

That is, if Connor doesn't nail the details to perfection.

The wedding also marks the end of the reality show. No more cameras. No more communal showers. No more Philadelphia townhouse.

Daisy picks the fuzz on a blanket, hardly watching the film. Returning to our Princeton house will be the hardest on her because it means that she has to go back home, to live with our mom and dad. These six months have been like one long, extended summer camp, and probably the first time that she's felt included in our group.

Before the reality show, she tagged along and asked to join us. For the past six months, it's been unspoken that she'd belong in any event we planned. I don't want to go back to the way things were. I want Daisy to be with us, but at the same time, she's only seventeen.

She has prep school.

I scroll through Twitter on Lo's phone, too curious. He glances over my arm, and he must realize it's *not* Tumblr because his gaze returns to the TV.

His feed is loaded with tweets from comic book artists and fans of TV shows like *Game of Thrones*. My eyes sting from staring so hard, about to shut the app. But I pause as I graze over a hashtag.

#CoballowayPornTape

What? My brows crinkle, and the first tweet near the top is from a credible news station.

@GBANews: Connor Cobalt & Rose Calloway have sold their porn tapes to a very large distributor. Clips already streaming online.

My heart nosedives to the bottom of my stomach. This can't be right. My breath catches in my throat. Rose would never share her own sex life on *the internet* if she can barely share miniscule details among her friends. I practically pummel Lo with my bony body, squishing into his space.

"Lil?" I hear the concern in his voice.

I hand him the phone, and at the same time, I switch the television to the other HD input, turning on cable.

"What's going on?" Ryke asks, his arm stretched on the back of the couch.

I answer by flipping to the news. I reread the headline at the bottom, over and over, expecting them to say *April Fool's*. But it's not April. And this is far, far from a joke.

SEX TAPE OF ROSE CALLOWAY AND CONNOR COBALT SOLD TO PORN SITE FOR $25 MILLION.

"Fucking hell," Ryke mutters.

"This can't be right," I say aloud what's been floating in my head. *No, no, no.* I never had videos of my sex life broadcasted to the entire world. This goes beyond what happened to me. This is—this is life-altering, earth-shattering bad.

I'm so sorry, Rose.

Lo shakes his head, in a fog. "It had to be Scott. They must have had cameras in the bedrooms."

"What?" I squeak. "*Our* bedrooms too?"

"No, Lil," Lo says quickly. "If they had a sex tape of us, it'd be on TV before Connor and Rose's." He's right. I'd be more "newsworthy" since we've been in the media much longer.

Still, the fact hardly lessens the enormity of the situation. My sister…

The reporter starts speaking, grabbing hold of my dispersing thoughts. "If you're returning with us, news just broke about the heir to a Fortune 500 company, Connor Cobalt and his girlfriend, Rose Calloway, selling a sex tape. Another Calloway girl in a scandal," she says. "This time there's legitimate proof."

"Oh shit," Ryke curses.

I follow his gaze over the couch, spotting my sister who marches down the staircase. Lo snatches the remote and powers off the television. It blinks to black.

Rose appears behind us, her cheeks concaved and her yellow-green eyes frighteningly focused. Like a lioness ready to devour an antelope.

She places her hands on her hips and sets her target on Lo. "I'm not five-years-old, Loren. You can turn on the news."

My throat swells. Does she already know? I can't hide the pained expression on my face.

"No," Lo says, his voice edged in nervousness. "I'd rather not."

Daisy cups her hand to her mouth, whispering to me, "Should we tell her?"

I mimic the discreet gesture so Rose can't read my lips. "Maybe not until Connor comes downstairs too." He's a crisis solver. He'll make everything better, right?

Rose refuses to wait any longer. She's already halfway across the room, her back arched like she's building her defenses. She tries to steal the remote from Lo, but he won't release his grip. They end up having a tug-of-war.

"Let go, Loren, unless you'd like me to dislocate your arm."

"Aren't you tired of making all these empty threats?"

She twists his forearm, and pain flashes in his face, wincing. He loosens his hold, and she claims the remote.

He rubs his arm. "Bitch."

Not nice.

"Yes, but I'm a bitch with *real* threats." She powers on the television, and the news explodes once more.

"Bet you feel like a bigger bitch right now," Loren adds.

"Shut up, Lo," I snap. This is *not* the time to attack my sister. "Rose…" She has frozen to the middle of the floor. I know, better than anyone, how horrifying and gut-wrenching it feels to see your dirty sex laundry scattered all over the media.

She waves me off and increases the volume to an obnoxious level. "The producer is none other than Scott Van Wright, Rose's ex-boyfriend."

They're still perpetuating the ex-boyfriend lie? Rose remains transfixed to the screen, her posture tight, just livid, pure heat radiating off her stance.

Rose…

Tears almost threaten to rise. It wasn't supposed to be like this. Our lives. She was supposed to have the perfect wedding with the perfect guy with the perfect happily ever after. Being taken advantage of in pursuit to strengthen her career—it's not fair. It's not right.

People just suck.

Lo rises and seizes the remote from Rose, and she jerks back and hits another button.

The TV blares, and I cringe at the shrill sound.

"I'm watching this," Rose says, managing to enunciate over the noise. The reporter plays clips from the actual sex tape. On screen, her arms are tied to the headboard with a belt, a glittery diamond choker around her neck. Black bars censor all the naughty parts, but the uncut video streams online somewhere.

"Rose," Lo complains, pressing his hands to his ears.

I stand up and reach for her arm. "Rose."

She recoils. "Don't touch me."

She scares me, more now, than she ever has before. It's like she needs to explode, but she's containing this raging fire inside her body.

The news channel blisters my ears. "Scott Van Wright has sold the sex tape to Hot Fire Productions for a multi-million-dollar deal. There's been no comment yet from either Connor Cobalt or Rose Calloway, but it appears to be a legal transaction between all four parties."

How can that be right?

"The summary of the film says the hour long session is rough and for mature audiences only."

Rose increases the volume to the highest level. Why does she insist on listening to it like this?

"What the fuck are you doing?" Ryke asks, his hand rising to his ear.

"Maybe she's like…having a mental break…" Daisy says.

Rose retreats to the kitchen, more *on attack* than anything. She disappears from view as she digs through a lower cabinet.

"Seriously though, Rose!" I yell. "Are you okay?"

She pops up with a bottle of whiskey. I forgot that Brett hid his booze with the dishwasher soaps. She spins her heels and collects a wine glass from another cupboard, pouring the whiskey to the brim.

It's like watching a fissure run through a person made of stone.

I don't like it.

"Rose, not to lecture you at this really sensitive time in your life," Lo says, "but that's not how you drink whiskey. And as an expert in liquor, it offends me."

She glowers, one so fierce that my breath dies in my chest. "You're not an expert in liquor. You're an alcoholic." She sets the whiskey bottle on the table and takes a *giant* swig from her wine glass.

She doesn't even cringe.

"Which makes me an expert," Loren argues. She waves him off like she's shooing away an animal.

"What's going on?" Connor's voice emanates from the stairs. His gaze travels to the television, the source of the cacophony. No…

That's why she turned the television up so loud? She decided to deafen everyone just to call him downstairs.

"Look honey," Rose says. "We have a sex tape together."

She's lost it. Officially.

Chapter 37

0 Years : 10 Months

June

LOREN HALE

Want to know the most deplorable, heartless thing in my head?

I am so fucking relieved that wasn't Lily on the news. Extending empathy for my best friend, Connor, or for Lily's sister—I can't do it. Deep down, I just think: *finally* it's not us, *finally* the world has shit on someone else.

It's a thought that turns my blood cold, my forearms on my knees, sitting on the couch and waiting for the guilt to come crush me. I wish that I was like my brother. Ryke stares at Rose with so much concern that you'd think he was dating her.

"I'm on the phone with my attorneys and Cobalt's," Greg Calloway says through the cell's speaker in Connor's hand. "We're looking through the contracts all of you signed. Until we can come to a clear picture of what's going on, I need you to get my daughters out of that townhouse. No more cameras."

Goodbye, Scott Van Wright. I thought Scott would go further and further until he reached an unbearable point with us, but leaking a sex tape with Connor and Rose—it never crossed my mind.

Connor has been unsurprisingly stoic during the whole ordeal. Sometimes I just want him to scream like the rest of us. Most of the time, I don't want to see it. Because if someone like Connor ever breaks to that degree, then the whole world is headed for hell.

He places his hand on Rose's shoulder, but she barely relaxes. "We'll pack today and leave," he tells Greg over the phone.

"Let me know when you make it safely back to Princeton. If there's too much press around the house, you should all stay at our place in Villanova."

My frown deepens, waiting for Greg to add, *I need to have a serious talk with you, Connor.* He just watched Connor screw his daughter on national television, albeit censored. And not only that—they're into bondage and kinky shit that I'd think would have Greg tapping into his paternal side, ready for an hour-long conversation.

It never comes though.

"Do you know where Scott is?" Connor asks him.

My ribs burn when I inhale.

"No idea," Greg says, "but Loren's father is about to rip him a new asshole." *Good.* "To be honest, I'd love to see it happen." He pauses. "Is Rose around?"

"She's on speaker."

"Rose, honey, how many lawyers looked over the contract before you signed it?"

I presume he's talking about the reality show contract—the one we trusted Rose with before we all signed the bottom. What the fuck did she do? I glare at her with everything inside my soul. *What the fuck did she do?*

She cradles Sadie in her arms, Connor's orange tabby cat that usually scratches Rose. Instead, Sadie purrs. The world is backwards today.

"Just me," Rose suddenly announces.

"What…the fuck?" Ryke says, stunned.

I groan and lean back against the couch, my hands on my head. "Why did we trust you?" I snap. I should have realized that she'd be too conceited to actually hire a real lawyer.

"I've taken multiple law classes at *Princeton*," she refutes. "I understood every line of that contract." *Sure. That's why you now have a sex tape released to the public, Rose.*

I shake my head repeatedly. So they could film in the bedrooms then? A weight bowls straight into my chest, the pressure knocking the wind out of me. If they filmed us—that means they have tapes of Lily and me.

Scott's just waiting around to release them then?

Lily breathes choppy, sporadic breaths beside me. I reach out and hold her hand. "It's okay," I whisper to her. *It's okay.* She can read my uneasiness through my features, her eyes growing bigger and bigger. "It's okay, Lil." Repeating it doesn't help. *We're going to be okay.*

"I thought you took my lawyer to the meeting," Connor says, already off the phone with Greg. "And I thought he read the contracts."

"I thought I told you I left him behind," Rose retorts.

Connor frowns, shaking his head. "You must have mentioned that to someone else, darling." He snatches her whiskey-filled wine glass and drinks the rest in one swallow.

I concentrate on him. It takes my mind off what seriously could be the end for us. "What the hell was that?" I ask him. "Greg gives me a two hour speech about sobriety after our scandal, and he doesn't even acknowledge yours."

"To be fair," Connor says, "you lied to Greg and Samantha about being addicts. That news is a bit more jarring than a sex tape..."

I don't see how.

His attention and voice drifts across the room. I follow his gaze with everyone else, and all oxygen is suddenly caged in my lungs.

Scott stands by the staircase with his hands in his khaki, tailored pockets, like he didn't just screw over a bunch of people over. Like he's never done a wrong thing in his life. Like he can't feel remorse or regret or guilt.

I envy him on that account. How goddamn easy life would be if I wasn't saddled with all of *that.*

"Did I miss something?" Scott asks with a sleazy grin.

With an unreadable expression, Connor walks towards Scott, the only person even moving or breathing at this point. I've been waiting for him to do *something* more to the guy that's just hosed him during the show. If anything, these past six months have taught me that Connor Cobalt and I fight different battles in different ways.

Connor stops right in front of Scott and holds out his hand to shake the producer's. "Congratulations," Connor says. "You outsmarted me. Not many people ever do. And I admit...I never saw this coming." His voice is humorless, emotionless—frighteningly dead.

Scott glances between Connor's hand and his face. Then he clutches Connor's palm.

What a fucking weird way to end—

And then Connor punches Scott in the jaw with his free fist. His body hits the wall hard. My lips rise.

"Thank you," Ryke says with an exhale, near me. We've all been waiting for that to happen.

"That's from me," Connor sneers at Scott, brutal anger flashing in his eyes, something that I've never seen before—something he has been keeping to himself.

Scott tries to swing back, but Connor dodges the attack with ease. And then he knees Scott in the dick, the contact audible. Scott groans, his hands instinctively reaching for his crotch. I cringe at how painful that must've been. And Rose is practically celebrating like a fan in a football stadium. I'm shocked she hasn't raised her fists in the air and twirled in a circle.

"That's from Rose," Connor says lowly, venom in his voice.

Scott crouches, almost close to a fetal position. His eyes water, and it takes him a moment to slowly stand back up, bracing the wall so he doesn't tip over.

Connor never backs up, confident and pissed. This isn't a guy I'd want to fight, I realize. Not like this.

Scott coughs into his fist and then he says, "...I'd love to see your face when you realize what you've signed."

Something bursts in my chest, and I open my mouth to scream at him. But Ryke covers my lips with his hand, blocking all noise and future regrets from escaping.

"You're seeing it now," Connor tells him calmly. How can he not be more upset? Even the thought of Lily being swept up into the rabid media, with sex tapes of our own, is killing me inside. I can't see any light among that darkness for us. It's one brick too many, one push too hard—it feels catastrophic.

"I'm positive you have full rights to anything we ever film," Connor continues, "which gave you permission to sell the sex tape to a porn site without our signed consent. I don't have the contract in front of me, but I'm sure there's something misleading about the part where you weren't allowed to film us in the bedrooms."

"I *read* that line correctly. I know it," Rose says, pointing at the ground.

Scott is still partially doubled-over from Connor's two hits. "It said that we couldn't *air* anything from the bedrooms on *television*. We never did. The contract said nothing about filming. And any of the footage from the bedrooms and the bathroom can be used for movies and web content. Just not network TV."

The bathroom. I glance at Lily while she stares at her knees, pale and cold to the touch. I rub her back and rest my chin on her head, holding her closer to my chest. She wore a bathing suit in the shower for six months. She was that uncomfortable. One silver lining.

Scott adds, "Lily was almost always in her room." He pauses. "We weren't able to install any cameras to catch anything."

I shut my eyes, both of our shoulders dropping with the release of this immeasurable weight. *Thank God.* I suck down the sadness that wells with a rough inhale and kiss Lily outside her lips. She holds my face quickly and kisses me for real, a deep one that grips me.

"It's illegal to film minors in pornographic situations," Connor says.

Both Lily and I break apart at that. Connor is talking about Daisy. Did she…did she really screw someone in her bedroom? A series of emotions pulls my face in a grimace. The most lasting one is shock.

Daisy blanches, and she actually meets my eyes, over everyone else. Maybe too mortified to look at Ryke. I nod at her like *it's okay.*

She shakes her head like it's not.

Lily crawls over my lap to sit beside her sister again, and she wraps her thin arms around Daisy's neck.

"We didn't," Scott replies. "All that footage was destroyed."

There was actual footage of Daisy…in her bedroom with another guy? She must have been doing things with Julian, but not *it.* I can't even say the word in context with her. I rub the back of my neck.

"You're disgusting!" Rose shouts with another scream attached.

I glance over my shoulder to see Ryke on his feet, restraining Rose from the other two guys by grabbing her shoulders.

My head just rattles as Scott keeps talking. As he spills all the things he planted with production.

"Lily and Lo in the bathroom with the slurping audio?" Connor asks.

"Edited," Scott says. "We did it in advance and uploaded it on the camera for you to find." At least everyone will believe us now.

"The alcohol in Lo's closet?"

"Planted. Savannah and Ben put it there when Lily was taking a nap. They were supposed to install a camera too, but they ran out of time."

How many bullets did we actually dodge this time around?

I can't get off the couch to help them or to shout another expletive. Ryke has said them all anyway. I've known what everyone is just finding out. In fact, I've known for a while that production was behind all of this shit. I guess they couldn't one-hundred percent believe in that truth because they had other options to consider. Like us. Lily and I—we could have lied to them.

"I'm going to let Ryke go if you don't get out of this house," I hear Connor tell Scott. "And his fists are going to hurt a hell of a lot more than mine. So take what's on your back and *leave*."

Not long after, the door slams shut.

I can only hope that's the last cancer in our lives, but my dad would tell me that I'm being a little fucking fool. For believing in that impossibility. When you have money like we do, there will always be people ready to bury you for a payout.

It's how the world turns.

Chapter 38

0 Years : 10 Months

June

LILY CALLOWAY

Connor never once hesitated, not even for a moment did he second guess his plan, which is on a grand, massive scale. Even with the sex tape and a lawsuit being flung in Scott's face, Connor said, "There is no better time than today."

Both Lo and I strongly disagreed. Rose was going to claw his face the minute we did the wedding switcheroo.

I think my doubt vanished about the same time I stepped into the "Château de Fontainebleau"—a French palace fit for a queen.

Every single detail resembles my older sister. The simple pale pink bridesmaids gowns, like ballet dresses. The hundreds of attendees, showering her with compliments. The lavish antiquity of it all. Diamonds, roses, red velvet cake and classical music.

It's a dream wedding that she never dreamed of until now.

I couldn't be happier for her, especially since she said *yes.*

I stand beside Lo in a grand ballroom that resembles a royal castle in a history book. Paintings engulf every wall with gold ornate frames. The ceiling is just as fancy, and a row of chandeliers twinkles overhead. Giant red rose bouquets line the room, classy and elegant like my sister.

Ryke comes up beside his brother while clusters of people enter the ballroom after dinner, a stage setup with violinists, cellists and a pianist.

"When you two get married, should I be prepared for something like this?" Ryke asks us. He downs a champagne flute filled with water in two seconds and a server collects it before he even turns around.

"No way," Lo says. "There will be a finite number of people."

"And no press," I add. Connor let the media squeeze through the doors so they could blog about the event. He said something about needing "good" publicity for Fizzle and Cobalt Inc.

"Exactly." Lo gives his brother a half-smile before putting his arm around my shoulder. I lean closer to his body, waiting for Rose and Connor to take to the empty floor space for their first dance as husband and wife.

"I'm not trying to pressure you," Ryke says, "but are you going to set a date for it?"

Lo and I haven't really talked about it. We got engaged because our parents ordered us to, and they also said we had to be married *today.* And then when all of that changed, the timeline kind of dematerialized with it.

"No," Lo answers. "We're going to wait until the media dies down."

Ryke's jaw hardens and he nods a couple times. "And if that doesn't fucking happen? What then?" I don't like his tone one bit. Like he believes it won't *ever* come true. I just hate thinking that this could be our new normal. The frenzied cameras, the invasiveness, the never-ending questions and rumors. The reality show is over so everything should return to the way it was, right?

Lo's cheekbones jut out a little more than usual, irritated. He licks his lips and shrugs. "I don't know. Maybe you should worry about your own future wife. Oh wait, she doesn't exist."

Ryke raises his hands in defense. "Hint fucking taken. I'll stay out of it."

Lo lets out a short laugh. "When have you stayed out of anyone's business?"

He nods. "Good point."

"Shhh," I whisper, swatting Lo's arm. The violins have shushed, and Connor saunters into the open space. When he stops in the center, his deep blue eyes lock straight on Rose.

I am full-blown smiling. The way he's staring at her—it's beyond magical.

"I just want everyone to know," I whisper again, "that I predicted this would happen the moment I saw them together."

Both Lo and Ryke clap for me at the same time, mostly in sarcasm. Yeah, yeah, they can team up against me, *but* I was right. It doesn't happen often, so I pocket that small glory.

Connor holds out his hand, and Rose approaches with a narrowed, passionate gaze. She takes his hand in hers. She's still in her white wedding dress with sheer material around her collarbones. A high slit runs up her leg, but the tulle netting flows around her limbs so much that you can hardly tell until she walks. Sexy *and* classy.

She designed that dress, sewed it together for me, but it's her style and something she loved with each last thread. Daisy stole the gown to have the bust altered to match the measurements of Rose's bridesmaid's dress. It fit her perfectly.

They wait for the music to start, questions flickering in Rose's gaze about Connor's song choice. The moment the instruments create a sweet, silky noise, Rose's hand flies to her mouth. And her eyes begin to glass.

Connor pulls her closer to his chest, his grin so bright. Her hands tremble. Both have now risen to her lips that part with unrestrained surprise.

She shakes her head, and I start crying as soon as rare *happy* tears stream down her cheeks. French lyrics leave the singer's mouth like honey.

The music is gorgeous, even if I can't understand a single word.

"What song is this?" I murmur, wiping my eyes quickly.

"No clue," Lo says, the corners of his mouth lifting the longer he watches Connor and Rose in the center of the room. There aren't many dry eyes around here.

Connor kisses Rose's forehead and I read his lips: *I love you.*

I bite my gums to stop the waterworks from beginning all over again. Every moment of Rose's wedding has been a surprise, and with each one, I think that we've all realized how well Connor knows her and how much he truly, truly loves her.

"La Vie En Rose," Ryke suddenly says with a French lilt.

"What?" My brows pinch together.

"The song," he says, "it's called *La Vie En Rose.*"

"How do you know that…?" I ask, my voice trailing off, distracted for a second by my sister. Rose calms after the initial overwhelming shock of the song choice. And they begin to slow dance together.

"It's a popular song," he says before walking backwards. "I'm going to get another drink. You two want anything?"

"Bourbon, no ice," Lo quips dryly.

"Hilarious," Ryke says with zero humor. He nods to me. "What about you?"

I can't get over how he said *La Vie En Rose*, like he understood exactly how to pronounce each syllable in the foreign language. If I said the song title, it'd sound like an American butchering the words. "Do you know these lyrics?" I ask.

"They're in French," he says, glancing over his shoulder at the growing line to the bar. "Last chance, Lily."

"Fizz Life," I place my order, letting my suspicions go with it. He weaves between the guests, and I focus my attention elsewhere. "Do you think they'll be okay?" I ask Lo as we watch Connor spin Rose with poise and masculinity. They haven't confronted the serious repercussions of having a sex tape floating on the internet.

Once they start Googling themselves and the hatred and criticism pours through—they'll feel the real sting. It's not fun.

"Yeah," Lo says. "They're Connor and Rose." He says their names like they're a fortress of steel. While I agree on some accounts, he hasn't calculated the fact that negative cannon-blasts from tabloids can easily knock down their defenses.

"Yeah but they'll need us," I say with a nod. "We've been through this before." We'll pay it forward, be a friendly shoulder to cry on like Rose was to me. Not that she sheds more than a few tears a year.

He stays quiet on the matter, his eyes darting to alcoholic beverages in almost everyone's hands. It's an open bar. He wears that mildly annoyed look that he used to get in college, when happy people flaunted their enthusiasm in front of him.

Just as the first song ends, guests begin to join Rose and Connor on the dance floor. Instead of rushing to the middle, a hoard of people edge closer to us. They unfortunately linger, as though to eavesdrop. We haven't had a single reporter bombard us with questions because Connor ordered them not to, but they're studying our movements from afar…well, now they're doing it from five feet.

I press up against Lo's hard, lean body. The spot between my legs pulses, and my arm latches around his waist. If I shift just a *little* close I can feel his bulge—

"Lily," he says softly, staring down at me. He fixes a piece of my flyaway hair. "If you rub up against me anymore, I'm going to get hard."

Ohmygod. I let out a shallow breath. "That's the point…" Or is it not the point? We're not allowed to have sex at my sister's wedding, are we? That's old, bad Lily.

This is Lily 2.0. Scratch that—this is Lily *3.0*. Brand *spanking* new.

He groans a little. "Lil…" He pries my fingers off his toned ass. Oh Jeez. I redden. "Spanking" is a very dangerous word. The intensity in his amber eyes magnifies when they bore into me. His chest falls heavier than before.

Lo doesn't distance himself from me. Not once. Instead he closes the gap, kissing me with an urgency that I've missed dearly.

My limbs shake as his palm cups the back of my head, his fingers gripping my hair, his tongue skillfully sliding against mine. We part for one single breath.

"Lo…" *We're in a room full of people.* It's a thought that disintegrates in the back of my brain.

"Lil…" He rests his forehead on mine. Then he kisses my cheek, and quickly clasps my hand, leading me in a new direction, swerving between people. I realize we're aimed for a hallway or a bathroom. He glances back at me once, his lips rising in a gorgeous, devious smile. We're going to have sex!

Yes. Yes. Yes.

My body thrums with victory and applause. It's not wrong. It's *so* right. I hold onto his one hand with both of mine, afraid that we'll break apart and I'll lose him.

And then a sloshed guy with black Ray-Ban sunglasses on—indoors—haphazardly cuts through us, tearing my hand right from Lo's. Another guy in a white button-down rushes through the same space. "Wait up, Luke!" he shouts after him.

His momentum forward pushes me backwards. I nearly stumble into an old lady with oversized jewelry.

Three, four...*five* other people follow the two guys like a wolf pack.

Luke essentially created a pathway right between Lo and me.

What's worse: I can't see Lo anymore. It's like he's vanished from the building, lost in the sea of bodies. I spin around, my heart pumping, the *need* thrumming for him. Where'd he go? I rotate one more time and catch eyes with a woman in a maroon dress. My attention narrows straight to her honey-colored curly hair that's strangely tamed despite the large volume.

She stops mid-sentence in a conversation with another woman, white wine in both their hands. Her face just lights up when she sees me. For a brief moment, I wonder if I personally know this woman. She takes a few tentative steps forward, like she's a vampire I haven't invited in my house yet.

"Hi, Lily, I've been wanting to meet you for so long. I'm glad I caught you here." She holds out her hand for me to shake.

I hesitantly do, a foreboding feeling in my gut. I scrutinize her deep red lipstick, darker skin and perfectly matched high heels, jewelry and dress. Very fashionable. "You must be Rose's friend," I say. "From Princeton?" Though she seems a little old to be a college graduate with Rose, probably in her early thirties.

She lets out a small, weak laugh like *are you serious? You don't know who I am?* Oh God. Is she famous? A celebrity?

Shit.

I suck. I really wish Lo was—

"I'm Wendy Collins, a staff writer at *Celebrity Crush*."

My face plummets. Wendy Collins. The one who posted my letter that I sent *to her*, online for the whole world to see. The one perpetuating any and all rumors that I'm sleeping with Loren *and* his brother...at the same time.

Wendy Collins. *I have nothing to say to you.* Any harsh, horrible insults that stick to the back of my throat must stay there. I don't have one of my family's publicists to help redirect the conversation. If I spout anything wrong, she'll just twist my words for a better headline.

I know that now.

Maybe she can read the horror on my face because she adds quickly, "You have to realize that I'm just doing my job. If I didn't write those stories, somebody else would have, and I wouldn't be paid nearly enough to afford rent in New York City. We don't all come from money."

Right. I don't know if it's my civic duty to let people berate me on the internet so they can afford their apartment. Maybe it is. Maybe this is the cost of growing up in luxury.

"I have to go," I say, about to turn around. "I have to find my best friend." *Wrong term, Lily.* I redden. "My boyfriend," I amend and then wince. *Still not right.* "My fiancé. And *yes,* they are all the same person." So there.

"We were just talking about your sister," she says, freezing me in place.

I turn back, taking the bait too easily. Wendy motions to another woman by her side, older with a short blonde haircut and a pointed chin like a wicked witch. "This is Andrea DelaCorte an Executive Editor at *Celebrity Crush.*"

"Pleasure," Andrea says, sipping her wine. Her needled brown eyes cast judgment from my toes to my face, probably speculating how many bodies touched mine.

Wendy doesn't seem so evil compared to Andrea.

"What about my sister?" I ask, a little defensively, considering her name will most likely crop up on their front pages soon. And not only because of the wedding switch.

"Andrea and I were discussing how great it is to have someone like Rose in the public eye. She's a female figure that we believe a lot of women can rally behind."

What…?

Off my frown, Andrea says, "She's been with Connor Cobalt for over a year, and she's stayed committed to him through everything."

Wendy nods in agreement. "Especially after her ex-boyfriend tried to break them apart. It's empowering to have someone like Rose out there—she's independent, driven, and sexually open. I wouldn't be surprised if women start asking her for relationship advice."

Rose? Relationship advice? I never thought I'd hear those words. Or that a sex tape could be spun positively rather than negatively.

I don't understand. Wouldn't she be slandered and outcast like me? A weight just drops on my chest.

"That's a great idea actually," Andrea says. "Do you think your sister would be open to a short column on the blog? It can be about sex tips, a guide to dating, anything in that field." *Sex tips?*

"I don't know," I say in a small voice. Rose is being lauded for having a boyfriend for over a year, for only sleeping with him. But I've been with too many no-named guys. She's a model that other people can copy whereas I'm dirty, right? No one should follow my footsteps.

I never thought of it like that.

I never thought that she'd be praised and I'd still be condemned.

It's not fair.

If I had been committed to Loren Hale all my life, would people love me more?

Probably.

Andrea and Wendy examine all of my reactions like they're going to jot this down for an article. I think I mumble a goodbye, and then I just kind of drift away in a daze. Minutes must pass before I hear a familiar sound.

"Lily." Lo's concerned voice seems so distant. "I've been looking for you…Lil?" His hands go to my face, still standing in the ballroom, closer to the ornate wall.

"You were right," I breathe. He was so right.

"Right about what?" His voice is low, like the hollow of a cave.

"Connor and Rose don't need us." They never needed us like we need them. Are we leeches then? We suck the life out of our friends and will never, ever be strong enough to pay them back.

I'm in his arms before I can even ask. He carries me in a front piggy-back. My legs tighten around his waist, sex sounding better and better. To at least give me a rush, a high of something good to drown out the bad.

But I know how this ends.

I will never satisfy this craving.

Very softy, I say, "We can't have sex." The words drive a nail into my heart. Because it aches to be denied it, even by my own lips. Because it's all I feel like I need.

"I know," Lo whispers, bringing me to an empty hallway with globes and more paintings overhead. He sets me on a bench and kneels in front of my spread legs.

My breath hitches, and I lean forward to kiss him, to grab a fist-full of his shirt and pull him even closer.

Just as my fingers clench the fabric, he puts his hands on my knees, shuts my legs tightly and rests one of his palms on my collar, pushing my back into the wall. The rejection stings. "Lo," I say in a breath, his features sharp and severe and forceful.

A tear rolls down my cheek.

He's not backing down from this. It's like he could see this outcome from the very moment the wedding started. It's like he was preparing all day for my descent.

Here it is.

I'm ashamed of myself and embarrassed. I just feel gross.

"The world is never going to understand us," he tells me, his eyes so impassioned that I can't look away. "But it doesn't matter, Lil. We have each other, and I get your pain, I understand how badly it hurts, so I need you to block out the other people today, okay? They don't exist in *our* world."

Our world.

There is no going back to a life with just Loren Hale. Even though it's harder to have real friends, real connections with other people, it's the right thing. But it's what causes so, so much agony inside. Every day in their presence, we stare at reflections of what we should be and know that we can never become them.

My shoulders relax, and I whisper, "Do we have superpowers in our world?"

"Yeah," he says, "but you're not invisible."

Damn.

"What can I do then?"

"Fly," he says, "with me." He lifts me up quickly, onto his back like we always do. And he races towards a door, my hair blowing behind me. My lips rise in a weak smile.

He says, "Want to get lost with me in a palace?"

I rest my chin on his shoulder, a couple tears dripping but they come from a fuller place in my heart. "Yes."

It's a good kind of *yes.* The best kind.

One filled with a thousand *I love yous*, the type of love that can make you fly.

Chapter 39

1 Year : 00 Months

August

LOREN HALE

Her lips swell underneath the pressure of mine, her fingers clenching my light brown hair, yanking hard. I slam her back into the bedroom wall. *Our* bedroom. *Our* wall.

She reaches out for stability, her fingers finding the wooden edge of our dresser. My cock deepens in between her legs, and she lets out a sharp, ragged breath followed by a cry of pleasure. I kiss her strongly as I rock against her, and her body spasms with pleasure. Her hand slides, knocking a lamp to the floor.

The crash is barely audible.

My head bursts with light, overcome with her body, her sounds, and the emotions that we exchange through our lips. I never want to stop kissing her like this, while I'm full inside of her, our pulses in sync and this desperate urgency pumping our blood.

I don't stop. The intensity smashes into me, black and white spots dancing in my vision. Nerves that I didn't know existed explode, and my movements become hungrier, harder, eking out every ounce of energy she has left.

I hold the back of her head, pushing up into her over and over. Our lips are so close that our noses brush.

"Lo," she cries out. She tries to grab onto the dresser again, but her hand, slick with sweat, glides right off.

In a heavy grunt, I say, "Up." I lift both her thighs higher over my waist and let go to brace a hand on the wall, pinning her with my body.

Her legs limply slide right back to the floor. "I…" she trails off, too tired for words. But her eyes are alight with cravings, wants and desires.

I raise only one of her legs this time and hold it above my hip. The angle slices her breath and lolls her head to the side.

I slow my thrusts, and a moan escapes her parted lips. Tears crease the corners of her eyes. I wipe them away with my thumb as I begin the perilous ascent, speeding up and climbing towards that high.

I turn my attention onto her small breasts, kneading one. Her body arches towards me, and I pinch her hardened nipple. She gasps.

"Lo," she pleads. "Pleaseplease."

"Almost, love," I say and then let out a long groan. Sex with Lily Calloway just may be the most toxic, mind-altering experience of my life.

I do it pretty much every night and every morning, and together, we still manage to go into another dimension of pleasure. She clenches tight around my cock, and it's over at that. My breath staggers, and my thrusts turn determined and even harder.

Her hands wearily grip my biceps, not even attempting to really hold on.

I'm the only thing supporting her at this point.

When I finish, I carefully pull out, my hands still firm on her waist in case she can't stand. Her eyelids flutter in exhaustion, and I lift her in my arms.

She struggles to fight sleep that finally weighs on her. "Lo, I'm…" she yawns. "…really sorry."

My muscles sear at her sincere apology. I wipe the strands of wet hair away from her eyes. "Don't be sorry, Lil. It's my choice too. Only for tonight though, okay?"

"Mmmhmm." She can barely nod. We've been fucking for a little over four hours with few breaks in between. All to wear Lily down to the point of mental and physical exhaustion. Giving her sleeping pills would have been easier, but her therapist was worried she'd start being dependent on them.

I doubt she would've approved of this alternative, but it's just one night of insane sex. I won't let Lily get used to this and make it a new routine.

I set Lily on the bed, open her legs a little, just enough to wipe her clean with my crumpled gray shirt. Then I pull the black and white comforter to her chin. Her eyes fight to stay open.

"Where's my spoon?" She pats the mattress beside her.

I kiss her forehead. "I'm going to take a shower." I trust that she won't masturbate while I'm gone. I had to have satiated her enough, only sleep on her mind. I tuck the edges of the comforter around her thin body. "I love you, Lil."

"I love you…" Her eyes close, and she breathes out the last word. "…too."

I watch her fall asleep for a couple seconds before I turn towards the bathroom, battling against the same fatigue. Before I even reach it, someone knocks on the door. I hesitate to answer right away.

"Lo?" I hear Connor's calm and controlled voice. "It's just me."

Those last words are the only ones that reanimate my body. Slowly, I step into a pair of drawstring pants and slip out of the door, leaving it cracked.

Our house in Princeton is eerily quiet, mostly because Lily has finally fallen asleep.

Connor studies me with a long once-over, as though he's examining a patient. I comb back my wet, sweaty hair with my hands and lean my shoulder on the wall. "She knocked over a lamp," I say, figuring he heard the crash since his bedroom is on the main floor.

"You've been having sex for four hours." He states it as a fact.

"Yep," I say. "You've been timing me?"

"It's hard not to." His eyes never waver from mine. I don't see judgment in them, which is why we've become best friends.

"Because Rose is worried about her."

"Because I have better hearing than most people," he says, "and you two fuck without restraint."

I produce a half-smile. "We all can't be into ball gags and handcuffs." I have tied Lily up before though. That's not new to me. Connor and Rose's sex tapes, however, go beyond anything I've done. I haven't actually watched them, nor do I ever want to, but the internet still talks.

"No, we can't," he says softly in agreement. "And I've never been a fan of ball gags, though I appreciate their purpose." He pauses. "Can I talk to you in the kitchen?" His eyes flicker to the office across the hall, the door ajar. In the shadows, an outline of a body moves behind it. Rose. Her mere presence clenches my stomach.

For the past couple of weeks, Lily and Rose have barely spoken more than a few words in passing, on a quiet streak. Ever since Rose and Connor returned from their honeymoon in Bora Bora, the atmosphere has been…tense.

I glance back at my bedroom, the door cracked, Lily still fast asleep underneath the covers.

"I'll save you the time," I tell him, speeding up this lecture. "This was a one-time thing. I'm not enabling her. I know what I'm doing. The end. If you'd like any more information than that, then you're going to have to spill details about your sex life." Not that I want *any* more than what I've already received from the tabloids. But fair's fucking fair. I cross my arms, waiting for his reply.

"I'm not Ryke or Rose," he reminds me. "I trust that you won't enable Lily and vice versa."

Then what's this about? I frown.

To convince me more, Connor says, "Just a few minutes downstairs."

"If you don't mind my stench."

"You smell lovely, darling." He already aims for the staircase. "Just how I dream of."

I snort into a smile. "Alright." I follow his lead.

Once we pass through the living room, the archway and into the kitchen, Connor starts the coffee machine. I catch the time on the oven. 4 a.m. Morning for him. The dead of night for me. He still wears pajama pants, so at least we're on equal footing there.

I hoist myself up onto the low counter and lean back into the cabinets. "Does this conversation happen to involve two very stubborn Calloway girls?"

"It does." He opens a cupboard by my head. He's so tall that we're actually eyelevel. "It's really trivial." He retrieves a black mug. "If they both sat down and talked, they'd realize that they're on the same side. But instead, your girlfriend isn't getting any sleep and neither is my wife."

"How do you know Lily isn't sleeping?" My edged voice hurts my ears at this time of night.

"You just had sex for four hours," he says, knowing everything before I even tell him. It's not as annoying right now as it could be. "And I've also seen Lily awake in the living room at 2 a.m. a few times."

My lips downturn, worry coating my features. "What was she doing?" I must have fallen asleep already, and she crawled out of bed.

"Reading Kafka," he says. "She said that she was hoping my reading material would bore her to sleep."

I let out a heavy breath. When Rose and Connor left for their honeymoon, the words "slut" and "whore" and "gross" were never thrown around in the media. The headlines commended Rose for being monogamous, strong and open enough to defend her right to be submissive in bed.

The polar opposite happened to Lily. She was degraded, humiliated and dragged through the mud. Still is. Every fucking day.

She can't sleep and forgets to eat sometimes. I've already talked to her professors for next semester, setting up her courses so she can watch the lectures online and attend the classes for exams. While my girlfriend sinks under the weight of the world's hypocrisy, she bears this immeasurable guilt that no one understands.

No one but me.

Deep down, she wishes that Rose had the same outcome as her, so at least she could feel less singled out, less repulsed by herself, less like a spot on the world that should have been wiped clean. And she can't destroy those feelings or try to explain them. Because they seem completely fucked up.

But I know what it's like to have emotions that war within you. To want something so cold and callous, only to feel a shred of self-worth.

I get it.

I fucking get it.

Rose is willing to give Lily time to sort through her feelings and come to terms with what's happened. But that means a stalemate between them. When they walk into the same room, they withhold most conversation and barely meet eyes.

Connor pours coffee into his mug. "I've tried talking to Rose, but she believes that Lily needs to work this out on her own." He waits for me to add something, and I realize that he brought me down here to see where Lily's head was at. Maybe to gauge how long this tension will last.

"I think Lil just needs some time," I say, not sure how *much* time. "She's going to her therapist every other day now."

Connor sips coffee from his mug, and I notice his ring on his left hand. Lily and I discussed our living situation with Rose and Connor after their wedding, and it lasted about two minutes. They don't feel comfortable moving out, even though they both should be closer to Philly. Their work is there, like Cobalt Inc.

Connor stopped pursuing his MBA so he could take over as CEO. The only tie they have to Princeton is Lil, who's still in college.

Since the paparazzi have increased exponentially after the reality show and now Rose's sex scandal, they both said: "it's best if the four of us still live together." A united front—or whatever. I didn't refute. Because even though it's harder with them here, I like having Connor around for advice. And Lily needs her sister.

He rests against the center island, facing me, and he stares at his mug with a lost look in his eyes, one I don't see often from him.

"What is it?" I ask.

"My mother is dying," he says out loud. "She'll be gone within the week. Breast cancer."

My jaw slowly drops. I can count on my hand the number of times he's mentioned his mom. She stepped down from her position as CEO of Cobalt Inc. a few days ago. Now I know why. "I'm sorry," I say, my brows bunched in confusion and a bit of hurt for him.

I can't read his expression. He's not letting anything pass through his features for me to hold onto. All I see is a blank surface, my own emotions ricocheting back at me.

"Don't be," he tells me. "She wouldn't want your apology."

"She sounds…"

"Cold," he finishes.

"I was going to say like Rose, no offense."

His deep blue eyes rise to mine. "They're not alike. Katarina doesn't have the capacity to love someone other than herself. If anything, she's more like me."

"*Was*…like you," I say. He's finally admitted to loving Rose.

He smiles. "Love still seems like an irrational concept to me." He pauses. "But in believing in it, I've become like everyone else."

"Are you okay with that?"

"More than okay," he admits.

I nod, happy that he's not such a cynic on a matter that seems obvious to the rest of us. "Are you going to the funeral?" I scratch the back of my neck. "I mean, when it happens…" I cringe. Everything sounds wrong. Is there even a right way to talk about someone's mother dying?

"She doesn't want one."

I open my mouth to ask why, but he cuts me off.

"She doesn't want people from Cobalt Inc. to waste their time mourning a corpse when they should be working. Her words."

Ouch. I change the topic as soon as I see stress tightening his shoulders. "How's the lawsuit?" I ask. They've been trying to take Scott Van Wright to trial for weeks, or at least come to a settlement out of court. A whole team of lawyers gathered evidence while they were on their honeymoon.

"It's complicated," he tells me. "The videos are already online. Winning the lawsuit won't win us back our privacy. It may destroy Scott, but it doesn't gain me anything." He sets his mug on the counter. "I've never had to use so much energy on an outcome that has no direct benefit for me."

I frown. "The benefit is watching that douchebag burn."

He lets out a short laugh and rubs his lips. When he drops his hand, he says, "Revenge isn't a benefit, Lo. It's self-gratification, an emotional response with very little logic and even less reward." He exhales and shakes his head. I've never seen him this conflicted. "I'll figure it out. I always do." He flashes his billion-dollar smile, reminding me in one single second how different we truly are.

And how grateful I am to have him as a friend. And a roommate.

Chapter 40

1 Year : 01 Month

September

LILY CALLOWAY

"Should we walk?" I ask my bodyguard, whose mammoth body occupies *two* cushions on the couch. Garth reads a gardening magazine (I don't question it) in the break room of Superheroes & Scones. "Or maybe we should drive? Have you seen the crowds outside? Are they big?"

I reach over the blue couch with red pillows, flipping a blind to peek outside. A long line of bodies winds across the sidewalk, black velvet ropes barricading them from the street. The line never shortens until thirty minutes from closing.

"Whatever you want, Lily," Garth tells me.

"It's just across the street," I mention. "It'd be kind of silly to drive, right?"

He shrugs, not giving me an answer.

My nerves are already heightened, and I've practiced my apology into the mirror about a million times. I don't want to pussy out though. Not like yesterday and the day before that.

I value my relationship with my sister too much to keep going on like this. "Okay." I jump off the couch. "We walk. Quickly. And we don't make eye contact with any of the cameras." Paparazzi always linger outside the store to catch footage of me leaving.

"All right." He closes the magazine and stands, just as the store manager breezes into the break room. Michelle, a curvy college grad, has on a Superheroes & Scones T-shirt with the slogan: *Channel your inner superhero.*

"Hey, are you leaving?" she asks, her brown bangs nearly hiding her eyes, but I catch her looking to Garth who rarely ever moves off his post on the couch.

"Yeah, I'm going to finish the day at my house. Do you need anything?"

"We just sold out of the *Guardians of the Galaxy, Volume 1: Cosmic Avengers*, but I can make a note of it in the inventory list."

Michelle used to help run this small Indie comic book store in D.C., and after many, many interviews with other potential store managers—and having to let go of a few others before her—we've hired Michelle full-time.

I wave her goodbye. The biggest benefit with Michelle, she never asks about my personal life. Our relationship is purely professional and comics based. I kinda love it. "See you tomorrow." I push through the door and Garth follows, keeping up with my quick stride.

When the crowds spot me, the familiar screams of glee and *click, click* of cameras overwhelms my senses. *Focus on the ground, Lily. The gravel is your friend.*

I concentrate on the pavement, crossing the street with little traffic and then reach a new store window. I dig into my pocket and try to find the right key on my jangling ring.

Last week, Rose set the key on the counter with a note.

Lily,
This key is for you if you ever want to stop by.
Love you, Rose

Our relationship hasn't mended enough for her to hand me the key in person or for her to say those words to my face. Today is the day that everything changes. It has to.

The brick store has newly-painted letters up above: *Calloway Couture.* After the sex tapes, as in plural (the online porn site has already released *two*), Rose gave up her dream of having a fashion line in thousands of department stores. She settled for a boutique in Philly.

The *coming soon* sign hangs across the front window, and my hands sweat as I struggle to open the door.

"Lily! Where's Lo?!" a camera guy shouts behind me.

"Lily! Have you watched Rose's sex tapes?"

No. Never. Everyone has this stupid theory that I've seen them, that I'm *so* addicted to porn, I'd watch my own sister banging her husband. Even if I was in a very bad place, I'd never want to watch that. We're *related.*

"Do you need help?" Garth asks.

The lock clicks. "Ah-ha!" I smile. "Got it." The success almost distracts me from my current mission, a bundle of anxiety attached. With one deep inhale, I enter the store.

I expect to see workers bustling around, hanging clothes and fixing up mannequins, but the white marble floors are nearly bare, no pitter-patter of hurried feet. I wonder if she just wants a quiet, less hectic job than the one she had.

The empty store is only brightened by the chandelier lamps hanging from the ceiling.

The bells on the door clink together as Garth shuts it.

"Poppy, if that's you, I need your opinion on the mannequins." Rose's voice sounds further back in the store, and I hear paper crinkling and the clap of her heels. "Do you like the headless, faceless or realistic ones?"

My stomach flips a little, and I notice the three mannequins she's talking about. The middle one has a smooth head. "The faceless one is really freaky," I say, my voice squeaking out.

Dead silence fills the room. Maybe this was a bad idea.

Before I can make a decision, Rose walks into view, carrying a half-opened package with tissue paper and plastic falling over the sides. The tension stretches and is only broken by Garth, who clears his throat and says, "I'm going to go sit down."

He motions to the champagne-colored couches beside the row of dressing rooms.

When he disappears, I try really hard to keep my focus on Rose, even if my heart wants to jettison out of my body. "So, I came here to apologize, and I had this whole speech planned, but now that I'm here, I've kind of forgotten it. It's like that time I played a teapot in an *Alice in Wonderland* play in the fifth grade. I only had two lines but still managed to forget them. You remember that? I think school plays are designed to embarrass little kids." I cringe and shake my head. "I'm rambling. I'm sorry."

"Just take a breath and slow down," she coaches in her icy voice, but her softened face says differently.

Right. I regroup and meet her yellow-green eyes once more, the deadly poisonous ones I've avoided for many weeks. A wave of emotion floods me all at once. "I miss you," I blurt out, tears welling. "I know you may never forgive me. I was cold and—"

"You should be cold," she snaps, taking a few steps forward. She tentatively stops, still ten feet separating us. "What happened was fucked up."

I shake my head. "I should be happy that people admire you," I choke on the words. "You're my sister, and I love you." Tears slide down my cheeks. "And I should be so, so happy that you didn't have to experience what I did." But deep down, I've been wishing for a different outcome. That desire to place pain within my sister has festered guilt too vast to handle. It eats at me every day, tearing at all the good parts.

I haven't been able to talk to Rose. She'll justify my feelings, telling me that it's okay. I don't want it to be okay.

"Lily," she says forcefully. "The media shouldn't have shamed you to begin with. And since they did, they *shouldn't* have treated me any differently. If our roles were reversed, I'd be so fucking furious that I'd have stormed twenty news outlets by now and wrung their necks." She flips her hair off her shoulder. "I'm not going to lie to you, I called seven of them to bitch, and the only reason I stopped was because Connor told me that I was making the headlines worse." She takes a strained breath. "It's not right, and you know…I wish, more than anything, that you were treated like me and I was treated like you."

My chin quivers, and she looks away from me so she doesn't start crying too. I sniff loudly, trying to halt the waterworks.

"Stop," she snaps, wiping underneath her eyes. "I'm not wearing waterproof mascara."

I smile weakly and step closer to her so we're only a few feet away. "I'm sorry…" My face breaks even more. "I don't want this to tear us apart. I can't lose you. So I'm really, *really* sorry for being so…"

"Human," she tells me, tilting her head as she looks at me again. "I can't tell you how many times I wished ill for other people. It's completely normal, Lily."

"But you're my sister—"

"So? I'm certain I wished Connor would fall on his face when I was fifteen, break his nose and lose at Model UN. Envy, jealousy—I know them probably better than you do." One step closer. We're in hugging distance. "And guess what, little sister, *you* are better than me. I rarely feel guilty by those emotions, but you beat yourself up about it. So tell me, which one of us is the real cruel bitch here?"

I would never trade Rose for another sister. Not for anything. I wipe my nose with my arm. "Can I hug you?" I ask.

She scrunches her nose. "Is that what happens now?"

"Yes," I nod.

She sighs and then places the box on the floor. "Don't make it last too long."

I smile and wrap my arms around my stiff, rigid sister. She pats my back like she's giving it a golf clap.

When we part, she points to the three mannequins. "Do you think the faceless one will scare off kids?" Her eyes twinkle at the thought.

"Or just make them cry in your store."

She grimaces now. "I wish I could have a sign outside that says: *No strollers. No babies. No dogs over five pounds.*"

"What about cats?"

"If you've taken your cat shopping, you have a serious problem," she says and then appraises the mannequins once more. "You're right though. The faceless one is creepy."

I rub my tear-streaked cheeks. "You really thought I was Poppy?" I ask. Rose is my main line of communication where family matters are concerned. Our silence has pushed me out of the loop and into a dark black hole, and I'm worried now that I'm crawling out, things will be changed.

"She stops by sometimes." Rose picks up her box and sets it on the checkout counter. "Mother does too, but I think she just likes the attention from paparazzi."

I frown. "She does?" I haven't noticed all that much. But maybe that's because I purposefully don't make eye contact with our mom.

"She doesn't want it to go away," Rose says. "She's even been feeding stories to the media so we'll stay relevant."

My lips part. "What?"

Rose sighs. "I'm not sure what she tells them. She definitely leaks where she's eating lunch during the day so they can take photos. She says the attention is good for Fizzle, but really she likes the status. She has way too many fake friends fawning over her now."

I realize that we may never distance ourselves from the spotlight, not if our mom purposefully brings us back in. All for the "good" of the family. The weight sinks low and I let it settle there.

"I missed a lot then," I say softly.

She gives me a sharp look like *don't think about it too much.* And to distract me further, she says, "Maria is in the Nutcracker this December. The entire family is going in support."

"I'll be there." I pick up the hint. "Umm…" I scan the half-decorated store. "Do you need any help here?"

"I have it under control," she says quickly, almost like a reflex. She spins back on her heels, and as I turn to leave, she pauses. "Wait."

I glance back.

"I'm starving." She grabs her keys off the counter and her clutch. "Let's go eat lunch."

I smile softly, kind of loving that it wasn't a question. It's more like Rose to demand your company than to ask for it. "Okay."

The knots in my stomach slowly begin to untangle.

Chapter 41

1 Year : 04 Months

December

LILY CALLOWAY

Our limo driver slams on the brake for the third time, and I fall backwards on the leather seat, laughing so much that my chest hurts. Lo breathes heavily, his hand gripping the seat above me, and as he stares down, he shakes his head. But his own smile envelops his face and dimples his cheeks.

"You think he's doing it on purpose?" he asks, his amber eyes flitting down my body, creating hot trails.

"He'd be a grade-A cock-blocker," I say.

"Well, I *refuse* to be cock-blocked tonight." The headiness, the desire in his gaze sweeps me into a bigger, better ride than the swerving limo ever could. "You ready?"

As he says the words, the car careens forward once more, and he nearly slides off the back seat. He grips my shoulder, his body pressed against mine, and fixes a sturdy hand to the door above my head.

I laugh more, especially as he nuzzles his forehead in the crook of my neck and lets out a long, agonizing groan.

I love that he's hornier than me.

I love that I can laugh during sex.

But mostly, I love that being tangled together in the backseat of a car is no longer wrong. It won't turn me into a compulsive monster anymore. It's a level of control that I never thought I'd reach.

Yet, here it is.

I'm starting to feel normal. Or at least, *our* kind of normal.

Lo's groans turn into kisses on my neck, ones that soak my underwear and rouse so many sensitive places. My laughter burns out, replaced by deep breaths.

He rolls my velvet black dress up to my belly and hooks his finger in my panties, pulling them aside. When his lips reach mine, he fills me, his hardness slowly lighting up every single nerve. My chin rises with a silent gasp.

And then he kisses me deeply, in immeasurable increments that weld our bodies together. Like they were made to never break apart.

The car whips left like the driver missed the turn, but Lo has braced himself to me. And he uses the momentum to drive deeper between my thighs, my body electrifying. I let out a ragged moan. Everything clenches, my legs tremble, and he just holds me tightly, creating a fullness inside me that didn't exist before.

I can feel Lo's smile on my lips. I return the kiss, trying to wipe away his grin, making it a goal. He cups the back of my head, and the more aggressive I become and swell his lips, the harder his cock pounds into me.

When I come for the second time, it's short, sporadic, and leaves me utterly breathless.

Lo laughs between his heavy groans, still rocking against me, building his own climax and rousing a new one for me. "You would be an awful lay if you were a guy," he explains the source of his humor.

"Huh."

He kisses me and clarifies, "You wouldn't be able to last that long."

True. "How am I as a girl…?" I grip his biceps, distracted as his thrusts turn slow and deep. *Oh God.* My back arches, and my lips part in need.

His amber eyes graze me as though I'm the most beautiful broken thing he's ever been a part of. "You're perfect."

It's a lie, but he makes it sound so true. I cry as he hits another sensitive place. My hand drifts to his ass that tightens with each push into me.

He snatches my wrist and reads my watch. "Dammit."

"Are we late?" I ask, shutting my eyes and gliding into another world. "I don't mind…so much…" *Oh God.* My toes curl.

"Not yet," he tells me, and I take it that he's talking about the time. Not my climax, because I can't restrain it like he can withhold his.

There is no warning before he quickens his pace, slaying every nerve and seizing my breath. I'm his for the taking.

My eyes stay closed, focusing on his husky grunts that are primal and needy. My core thrums with deep-seated attraction. Physically, mentally, emotionally—Loren Hale has all of me.

"Open," he whispers in a coarse voice.

Oh. I open my eyes.

And drown beneath his amber ones.

When we exit the limo, the wind whips my shoulder-length hair, snowflakes settling on my black pea coat. Fifteen minutes early to Maria's ballet. Must be a record.

Lo's breath smokes as he shuts the door and nears me on the sidewalk. No cameras around. It's one of those rare nights where no one paid attention to what the Calloways were up to. Other families excitedly head into the theatre, and I'm about to follow when Lo grabs my arm.

"Wait," he says.

I spin back around. Wreaths hang on lampposts, dim light casting halos on the street. I have a sudden flashback, remembering the snow, the wreaths. Lo was twenty-one when he went to rehab, on Christmas Eve. And now he's twenty-three.

He must read my faraway expression because he says, "Can you believe I've been sober for this long?"

"Yes," I say definitively. His light brown hair is dusted with snowflakes, some flutter and land on his eyelashes. His face is flushed more from earlier than the cold. He's beautiful, seductive even. I could kiss him again.

"We're doing well, aren't we?" he asks. "This…" He motions between the two of us. "It's working." He's been so confident about our new routine—sex almost three times a day and wherever we like—that it's a surprise hearing him question it now.

"I think so," I say. "It feels right." Not every time is easy. Sometimes I'm a little compulsive and grabby, but I don't think either of us expects it to be good twenty-four-seven for the rest of our lives.

There will always be bad days, but it's how we live those bad days that counts.

He says, "Can you believe you've learned how to control most of your compulsions?" He rests his arms on my shoulders, like we're about to dance.

"It still feels like a dream," I whisper.

"It's real to me," he says. "It took you years. It wasn't an overnight thing, Lil." His gaze falls to my lips. And after a long moment, he breaks the quiet. "I want to marry you."

The words rock me back a little. He holds tighter.

"Soon," he continues on. "In the next year maybe?" His eyes rush mine, searching for confirmation, to ensure we're on the same page.

"Next year," I smile and slap his arm in excitement. "What if we get married on 6-16?"

He's grinning. His sharp jawline and cheekbones just plain gorgeous. "Whatever you want."

He leans down, kissing me with the Christmas lights shimmering overhead. With the snow falling, it's a picture perfect moment.

I wish I could snap-shot it and save it for later. Maybe because I have a feeling. One that hits me as he hugs me to his chest. We've never let ourselves be excited about something further down the road. Two addicts constructing a future together: when I think of it like that, it all begins to sound like make-believe.

Too rooted in fantasy to ever come true.

Part Three

"Love is for souls, not bodies."

– Scarlet Witch, Giant-Size Avengers Vol 1 #4

Chapter 42

1 Year: 06 Months

February

LOREN HALE

Daisy bounces on the diving board with a devious smile, staring right at my brother. He sits with me at a black iron patio table with plates of burgers and fries.

"Just because she's eighteen—" I can't even get the words out.

"I fucking know," he says.

She does a cannonball close to the wall's edge, splashing our feet. My father's indoor pool is decorated with yellow streamers to celebrate her eighteenth birthday.

According to Lily, Daisy's initial plans had been to tube down the Delaware River, but it's too cold for that, so my father offered his estate instead. It took Rose seven days to convince their mom to let Daisy have a small party with just family and close friends.

"I'm only looking out for her," I say with edge. Daisy doesn't know my brother like *that.* She can't possibly see how many girls he screws. I don't think "long-term relationship" is even a word in his vocabulary.

He quickly changes the topic. "You never mentioned that Dad has an indoor pool." He dunks a fry in barbecue sauce. Ryke usually stays a hundred feet away from this house at all times, hating our dad that much. Even though Ryke is physically here, he won't make eye contact with Jonathan Hale, who stands by the bar with Greg Calloway.

"He also has a putting green outside, a home theatre, and a spa." I flash a half-smile.

My biting tone just rolls off his back by now. "Did you swim here a lot?" he asks, prying. Like he wants to make up for lost time.

"When I was a little kid, Lily and I used to sneak down here a bunch of nights," I say, offering him something.

His hard features darken. "If you say *to have sex*—"

"We were like…seven." I scowl. "It was innocent." We'd dare each other to jump in, all the lights off, the bottom black and murky in the darkness. I'd always end up pushing her in, and she'd scream and try to kick back to me. "One night we woke up the staff, and the butler ended up telling my dad that we'd been swimming."

"What'd he do?" Ryke asks, his elbows on the table, his focus set on me. Whenever we talk about our dad, it's always in context with *me.* His past with our father—it's like an abyss, a hazy picture that I can't see. It's still weird that he's had conversations with Jonathan Hale where I wasn't there, talks as a young kid that I know *nothing* about.

"After he found out?" I say. "He locked the pool." I toss my crumpled napkin on the table.

"He was worried about you drowning?"

"No," I say sharply, irritation bearing down on me the longer we discuss this shit. "He asked me if I wanted to swim competitively. I told him *no.* So he told me that the pool wasn't a privilege that I'd earned yet." Before my brother can say anything, I ask, "Was he like that with you?"

"Kind of," he says vaguely, staring off at the glass walls that overlook a courtyard. Rain beats against the panes.

"How's your mom?" I prod a bit further.

"I don't know. Fine, I guess." He hasn't talked to her in forever. Not since she leaked Lily's sex addiction to the press.

"Wow, it's nice talking to you, big *bro*. Let's do this again sometime. I get so much out of it."

He shoots me a look. Yeah, he's been there for me many times, more than I can describe. "I don't talk to my mom, and I sure as fucking hell don't talk to my dad, so I don't see what there is to say."

"Did you ever like Dad?" I ask. "Like growing up?" That's what I want to know.

"Sure," he says. "In the beginning." He chugs his can of Fizz and then nods to me. "Have you heard anything from Scott?"

I'll take the deflection, only because I *do* have an opinion on this. "He texted me twice, once to say: *I'm in Barbados, bitch.* And then another time to send me an actual picture of himself tanning on a damn yacht." I blocked his number after that. Like I need to be reminded that he's profiting off of Connor and Rose's sex tapes.

"Motherfucker," Ryke mutters under his breath. "I hate that Connor threw out the lawsuit. I tried talking to him about it, and he told *me* to fuck off."

I actually laugh.

Ryke extends his arms. "Why is that funny?"

"Because Connor told me that you yelled at him like 'a Neanderthal trying to debate higher knowledge'—it was funny."

"Hilarious," Ryke says dryly. "You can't honestly agree with him."

"No way," I say. "I don't care if he's using the publicity to grow his diamond company. Scott is sunbathing on a *yacht* and swimming in his pools of cash. That sick fuck deserves to be in a prison."

"Or at least bankrupt," Ryke says with tense muscles.

Lily squeals, and we both turn our heads to the pool. She's on Daisy's shoulders, trying to knock off Rose who sits on Connor's, playing a game of chicken.

"Get her bikini strap!" Daisy yells.

Lily tries the dirty move, unclipping Rose's black bathing suit top, but Rose swats her hand away.

"Cheating!" Rose accuses. "I win."

Connor grins and speaks to her in French.

"Nooo way," Daisy says with a laugh. "That is so legal."

Lily is in a one-piece, so Rose can't retaliate.

"Are we just going to leave Scott Van Wright to him?" Ryke asks me.

"Isn't that what you've always done?" I turn back to my brother.

He nods. "Yeah, I guess it is. We have to choose our battles, don't we?"

"Yeah." And Connor wouldn't want us stepping near that one.

Chapter 43

1 Year : 06 Months

February

LILY CALLOWAY

I heave my body out of the pool, water splashing on the indoor stone floor. I carefully walk to the stack of white towels without slipping, but five-year-old Maria darts out of nowhere, skirting straight in front of me.

"No running!" Sam yells at his daughter. He sits on one of the wicker sofas next to Poppy, her cheeks a little flushed from the mojitos that the servers carry around. The raspberry mojitos were tempting, but I passed on them, as did Lo and Ryke.

Maria tries to slow her stride, a piece of paper with crayon drawings in her hand. She comes to a halt by Daisy, who's on the pool ledge.

"Aw is this for me?" Daisy asks with a smile.

Maria nods and then whispers in her ear.

Thankfully I make it to the towels in one piece. No broken bones. I wrap the soft cotton around my waist and near Lo and Ryke at their iron table. They both look to me when I approach, their conversation ending.

Lo opens his arms, and I take a seat on his lap.

"Who won that game of chicken?" Ryke asks me.

I steal a fry from Lo's plate. "Daisy and me, definitely. Rose and Connor will say otherwise though."

Daisy steps out of the pool with her card from Maria, hearing me. "Yeah, there's no rule against elbowing someone in the boob." She locks eyes with Ryke, reading his confusion. "Lily's elbow. Rose's boob." She wags her brows with a growing smile.

Ryke gives her a hard, unamused look—his normal, brooding expression. "At least we all know which Calloway girls play dirty," he says. I easily read into the sexual innuendo.

"No dirtier than you," Daisy says, passing us.

Ryke stiffens, realizing that conversation went south…closer to his penis than he probably intended. Or maybe he *did* mean it. Ryke watches her open the glass sliding door.

I lean forward and whisper-hiss, "Are you staring at my sister's butt?"

"What?" He cringes at me like *I'm* the crazy one.

Daisy disappears inside.

Lo shakes his head at Ryke. "Just no."

Ryke sighs heavily and rolls his eyes, visibly frustrated.

I clear my throat, realizing that this is the best time to discuss a certain subject on my mind. "Speaking of dirty things," I tell Ryke. I straighten on Lo's lap, folding my hands on the table. Seriousness intact.

Ryke's brows rise. "Do I need to step out of the room?" He looks between Lo and me.

"No, this is about *you*," I say.

Ryke looks to Lo. "What the fuck?"

Lo raises his hands. "I'm not involved in her suspicions."

"They're facts," I say. I focus back on Ryke. "I've been observing you…" That came out so wrong. "I mean, watching you." Nope. Not better. I redden while both guys now stare like I've sprouted wings. *Dear God, help me out a bit.* "You know what I mean."

"I fucking don't," Ryke says easily.

This is going badly. I take a sip from a Fizz Life can and gag. Ew. That was flat. And not mine.

"Lily," Ryke growls, impatient. He picks up his water.

"We need to talk," I say, "about your sex addiction."

He chokes on his drink, coughing hoarsely.

Lo and I pat his back at the same time. "It's really, really out of control," I tell him.

And then Ryke wipes his mouth with his arm. "You can't be serious."

"We just had to let go of Michelle. That's the *third* store manager you've slept with. And I *really* liked Michelle." I would've kept her around, but it complicates things. "And I completely understand. You can't control yourself, but if you wanted to get away with hiding your addiction, you shouldn't have slept with people we know. That's sex addiction 101."

Ryke leans back in his chair. "That doesn't make me a fucking sex addict."

"It's okay," I say. "I know it's hard to admit, especially since you've been with *so* many women. But we're here for you now. You can get this under control." I put my hand on his arm in comfort.

His lips part a little. I think he's finally out of the denial stage. And then he says, "I can't tell if you're being fucking serious." He looks to Lo. "Is she for real right now?"

That should've worked. I did all the serious things that serious people do. The complacent face. The folded hands. The stiff spine.

Check, check, double check. "You don't have to be afraid anymore," I add.

"Lily…" Ryke's eyes darken. "I'm not a fucking sex addict. I know you wish I was, so I could join in your little sex addicts not-anonymous club, but it's not happening."

I thought I'd crack him this time.

Damn.

I slouch again. Fuck sitting up straight. "Can you at least admit that you screw more than the average male?" I ask. He always gets numbers from waitresses when we eat lunch out, and I've seen him slip into so many bathrooms with girls. He does one-night stands with zero shame. In and out. Sex, sex, sex.

Wow.

That does sound like me. Except for the zero shame part.

"No," Ryke snaps back and points to Lo. "Your boyfriend fucks more than the average male and *way more* than me. You two have sex once every night."

Twice. Sometimes three or four times.

"He has an excuse," I defend. "He's dating a recovering sex addict."

Ryke laughs into a grin. "Don't fool yourself," he says kind of meanly. His eyes flit over my shoulder to Lo. I can feel his smile as they both gang up on me. "He wants it just as badly as you."

I would have disagreed with him months ago, when Lo feared pushing me over the edge with his own needs, but now Lo shows his arousal way more. So it seems like the truth.

"So is Lo a sex addict?" Ryke asks me, his brows raised in combat.

No. He's not. They're both just horny. "Fine," I surrender, "but can you not sleep with our next store manager? It's hard trying to find the right girl for the job."

"Then hire a guy," he says.

"We just went through this," Lo says. He touches my head. "Sex addict." He motions to Ryke. "Not a sex addict."

"How about this?" Ryke refutes. He waves to me. "In a relationship." His hands lie flat on his chest. "Single."

"He has a point," I mutter.

"No way," Lo says. "We're not hiring a guy because of him." He looks to Ryke. "Keep your dick in your pants or get a girlfriend, man."

"Or…" I say, a light bulb blinking. "What kind of girl are you *not* attracted to?" We can just hire someone Ryke would never sleep with. Problem solved.

"I like all women," he proclaims.

Problem not solved.

"That's so something a sex addict would say," I tell him.

He chucks a fry at my face.

I eat it. So there.

"I can tell you point-blank why I'm not a sex addict," he says, crossing his arms and rocking back on two legs of his chair. "When I come, I don't *have* to do it again."

"The real issue," Lo says, "is how you've actively slept with Lily's store managers." Lo's hands dive to my waist. I hold them there as they slip by my thighs.

"It's not like I was actively…" He trails off, his gaze rising behind our chair.

We don't have to turn our heads to find his distraction. Daisy scrapes the chair back beside Lo, her plate full of raspberries and apple slices. She senses the awkward tension almost immediately and hesitates to touch her fruit. "Am…I not welcome?"

"No," I say and then redden. "I mean, *yes*. It's your birthday."

Ryke runs his hand through his hair, looking rather uncomfortable.

"You were saying?" Lo prods.

He meets Daisy's eyes for two seconds, but I can't read what passes through them. "...I wasn't actively seeking her out."

Daisy crunches on an apple, not prying.

"So how'd it go?" Lo asks.

"How does anything like that fucking go?" Ryke says. "We made eye contact. We talked for a couple minutes. Exchanged numbers and hooked up. The fucking end."

"Whoa, don't get so hostile."

Ryke takes a deep breath, glances at Daisy once or twice and then shakes his head. "I didn't realize that's why you were firing the girls. I wouldn't have gone near them if I knew that was the case."

"Who'd you sleep with?" Daisy asks like it's everyday conversation.

"Their store manager." He doesn't even lie?

Lo and I glance between them. What kind of relationship do they even have?

"Bad call," she says.

"No fucking kidding."

And then a shadow casts over the whole table. I look up and there's my mother. My veins ice over, realizing that we have not talked. In so long. Still, she barely gives me the time of day. Her attention remains fixed to my little sister.

"There's too much sugar in that, Daisy. I thought we agreed to just eat the vegetables."

"I didn't think—"

"It's fine. I'll get you a new plate." Our mom collects the dish right in front of Daisy's face and marches inside.

Daisy looks ill. She sets her half-bitten apple slice on the table, silence weighing down on us all. I don't know what to say. Our mom has no self-awareness. If she did, she'd realize how much she suffocates Daisy...and how much she ignores me.

But then again, maybe she does realize it. And she just doesn't care.

I want to give her the benefit of the doubt though. She hasn't cast me out of the family. She's just…dealing. In a very passive aggressive way.

Daisy breaks the silence. "She's right. My agent said I need to lose ten pounds."

"You're already too skinny," Ryke tells her, his features downcast like the storm outside.

"In your eyes, maybe," she says softly. "To the people that matter, I'm fat."

"Do I not fucking matter?" he asks, hurt passing through his voice.

"I didn't mean it like that."

"Lay off her," Lo interjects, glaring at his brother in warning. "It's her birthday."

"I'm not trying to lay *into* her," he retorts. "You do realize that she's moving into *my* apartment complex when she graduates in May?" Oh yeah. Ryke proposed the idea since Daisy doesn't want to go to college, and our mom has been scheming to extend Daisy's stay at her house for an extra two or three years. Which means more plate grabbing and general hovering.

Lo, surprisingly, has trusted Ryke with this idea, but it comes with some suspicions. How much of what Ryke is doing because he cares for Daisy as a friend? And how much of it is because he wants to have sex with her now that she's legal?

I want to think better of Ryke, but his track record with women points big neon arrows to the latter.

"So?" Lo says. "Does that mean you can be a dick to her?"

"I'm a dick to everyone," Ryke states, extending his arms again.

"Loren!" Jonathan Hale's rough voice echoes against the glass ceiling and walls. One hand in his charcoal slacks, the other clutching a crystal goblet of scotch, filled to the brim. "Come here, son." He practically chugs three-fourths of his drink, standing tensely next to a hanging fern and pool bar.

"Don't," Ryke says under his breath to Lo.

Jonathan's eyes pulse with something familiar, something inhuman and soulless, like he's ready to slaughter any man in his wake, like he's ready to verbally tear through his son. My heart sputters in panic.

"It's fine." He picks me up off his lap and stands with me at the same time, the chair scraping back. Then he forces me in the seat and gives me one deadly look that says: *Don't follow me.*

"Lo—" I start.

"It's probably just Halway Comics," he cuts me off. "I haven't talked to him about my company in a while. I'll be right back."

This seems so much larger than that.

Chapter 44

1 Year : 06 Months

February

LOREN HALE

On the short trek to my father, I look back at Ryke once. He shakes his head at me like I'm going in the wrong direction, facing the wrong man. But I'm not filled with false bravado. This is a person I've faced my *entire* life.

He's my future if I'm not careful.

And he's Ryke's biggest demon that he's buried.

I'm not even five feet from my father before he starts talking, out of hearing distance from everyone else. "How tough are you?"

My face contorts in malignant irritation. He did not call me over here for this shit. "Tough enough to not roll my eyes at *you*." I don't have a chance to flash a dry smile.

When a foot separates us, he clamps a hand on my shoulder, his fingers digging in. I hear *little shit* on his tongue, but he swallows that insult down with his drink. "How fucking *tough* are you, Loren?" he asks, the bar behind him.

I grit my teeth. "Is there a fucking level? Scale one through ten? A numerical system? What do you *want* from me?"

He breathes heavily, his nose flaring. "In a few weeks, we're going to see what kind of man you really are. You can sell me down the river, son." He sets his glass too forcefully on the bar, and a fissure snakes through the crystal.

"What are you talking about?" My pulse kicks up a notch.

"You're going to be hearing some things soon," my dad says with a curled lip. He's drunk. Wasted. I can see it in his glazed, pained eyes. "Maybe it's punishment, on my part. For thinking that I could raise a bastard as anything more than what you are." His tongue runs over his teeth in distaste. No guilt flashes. No fucking remorse.

His words slice straight into me. My jaw locks, my muscles burning as they tighten. *I'm just a bastard then.* "Tell me what's going on," I sneer. "Is it about Lily?" I hate the desperation in my voice.

"Don't *whine* like a little girl," he says with a grimace. His hand lifts off my shoulder and clutches the side of my face. I can see Ryke stand up from his chair in my peripheral.

He can't get in the middle of this. I need fucking answers. I try to give my brother a look that says: *don't come near me.* But my father forces my face towards his.

"Look at *me*," he growls.

I have no other choice. Our foreheads almost fucking touch we're so close. I smell the alcohol on his breath, and it grips my stomach in new, horrifying ways. His hand drifts to the back of my head. "Are you tough, son?" he repeats, drunk out of his fucking mind, upset about something he heard.

"Just tell me," I say lowly. "Why can't you fucking tell me?" He has all the answers. He's always had the answers, and he *keeps* them from me. He always does.

He opens his mouth like he may let it out, but anger just warps his hard, coarse features. And then he says, "We're going to burn, you and me."

I search his eyes, and all I see is blackness. Mine begin to cloud. "What could be worse than what I've already been through?"

"You have no idea."

I stifle a scream that tries to reach my throat. "I deserve answers."

"You deserve *nothing*," he says. "I've given you *everything*, Loren, including your life. You realize that, don't you?"

A pain crashes into my chest. I lick my dry lips. "Yeah," I say. "I realize that you're the only one who wanted me. I get it. I'm just a bastard. Thanks." I wait for him to let me go. I just need to walk away. I need something to drink—*Christ.*

I rub my lips.

I have to get out of here. He's not going to tell me anything. He never does. I feel like I smashed my head against a wall.

I breathe heavily. "Lily…" I try to turn, to find her, but my dad grips the back of my head, harder.

I've given you everything, Loren.

I forgot what it feels like to stand against him when he's *this* wasted and I'm not. It's easier when I'm numb. It's easier when we're sinking in the same fucked up black hole. But he's dragging me down, and every brutal cut tears into me. The weight of every word pummeling me.

I am sinking beneath it all.

Like quicksand I should've seen in front of me.

"Grow *up*," he sneers. "You shouldn't have to call your goddamn girlfriend when you're feeling weak." He removes his hand off my head, and taps my cheek, twice with force. My head jerks back on the second contact. And disgust lingers in my dad's eyes. For not being strong enough to withstand a fucking slap to the face.

"Hey!" Ryke yells at him.

I feel Lily's hand in mine almost immediately. And I spin around, done with this shit. Just over everything.

"Lo…" she says, hurrying next to me, but I readjust our hands, lacing my fingers with hers.

"Don't leave me," I whisper. I'm afraid of myself, I realize. *I don't want to drink.*

Yes I do.

I do so fucking badly.

"Lo," Ryke says forcefully, about to take a few steps towards our father. I put my free hand on my brother's chest.

"Don't start a fight with him," I say.

"He fucking *hit* you!"

The pool is dead quiet.

Our dad retreats inside with a new glass of scotch while Sam lifts Maria in his arms and brings her into the courtyard. The rain has stopped.

"Lo!" He grabs my shoulder, practically pushing me to face him.

"You don't understand!" I shout back, squeezing Lily's hand. "You don't get it."

"What don't I get?" he growls. "How can you put up with that shit and then defend him?"

"Because he's just like me," I retort.

"He's *nothing* like you."

"He's in pain!" I shout. *I've given you your life, Loren.* "And he's hurting me before I can hurt him." *You can sell me down the river, son.* I have no idea what's wrong with him, what he heard to make him bitter and malicious. Why he thinks I'm going to fuck him over. I hate that he can't just tell me. I hate that *everyone* censors parts of my life from me.

"You're an idiot if you think that."

"Then I'm a fucking idiot," I retort, my blood pumping so fast.

His face twists and he rests his hands on his head. "I didn't fucking mean it like that."

"I think we should go," Lily says, wrapping her arm around my waist. I look down and realize her fingers are purpled from my grip. I loosen my hold.

"Do you want to drink?" Ryke asks.

He's killing me. "Please, *stop*," I sneer, my voice scratching my ears. "I just need…air." I breathe heavily, trying not to imagine what's going to happen in a few weeks—my father's fucked up version of a warning.

I go outside with Lily, to the courtyard gazebo, away from Maria and Sam. I stopped taking Antabuse about four months ago. This time I sat everyone down and told them before I did it. I wanted to test myself without the pills. A challenge that I was sure I could defeat. They agreed that I'd been sober long enough to toss the pills. To try.

I have no voice in my head that says: *you'll puke if you take a sip of whiskey. You'll be sick. It's not worth it.*

This is the hardest day I've had in *years.*

And according to my father, it's only going to get worse.

Chapter 45

1 Year : 07 Months

March

LOREN HALE

Its 2 a.m. and my phone won't stop ringing.

Lily is hogging our comic book in bed, flipping through it too quickly. "Are you going to answer that?" she asks, licking her finger, about to turn the next page.

"I thought we talked about licking the pages." She puts fingerprints all over the panels when she does that.

"I'm not licking the pages," she refutes. "I'm licking my *finger*. Smart people do it."

"Like who?"

"Connor Cobalt," she notes.

"Yeah? Well he's a weird smart person, so he doesn't count." My phone rings *again*. I internally groan and shut it off, not recognizing the number.

"I'm going to tell him you said that."

"He'll probably take it as a compliment," I say, scooting closer to her. And then my phone goes off *again*. "Jesus Christ. Who gave my number to a telemarketer?"

"Not me," she says quickly. "Maybe someone posted it online. That happened to Ryke, you know."

"I'm also not sleeping with random girls who've decided to share my number with the world," I say crossly, more because of my cell than anything. Ryke should also be more careful with shit like that. He doesn't care though. He barely cares about what anyone thinks of him.

I can't be like that. Not completely.

When the next ring comes, I groan out loud. About to silence my cell. Instead I answer the call. My eyes narrow at the comforter, the cold speaker to my ear. "Who is this?" I snap.

"This is Mark Johnson from GBA News. How are you today, Loren?"

A chill sweeps the back of my neck. It's been about three weeks since Daisy's pool party—since my dad lashed out at me with seemingly no goddamn reason. *This is why.* I deduce in two seconds flat that a series of reporters have been trying to reach me.

I can't do this here, in front of Lily. I lick my lips. "Hold on a minute," I tell him. My chest constricts, and no matter how hard I tell myself to relax, my muscles just keep tightening.

Lily frowns at me. "Who is it?"

"Can you save my spot in the comic?" I ask. "Don't dog-ear it; just remember the page."

"Yeah," she says softly while I swing my legs over the bed and exit our room, shutting the door behind me. I practically skip steps downstairs and make my way to the kitchen, out of earshot from Lil. If this has to do with her—I need the answers first. So I can break it to her gently.

I try to inhale, to breathe a full breath, but the pressure on my ribcage only pains me.

"Okay," I say to Mark, standing between the kitchen island and the sink. "What's this about?"

People holler in the background—on his end, not mine. "Sorry," he apologizes with a heavy breath, like he's walking somewhere else. The interfering noise suddenly dies out. I hear a door close. "The newsroom was going crazy when you answered the call. We know that other networks have been trying to get in touch with you too." And he's the first one I clicked into.

"Don't flatter yourself," I say coldly. "It was random that I picked up your call."

"And I appreciate it one-hundred percent," Mark says quickly, as though to keep me on the line. "I know this has to be a tough time for you and your family, Loren, but we'd love to hear your side of the story. Do you have a statement or anything you'd like to say? If you don't have time, we'd be more than happy with just a short quote."

What could be *this* newsworthy that he'd grovel for a fucking statement? When Lily's sex addiction became public, reporters didn't even hound me like this. "How about you start by telling me what's going on."

His shock amplifies this heavy silence, and it builds an unbearable amount of tension. I try to exhale, like razors cutting through me.

"It's been breaking news since 1 a.m." He pauses. "I thought you'd heard by now."

I grip the sink counter, leaning over. I could hang up on him, read a news article online. See the headlines. Turn on the television. But I have the answer in the palm of my hand. Right now. And nothing motivates me to drop the cell. If I let go, I may lose my shit. "Just tell me." My voice is achingly deep.

He clears his throat. "Your father is being accused of molesting you." He keeps speaking, but the words don't register in my brain. I stare blankly at the white sink. *Your father is being accused of molesting you.*

There is a pain buried so deep inside of me. I've never tapped into it, never felt it until today. "It's not true," I say, shaking with emotions that I can't sort through. "It's *not* true. There's your quote." I hang up and immediately dial my dad's number. My hand quakes as I rub my lips. The line clicks. "Dad?" And everything begins to pour out of me. "It's not fucking true. What sick fuck would say this?" I almost scream. It rises to my throat, and it turns into a silent one, the sound completely lost. Hot liquid creases my eyes, and I sink to the floor, leaning against the island cupboards.

"Loren Hale" has always been synonymous with: *failure, fuck up, bastard, alcoholic, Lily Calloway's boyfriend.* Those are the titles the world has given me. I never, in my life, believed that this could be attached to my name, to my father's.

"It was a family friend," is the first thing my father says. "He made these allegations to tarnish my reputation, my company's name." He lets out a weak, irritated laugh. "Hale Co. produces baby products, and whoever believes in this lie will likely boycott us." He doesn't say: *because who wants a stroller made by a pedophile?* He can't utter the words.

I rest my head on the wood, realizing that he couldn't tell me at the pool because he couldn't stomach it. He tried, but it wouldn't come out.

"No one will believe it," I say under my breath. "I already made a statement. I said it didn't happen." It'll all just pass like every other rumor.

"There's an investigation, Loren," he says.

"What?" My nose flares, hot pools welling in my eyes.

"They'll talk to your teachers from Dalton Academy, maybe some of your professors from Penn before you were expelled. Any friends."

I bury my face in my hands, a wave thrashing against me. The riptide swallows me whole.

"I'm not going to sugarcoat anything," he says with a rough voice. "You're old enough to hear the goddamn truth." He inhales loudly. Exhales coarsely. "I've already filed a defamation suit, but after what our family has been through…with the reality show." I hear ice clink against his glass. "We became celebrities with almost no privacy, and to ever win a defamation case, we're going to have to jump through fifteen-hundred hoops."

"So what do we do?" I ask, anger rising. "We just wait around? We just *hope* that these allegations go away? I told the reporter that *it never happened*, and it's about *me*. Case closed."

"No, son," he says. "No."

A scream almost breaches my throat this time. I force it down, the pain swelling my stomach. "Why not?"

"You're twenty-three. You went to rehab. Your word means nothing to anyone because I could've manipulated you." He pauses, more ice hitting glass. "This surpasses the both of us, Loren. It's about the people around us, who can vouch for our relationship as father and son."

It's over, he's saying. No one understands us. He's not the greatest father, but he's never touched me like that. He's never abused me—not in that way. And I hate…I fucking hate that this is going to be a part of me, for the rest of my life.

And every day, I'm going to have to repeat the same words over and over: *my father did not molest me.*

I rub my eyes that sear and water with emotions that I've never felt. I wish I was like Ryke. I wish I didn't give a fuck about how other people see me. How does someone even get that kind of strength?

I grasp at a sliver of hope. "The people close to us will vouch—"

"No," he snaps, shutting me down. "Stop being delusional. They're looking for answers from two people. They matter most. Not you, not me, not Greg Calloway or your girlfriend."

I swallow hard. "Who then?"

"My bitch of an ex-wife and my other son."

Sara Hale.

And Ryke Meadows.

They both hate Jonathan. Can't stand to look at him. Why would they ever testify *in favor* of him? It's over. There is nothing we can do but live with this news.

"I get it," I finally say. I just want to drown. To numb the parts of me that can't withstand this reality. I just want to go away for good.

Maybe when I wake up my life will be different. Everyone will be happy. There will be no more pain. A scalding tear rolls down my cheek. My phone slips from my hand, thudding to the floor. I reach into the cupboard behind me and find a bottle of Glenfiddich. Three-fourths full.

I pop off the crystal stopper and put the rim to my lips.

I hesitate for only one second before the sharp liquid slides down my throat.

Chapter 46

1 Year : 07 Months

March

LILY CALLOWAY

I snoozed with the comic book open on my chest. I startle myself awake, in a half-sleep. “I’m up,” I practically snort the words and blink quickly. Oh shit, what was his page number? Forty-seven? Or forty-nine? Somewhere in the forties, for sure, right?

I flip through the comic hurriedly. “I remembered your page,” I fib. *I’ll find it.* “I didn’t get that far when you left…” I trail off as I see his side of the bed. Bare. The comforter rumpled where he had crawled out. I read the clock on the end table.

5 a.m.

Maybe he fell asleep on the couch, I think first. But I can’t recall a time where he’s done that before. My heart skips, and I slip off the bed, in black cotton panties and a white tank top. The probability of running into Connor is about fifty-fifty since he wakes up early for work, but I don’t waste the time hopping into pajama pants.

I just briskly walk out the door, my bare feet padding against the cold floorboards as I descend the stairs. The living room is pitch-black, and I flip on the overhead light. My eyes dart across the furniture, pillows fluffed, no butt indentions.

Okay. I pass through the archway into the kitchen, the microwave light turned on. "Lo?" I whisper, walking further.

And then I freeze, my eyes growing big. "Lo?" His limp hand sticks out from behind the island. I awaken with pure panic, my heart on a freefall. "Lo!" I rush to the space between the sink and the island, and I find Lo half supported by the cupboard, his head drooped to the side, his body slumped.

I drop to my knees and touch his face, his eyes closed like he's sleeping. I feel his slow pulse, beating sluggishly.

Tears stream down my cheeks. "Lo, Lo…" *What'd you do? What'd you do?* I spot the whiskey bottle next to him, almost all gone. "LO!" I scream. He's passed out. But this is different. He hasn't had alcohol in so long. "Wake up!" I rattle his shoulders a little. Hopefully he'll open his eyes. He's not dead. He's not dead. I lift underneath his arms. *We're going to the hospital, Loren Hale. Just you hold on.* "You wait for me, okay?" I cry, trying to heave his body with mine.

I'm not strong enough.

I fall back down, the weight of his muscles outsizing my thin arms.

"Lily!" Rose rushes in the kitchen, dressed in a black robe. "What…" Her voice dies off.

I'm tangled with Loren Hale's limbs while he's completely, dangerously unresponsive.

"Connor!" Rose shouts, fear breaching her voice.

It terrifies me ten times more. "I'm trying to get him to the car," I tell her, my body trembling. "I'm taking him to…to the hospital."

"CONNOR!" Rose screams.

He runs into the kitchen, his hair wet, shirtless, navy pajama pants like he jumped out of the shower. He moves into action faster than Rose. "Go start the car, Rose," he orders, his voice stoic. But there is something behind Connor Cobalt's eyes that I don't like.

"We have to go," I say through a cascade of tears. I try to lift Lo again, but Connor squeezes into the small space.

"I have him, Lily. Can you go with Rose?" He glances back at my sister, who is staring wide-eyed at Lo. "*Rose.*"

"Whose bottle of Glenfiddich is that?" she asks in one breath.

Connor easily lifts Lo into his arms, his head hanging like he's…I hold his neck so it doesn't look like that. Then Connor adjusts Lo's body, his head resting against Connor's bare chest. Better. I lead the way, grabbing Rose's arm so she'll follow.

I have seen Loren Hale passed out drunk, more times than I can even count. Rose hasn't seen him like this. And even though something brutal terrorizes every nerve inside my body, I only think one thing: *he needs help.*

I don't want to wake up tomorrow and realize I didn't do the right thing for him. I don't want to regret not moving faster. I don't want to open my eyes and see that he's gone for good. So I suck down this pain and I trudge forward. To the garage. To Rose's Escalade.

"Connor," Rose says under her breath while he carries Lo, two paces behind us. I glance back, just to make sure Lo is still there.

"You need to drive," he tells her, admitting that he can't.

Rose nods quickly and takes a deep breath, her game face returning. She unlocks the car and heads to the front seat.

I open the backdoor, and I slide in first. Connor gently rests Lo next to me, his head on my lap. I concentrate on the way his chest rises and falls, so discreetly that it's hard to see. *Just keep breathing, Lo.* I comb his hair out of his face, and by the time Connor shuts the passenger door, we're speeding to the hospital.

Minutes must pass, in the quiet of the car, before someone speaks.

"It was mine," Connor says. I can't see his expression from the backseat, but he covers his eyes with his hand. Something he almost never does. "It was my alcohol."

Rose reaches out and holds Connor's hand between their seats.

I kiss Lo's forehead. *You wait for me, Loren Hale.* "Promise me," I whisper, blinking back tears. I can try to hold him as tightly as possible, but in the end, he can slip through my grasp at any moment. He can drift away without me.

Please not today.

Chapter 47

1 Year : 07 Months

March

LILY CALLOWAY

I forgot that I was only wearing panties and a see-through tank top. And I really don't even care. Though the hospital staff made me put on blue scrub pants. I've scooted a chair as close to Lo's bed as I could, and I hold his hand, tubes stuck in his skin and running to an IV bag with fluids.

They pumped his stomach. Now he just needs to wake up.

"You shouldn't have had alcohol anywhere in the *fucking* house!" Ryke yells.

"I brought it home after a company party. I didn't think—"

"You're living with an alcoholic, Connor! Do you not even care about him?" Their shadows stand tall behind a gray curtain, inside the nice hospital room with a couch and a bathroom. The door is shut so hopefully no one can hear them in the hallway.

"I know you're upset—"

"*You* should be upset!" His voice shakes, and his shadow paces back and forth while Connor remains fixed in one place. "Do you even know what you did?!" While Ryke stares straight at Connor, there is the longest pause in history of pauses.

And then their forms collide, Ryke's silhouette shoving Connor roughly. Something clatters to the floor while Connor defends himself, pushing Ryke back. My heart races, especially as an elbow or arm whacks into the curtain. I can't see a thing, really.

I'm mostly surprised that Connor doesn't talk Ryke down. He's letting Lo's brother attack him this once. The more aggressive shadow pins the other into the wall, both breathing heavily.

"I trusted him," Connor says in a low voice.

"You can't trust a fucking alcoholic," Ryke growls.

"I trusted my *friend*," Connor retorts. "I see him every day, Ryke. If I knew about the allegations, I would've never kept him out of my sight."

"You know what I fucking think?" Ryke asks, fuming. "I think you get off being the superhero to my brother. I think you like the way he looks at you—like you're invulnerable. While he stands beneath you, weak, looking for guidance and you take advantage of all of that—"

"*Stop*," Connor says forcefully, and I can see his chest rising.

"Tell me that I'm wrong," Ryke says. "Tell me that you're *not* destroying him."

"I love him," Connor says with so much conviction. "I would never intentionally harm Lo."

The door suddenly swings open, and the guys immediately separate.

I hear the clap of heels. Rose stops midway into the room. "If I interrupted something, then maybe you two should realize that you're fighting in front of my little sister. She has fucking ears, you know."

Rose has dropped more f-bombs today than usual. I almost wonder if Ryke is rubbing off on her. She flings the curtain aside, and everyone looks at me.

Dried tears, my hand clasped in Lo's. I'm just waiting, is all.

Rose has four coffees in a carton, and she marches over, passing me one. "Dr. Banning wanted me to ask if you've been thinking about sex at all."

My therapist. I talked to her a little bit ago. My cheeks redden, and my eyes flicker to both Connor and Ryke who stand unwaveringly at the foot of the bed.

"No," I whisper. I've been sad, and usually I cope with sex. Not this time. I've suppressed most thoughts about orgasms, about that rush that would take me away from here. "Lo has been there for me for so many months." Saying the words out loud makes them unbearably real. "I want to be strong for him." It's my turn now. I'm ready for it.

"I'm proud of you, Lily," Rose tells me, even giving me a smile. When she turns back towards the guys, they both reach out to collect their coffees. She tucks the carton tray to her chest. "No coffee for either of you. Not until you stop fighting over something that is *no one's* fault."

"Rose is right," I say softly. "Lo wouldn't want you both to argue about this." He'd blame himself if he woke up and heard Connor and Ryke going at it.

They all asked me if the allegations were true. We heard about them around the same time the doctors began pumping his stomach. I said *no.* I can't even, for a second, believe they're true. Lo would've told me.

Rose and Ryke seemed doubtful. And it hurt me to think that our own friends, his brother, may never believe the truth. We're both known liars. It's hard to accept anything we say as fact. So I understand, but it doesn't hurt any less.

Everyone stays in the room, taking the day off of work while I skip all my college assignments. I don't join them on the couch. I just hold Lo's hand while he sleeps.

An hour passes before he finally stirs. His eyelids slowly open, and he blinks a few times to orient himself. Connor, Rose, and Ryke leave the room before he even wakes fully, afraid their presences will overwhelm him.

It's just Lo and me.

When he finally turns his head to see me, there is something so vitally heartbreaking about those amber swirls. We've been in this place before. Him on a hospital bed. Me on the chair. I do what I did when we were teenagers. I pass him a glass of water.

He shakes his head slowly and says, "Lie next to me."

I set the water on the small tray table and climb onto the wide bed. His arms wrap around me before mine tuck around his chest, tangled up in a few wires. Our legs intertwine, sufficiently embraced and connected together.

It's quiet, and we listen to each other's breaths for a few minutes.

"Lo," I whisper, my fingers making circles on his black shirt. "I just want you to know that if you leave this world, I won't be in it for much longer." He's a piece of me. You cut it off, and it's like going through life with no lungs.

That is how deep our love really goes.

"Lil…I didn't…" He cups my face, our lips inches apart. "That wasn't my intention. I would never do that to you."

I wipe his tears before they fall far down his cheek. "How much did I drink?" His face contorts. He didn't think he drank past his limit, I realize. Initially, I didn't either.

"Most of the bottle," I say.

"I should've just passed out," he says in confusion.

"You drank too fast, and you haven't had alcohol in *years*, Lo. That matters." The doctor said that his tolerance is different. He can't function drinking the same extreme amount that he used to consume.

He shuts his eyes. "I'm sorry."

I hold him tighter. "I would've been upset too," I whisper, "but it's going to be easier than you think."

"Yeah?" he asks.

"Yeah."

His eyes open but look faraway, lost to the rumors that have been spreading like wildfire. "They're not true, you know."

"I know." I kiss his lips, and he pulls me even closer and kisses me back more forcefully, full of eager desperation that tears at my soul. My legs clench around his waist. I break apart first. "Lo…"

He breathes heavily. "Maybe you shouldn't…be near me for a while."

"No," I say. "You can't enable me."

"Why is that?" he asks, tucking a strand of hair behind my ear.

"Because I can withstand your charm, Loren Hale." *Unless he layers it on, in which case, I will have to turn away to collect myself.*

He laughs into a weak, pained smile, and then he shakes his head, his features just shattering. "I don't want to be the weak one."

It's one of the most human things he's ever said.

I kiss his forehead, and he kisses my nose just as quickly. I smile a smile that is filled with tears and hopes and unspoken promises. "You won't be. Not for long."

Chapter 48

1 Year : 11 Months

July

LOREN HALE

June 16th passed. I remember Lily picking out the date for our wedding like a dream. I'd think it wasn't real if Lily hadn't marked the day on our calendar with stars. Before I drank, we briefly talked about a location, somewhere on the coast, but after I broke my sobriety, we just forgot about it.

Our energy has been focused other places. I wish I could say that I haven't tasted alcohol after that one night, but it's so much easier to break my sobriety again now that I've done it once.

I haven't been right for a while, not since March. Some days I can barely stomach the thought of starting a morning without something to get me through it. I can't force myself to take Antabuse. The only thing keeping me here is Lily. I try to make every day count for something. For her. When I fuck up, she doesn't act like it's the end of the world. She tells me that the next day will be better.

But sometimes I think that my dad was right. I was never going to be anything more than a bastard.

Chapter 49

2 Years : 01 Month

September

LOREN HALE

I run after my brother, down the suburban street in Princeton, New Jersey. He never even tries to slow. Not when my tendons scream to stop. To take a single break. My chest blazes like an animal wants to crawl out of me. And he just glances back, as though to say, move your ass.

I can't run as fast as him. I can't keep up, not even when my calves burn. Not even when I force my foot in front of the other, each one heavy like lead.

He reaches the oak tree at the end of the street first—of course. I slow to a halt and rest my hands on my head, my jaw locking as I glare at him, pissed. At me, mostly. For not being able to run right by his side. I want to.

God, I want to.

"You can't go easy on me just once?" I ask, pushing damp strands of hair off my forehead.

"If I slowed down, we would have been *walking*," Ryke retorts, not even winded. He stretches his arm over his shoulder. If I told him to do a hundred push-ups right now, I doubt he'd even break a sweat.

I roll my eyes and scowl. I want to let go of everything, to just move on from the allegations—the stupid shit online, the way people *look* at me when I walk down a street—but I can't. I don't know how to release this tension in my body. It *never* goes away. Not with anything but alcohol.

I squat to try to breathe right. And then I rub my eyes.

"What do you need?" he asks me.

"A fucking glass of whiskey. One ice cube. Think you can do that for me, big *bro?*"

He glowers back. "You want a glass of whiskey? Why don't I just push you in the front of a fucking freight train? It's about the same."

I stand up and let out a short laugh. "Do you even know what this feels like?" I extend my arms, my eyes *on fire* like I'm halfway between crying and rage. "I feel like I'm going out of my goddamn mind, Ryke. Tell me what I should do? Huh? Nothing takes this pain away, not running, not fucking the girl I love, not *anything*."

I wish to God that I could find an easy out. An easy fix. Anything except alcohol. I'd take it in a heartbeat. But there's *nothing* that I can do except deal with this shit. Try and move on, to let go. It's just taking a lot longer than I ever thought it would.

"You relapsed a few times," he says. "But you can get back to where you were."

I shake my head, a knee-jerk reaction.

"So what? You're going to drink a beer? You're going to chug a bottle of whiskey? Then what?" he continues, eyes flashing hot. "You'll ruin your relationship with Lily. You'll feel like *shit* in the morning. You'll wish you were fucking dead—"

"What do you think I'm wishing now?!" I scream, pointing a finger at the fucking ground. "I *hate* myself for breaking my sobriety. I *hate* that I'm at this place in my life again." I wish I could take back the day I broke my sobriety a million times over. I wish I never answered that phone call. I wish I walked back upstairs and crawled in bed. I wish I held Lily and just disappeared from the world with her.

I wish.

I wish.

I wish. And nothing ever comes true.

His face falls and he raises his hand like *calm down.* "You were under a lot of scrutiny."

"You're under the same scrutiny," I retort. The media asks him for a statement about the allegations almost every day. "And I didn't see you breaking your sobriety." My brother—unbreakable, unbendable like the rocks he climbs. Nothing can topple him.

The jealousy and resentment tastes horrible.

"It's different," Ryke says, his voice less hostile and aggressive. "The media was saying some pretty awful shit, Lo. You coped the first way you knew how. No one blames you. We just want to fucking help you."

Sweat collects on the back of my neck. It's not from running down the street. "You don't believe them, do you?" I ask. I can see the answer in his eyes, almost every time we talk about the molestation rumors.

"Who?" he asks.

"The news, all those reporters...you don't think that *our* dad actually did those things to me?" *Say no. Just say no.* I need him to believe me.

He looks physically pained, his answer so clear.

"It's not fucking true!" I shout. Why can't my own brother believe me? I've known him for three years now. *Three* years. That should count for something.

"Okay, okay." He raises his hands again. "You just have to move fucking forward. Don't worry about what people think."

I internally laugh, one full of agitation. *Don't worry about what people think*. I inhale deeply and stare at the sky with the darkest glare I have. "You say shit, Ryke, like it's the easiest thing in the world. Do you know how annoying that is?" I turn my head, meeting his eyes.

"I'll keep saying it then, just to irritate the fuck out of you."

I let out another deep breath. Okay.

He rubs the back of my head and nods towards my house down the street. I follow him for a few paces, and I see the way his muscles cut in defined lines—reminding me that he's an athlete. A different kind. He might not have a nine-to-five job, but he has goals.

Goals that he's put on hold to be there for me. I don't want anyone to pause their life because I had to slam on the brakes for mine.

I stop in the middle of the quiet road, morning. No cameras. It's the best time to run. I lick my lips. "About your trip to California…I know I haven't asked about it in months. I've been too self-absorbed—"

"Don't worry about it." He gestures with his head to the house. "Let's go make some breakfast for the girls."

"Wait. I have to say this." I swallow hard. "I need you to go." He tries to cut me off, but I barrel ahead. "I can already hear your stupid fucking rebuttal. And I'm telling you to *go*. Climb your mountains. Do whatever you need to do. You've had this planned for a long time, and I'm not going to ruin it for you."

I can't hurt anyone else.

"I can always reschedule. Those mountains aren't fucking moving, Lo."

I put my hands on my head again. He's wanted to free-solo climb these rock formations in California for months, maybe even longer than that. "I will feel like *shit* if you don't go," I say. "And I'll drink. I can promise you that."

He just glares.

Why doesn't he get it? *Leave me.* "I don't need you," I sneer. It's a complete and utter lie. But I can't hold onto him like a life vest. I have to let my brother have a fucking life without me in it. "I don't fucking need *you* to hold my hand. I need you to be goddamn selfish like me for once in your life so I don't feel like utter shit compared to you, alright?"

He stares at me for a long moment, with this rock hard expression that turns darker by the minute. *Please. Give up on me. Just this once.* And then he says, "Okay, I'll go."

I exhale, a pressure actually lifting off me. I didn't realize I'd been carrying around that guilt for so long.

Ryke wraps his arm around my shoulder and says, "Maybe one day you'll be able to outrun me."

Yeah. Maybe one day.

Chapter 50

2 Years : 01 Month

September

LILY CALLOWAY

"What'd I do?" I ask, my shoulders curving forward. Rose dragged me into the downstairs bathroom like she was plowing through bulky Spartan warriors. Whereas I'd most likely turn beet-red and surrender to their swords, Rose just knocked them all down, a woman on a mission. No man can stop her. Not even three-hundred of them.

"This isn't about you," Rose says, fixing her hair into a sleek pony.

I frown. "Are you preparing to unplug a toilet?"

She gives me a look.

"What? You're fixing your hair. That's all I have to go on." She's not providing me with any information.

Right when she opens her mouth, someone knocks on the door. "What are you two doing in there together?" Lo asks, suspicion in his voice. This *is* very suspicious, I'll admit. Joint bathroom sessions only happen when there are multiple stalls. Unless, you know, *sex*. But that can't be one of his thoughts. Because, incest.

Uh. I redden instantly. I need some bleach for my mind.

I picture Lo leaning against the wall, arms crossed, and I almost invite him inside. But Rose smashes her palm against my lips and gives me humongous crazy eyes.

It both scares me and propels me to my sister's side of things. Her yellow-green eyes are very convincing. Plus, even though she has a flair for the dramatics, this seems serious.

Rose drops her hand, trusting me to stay quiet, and then she cracks the door and sticks her head out. "Two words, Loren: *Female menstruation*." She slams the door right in his face.

"Great," he calls back with irritation. "I'd say talk to me again when you're done PMSing, but you're always a bitch." I wince at that comeback. He's been a lot meaner since he relapsed, but that also comes with an even bigger portion of guilt. I imagine his face twisting with it, and it hurts my stomach even more.

His footsteps sound on the floorboards, drifting off.

"Female menstruation?" I ask with the rise of my brows. "What's this about, Rose?"

She passes me with fire in her eyes and crouches to the cabinets beneath the sink. Her silence makes me nervous.

I almost bite my fingernails, but I drop my hand quickly. "Should I go get Daisy?" I ask. "If this is like a sister thing, we should include her, right?" I feel badly leaving her alone with the guys, especially since we're all together to celebrate her trip to Paris. In a few days she'll be off to Fashion Week, her first time attending without our mom. It's a big deal for her, and Rose likes any reason to throw a party, even if only close friends attend.

Rose rises to her feet, brandishing a box of tampons.

I squint. "So this *is* about your period?" I feel like there's a mystery here. One that I am not programmed to solve.

"No," she says like I'm an idiot. I don't see how *I* could be the stupid one. She pops open the flaps and takes out a familiar looking stick.

My rushed thought spills out of my mouth. "Who mixed up a pregnancy test with tampons?"

Rose purses her lips. "*I* put the test in here," she says flatly.

Oh.

Ohhhhhh. My eyes widen in alarm, never believing or registering that *this* could actually happen: Rose pinching a pregnancy test between two fingers. "You're not…"

"I'm late."

Oh my God. This is really happening.

I just don't understand why she's keeping it so secret. Sure, I've had to sneak around pregnancy tests more than I'd like to admit aloud or even to myself. Rash-like welts start springing up if I go back that far to my past. But this is coming from Rose—my sister who used to buy tampons for me because I blushed too hard at the checkout counter.

"Why the incognito pregnancy test?" I ask with the tilt of my head.

She points a manicured nail at the toilet. "Sit."

What? "Um, Rose," I say hesitantly. "*You're* supposed to sit on the toilet, not the sister of the person who may be pregnant. That's how pregnancy tests work…"

She glares like she's trying to shrivel me. Like I'm *Loren Hale*—her one true nemesis.

"Team Rose." I point to my chest. In the mirror, I catch my bony arms and flushed skin, looking very much sunburnt by now.

"I need you to take the test first," she says, pushing the stick into my hands.

Now I go pale, blood rushing out of me. "Why?"

"I need a baseline," she says. "To know that they work before I try."

That sounds…ridiculous, but Rose has begun to pace, worrying me a little. Her eyes dart around the room like she's thinking *way* too hard about the future. It's not a secret that Rose dislikes children, babies even more.

"I thought you and Connor talked about children," I say softly, tiptoeing very carefully on the topic.

"*Thirty-five*," she says. "We agreed to have kids at thirty-five. This isn't part of the plan."

She's only twenty-five.

"You know," I say, "lots of women have babies at your age." I try my best at being supportive, but she shoots me another withering glare.

"*Piss* on the stick." Each word sounds like a threat.

I take a deep breath. She's done far more for me. I can definitely do this for her. "But you can't tell Lo that I took a pregnancy test—even one in camaraderie. He'll freak out."

"It won't ever come up," she promises.

I approach the toilet, roll down my leggings and sit on the cold seat. I concentrate on the task, really careful not to pee on my fingers (that's the trickiest part). When I finish, I pull up my leggings, set the stick on the counter and wash my hands, waiting for my results.

"You next," I say with a smile, like *see it's not so scary, Rose.*

She inhales sharply. "I'll wait until we read yours."

"It'll be better if you just get it over with." She's going to wear down her five-inch heels to three-inches if she doesn't stop pacing. I delicately hand her the tampon box, showing her that it's not so bad after all. "It's probably negative anyway. You're on birth control, right?"

"I haven't missed a single day, so you know what this means?"

"That there is no way you could be pregnant." I exhale for her and smile. She's being dramatic for nothing.

"That I'm *unlucky*. Very, *very* unlucky, Lily. Birth control is 99% effective, so Connor's superhuman sperm somehow penetrated my body's defenses. He *won*. His sperm reached my egg and now I'm going to have this *thing* growing inside of me for nine whole months while he gets to parade around the fact that he impregnated an impregnable woman." She exhales after that rant.

My eyes are saucers and I pat her iron-like shoulder for support. I try not to think about Connor's sperm or his sperm wearing a superhero cape. "If you have a baby, just think of all the cute clothes you can dress her or him up in." It's the only *pro* that I can think of.

"A baby isn't a doll," she refutes in a chilly tone. She struts forward, forcing my hand to fall. I doubt it was that comforting anyway. She reluctantly pulls out the pregnancy test from the tampon box.

"Okay," I say, regrouping. "Then give me a reason why you don't like children that has nothing to do with tantrums and dirty diapers."

She pulls her black panties down from her dress and stares at the stick before taking the test. "Besides the fact that they'll freakishly look like a hybrid of Connor and me," she says, "children are reflections of their parents. Anything they say or do is going to be seen as a product of my parenting choices." She shakes her head and this foreign fear darkens her face. "It's not like fucking up a math test, Lily."

She rolls her eyes, her guards rising again. And then she pees on the stick. "What does yours say?" she asks.

"Negative," I declare before I even pick it up. She flushes the toilet, and I grab my stick. "Two lines that's…" I snatch the directions, my heart catapulting to my throat. *No…*

After scrubbing her hands with soap and rinsing, Rose steps forward and leers over my shoulder to read the test. "*Lily*." Her brows rise in accusation.

"It's broken!" I point at the stick like it has betrayed me. I toss it into the sink. There's absolutely *no* way I'm pregnant. Right. Right?

Rose grips my shoulders, spinning me towards her. "Stay *calm*," she says in her unsympathetic voice.

I breathe out a long breath. Like I'm in a maternity class. Oh my God. I'm already doing pregnant things. I touch my cheeks that roast. "Am I burning up? I think I have seven-degree burns."

"No such thing," she says.

"What does yours say?" I ask, about to look over at the counter.

She clutches my shoulders harder. "Concentrate. One issue at a time."

Okay. But I can't help but notice her change in demeanor. My morose, panicked sister has put on her problem-solving attitude with a little too much excitement. She's avoiding her issues by focusing on mine.

"Has Lo been using protection?"

"No," I say. "Has Connor?"

Her glare ices over. "I'm on birth control. We've discussed this already."

Oh yeah. Okay.

"Breathe," she tells me.

I blow out a breath. I may be pregnant. "Oh my God."

"How late are you?" she asks, still quizzing me. My brain is trying to cross five different pathways at the same time.

"Um…" I blink repeatedly. "Oh um." I shake my head to collect my thoughts. "I skip my period with birth control." I don't know how late I am. I'm not Rose. I bet she has alerts in her cellphone for her next cycle.

"And you took all of your birth control? Every day? You didn't miss once?"

"I'm good about it," I say. "I always have..." I cringe. Shit. My head hurts as I wrack my brain for answers. When Lo relapsed and when the molestation rumors ignited instead of fizzling out, everything became really confusing and stressful. I must have been distracted and forgot.

The realization knocks me back a couple steps, but Rose holds onto my shoulders still, so I just sway a little like I've had too many morning mimosas. This can't be right. "It's wrong." I can't believe in this outcome.

If I'm pregnant...Lo will be devastated. He has expressed that he doesn't want children, not when alcoholism is hereditary. And we're not in a good place to have a baby. I don't know if we ever will be.

"It has to be wrong," I say again, this time meeting my fierce sister's narrowed gaze.

I wait for her to say: *it probably is.* Or: *there's no way you're pregnant.* But maybe it seems unrealistic. I'm a sex addict. I should've had an accident a long time ago, right? "We have anal sex," I blurt out, even raising my hand like it solves everything.

"So?"

"So we have lots and lots of anal sex, and the sperm can't go to the right place in that position." I am shrinking into myself, dodging the word "vagina" and "eggs" in one swoop.

"All it takes is one time *vaginally*," she says. "And what are you doing having *lots and lots* of anal sex? You shouldn't be having lots and lots of *any* sex. I thought you two were being more careful."

We weren't.

We haven't been careful since we ditched my therapist's blacklist. Nooners. Public sex. It has become our new routine. One that has filled us both with a sense of joy and normalcy.

"There's something that I have to tell you. Please do not scream." I tuck a piece of my hair behind my ear. "A little before my twenty-first birthday, Lo and I weren't doing so well. We had a major fight about sex…" I swallow a pebble in my throat. "I felt guilty for keeping him from it, and he was always restraining himself around me." I pause to gauge her reaction.

Anger has already shaded her face into something kind of demonic, her cheeks concaved and her arms crossed.

Shit. I just keep going. "You see, I didn't want the guy I'm with to be scared of me. And that's what it was starting to feel like. So…"

"You've been having *lots and lots* of sex," she finishes for me, her words crystalizing.

"Yeah, and we ditched my therapist's *suggested* rules."

Her mouth falls. "You did not."

"They were *suggestions*," I emphasize this part.

"Did you tell Dr. Banning? Did you let her in on what you've been doing or have you and Loren kept this from *everyone?*" *Well Daisy knows…*but I don't throw my youngest sister under the bus. Her loyalty must be rewarded.

"It's our sex life," I say softly. "We thought we had it under control."

"Now you're pregnant," she snaps. "How is that *under control?*"

Tears start to brim, and I wipe them quickly. "The test could be wrong…"

When she sees my tears, she rolls her eyes but stops attacking with every weapon in her arsenal. "How much is a lot?" she asks, planting her hands on her hips.

"I don't know…" I blink, trying to recall the amount. "Maybe two times, three, sometimes four."

"Every *day?*" The word is laced with acid.

My answer won't bring kind sentiments and good cheer, so my lips stay closed. I just nod.

"For two years, Lily?" She looks like she's going to cry. Maybe because I never trusted her with this information.

"I'm sorry," I whisper. "It was working..." Until now. I can't touch my abdomen. Is there really something in there?

"I'm surprised you haven't been pregnant ten times already."

"The test could be wrong," I exclaim, sticking to this one bit of hope. How can I tell Lo? It will send him off a cliff that I've been trying to draw him away from for months.

"I'll schedule an appointment for you so we'll know for sure," she says.

I nod, and my gaze drifts to the counter where her test lies. She is fixed to the floor, too scared to confront her own fate. So I do it for her, approaching the pregnancy stick.

Two lines.

Just like mine.

I shake my head, a weight lifting off my chest at a single thought. "These tests have to be broken, Rose. What's the probability that we both got pregnant at the same time?" It's all wrong. We're okay.

"Not impossible, obviously," she says, her body rigid like a board. "I'll schedule an appointment for me too."

I blow out another breath, this time it quakes my chin. "I can't tell Lo," I realize. Even if it's true, I don't know if I can tell him right away either. It'll crush him so much. I don't want to cause him any pain.

"I know," she says. "I'm not telling Connor."

My mouth falls. "Why?" He *wants* children. They've been married for a little over a year, and they've withstood a lot together, with no signs of parting. They channel power from the universe that only nerd stars can access. I'm sure of it.

The galaxy is on their side.

"He'll be *happy*." She says the word like it's disgusting. "And I want to process the awfulness of this situation for as long as possible without him gloating and grinning." She raises her chin like a declaration. "If he's truly as smart as he claims to be, he'll figure it out on his own."

I wonder if she really just wants to pretend like it's not happening for a while. It's weird, but Connor will probably like the challenge. Then again, maybe it isn't so weird. He's Connor Cobalt.

She appraises my mental state for a second, returning her worries back to me. "We'll help each other," she says. "And we won't tell anyone else until you're ready to tell Lo."

"*If* I'm pregnant," I say, but the waterworks have already begun again. Rose is usually right. She's the smart one, so the fact that she's not even considering an inaccuracy in the test—it makes it more real than I want it to be.

She rips off a piece of toilet paper and hands it to me.

I dry my eyes, realizing that if we're going to have any chance at hiding this, I can't leave the bathroom distressed and upset. I sniff.

"I'm here for you," she says in that icy, Rose Calloway voice. Strangely, it's become more than comforting. "We won't let each other down."

I nod. In the end, I have to do what's best for Lo. Even if it hurts.

Chapter 51

2 Years : 01 Month

September

LOREN HALE

"Where's Daisy?" Rose asks, strutting into the kitchen with Lily after they spent probably fifteen minutes together in the bathroom. Connor is right. I shouldn't question these things. It's Rose. She could've been asking Lily about sex, just overly concerned.

Connor dumps bacon into a bowl. Breakfast for dinner, Daisy's choice for her going away party. "The garage," he says. "Ryke went to check on her."

I watch Lily approach me. Her gaze rakes me in a slow once-over, landing on my crotch. I don't even think she realizes that she's doing it. Which actually makes me smile. She stops a foot from me, hesitating.

Screw that. I hook my fingers in the band of her leggings and pull her to my chest. She knocks straight into me, a gasp escaping her lips, and she sets her palms flat on my abs. I kiss her nose, and she blushes.

"Lo," she whispers, her heart beating quickly against me. Mine matches her speed, and I kiss her cheek. She breathes deeply, need flickering in her eyes but also something else…

She looks away from me, focusing on Connor and Rose who have a good five feet between them.

Rose has her arms crossed. "I hate your smile."

"You love my smile. That's why it annoys you, darling."

"Your backwards logic wouldn't make it past the first round of the Quiz Bowl Tournament."

He takes a step closer to her. "My logic is what won my team the Quiz Bowl Tournament. Four years. In a row."

She glares. "I hope your cat scratches your face tonight," she deadpans. Rose even mimics the claws with her hand.

He grins like she gave him the best compliment.

My eyes fall back to Lily. "Lil?"

"Did you talk to Ryke about dating?" she asks, dodging my teasing like I'm not even kissing her. Usually she'd at least smile back.

"Yeah…he says that he's not with your sister." We've *all* speculated that something's going on between him and Daisy ever since she moved into his apartment complex. He hasn't dated one single girl since then. He even *rejects* girls when they try to flirt or offer their number. It's weird.

"Maybe he has a secret girlfriend that's *not* Daisy," Lily offers a theory. He's with Daisy almost every day. Connor doesn't even think that's possible.

"I don't know…"

Lily anxiously rubs her arm, and her leg rises towards my hip, more out of impulse, a bad one. I can tell the difference by now.

"You okay, Lil?" I ask.

"Yeah," she breathes. She drops her leg, catching herself.

"You'd tell me if I was pushing you too far?"

She nods quickly. "I'm okay, really. A little…" She leans close and whispers, "*aroused*." Then she blushes again, but she ends up smiling nervously.

My lips rise. "I had no idea," I say. "We'll have to do something about that later." I kiss the corner of her lips, and her body curves into mine. My hand lowers to her back, sliding underneath the band of her—

"Loren," Rose snaps, completely ruining this.

I internally sigh and put some space between us. "Yeah?"

"How about you not grope my sister when I'm in the room?"

The irritation just storms right back inside of me. "How about you *not* verbally fuck your husband when I'm in the room, thanks?" I flash a smile.

Rose looks at me like I'm crazy. "I don't even know what you're talking about."

Connor leans against the kitchen counter with a growing smile, popping a grape in his mouth. Yeah, even when he eats, his lips pull upward in a rich grin.

"*I hate your smile*," I mimic her in a high voice. "*Your backwards logic wouldn't*…whatever." I can't even mimic her right. I wave her off and head towards the door. I need to get my brother and Daisy anyway. The food is all cooked.

As I open the door, I hear Rose's voice in the background. "I was not flirting with you, Richard."

I can pretty much feel his grin overtake his whole face.

"Hey," I call, stepping into the garage and shutting the door behind me. "Dinner is…" My face falls, morphing into a series of emotions.

Ryke and Daisy are on a parked motorcycle together, her legs wrapped around his waist, lying almost flat against the gas can near the handlebars. His body is pushed up against hers, no space between them. It's miles and miles away from innocent.

The worst part: just minutes ago Ryke told me that *nothing* was going on. I don't get it. I don't fucking understand why he has to lie to me. I ask him if he has feelings for her. He says no. I ask him if they're fucking. He says no. I ask him *anything* and he gives me responses he thinks I want to hear. He's walking on egg shells for me, and I just need the fucking truth.

Every day, I feel like I'm going out of my goddamn mind.

Anger drives into me. From so many places. I can't stop it. Ryke climbs off the bike, acting guiltless about the whole ordeal. Daisy follows suit, and when they're both standing on the concrete, I go off.

"Did I interrupt something?" I ask my brother.

"No," Ryke says. "We were just talking."

I nod repeatedly. There are fears so deep that I can barely touch them. He could fuck over Daisy. Break her heart. He could betray me. And break mine. I just need him to give me *something*. Tell me that he loves her. Tell me that *this* is more than what I think it is. *Anything* that can put these doubts to bed.

I ask, "If you were *just* talking, then why were her legs wrapped around your waist?"

"Lo," Daisy cuts in. Ryke raises his hand, silently telling her to stay out of it.

"We're friends," Ryke says to me.

That's all he gives me: *We're friends.* I shake my head. "Friends don't do shit like that." I point at the Ducati that they were *just* on together.

Ryke pinches the bridge of his nose, his jaw hardening. "What do you fucking want me to say?"

Anything. "That what I just saw was a mistake!" I shout.

His lips tighten. He just stares at me. I want to punch him right now. Maybe then he'll tell me the truth.

"It was a mistake," Daisy says. "I wanted to see what it would be like to ride on a motorcycle backwards. I needed his help."

I look between them. Is she serious? "That's the best lie you can come up with?"

She smiles. "It's actually the truth."

"This isn't a fucking joke, Daisy. He's seven years older than you. He's been with more girls than you probably even realize." I don't want to bring a person in her life that'll just screw her and leave her. I can't handle that.

"No," she says, "I realize that he's slept with a lot of women, but his number is probably one that I would have easily reached at twenty-five too."

I grimace. Sometimes I think she puts on this act like *"I'm so old and experienced"* just for my brother. "I'm in an alternate universe right now."

"Really?" Daisy says with a lopsided smile, one that brightens her whole face. It reminds me that she's still young and may be able to escape all of this. I want something better for her than my brother. She has the opportunity to leave Philly behind, date a guy without so much baggage. She can be so fucking free. "Cool," she nods. "Is it more fun here? I think it is." She turns to Ryke. "What do you think?"

His eyes never leave me. "Tone it down." And then he says, "Lo—"

"You're not good enough for her," I interject. "You realize that, right?"

Ryke's muscles flex, as tense as me. "I care about Daisy just as much as you, if not more, so you don't need to pull this overprotective bullshit on me."

I want to believe that. So badly. The side of me that I hate most never will. "It's not bullshit if you're fucking her," I say.

"We're not fucking!" he shouts.

The door opens, and Connor, Rose and Lily slip into the garage.

Lily stands next to me with a heavy frown. "What's going on?" she whispers.

"I caught them fucking on her motorcycle." I literally say it to be mean.

Ryke groans. "Come on! We were both on the bike, fully fucking clothed. We've *never* had sex!" He shakes his head. "How many times do I have to say it?" *I don't know. I don't know how to give you a fucking break when I rarely get one.* It's the cruelest part of my soul. "You know what," he says, "we might as well fuck if you all think we've done it a thousand times already."

"Whoa, whoa." I cringe and raise my hands. "I can't stomach you guys doing it once. So please spare me the goddamn picture of it happening a thousand times."

"Both of you," Connor chimes in, stepping off the short stairs that lead down into the garage, "stop for a second." He stands between us. "You're overreacting."

Probably. But sometimes it feels good to see the anger flash in my brother's eyes. Like we're on equal playing fields. It's sick, I realize.

"I don't like being accused of things that I didn't fucking do," Ryke growls.

That just about kills me. "Yeah? How do you think Dad feels?!" It comes out before I can stop it. The garage deadens with silence, my hostile voice echoing. I have not *once* pressured Ryke for a statement. I won't either.

But every day he remains quiet is another day I fight this alone. All he has to do is go to the press. That's it. If he can't vouch for our dad, then why can't he at least vouch for *me?* Yeah I'm not the greatest person to be around, but he's been by my side for three goddamn years. That has to count for something.

I swallow, realizing he's not going to say anything. I can't force him to speak out. It's too big of a deal. "She's eighteen," I tell him, sticking to the topic.

"Here we go." Ryke tosses his arms in the air. "Let's fucking hear it, Lo. She's eighteen. She's like your little sister. Her mom hates me. I know. I know. I fucking *know*."

Pain ripples through me. *I'm sorry.* Am I though? I just feel like shit. Lily's arm slides around my waist, and my shoulders begin to relax. I exhale.

It's not over though. I've always been a machine gun, another bullet ready after I press the trigger. Most of the time, I'm just waiting for it to ricochet. And finally hit me.

Chapter 52

2 Years : 01 Month

September

LILY CALLOWAY

I skirt past the kitchen, training my focus on the living room and the remote. Not Loren Hale, who closes the fridge, a water bottle in hand. I am *not* even going to glance at his gorgeous bone structure, those sharp-as-ice cheekbones or the pink lips that turn into a sexy pout when he glares. Or his intense amber eyes that always stare *straight* into me.

It's just me and the remote.

Right on the couch cushion.

"Hey," Lo calls after me.

"Hey back," I reply, not slowing down. *Hello, remote.* I sidle to the couch and before I even plop down, Lo runs to catch me. In a flash, he clasps my bicep, stopping me. I let the surprise float across my face. "Do you have Peter Parker reflexes? Why didn't you tell me you were bitten by a radioactive spider?"

He doesn't laugh or even acknowledge my joke. "Why are you acting so weird?"

"Weird how?" My stomach does a dance, the kind of nervous dance that only middle school students can relate to.

"You're avoiding me."

Okay. He's right on that account. On my way to the doctor with Rose, we had a major flat tire, which was a bad, bad sign, doomed from the start. So by the time the doctor said *you're pregnant* to both of us, I resigned to the fact that this was some real cosmic injustice.

And that I better get my shit together so the news doesn't break Lo. Rose is two weeks further along than me, so she may have to announce her pregnancy before I do. But I just have to wait for the best moment, the perfect time where Lo is in a better place. I'm hoping it'll come before I start showing. It has to.

"Lily," he snaps, waving his hand in my face. "Are you even with me?"

Keeping this from Lo is like carrying around a grenade, not knowing when it'll blow up. "I'm not avoiding you," I say swiftly.

"You *just* walked right past me," he argues, "and yesterday, you didn't even wait to shower with me." Shower sex. I skipped shower sex. That had to be a big red flag. His eyebrows pinch together, hurt coursing through his features. "Did I do something? Are you mad at me?"

"No," I say, a knife wedging itself in my ribcage. "I just wanted to go longer without having sex so frequently. You know, see if I can do it. Like a personal goal or something."

His muscles loosen in an instant. "Can you let me know when you're planning these personal goals?"

I nod. "Good news," I say, rising on my tiptoes and hooking my arms around his neck, "I've completed it."

His lips curve upward, and his hands fall to my ass, squeezing and building a strong pressure like sexual magic. He walks me back into the couch, and I lie against the cushions, the remote digging into my shoulder blade. I toss it on the floor and feel the weight of Lo's toned body bearing down on mine.

A noise catches in my throat, and my heart skips, utterly transfixed by his lips. I try to lean up to touch them with mine, but he places his palm on my chest, flattening me against the couch.

"I don't like this game," I tell him.

His knees rest on either side of my hips, straddling me and making it near impossible to roll off the couch or to acquire a long, sultry kiss.

"You don't?" His brows rise, and his hand disappears up my thin cotton shirt. Gliding over my skin, teasing me. It's a rush that fills me with need.

"*Yes*," I breathe. Yes? Was that the right response?

"Looks like you're stuck here," he says.

Yes. I try to focus, but that hand is creeping up my abdomen at such a slow, intoxicating pace. "No kissing?" I whisper.

He bends down, and his lips brush the nape of my neck, his nose nuzzling me. I cry a little, the sensations blistering and pulsing inside of me. His tongue slides against my soft skin, and I shudder, my limbs trembling beneath him.

Not fair. So not fair. I am a goner. I let out a hoarse ragged breath, and then wedge my arm between our bodies, enough that I can place a hand on the outside of his pants. When I begin rubbing, he groans into my neck.

Ha! I take it a step further and slide my hand underneath the elastic of his gym shorts but over his tight compression shorts, like spandex that most guys wear to keep their stuff in place when they work out. Very little fabric lies between my palm and his cock.

Lo rocks his pelvis, sucking gently on my neck, and his lips travel to mine in a brief moment, attacking with feverish hunger. *Yes. God yes.*

Instead of moving my hand, I let him grind his body against me. My lips ache and swell, and my panties begin to soak. When I feel him harden, I let out a sharp breath and try to slip my fingers beneath his compression shorts.

But he rests his palm on top of my hand, silently telling me to keep it there.

He kisses slower, and his tongue flicks in and out of my mouth, the best French kisser in the whole wide world. I think I could do this forever. Well, not *forever.* I need a release sooner or later, but foreplay has never been better between us. I revel in the beforehand now. Each moment means something. It's not just about the climax.

Though something hard, *really* hard, right inside of me would be just about perfect.

"Hey, get the fuck off each other." Ryke's voice wakes me from my blissful thoughts. A pillow assaults my side.

Lo props his body up with one arm, just enough to detach his lips from mine and reveal exactly where my hand has journeyed. In Lo's shorts. On his cock.

Should I look over? I do. I glance at Ryke, who towers over the couch. My elbows heat in a shade of rash-red. Ryke crosses his arms, a dark accusing look on his face. "The couch is a public area."

"We weren't fucking," Lo refutes with a half-smile. "Thanks for the concern, *bro.*" He helps me retrieve my hand from his shorts because I have frozen in a pit of embarrassment.

"Ten minutes later and you might have been," he notes. "I really want to fucking go. The weight benches are probably all taken, so can you hurry up?"

"Yeah give me ten minutes."

"Not *with her*," he says. "It's the middle of the afternoon." Shit.

Lo's jaw muscles tic, and he rises to his feet. "Ten minutes *alone*, I got it."

I cover my hot face with my hands, watching out of the cracks of my fingers. I can't touch myself. For other people, it's not so dangerous. For me, it may trigger my compulsions. Losing thoughts and time to porn and masturbating—not again. I don't want to regress, not with this baby ticking inside of me.

I just need…to forget about the pulsing between my thighs. *Do not think of what it feels like to climax, Lily. Think about ugly thoughts. Unattractive things.* I glance at Ryke, his scowly unshaven face and general broodiness. It almost kills my arousal. *Almost.*

Lo pauses beside the couch, and his eyes fall to me. "You're coming with us, Lil."

"Nonono," I say. "I'm coming with you, not him." I point a finger at Ryke, thusly removing a hand-shield from my face.

Ryke groans. "Really, Calloway?"

"Not that type of coming, Lil," Lo says with a small smile, making me like less of a sex-crazed freak. He nudges my shoulder with his knee. "To the gym, okay?"

I nod, nervous flutters in my belly. I can hold out.

I realize I've crossed my legs. I'd like something very, very hard still. *Don't think about it.* Right. Unattractive things. *Ryke Meadows. Ryke Meadows.*

I breathe out.

"Don't leave her," Lo tells Ryke. It's not a question.

His fear lingers long after he leaves, like a dust storm he kicked up in his wake. I think I'm okay. Wet, aroused, but I can wait until tonight. No porn or touching. It's not what I really want anyway. Loren Hale is my one true desire.

A couple seconds pass, the silent, awkwardness in the room disturbs me. I still lie on the couch, afraid to uncross my legs at the current moment.

"Can you talk?" I ask, tempted to just burrow in this couch like a naked mole rat and never return to see daylight.

"Sure," he says roughly, which makes me a little scared of what comes next. "We should talk about how I now have to wait for your boyfriend to jerk off before we can go to the gym."

I cringe and let my other hand fall from my face. "Doesn't it skeeve you out that you're talking about your *brother* jerking off?"

He rolls his eyes and throws another pillow at me. Seriously annoying. Mood killer. I brighten. It's working, and I don't even think Ryke meant to be my sexual repellant.

"Who instigated that?" He gestures to the couch. "You or him?"

"It was mutual," I reply defensively.

He opens his mouth and then closes it quickly, as though trying to choose the right words. That doesn't happen that often. Ryke speaks on impulse with me. Finally he lands on this: "Are you okay?"

My lips part, not able to say anything, half out of shock.

"Don't look so fucking surprised," he says. "I care about you. It's just…Lo has been in a bad place. All my concern has been directed towards him for a while."

"Mine too." Slowly, I sit up and hug one of the pillows to my chest, able to sit Indian style well enough. It's not so bad. "I'm really worried about him." I pause, collecting my thoughts. "He told me that he's going out west with you and Connor, on a road trip, instead of going to rehab." When he uttered those words, I started to cry. Anytime we're separated it feels like someone has ripped a piece of me away, but this time, the tears were more from the shock of the situation. The longer we sat and discussed it, the more it felt right.

I hope that when he returns he'll be in a much better place, enough to handle more news. I'm not even sure if keeping this secret will be easier or harder with him absent.

"I didn't think rehab was a smart choice," Ryke says. "Not with the press. I don't think he can deal with more attention from the media."

"I know," I say, remembering every headline about his hospital trip. It's bad enough that he broke his sobriety and landed there, but to have the whole nation in on it—it's ten times worse. It made his recovery harder, and it was one reason why he drank again afterwards. He even told me so. "Thanks for that." I look to Ryke. "For offering an alternative."

He shrugs like it's nothing. But it's not nothing. I saw the relief in Lo's eyes when he told me about this pseudo-rehab away from cameras and the press.

Ryke takes a seat beside my feet, and he runs his hand through his dark brown hair. "Do you miss public sex or something?"

"Huh?" I frown at the quick subject change and tense at the actual topic.

"You were practically fucking in the living room," he says, keeping eye contact with me. Which makes the awkwardness amplify by about ten notches. "Is it because you miss it? The public sex, I mean."

I sometimes forget that Ryke is comfortable by most things. "Yeah…I miss it a lot," I lie. The truth: Lo and I had sex in the pool a few weeks ago while Connor and Rose spent a long weekend in London.

"You know that you shouldn't be ashamed of liking it. It's not wrong," he tells me. This is definitely a Ryke Meadows ploy to make me comfortable.

My cheeks heat. Half out of embarrassment and the other half out of fear. This is not how I want Ryke to discover my "extra sex" secret.

He can learn the same way as Rose, when I eventually tell him that I'm pregnant.

"Not that this makes me a sex addict," he prefaces, "but I prefer to have sex in places besides a bed."

I perk up, more interested. *I knew it.* All of those bathroom breaks with Melissa during a Cancun trip years ago suddenly make more sense. He even did it on the plane. It's very rare for me to find someone who enjoys these things. Maybe because I just don't talk about sex all that much.

"Like where?" I ask.

"I've fucked all over," he says conversationally. I must admit, he has a gift in speaking without restraint or shame. It's like he owns who he is to the fullest degree.

I wish I could be like that about sex. But I think it's a little different being a girl.

"The beach," he lists.

I shake my head. "Sand is evil."

"But in the early morning, it's so fucking beautiful."

I can't recall a morning beach hookup for myself. Night, most definitely.

"Bathrooms," he continues.

"Even the dirty ones?" I ask.

He shrugs. "Honestly, I don't really notice." He adds, "Parks, elevators, golf courses, locker rooms, the woods—love the woods."

"Did you ever have sex at your high school?" I ask.

He nods. "Under the bleachers like a cliché."

I smile. "Me too."

He raises his water bottle in a toast.

"Lo and I had sex in a movie theater once," I tell him. "He actually bought every ticket just so we could do it."

Ryke's brows shoot up. "Before you went into recovery, I assume."

I nod. It was when he wanted to satiate my every whim and desire, which turned into one big enabling factory. But it was fun. I can't deny that. Even though we're having public sex, I doubt Lo would ever buy out a theater again. Some things go too far.

"I fucked this gypsy at a carnival once," he says, his arm stretching over the back of the couch, "right underneath her table. We knocked over the crystal ball." He smiles at the memory like it's a good one. Like the whole event was more than just a climax for him. That's not how I ever saw sex. I didn't seek out wild places to fuck. They were just convenient at the time. Settings to get me what I wanted.

"I did it at a carnival or amusement park or…whatever," I say. "On the Ferris wheel though."

"While it was moving?" Surprise infiltrates his voice.

"Yeah, I mean, he didn't last long." My throat tightens, trying not to think about the messy details.

Ryke's face falls a little. Maybe he's just now realizing that I'm not talking about Lo. I test out this theory by saying, "I also did it with a guy I met at a cotton candy booth. Same night."

He shifts forward, removing his arm from the couch, darkness clouding him. I can tell he's trying to push it away, but when his gaze meets mine, there's more understanding, more empathy for my addiction than I've ever seen before.

Me and him. We're not the same. He can reminisce about all the places he's fucked with laughs and smiles, rehashing stories that involve beginnings, middles, and satisfying conclusions. With orgasms and no shame in the end. My past is littered with hurt and regret. I'd rather leave it all in the fog.

He was right. He won't ever join my club.

It's just me.

By my lonesome.

How it should be.

"You ready?" Lo's voice wakes me from my reverie. He stands in the doorway with wet hair and a sharpened jawline. His eyes flit from my head to my toes, assessing my state. And then he nods to me like *you're okay.* I rise to my feet and gladly walk straight into his arms.

Maybe I'm not so alone.

Chapter 53

2 Years : 01 Month

September

LILY CALLOWAY

Landed. Flight was pretty good, almost no turbulence. – Lo

Rugby World Cup is going on in Paris this weekend. Horrible traffic. – Lo

Daisy looks shaken up. – Lo

I scroll through my old text conversation with Lo, rereading each word. His road trip with his brother and Connor had to take a major detour and pit stop for my little sister.

She had some sort of night terror...are you sure you don't want to come up? – Lo

Is Rose raging right now? – Lo

Rose paces in front of me, slamming her fingers violently on the screen of her phone. Raging, yes. Fuming, yes. She growls and looks like she's ready to chuck her phone across the room. "Connor won't snap a picture of her and send it to me," she says. "How am I supposed to verify that Daisy is okay without *evidence?*"

I rest an elbow on the checkout counter at Superheroes & Scones, the store opening in a couple hours. "Trust," I say, a pit in my stomach. "We have to believe that they're telling us everything." I scroll through my messages again, silently cursing Lo for being such a brief texter.

I should just focus on my book that's cracked open for my Options, Futures and Financial Derivatives course. Every page is highlighted with neon yellow marks, my fingertips stained that color. But the sentences blur together, my mind in Paris with the guys and my little sister.

"We can fly in tomorrow," I suggest.

Lo did call to deliver a more detailed account of what happened. Daisy was thrown out of a runway show only minutes before she was supposed to walk, and the designer basically ripped off her clothes. In front of everyone backstage. I would have been mortified if that was me, so I wasn't surprised that she was upset. But I am a little shocked that she chose to call Ryke and *only* Ryke about the incident.

He immediately wanted to check up on her in person. And when they spent the night, Daisy woke them up, screaming like she was being murdered. Apparently she was "stuck" in a nightmare…or something like that.

Chills still prick my skin every time I imagine it. Lo said, "It was horrifying." *It was horrifying.* I want to jump on a plane and hug my sister, not leave her with our significant others and Ryke.

"We can't fly in tomorrow," Rose tells me, her eyes still narrowed at her cellphone. "You won't graduate."

After being delayed for so long, I can almost feel the crisp paper of my diploma, so close. But I have a huge exam, and if I don't make the date, I'll be given a big fat zero. My professor said, "In order to be excused, you need to be dying in a hospital." This particular professor isn't fond of the "celebrity special treatment" either, so I have to be there.

In the flesh.

"You can go," I remind her, already feeling a bout of guilt for not being present for Daisy. I don't want to hold Rose back too.

She pockets her phone in her clutch and sidles up to the counter. I smell coffee being brewed by one of the employees. "I'm not leaving you," she says. I read into the rest: *not while you're pregnant.*

I give her a weak smile.

Rose straightens up. "Now where are your notecards? I'll quiz you."

I fish them out of my backpack at my feet and pass the disorderly stack to her.

She snorts. "Connor is a horrible tutor. He didn't even teach you to rubber band these."

"He did," I say, even though I thought that "helpful tip" was pretty self-explanatory. "I just always lose the rubber bands." My tablet pings on the counter. I've been entrusted with the internet to study for my exam, but I may have also setup notifications for certain tags on Tumblr.

I don't deny it.

I'm still a little obsessed.

I just don't want another surprise like the one about Lo's dad. Plus, I sometimes fear that the pregnancies will just pop up online. That *cannot* be the way Lo finds out.

Swiping my finger across the screen, I power the tablet on and check the alert: *1 New from #Coballoway*. I click into the tag, and my cheeks burn at the gif of Connor's hand gripping Rose's bottom, her ass already a little red. I quickly click out. *I didn't see it.*

Rose finishes straightening my cards together and gives me a look. "Why are you all flushed?" I'm flushed in embarrassment, not arousal, just to be clear. Her eyes flit to the tablet. "Lily, do you have *internet* on there?"

"Just a little bit," I blurt out.

"Okay"—she snatches the tablet from me—"you can't have a little bit of internet." She logs into my settings.

"It's for work purposes, and you know, *studying*." I tap my highlighter to my book for further emphasis.

"Stick to your notecards."

She just doesn't trust me as much since the doctor's office. I think she's waiting for me to slip back into my old, destructive porn-filled routine. Which is understandable. But she's pregnant too and…

My eyes grow big as my thoughts take a dangerous turn. "Rose," I whisper, leaning close, "are you going to be able to have sex now that you're pregnant?" I frown, thinking harder. Oh my God. "Can I have sex when I'm really, really pregnant? *Oh my God*. What about right afterwards?" I lunge for my tablet. I need answers. Answers that the worldwide web can provide.

"Lily," Rose snaps, raising the tablet over my head. Damn her heels. "Be calm."

"Aren't you freaking out? Just a little. Even internally?"

"Internally I'm rolling my eyes at you," she deadpans.

Oh. "These are valid questions." I point at her. "You should be more worried. I mean, you and Connor do it like…" I trail off.

"Like what?" Her eyes pierce me through the skull.

"Like…rough, and you're into bondage."

"So?" she says.

"How is it?" I suddenly ask.

The break room door breezes open, drawing our attention to a makeup-less girl with straight black hair, big rimmed glasses and rosy cheeks. She flashes the Vulcan salute, a clipboard tucked underneath her other arm. "Live long and prosper." She smiles and then says another greeting in Korean.

Did I mention that I am in love with our new store manager? Ryke can't have her.

Rose taps her nails on the counter, watching Maya Ahn slip behind it. All our conversations about babies and sex have disappeared with the threat of eavesdropping. Worst case scenario: The news is leaked to the press before we tell Connor and Lo. That is a nightmare of hellish proportions.

The silence drags and Maya spins around from the coffeemaker. "Did I interrupt something?" She pushes her glasses up with a finger.

"No," I say quickly. "We were just talking about…breast implants." Ohmygod. I clear my throat. "Mine are kinda small…" I actually don't have a problem with my boobs, but it was the first thing that jumped from my lips.

Rose stares at me like I just purchased my one-way ticket on the crazy train. "And *I've* been telling Lily that her boobs are fine how they are."

Maya doesn't look fazed by the conversation. "As long as you're happy with yourself, it doesn't really matter how you look, right?" She starts the coffee pot and it gurgles in response.

"True," I say with a nod. "I think I'm going to stick with these."

"Okay." Rose grabs her purse off the counter and starts towards the door. "I need to get to Calloway Couture to prep for opening. Come along, Lily. You can study in my break room."

"I have a break room," I motion to the backdoor.

"Yes, but my couches are better." Her eyes turn fierce. Okay. Jeez.

"See ya!" Maya calls out as we leave through the front door. The wind hits me and I release a large breath. Close call.

"At least we'll know how trustworthy she is," Rose says as we walk across the street. The people standing in line at Superheroes & Scones whip out their smart phones to snap pictures of us. I'm a little surprised no cameramen pop up out of the thin air.

"Why is that?" I ask. Rose unlocks her store door and I shut it behind me.

"Because if tomorrow's headline reads *Lily Calloway is getting a boob job* then you can fire her." She pauses in thought. "Actually, that's not a bad idea. Plant a lie for your staff and see if they feed it to the press. Weed out the betrayers." She grins like she found her new tactic for her own store.

My phone buzzes before I can compliment her evil strategy.

Miss you. –Lo

I take a deep breath and try not to count the days until I see him again.

Chapter 54

2 Years : 01 Month

September

LOREN HALE

Loren, where did your father touch you?

I can still the feel the heat of the flashes as we walked down the Paris city street, the paparazzi bombarding us, a whole ocean away from where we live. Walking. Just walking. Became a nightmare.

Why hasn't your brother made a statement to the press? Does Ryke know the truth, Loren?

I sit on a barstool in a pub, gripping a glass with dark carbonated liquid. I try to focus on the Rugby World Cup playing on every television screen, but I can't distance myself from all the questions today. No matter how hard I try.

Connor says something to me, a plate of fries between us, but I lose track of his words.

"Whatever," I mutter, my voice biting and cold. I sip my drink, the bitter taste of liquor sliding down. Beginning to numb my head. But not fast enough.

Connor has to know I ordered a Fizz and whiskey when he went outside to call Rose. He's not an idiot, and while his demeanor never changed, he stepped out again. I'm guessing to call my brother.

Lo, what about Lily?!

I grit my teeth. My eyes sear like someone rubbed salt in them. I glare at the rows and rows of bottles behind the bartender. I don't want to think about this.

Did your father ever touch, Lily?

I chug the rest of my drink. I flag down the bartender and then point to my glass. She nods, understanding. *Has your girlfriend been molested?*

Where did your father touch her?

Stop.

Thinking.

Today.

It was the first day that I've ever heard Lily's name thrown around with this mess. I just want everyone to see the truth. To realize how much damage they're doing to my family by speculating. Instead, every lie keeps growing into a bigger one. I don't see how it'll ever end.

Connor looks between me and the television, eating a fry.

"Did you hear," I finally say, "that Sara Hale is going to be interviewed on television?" Some sort of tell-all special. "She's going to bury my dad." And I'll be dragged down with him.

The bartender slides the newly-filled glass towards me. She avoids eye contact, fear in her brows. She's afraid of me. I must wear the worst fucking glare—like I'm sitting here hoping that the world burns with me in it.

I partly do.

And then I take another sip, a buzz barely even present.

"Sara has nothing to gain from that," Connor says easily, as if the matter is settled.

"Not everyone is like you," I retort spitefully, clutching the cold glass. "Everything Ryke's mom has ever done is because she hates Jonathan."

"I never said that she wouldn't lie on camera. I just meant that it'll solve nothing for her if she does. So revel in that fact. I am."

"You go ahead and revel in that, Connor." An acidic taste sears my throat. "You'll be the only one."

"I'm used to being the only person who thinks intelligently. I honestly can't expect everyone to reach my level."

His arrogance doesn't fuel me like I thought it would. Maybe because he takes my insults and just creates more of his own. It makes being an asshole easier. "Cheers," I say raising my drink and taking a long gulp.

It's not that sharp. If I could, I'd just drink whiskey straight.

The bar erupts in exclamations and overly energetic shouts at the rugby match. French chatter overwhelms the small pub. Just as the noise begins to die down, a hand rests on my shoulder. "Hey," Ryke says.

I just sip my drink.

"How was shopping?" he asks, his voice deep, like black, rolling clouds before the downpour.

"Boring." I eat a fry and glower straight ahead, ready for his onslaught of: *what the fuck are you doing? How could you break your sobriety again? Stop this stupid fucking shit.*

It doesn't feel stupid. He doesn't have to be rushed by cameras and *people* that see a victim of a crime that never happened. Doesn't he fucking get it?

I will always be Loren Hale: the guy who was touched inappropriately by his father.

And now Lily…

Ryke drags an empty stool between Connor and me, and I grind my teeth. I wait for Connor to move back, but he stays quiet.

Fine.

Whatever.

Ryke motions to the female bartender, and my muscles constrict. "What can I get you?" she asks.

"What he's having." He points to the glass.

The bottom of my stomach drops, realizing his stupid ploy. All so I can admit, out loud, that I'm a fucking idiot. I'm a bastard. I get it! I know what I am, and it's no one good. I down the rest of my drink in one swallow. "I'm done. Let's just get out of here." I stand off the barstool. *This isn't happening.* I don't *need* him to do this. Why can't he just let me go this once? I just need to breathe.

His hand grips my shoulder. "Sit your ass down. I want a fucking drink." He literally forces me back onto the stool.

"You sound like Dad, you know that?" I retort. *Just tell him. Just say the fucking words*: I drank. They rise in a jagged ball to my throat. And I keep swallowing them.

The bartender begins to make his drink, setting ice in a glass.

"Ryke," I snap, forcing his gaze towards mine. A purplish bruise mars his cheekbone, from when Daisy slapped him while she was having a night terror.

"What?" His jaw is hard. His eyes never softening. He reminds me of our dad. And it makes this more difficult. It makes it worse.

I inhale a strained breath, the oxygen never meeting my lungs. In my peripheral, I see the bartender grabbing the whiskey. "Let's go."

"I told you. I want a fucking drink."

Why is he doing this? I tug at the collar of my shirt and turn back around, setting my forearms against the cold bar. Ryke has been sober for nine years.

Nine goddamn years.

Why would he even toy with the idea of breaking that? For me? My stomach roils, the alcohol making me more nauseous than anything.

"Refill?" the bartender asks me.

I shake my head. "No, I'm good." I hate him. I hate that he's pushing me this hard. I hate that he won't leave me alone. I hate that he expects more out of me than I can ever give.

I am falling.

Beneath every sentiment I expel.

"Cheers." Ryke raises his glass, pausing for a brief second, giving me an out. Telling me to stop him.

Stop him.

Stop him.

The rim hits his lips.

I am rigid. I am screaming at myself to move. To be a goddamn decent human being. To be worth this life that I've been given. And yet, I watch him, with deadness inside of me.

He drinks alcohol.

And I think: *now we're even.*

For having the better life. For knowing about me for so long and doing nothing. For not standing up for me in the media and ending this torment.

It's a thought that twists my face with brutal guilt.

He licks his lips, disappointment flashing in his eyes. Why does he have to be so goddamn good?

"I hope you enjoyed that," he says angrily.

"Which part?" I snap on impulse. "Me drinking or watching you do it?"

Hit me. His muscles flex, a vein pulsing in his neck. And instead of raising his fist, he grabs the glass, about to drink more.

My lungs explode, and I pry it from his fingers quickly and hand it to the bartender. "He's done." I start to slide off the barstool as I say,

"If you're this big of an asshole sober, I can't imagine what kind of asshole you are drunk."

Before I leave, he grabs my arm. "You can't do this shit." *Stop. Talking.* "You're supposed to call me if you have a craving to drink. I could have talked you out of it."

"Maybe I don't want to talk to you!" I scream. I climb off the barstool, and he follows suit, standing one inch taller. Face to face. Both wearing scowls so dark that you'd think we were mortal enemies, not brothers.

There is so much he's never told me about his past. And I keep waiting to hear it. I never push. That's not something I'd ever do to him. But the longer he stays quiet, the harder it's become for both of us. We've hit a roadblock in our relationship, and I'm banging my head against brick while he watches me bleed.

"Then call Lily," he says, "your fucking fiancée, who would be in tears if she saw you right now. Did you fucking think about her when you drank? Did you consider what this would do to her?"

No. I can't think about her when I drink. It hurts too much. "I'm done with this shit," I say. I try to walk away from this.

He grabs my arm.

Let me go. Please.

"You can't run from your fucking problems. They're there twenty-four-seven. You have to deal."

"Don't talk about *dealing*. You won't even text Dad back. You're ignoring him like he's not even alive." I shake my head. "You're doing the same thing to him that you did to me. So why don't you just do what you do best and pretend that I don't fucking exist."

I watch the pain take ahold of his features. I stabbed him the only way I know how, and then I just push right on by.

I just leave.

Wishing that I was someone else.

Chapter 55

2 Years : 01 Month

September

LOREN HALE

Outside of the pub, Daisy howls at the stars, standing on the sidewalk. “We’re in the land of tall people!”

My brother starts talking to her. He’s smiling.

I shift my dead gaze to the night sky. I want to be happy that Daisy isn’t as sullen as when we first arrived, though she looks frail and sleepless circles shadow her eyes. But she’s laughing.

That’s good.

Connor keeps a hand on my shoulder. I think if he takes it off I’m going to fall. He says something, but I barely register his words.

Sports fans in jerseys parade across the street in dead-stop traffic. The game must’ve ended.

I hate what I’ve done tonight.

It’s rushing back to me tenfold. Not enough liquor to numb this onslaught. A couple guys start screaming beside the curb, and I rest my hands on my head.

"Lo," Connor breathes.

I turn to him, but Ryke suddenly sidles up to us. Connor takes a step back so I can speak to my brother. And my eyes cloud with tears. "You shouldn't have had that whiskey," I say, the apology stuck in my throat.

Say it.

I can't. I pinch my eyes.

"One glass isn't going to make me fucking addicted, Lo."

I let out a weak laugh. "Lucky you." I cringe.

"We should go back to the hotel—" He suddenly careens forward, someone knocking into him from behind. I barely notice two beefy guys throwing punches.

And then a pair of knuckles decks my temple. I stagger to the side, almost tripping, my fingers scraping the pavement. The horrific screams bleed my ears, and in one instant, it's like a hurricane of people, arms flying, shoving—bodies slamming into each other.

My panic has shot up to a new level.

The end of an intense rugby match has brought the beginning of a riot. Ryke reaches out and grabs my arm. We lock eyes for an instant, exchanging a look like: *don't leave me.*

And then another fist pounds into the side of my face. The pain welling instantly. I grip his shirt, anything, and sock him in the gut, just so he'll get off me.

When I turn around, Ryke is being dragged backwards by his leather jacket. I try to sprint towards him, but someone clutches my shoulders and forcefully slams me to the ground.

A boot nails me in the ribcage, and my adrenaline drowns out the intensity of the pain. I elbow someone's shins, and I try to stand, but the boot side-swipes my head.

Fuck. Black dots burst in my vision.

"LOREN!" Connor yells.

Blood drips from my nose and to my lips. I taste the bitter iron. The screaming. Never ends. Glass shatters. Heat from fires blaze, but I can't see where they originate.

It's just pure chaos.

"LOREN!"

Another kick to the stomach, and I fall to my hands again. *Get up. You stupid bastard.* I punch back, meeting flesh. And I rise to my feet the same time that Connor reaches me with an unreadable expression, masking his alarm. Barely a bruise on his face.

"Where's Ryke?" My voice is filled with fear. I look around. "We have to find—" *Jesus. Christ.* Someone nailed me with something in the side. I cough roughly, and Connor is basically guiding me away from everything.

"Stop," I cough, my feet instinctively following his. I hold my ribs. "Connor, wait!" I scream.

"We have to go," Connor says, his eyes wide to tell me *now.*

"Ryke is out there!" I yell. I turn back around. *Daisy.* And I try to tear into the street, but Connor grabs my waist, two inches taller than me. And stronger. In almost every way.

He forces me back on the sidewalk, not the street where everyone has gone mad. Sirens blare in the distance, growing closer and closer.

"We have to leave!" Connor yells at me.

"I can't…" *I can't leave them.* I spin back to face Connor and shove him in the chest. "You would leave them?!" Tears wet my cheeks. I feel like I just put my brother to rest. And Daisy is gone with him.

"No," Connor says, his usually emotionless expression slowly unraveling. "I would save you."

Why.

I shake my head.

"He's strong," he reminds me. "He'll find Daisy, and we'll meet up with him."

He's strong.

It's hard to say no to someone like Connor. With his hand on my back, we push through the crowds, away from the fight.

Away from people who matter.

We walked for ten minutes before slipping into a drug store. I vaguely pay attention to Connor who disappears down an aisle. The cashier says something to me in English, about the riot. I think. I open my mouth to answer, but air catches in my lungs. I can't breathe.

I try to inhale.

I can't breathe. No bruise or welt amounts to this agony that pounds into me. I push through the doors, the cold night air blanketing me. And I gasp heavily, my hands on my thighs.

I puke on the curb.

Cop and ambulance sirens scream.

I wipe my mouth with the back of my hand, blood smearing from my nose.

"Lo," Connor says, appearing outside. He rests a hand on my back. His button-down is ripped by the collar. "Come on." He guides me along the sidewalk. It takes us more time to find a taxi, but when we do, we both climb in the backseat, the traffic horrendous. In French, Connor tells the driver our destination, and I zone out, patting my pockets.

"My phone." It must've fallen.

"Someone stepped on it back at the pub," he explains, digging in a paper bag. I stare at the headrest, slammed with tonight's events. With my brother being dragged by the jacket, away from me. I rewind to screaming at him—saying that I wish he never existed in my life.

I rewind further to forcing him to drink alcohol.

"Connor," I whisper, hot liquid pools in my eyes. What have I done? Connor holds the back of my head, but I can't stop these raging feelings. I can't stop the remorse or the fear of what's happened. He forces my gaze on his. "Please…" My chest falls heavily. "I can't…"

I can't deal with it anymore.

I don't want any of it.

Tears pour out of me, and I try to breathe—sharp pains stab my ribs with each one. My head floats from a lack of oxygen, and all I think is: *kill me.*

I am miles away from the one person who can talk me down from this edge. From the one person who has been with me every step of my life. Who has shared memories and moments that no one else will ever see. If I give up, she is gone.

I destroy this bond that transcends love, taking her soul with me.

It is the only thing that keeps me breathing.

I watch Connor bite a pill in half with his front teeth. His eyes flicker to mine, full of uncharacteristic concern that he rarely shows anyone.

"Are you putting me to sleep?" I ask.

"Not in the way you'd like," he says softly. He passes me half of the pill. "I can't take your pain away, no matter how much I want to." He pauses. "This is the best I can do for now."

Every moment of my life has been a mountain that I struggle to climb.

Chapter 56

2 Years : 01 Month

September

LILY CALLOWAY

"Lo," I say the minute Connor hands him the phone. He told me that Lo took a sleeping pill, so I only have a few minutes with him. Tears already stream down my cheeks, picturing them swept up in the Paris riot, footage on almost every news station. Rose and I didn't know that our sister and the guys were tangled up in it until we called Connor.

I sit on my bed with the comforter pulled up to my chest. Rose has left the room to tell Poppy that Daisy's in the hospital. Connor, Ryke, and Lo are in the waiting room, unsure of how badly her injuries are.

Rose and I already checked flights and threw clothes into carry-ons.

"Lily," he chokes. I hear the torment in his voice. I don't have to ask where it's from. The origins are most likely many, vast places.

My throat tightens, and I collect myself for him as much as I can. "I love you," is the next thing I say.

I can practically picture him pinching his eyes to dam the waterworks, his breathing sharper than usual. "I fucked up," he says.

"No," I tell him, as sternly as I can. "You didn't."

"You don't know what I did."

"It doesn't matter." I wish I could hug him. Why do we have to be so far apart?

And then he says with a broken voice, "I'm never going to defeat this."

"Lo," I breathe, licking my dry lips. "You're forgetting something."

He exhales deeply. "What's that?"

"We're in Earth-616. This isn't an alternate universe." I clutch the phone tighter, tears falling. "We're going to have our happy ending. It's just going to take us a little while to get there."

He told me that once. When I hit a low. Now he just needs to remember his own words.

He breathes out again, like a weight is slowly lifting off his chest.

"Do you believe me?" I whisper.

"Every word," he says. "I want to hold you."

I smile and wipe the rest of my tears. "You are."

"Yeah?" he murmurs. "Lily..."

I wait for him to finish his thought, one of my hands gripping my white comforter.

Very softly, he says, "I wouldn't be here without you." It is bigger than an *I love you.* It is a declaration that solidifies what I've known for so long.

We aren't connected by our addictions.

But by our childhood. Souls fused together from the very, very start.

Chapter 57

2 Years : 02 Months

October

LOREN HALE

Since the hospital four days ago, I haven't been able to produce a sentimental apology for my brother. Every time I try, something worse comes out of my mouth. Staying quiet has better results, but it also tears my stomach to shreds. I'm beginning to think that I hold back just to punish myself.

I run my hand through my hair before readjusting my baseball cap. I glance over my shoulder at the gas pumps, expecting a bombardment of cameras. It's quiet, trees rustling in the wind.

"No one is following us," Ryke reminds me, breaking a layer of tense silence. His eyebrow is stitched, the most severe of his wounds from the riot. I have two broken ribs, but I had to say no to pain pills. It'd be way too easy to rely on them.

Ryke and I stand outside of a gas station in Ohio, a grimy bathroom door in front of us on the side of the building. The road trip began in

New York and it'll end with Ryke climbing a few rock formations in Yosemite, California.

I've tried not thinking about that last part. Ryke never wears a rope or a harness. The probability of falling is greater than reaching the top. Connor even told me that. Heavy bricks set on my chest every time I accidentally process that end, the one where I outlive him.

The world is all fucked up if that happens.

"I can't help it," I say to Ryke, looking around for cameras just one more time. "I'm always going to be on edge." The media didn't have any footage of us in the riot, and we managed to leave the hospital without notice too. We were there for a while because of Daisy—she's okay. Not that okay. But she's walking. Breathing. And she quit modeling. Though…she would've had to regardless.

Ryke bangs on the bathroom door, the handle broken, which is why we're standing here, guarding it so no one walks in on her. "You need something, Dais?"

She's been changing her bandages. I check my watch. For fifteen minutes?

"The tape is stuck to one of my stitches." She sounds near tears.

Ryke doesn't even hesitate or ask, he just pushes through the door. He leaves it ajar so I'll follow him inside. I do. The space is cramped, and toilet paper is strewn on the damp tiles.

Ryke cups the side of Daisy's face and inspects the wound on her left cheek, half the bandage off. "Hold still," he tells her, peeling off the tape that pinches her skin and with it, a series of stitches. Her hands dig into his waist.

"Wait, wait a second," she winces.

"Dais," he says softly, his narrowed eyes on her. "This has to come off." Blood has soaked through the gauze and needs replaced.

I lick my lips. "Just think happy thoughts," I tell her.

She slowly starts to smile, which pulls at her wound. "Ow."

Wrong advice. "Think horrible thoughts," I say and then put a hand on my older brother's shoulder, "like your knight in shining armor falling off his pony."

She ends up laughing and touches her cheek, the pain barely reaching her green eyes that glimmer with something bright.

Ryke glares at me. "That's the best you have?"

"I don't see you offering anything, *bro*."

"Picture me beating the shit out of my brother," he says roughly, never looking away from me.

"Or the inverse," I snap back, our jaws locked. How'd we even reach this place? It's like a river of past history separates us, and I can't cross it without him.

Daisy's laughter has died out. "That's depressing," she tells us flatly.

Our attention returns to her. "That's the point," I say.

Her lips are downturned, and Ryke works on peeling back the tape, stitches still clung to it. Her eyes are already bloodshot at this point, and the signs of pain appear in the way she clutches my brother's green shirt.

"Are you sure you don't want your sisters out here?" I say to distract her. Rose and Lily are meeting us in a couple weeks, which'll be a surprise to Daisy. But they're adhering to her wishes as much as they can. Daisy just needs time to cope with what's happened.

"Lily has college," she says. "I don't want to ruin anyone's time."

Ryke rolls his eyes.

I tilt my head at her. "They want to see you."

"Not like this," she whispers, referring to her marred cheek.

And then Ryke removes the bandage completely. I scan her face, seeing the wound before, but not since she was asleep in the hospital. The large, reddened gash cuts from her temple to her jaw. Sliced but stitched straight through her cheek. Apparently she was hit with a board, something sharp on the end. The wound looks gruesome, especially on a girl as pretty as Daisy. It'll scar. There's no question about that.

She studies my reaction while Ryke unpackages a clean piece of gauze. "I'm happier, you know?" she says, her lips rising weakly. She's free from a profession that has been slowly making her sick for the past few years. And subsequently, she's free from her mom's ridicule.

I mask my expression by adjusting my baseball cap again. "I'm glad," I say. "But I'm never going to be happy that this happened to you." There could have been a thousand other ways for her to reach that point—to quit modeling. I'd never wish this for her, or any one of the girls.

"That's okay," she says softly, her long blonde hair falling at her waist. I have a feeling she's going to chop most of it off soon.

Ryke begins to cover her gash with clean bandages, and her arms slide further around his waist. To where his body is pressed against hers.

He whispers something to her, his lips brushing her ear, not discreet about it. They've never been. And then she smiles brightly, her fingers falling to the band of his jeans. Their embrace takes me aback, like a swift kick.

And it's in this single moment, that I know for certain, they're together.

So I ask: "Did I miss something?" I gesture between them, my jaw sharpening on instinct. I wait for my brother to tell me the whole truth. For once.

Please.

And then he takes a step back from Daisy with a pissed expression. Like I ruin everything. He's not even giving me a chance.

He says, "We're just friends."

Right. I nod a couple times. "I'll meet you at the car." Boiling. It goes beyond them together. It's that he can't be honest with me. He asks me for his complete trust, but it's becoming harder and harder when he builds walls between us.

He once said that I stand vulnerable in front of Connor, someone who wears layers and layers of armor while I bear all of myself to him.

Somewhere along the way, they switched places. I wonder what it'll take for him to finally see it.

LILY CALLOWAY

"I have been informed by higher officers at the Pentagon that there still exists a top secret UFO project. That's where your Roswell file is." – Brigadier General Richard Mitchell (Ret.)

I squint at one of the many quotes on the museum wall, each one about the Roswell aliens. I relax against Lo's hard chest, his arms draped over my shoulders. We reunited in the Smoky Mountains, and all seemed okay. Better than the phone call in the hospital. Even Daisy radiated with more life than usual, despite what's happened to her cheek.

She made it really hard to be upset for her—she's talented at that. But sometimes, I just want to hug her for an extended minute or two and put more attention on her, the good kind that she deserves.

"Did Wampa die from Tennessee to New Mexico?" Lo asks with a grimace. "It smells, Lil." Lo places a hand on my head—or rather on my Wampa cap.

"Shhh," I whisper.

And then he tries to snatch my white fuzzy *Star Wars* hat off my head. I hold the flaps of my Wampa protectively over my ears. "He does not," I refute and sniff just to make sure. Oh. It reeks of wood smoke from the campfire back at the Smoky Mountains. The moment my hands fall, Lo steals the hat from me, my hair poofing up from the static.

I pat it down, and he combs his finger through the messy strands. The Smoky Mountains didn't end on the best note, even if all the "before" parts were lighthearted enough. Though Rose did have a meltdown, brought on by hormones, and it got a little ugly.

I think Connor is onto her secret.

Not mine though.

Which means I *must* be smarter than her in this instance. I internally gloat at the idea.

The low moment in the mountains occurred right in the early morning. When we crawled out of our tent, the paparazzi sprung up out of the bushes. Literally.

In order to shake them off, we split up. Daisy and Ryke rode off together, and Lo, Connor, Rose and I drove our rental car the other direction. We're going to meet up sooner or later, but for now, we're separated from Lo's brother and my little sister.

"Do you think they're getting it on?" I blurt out. I should keep my thoughts to myself. "Nevermind," I slur together and grab his hand, quickly tugging him over to a glass casing of a spaceship model with dirt, labeled: **CORONA IMPACT POINT.**

"Whoa, slow down," he says, nearly running straight into me as I come to a halt.

"Look at this." I try to distract him from my statement by pressing my finger to the glass. "What if the dirt is real? Like from the actual crash?"

He gives me one of those cold Loren Hale looks that usually cripples people. I'm too used to them, really. They're more like pinches. Love pinches. "Who's getting it on?" he asks, his brows furrowing. He smashes Wampa in a ball, anger tensing his biceps.

"I was just thinking about how we all split up," I mutter under my breath. "Let's go listen to the radio recording." I try to tug him in another direction, but his feet stay glued to the floor.

And it clicks for him. "You mean your eighteen-year-old *little* sister and my twenty-five-year-old *older* brother?"

"When you put it like that, it sounds hotter than you think." I flush a little bit.

He doesn't make fun. "I don't see how. *Sister. Brother.* Immediately kills everything, Lil."

I shrug. "I kind of shipped them during *Princesses of Philly*. Didn't you?" He'll understand my fandom reference. To ship: aka, to fangirl hard over a prospective relation*ship*.

He cringes like it's a gross thought. "She was seventeen during the show. They're not even legitimately together."

"That's never stopped you from wanting a ship to sail." He's a not-so-closeted Sterek shipper from *Teen Wolf*.

He rolls his eyes and lets out a deep sigh. I think it's only appropriate that we're talking about fandoms and ships in a place that birthed one of my favorite television shows: *Roswell*. Aliens never looked so hot than on The WB.

"Lil," he says. "Let's just say, theoretically, they're together right now, doing…" The muscles in his jaw twitch and Wampa is a sad ball in one of his fists. "…whatever."

I could add evidence that they're doing *something* other than talking right now. Daisy had wild hair when she retreated from her tent in the morning, and I know post-sex hair. But just adding that fact will draw more irritated wrinkles by his brows.

"...then why," he continues, "have they not announced it to *anyone*?"

"They're scared of how you'll react," I say. And then I yawn. No one ever told me that being pregnant makes you tired. No one except Web M.D.

At my yawn, he steps nearer to me, our shoes touching. I didn't know yawns worked like magnets, but I'm liking it.

"Yeah?" He swallows hard and glares at the ground. "Then why hasn't Daisy at least told you or Rose, someone *else*?"

"I don't know," I whisper, thinking more about this. "Do you think they've told everyone but us?" The idea hurts a little. Sure, we've kept things from all of them. We all choose who to share information with, but it definitely stings being on the receiving side, the ones in the dark.

"She would've told you, Lil," Lo says with certainty. But I'm not so sure. It agitates him though—I can see it in his stiff posture. He hates that his brother would keep this from him. I worry, mostly, about Ryke's intentions with my little sister. If he's sneaking around with her, then their relationship can't be as real as something like Rose and Connor's. It has to be more sexual, and that makes me nervous.

I want Daisy to have the best guy out there. The one that gives her everything. Kissing in the dark, while fun, it's not the type of relationship that will last.

"Can we just forget about it for now?" he asks. "It's pissing me off."

"You're hurting Wampa," I point out.

He realizes that he's crushing my hat, and then he places it back on my head. His amber eyes flit over my face with a bit of longing, filled with more clarity than they have been in the past few months. I'd say: *now is the time to tell him about the baby*. But something dark swirls behind those eyes that frightens me. Pain that he has yet to deal with.

It's way too soon. The weeks are ticking down, but I still have some time, I think, before I start showing.

Lo tucks a piece of my hair underneath the fuzzy hat, and then his fingers brush the sensitive skin on my neck. Shivers run down my arms. I shudder and hold onto his biceps.

"I'm happy that you're here," he whispers.

Happiness is better than just *glad.* It's brighter and fuller and something I wish I felt more, but most of the time, I always sense it with him. "Me too," I breathe.

He leans in to kiss me, a smile playing at the corner of his lip. I may not get this kiss so easily. I try to close the gap. He quickly leans back and then plants a kiss on my forehead.

"Just take your time," Connor says.

I blush, but when we both turn our heads, Connor is standing in the middle of the museum with a phone to his ear. Rose sips an iced coffee and glares at a cheap cutout of an alien.

"We stopped in Roswell because Lily and Lo wanted to see the aliens," he says. "They spent four hours in the museum—excuse me, I mean the propaganda shit hole."

Spent. We're about to leave, I take it. And we haven't even reached the biggest exhibit at the end of the museum. There are extraterrestrial things left to be seen.

Lo wraps his arm around my shoulder and lets out a short laugh. "And you made us spend three hours at a graveyard," he says to Connor. "Between us, who's the super freaky one, love?"

Connor grins, that blinding white one, too pretty to stare at. "It was a war cemetery," he says to the person over the phone, probably Ryke. "And Rose and I were searching for our ancestors."

They were. The nerds were trying to find their once removed seventh-cousins.

"I won," Rose says, raising her voice so Daisy and Ryke can hear. She stirs her ice around her cup. "I have three more dead relatives than

Connor." They speak through their eyes now, something I've most definitely grown fond of.

"Follow me," Lo whispers, his breath hot against my skin, he motions with his head to the big exhibit behind a glass wall: an alien on a stretcher.

I smile and clasp his hand.

I want to believe that this road trip will end well, but a big heap of unresolved tension still pulls between Lo and Ryke.

LOREN HALE

We stopped at a gas station, not too long ago. The tabloid magazines were placed in a row at the check-out counter. The big bold print still flashes like blinding red headlights. I can't get rid of them.

SARA HALE TELL-ALL INTERVIEW LEAVES THEORIES OPEN-ENDED: INVESTIGATION TO CONTINUE.

She neither confirmed nor denied much. All doors and possibilities are still left open for belief.

"Lo, slow down," Lily says, sprinting to catch up to me as I storm as far away from the parking lot as I can. Red dust plumes in the air, my shoes kicking up the Utah dirt. A few couples scatter the hiking trail, and I veer off towards these red rock arches. My blood pumps full of adrenaline.

"I don't want to see him," I shout at her over my shoulder. I spot Rose and Connor following at a slower pace. Rose almost tips over, her heels caught on a rock, but Connor catches her around the waist and tucks her close to his chest.

She breathes with wide eyes, like she nearly fell off a mountain or something.

The other headline scorches my head.

**LILY CALLOWAY'S ADDICTION:
COULD IT BE LINKED TO SEXUAL TRAUMA
FROM HER FIANCÉE'S FATHER?**

I've seen that theory before on another tabloid, but being reminded of it—it tore something inside of me that I can't fix.

"Lo," Lily says, reaching my side.

"I can't..." I feel my cheekbones jutting out. In a few minutes, Ryke and Daisy are supposed to meet us at the start of the hiking trail. "He's *repeatedly* lied to me," I tell Lily, my bones throttling to march forward. Don't stop. I return my course, storming further and further away. "You want to listen to him, that's fine. I'm *done* pretending like everything is okay between us."

It's not.

It hasn't been since I broke my sobriety.

"It sucks," she says, rushing to keep up with me, panting for breath. "They didn't tell me either."

The last tabloid was the one that cut me the worst. The one I can't push away no matter how hard I try.

RYKE MEADOWS AND DAISY CALLOWAY CAUGHT KISSING!

Photographed outside of Devils Tower, a rock formation in Wyoming—she was on his shoulders, her hair chopped to her collarbones, with pink, purple and green streaks. Her head was dipped down, their lips touching, smiling.

They looked happy.

I spin around on Lily and she knocks straight into my chest. "What am I supposed to do?" I ask, my chest rising angrily. "Give him an easy time? Say *it's okay?*" I point at the ground. "It's *not* okay. I trusted him!" I make everything difficult for Ryke—being my friend, being my brother—but he doesn't see how much I've given him, how much I've let him in and how much I fucking loved him.

"Maybe you both can sit down and talk it out," she says hurriedly, reaching for a hand.

I take a couple steps back from her. "He had so many opportunities to come clean, to open up to me. To say *anything* that meant something to him." I feel like I don't even know him. Our relationship has been built off my addiction. He asks me about our dad. In relation to alcohol. In relation to my childhood. But I know absolutely *nothing* about his.

I don't need him to be a twenty-four-seven sober coach.

I need him to be my brother.

Connor and Rose join us, and I stand in place, glaring ahead. "I don't want to look at his face," I sneer. Because I'll see a guy that I desperately need in my life. He keeps me healthy. He's the kick in the ass that has propelled me forward.

It's why this hurts so much more. It'd be easier if he was Scott Van Wright or Julian. Someone I can just hate to hate.

His lies are like validations: *You're too weak to trust, Loren.*

You're just a little fucking kid.

Why would I tell you anything important?

"Hey guys!"

I rotate a fraction and spot Daisy waving as she walks down the red dirt, an unmarked path where giant rocks dot the landscape.

The sun has risen halfway in the sky, shade leaving us, sweltering my already boiling body. I watch Ryke approach, his unshaven jaw hardening the minute he meets my harsh gaze. Confusion coats his face for a brief second, and hate builds inside of me, prepared to launch it right at him.

My fingers curl into a fist. My heart is ripping to shreds. He just walks. Like nothing's wrong. It's my fault in the end, I remember. For trusting someone I shouldn't have. For letting him in.

I'm the real fool.

"Love the hair, Dais," Lily says, her voice spiking in fear.

They're nearer. I fume, my muscles taut, stretched to the max. My feet move before my head does. A target right on my brother. I aim for him.

Ryke stops and puts a hand on Daisy's shoulder. "Daisy," he says. "Go to your sisters."

"Ryke—"

"Fucking *go*," he growls.

She takes a few steps back, but she never joins Lily and Rose who stay beside a flat rock with Connor.

This isn't just about Daisy. It's so much more complicated than that.

"Lo." He raises his hands, already telling me to stand down. If I was *anyone* else, he would hit me. He would punch me. He would throw his whole *weight* into my body and pin me to the ground. I am sick of being treated like a broken toy.

I am a goddamn human being. When will I ever be worthy of the truth?

"What's wrong?" Ryke asks. "Let's talk about this."

We're so close. Ten feet away. "You wanna talk about it?" I say, my voice layered with too many emotions to untangle. "I gave you a million fucking chances to *talk* about it. I'm so done talking with you." I reach him, and I don't hesitate. I can't.

My fist pounds into his jaw. I rarely fight like this, but I just want him to put me on his level. For once. I knee him in the stomach, and he staggers, falling to the ground.

Ryke coughs, gripping the dirt.

Fight me.

"Lo, stop!" Daisy screams. She tries to rush us, but Connor grabs her around the waist and pulls her back with her sisters.

I can't stop. Penance—that's what I am to him. For all those years he never met me. I'm his way into heaven. Do right by me and all of his sins are absolved.

That's why he sticks around.

Something cold drills straight through me, and I punch Ryke in the face again. He turns his head and spits blood on the dirt.

"Lo, calm down!" Lily screams. I don't look behind me.

I just hit him again, my knuckles aching as they slam into his jaw, praying that he'll get up. *Get up.* And punch me back.

"Hit me," I sneer.

Ryke's fingernails scrape the red dirt, almost clenching into a fist. His gaze stays fixed on the ground, his muscles tense like mine. And yet, his hands start to relax. He's talking himself out of it.

"Come on!" I yell, my eyes burning, water brimming. "I've seen you beat the shit out of guys twice the size of me. I know you want to punch me." I step towards him. *Treat me like I deserve to be treated. Treat me like I can handle this shit.* "Fight back!"

He staggers to his feet, his face beaten. "I won't."

I slam my palms into his chest, shoving him hard.

He holds his hands up in surrender. "Lo—"

I sock him in the jaw. Again. He stumbles but stays upright.

"STOP IT!" Daisy cries, her strangled voice pitching.

I can hear Lily sobbing. It breeds more pain inside of me, clawing to get out. I can't back down. Not now. I point an accusatory finger at Ryke. "You're a goddamn coward."

His lips press closed, darkness clouding his eyes.

"You're so fucking scared to talk to our dad," I say coldly. "You're so scared to talk to your own mom." I barrel forward, and he actually steps back, keeping distance between us. I've *never* seen him do this. The aggression still exists in him; he just refuses to use it on me.

"What do you want me to say?" he growls. *Anything you feel.* "I'm fucking scared?" He points at his chest. "I'm *fucking* scared, Lo!" His eyes are bloodshot. "I'm so fucking scared they're going to manipulate me into loving them when all I want to do is forget!"

"What'd they fucking to do to you?!" I scream. I see Ryke Meadows with Sara Hale. And I see a doting mom. I see love that I never fucking had. I don't get what happened that's so horrible that he hates everyone *that* much. He just won't ever tell me. "I lived with *our* dad. You sat in your pearly white fucking mansion with a mom who loved you!"

Ryke shakes his head. Over and over. His lips pressed closed again. Why is this so hard for him? He pushes me to my breaking point every damn day. Maybe it's finally time someone pushes him.

"Tell me!" I yell, taking a step closer. He breathes like it hurts to inhale, a sentiment I'm familiar with. "Tell me how you had it so fucking bad, Ryke. What'd he do to you? Did he smack the back of your head when you got a C on a math test? Did he scream in your face when you were benched for a little league game?" Hot tears pour out. I am so close to him, with narrowed eyes, watching this brick wall crumble between us. "What'd he fucking do?"

He shakes his head again.

Goddammit, Ryke. I slam my hands on his chest another time, and he finally pushes back. I stagger but keep my balance, still standing.

"I'm not fucking fighting you!" he screams.

I grind my teeth and charge him again, hoping to knock him down, but his strength outmatches mine.

His forearm rams into me, and my back is on the ground in an instant. His hands grip my wrists, his knee putting pressure on my ribs, the couple that I'd broken. I stifle the pain beneath every aching emotion.

"I don't want to fight you, Lo," he chokes, his anguished face near mine.

I feel hot, raging tears roll down my sharp cheeks. "You spend so much of your fucking time trying to save me," I breathe, "and you don't even realize that you're killing me."

His hard, masculine face just contorts in pain.

"The news isn't just in Philly, you know. It's everywhere we fucking go. All the way to a gas station in Utah." I let out a weak laugh. "They think he molested me. The *whole* goddamn nation." Saying it out loud to him—the weight of the words smash into me, harder than any fist could. "People think my own father touched me, and you won't do a thing about it." I stare right into him, a question on the tip of my tongue, one I've wanted to ask. I never pressured him about the allegations. Never pushed him. Maybe I should have earlier. Like he's always done me. "Why do you believe them and not me?"

"I believe you," he whispers. Maybe I shouldn't trust him, not after all the lies. He could be placating me, afraid that I'm too close to this dangerous edge. But he wears a haunted look, one dragging him back to the past. This isn't about me. It's about the demons he's buried. It always has been. Finally, I think he realizes that.

"What the fuck did he do to make you hate him so much?" I ask, referring to our father. I expect another brush off, so I'm surprised when he finally talks.

"He chose you," he says with a hollow, dark voice. "He chose his bastard kid over me and my mom, and I fucking *lied* for him my entire life. I hid my identity for him. I had no mom in public because I was a Meadows and she was Sara Hale. I had no fucking dad to show for." His eyes drill into mine, filled with hurt that he's refused to come into contact with. Hate. For everyone. "I saved *his* reputation, and he buried me six feet in the fucking ground every single day he chose you over me, every day he paraded you around and shoved me aside. I couldn't breathe I was so fucking angry."

I find a real hole in his words, one that latches onto me like a parasite. "I thought you knew about me when you were fifteen." How many opportunities has he really had to come meet me?

"I told you that I met him at a country club every week. I knew his name. I knew he was my father. He was a fucking socialite, so I was smart enough to figure out that his son was my brother. They just didn't tell me until I was fifteen." His arms shake, not with fear, just pissed. He crawls off of me but stays on his knees, exhausted. His face is reddened everywhere my fist landed.

I stay on my back and stare at the blue sky. And I wonder. I wonder what it must've been like to be him. Alone, no real dad or mom. Friendships that mean less when you can't explain who you are.

"I hold grudges," he confesses. "But I think you do too, Lo." My jaw locks. I give him a hard time. Because I've been jealous of his strength, of the way people respect and trust him. Not because he showed up late in my life. The fact that he appeared at all is more than what I would've done. How could I keep holding that against him? If he feels any regret about that, then he's projecting it on me. Beating himself up about it.

Our dad has always been at the center of our grief, and I recognize how hard it must be to help a man that has shit on you, cast you away and chosen the bastard. I get it now. But I'm also a part of this mess.

A cloud rolls over the sun, and I say, "I just wish you could love me more than you hate him." I turn my head to the side, facing my brother's mostly hardened features that rarely break. My eyes glass again. "Is that even fucking possible?"

He lets out a deep breath. "I love you, you know that." He touches my leg in comfort.

My body tightens. "You didn't answer my question." Yes or no. *Will you stand up for me?*

"I don't know, Lo," he says. "I want to. I want to so *fucking* badly, but it's not as easy as wishing for that kind of peace. I hate him for things he did to me, for the things he does to you."

I sit up and wipe my face with the bottom of my shirt. "Jesus Christ," I laugh shortly. "You don't get it. I deserved every word he said to me. You didn't know me in prep school, Ryke. I was a fucking shit. I was *terrible*."

He glares. "Don't ever fucking tell me that you *deserved* it. No one deserves to be beat down every fucking day."

I feel like I did. Still do sometimes. I exhale, my eyes flickering up to his as I say, "He's never touched me." It's the truth. I know the whole world may never believe me, but I need the people closest to me to.

Ryke holds my face between both of his hands, his brown eyes boring into mine, flecked with hazel. "*Stop* defending him. Not to me, okay?"

He'll never love my father the way I do. It's impossible to even try to convince him. He just doesn't see the good that's hidden beneath all the bad. Or maybe, he just thinks the bad parts outweigh all the good.

I draw back, the tension loose between us. But there's still something left that we have to confront. I'm not leaving this desert with more things left unturned.

I gesture to the red welt on his cheek. "That bruise right there, that's for fucking my girlfriend's little sister by the way."

His lips part in horror.

Chapter 60

2 Years : 02 Months

October

LOREN HALE

"Tabloids caught you making out just outside of Devils Tower." I dig in my pocket for my new cell that I bought after the old one was destroyed in the riot. Then I scroll through *Celebrity Crush*, finding the picture of Daisy on my brother's shoulders, both of them kissing. I throw my cell at him, and he catches it in his hands. "The photograph is on every gossip site."

Off his shocked expression, I'm guessing he never saw the headlines. The longer he looks at the picture, the more his face settles on rage, his eyes glazing with this darkness. Then he chucks the phone back. It hits me in the jaw before thudding to the ground.

I pick it up and dust off the casing. "Pissed you got caught?"

He stays quiet. *Not again.*

I internally growl in frustration. "Please talk to me," I snap, "because I need to understand what's going on or I may just punch you again."

He shakes his head, his shirt covered in red dirt like mine. Bruises begin to form on his jaw. "It just happened." His voice is husky and lowered, like that's all he's ever going to give me.

It just happened. I blink a couple times. "It just happened?" I'm so tired of hearing that. "That's a really shitty thing to tell me." He runs his hand through his hair, red dust billowing. "You fuck Lily's little sister, and you say, *oh it just fucking happened?* What'd you fall on her? Did you add her to your tally of girls? Is it a one-night stand kind of thing?" My chest thrums in worry, in fear that all of this could be true. He's never said otherwise.

"That's not what I fucking meant." He grimaces and rubs his face with his hands quickly, like maybe he'll wake up and this issue will just be buried with everything else.

I won't let him. "Then what did you mean?" I ask.

He looks at me. "It's serious."

"So serious that you shared it with everyone."

"Because I knew you were going to jump down my fucking throat!" He springs to his feet with this fury, and I rise to mine, my ribs expanding with each heavy breath.

"If you cared about her, then you wouldn't be sneaking around like you're doing something wrong!" What am I supposed to think? He's an older guy. She's a younger girl. And if he liked her at all beyond just sex, he'd be with her. For real.

"Fuck you!" Ryke shouts, veins protruding in his arms and neck. "You've made this *impossible*, Lo!"

"She's EIGHTEEN!" I yell, nearing him. And even though his nose flares in anger, he forces himself to step back. "She's like my little sister. It wasn't supposed to be possible! But you didn't care. You still *banged* her." I trusted him. I accepted him into *my* life, and if he hurts her at all, it's partially my fault.

He cracks his knuckles, probably to stop himself from forming fists.

"Your cock finally got the best of you, didn't it?" I ask. "She turned eighteen and you could *finally* stick it in—"

"No, it wasn't fucking like that!" His muscles flex and knuckles whiten, hands balled into fists.

"I should leave you alone in this desert," I tell him. "I am *kicking* myself right now, for every time I let you near her, for every time I let you be alone with her—"

"You don't know what you're fucking talking about." He huffs in aggravation, but he never explains himself. I wait a second, expecting him to clarify. *I can't read your fucking mind, Ryke.*

"I don't know what I'm fucking talking about?" All I have to go on is what I see. And not all of it is good. Most of it is just inappropriate, starting from when she was fifteen. "How long, Ryke? Tell me that, how fucking long have you liked her more than just a friend, and let's see if it's all in my head?"

"I don't know." His hard gaze falls to the red dirt.

"I'm going to ask you *again*," I say, a tremor in my voice. "How long—"

"Stop," he grits.

I take another step towards him. "No, *how long*—"

"FOR YEARS!" he screams, blood rushing to his face, red and pissed and tormented. I don't want to believe him. Even if I have for so long. Even if I've seen it right in front of me. "Is that what you want to hear?! Years, Lo."

I wished that it wasn't true. That he didn't drag Daisy into our family. That girl deserves to be free from this shit. "You're lying?" I say.

"I'm not," he says, tears welling in his eyes. "I have been so fucking attracted to that girl. And I *never* planned on doing a fucking thing about it. I never was going to try. And I tried…I tried so fucking hard not thinking about her like that." The honesty pours out of him. "It was wrong. I knew it was fucking wrong. I suppressed everything as much as I could."

He liked her from the start. "Then why not stay away from her?" I ask. "Why not put a hundred fucking feet between you and Daisy? You flirted with her every day, Ryke. You became her *friend*." It sounds like a motive to end up with her, like he was just waiting around until she became the right age.

"I convinced myself that nothing would ever happen, so I thought it was okay to push further."

"You're a fucking idiot!" I shout. Seriously. The moment he decided to be a part of her life, it was over. "She was so hot," I say, "that you couldn't say no after she became legal—"

"No," he interjects, stepping forward with purpose and rage. "It *wasn't* like that."

"Then what was it fucking like?!" I shout, trying to pull something out of him that he won't let go.

And then he screams, "I FUCKING LOVE HER!"

My jaw drops, his words physically knocking me back a couple steps. I just—I scan his features, his eyes that plead for me to understand and scorch with emotion.

"I fell in fucking love with her," he finally explains. "It hurt to be away from Daisy. It hurt to watch her with other guys. Everything *fucking* hurt, and I didn't want to live with that pain anymore. I fucking couldn't." He takes a deep breath. "I can't tell you when it became unbearable, but it did."

I scrutinize him for a while, letting every single syllable sink in. *It hurt to watch her with other guys.* I spent years being the best friend of a sex addict. I spent years loving a girl who opened her door to every guy but me. And there isn't one day that I would wish that kind of torment on my brother or a friend. Not one.

So I say, "I understand, more than anyone, how painful it is watching someone you love be with other people." I pause. "But you can't really love her—"

"I've known her for over *two* years," he says. "I've spent so much fucking time with her, Lo. We've been through a lot together, so yes, I fell in love with her."

I look over my shoulder, at the girls. Lily has her thin arms wrapped around her tall sister while Daisy cries, wetting Lily's shirt. I turn back to Ryke, but he's still staring at Daisy.

His expression—it's beyond just caring for her. I remember him sympathizing with Daisy some years ago, in Cancun; I remember Ryke explaining how they were raised by similar kinds of mothers. But this is empathy reserved for one other person in your life, the type that some people may never even feel. It's just written all over his face.

No matter how weird it seems, this is how it'll be. I'm not going to separate two people that love each other. I wouldn't intentionally do that.

When he focuses back on me, he speaks again. "You can leave me here," he says passionately, "but I'll find a way back. I can't leave her, and I won't leave you, no matter how hard you fucking push me out." His eyes bleed with this distraught strength, an oxymoron that I can understand. I've had that same look in context of Lily.

"How much did it hurt?" I ask.

"Did what hurt?"

"Watching her with other guys."

He flinches back like air escapes him. After a short pause, he says, "It felt like someone was drowning me in fucking salt water and lighting me on fire."

I almost give him a weak smile. "Same." I steady my breaths. "I need some time." *To get used to them. Together.* Christ. It's fucking weird. "But I'm not going to hit you again. So revel in that."

"Thanks," he says.

I nod. "I wish you fell in love with another fucking girl." I'm going to wish it every day that my father attempts to use Daisy to get to Ryke. Just to try to patch up their relationship. It's something Jonathan Hale would do in a heartbeat. Maybe Ryke doesn't realize that yet.

"I'm sorry," he says. "I really fucking am. For lying."

I shrug. "You didn't want to get hit." What's past is past. I want to restart. Maybe we'll both have more faith and trust in each other after this.

"No," he says. "I didn't want to hurt you."

I know. "I'll get over it. Just…give me fucking time." I walk towards the girls who all huddle together, talking while Daisy rubs her eyes with the back of her hand. In his button-down, clean and undusted, unlike our clothes, Connor watches us with that impassive face, the one I can't read very well.

And I don't sense my brother behind me.

I stop and spin fully around, turning my back on Connor. The reddish marks along Ryke's eye start to purple underneath, winding my emotions. *I'm sorry.* I'm still not sure if he'll ever go to the press, to vouch for our father, for me. But I'm truly sorry that my existence caused him so much pain.

He lived the bastard life, in disgrace and hiding, all this time. And I didn't even know it.

He must read my eyes because he saunters ahead and stands beside me. We start walking together, towards everyone. And I reach out and put my hand on his shoulder.

He flinches at first, startled by the acceptance.

But then he rubs the back of my head, messing my hair roughly. "I'm glad you hit me."

"Why is that?" I ask.

"Not a lot of people stand up to me." Because he's intimidating, and if he wants to keep his problems hidden, no one is stupid enough to go up against him, just to let those things surface. "I'm happy you did."

"I knew you wouldn't hit back," I say. "And it's not like it was a complete selfless act."

He rolls his eyes. "Can't you take a compliment and not turn it into a character assassination of yourself?"

"Maybe someday," I say. *But not today.* I pat his shoulder and then drop my hand.

I'm more at peace with him now than I have been in years. It took blood and a hot desert, but we reached this place.

I can almost breathe again.

Chapter 61

2 Years : 03 Months

November

LOREN HALE

"Get away from the window, Daisy," I say with edge. She presses her forehead to the glass and clutches the door handle, peering out of the car as far as she can. But her view is blocked by cameras who attempt to capture us through the tinted windows. Paparazzi have swarmed my father's Escalade that's parked outside of the jail. Back in Philadelphia.

Anderson, my dad's driver, sits idly in the front seat while we wait for my father and hopefully my brother to return.

Not that long ago, Ryke free-solo climbed three rock formations in Yosemite without falling. All I wanted was for him to survive, and he looked tired but accomplished when he reached the bottom. I was proud of him.

And now he had to come home to *this* shit. Life sucks most of the time.

"I shouldn't go in there…" Daisy recognizes with a trembling voice. She wants to go retrieve Ryke from jail, but she can't do a damn thing. Neither can I. My father, however, has more power than us. We just have to be patient.

I rub my lips, irritated. Just at the whole situation we're in. "Ryke wanted you to go home with Connor and Rose, so I can't imagine that he'd be happy if he saw you walk into the jail."

"I know," she murmurs, wiping a stray tear quickly.

I wince, not liking when she cries, at all. I already sense a change in my relationship with Daisy since she's become my brother's girlfriend. She used to be like a little sister to me, but my obligation to her now feels larger when Ryke isn't here. Like I have to be a force that keeps her safe when he's gone. He'd do the same for Lily, and it's a role that I've easily accepted. I pat the leather seat next to me. "Scoot back."

Daisy reluctantly distances herself from the window, about to slide to the center seat.

"Not that far," I say before she reaches the middle. "The cameras can get a picture of you from the windshield." This way she'll be blocked by the front seat.

She nods, her eyes swollen from crying. Tear streaks are dried on her face, even her left cheek with the long scar. It's less red than it used to be, but it'll always be noticeable.

"I hate my mom for doing this to him," Daisy says softly.

"Yeah," I say, leaning my head back, "Samantha Calloway isn't a bright ray of sunshine." I think of all the pain she's caused Lily through this brutal silence and cold shoulder act. And now, with what she did to Ryke, who's completely innocent—

"No, I really, *really* hate her," Daisy cries angry tears, turning her head towards me. *Christ.* It's scary—seeing malice on a girl who's never worn it before, someone so full of life. "I quit modeling, and instead of being okay with it, she blamed Ryke and did *this*." Her phone is clutched in her shaking hand. "What people are saying…none of it's true. You know that, right?"

Yeah, I know. I'm also very familiar with defamatory allegations, being falsely accused. I snatch the phone out of her hand and scroll through her Twitter feed while she rubs her eyes.

@GBANews: Ryke Meadows under arrest for statutory rape. #BreakingNews

@PoPhillyFan12: #Raisy is dead :(I can't believe Ryke would do that! #TeamCoballoway

@Sucker3Punch: He's still hot imo. Why'd Daisy have to tempt him like that? #Raisy is dead bc of that ho.

@WendyBird_1: #Raisy is dead *cries*

"Raisy is dead" is trending on Twitter. I try to hide a grimace. Ryke and Daisy were one of the most popular parts of the reality show, for all the flirting that pushed boundaries but never crossed the line. I didn't think that their fans would revolt, not even over something like this.

"There's no evidence against him, Daisy," I remind her. "People will get over it." A camera lens taps the window, crowding too close. She barely even flinches at the noise.

"They didn't drop what happened to you," she says softly.

I stiffen. "It's different." There's an ongoing investigation for the molestation case, and they have family friends saying things like *Jonathan Hale has physically grabbed Loren in public.* Maybe just the back of my head. They're stretching what little they've seen.

"It's not the media that hurts the most," she whispers. "I just..." She tucks a piece of her hair behind her ear, the strand dyed pink. "I feel so betrayed by my mom." Samantha was the one who tipped off the police.

I shut off her phone. "Ryke won't be charged with statutory rape. They have *no* evidence, Daisy. Just concentrate on that." It's the one silver lining. Samantha just wanted to throw Ryke into the media hellfire, let them tear at his character for a while since he's dating her daughter. I don't want him to have to deal with this anymore than I want Daisy to.

"Maybe I pushed him too hard...that's what everyone says, you know? That I tempted him."

I glare at her. "First of all, you both didn't sleep together until you were legal." I internally cringe at the thought of them doing *anything* other than holding hands. *I can't believe I'm having this conversation with Daisy Calloway*. "And secondly, Ryke is going to bitch you out the minute you blame yourself. So rethink your first statement to him."

Her chin quivers. "No, I blame my mom...more than anyone."

I don't add what she probably already knows. This goes beyond Samantha being pissed that Daisy quit modeling. She hates Ryke's mother, so she wasn't ecstatic upon learning that her daughter was dating the offspring of Sara Hale. I don't even think Greg Calloway is all that excited about the idea. For the same reason I wasn't: Ryke expresses himself in an aggressive way with very few words. I wouldn't want that kind of guy dating my daughter. Not that I'll ever have one.

Suddenly the cameras break from the Escalade in a wave, rushing towards the jail. Daisy slides closer to the door and grips the handle.

"Don't leave the car," I warn.

She inhales sharply and says, "He's coming out!" Tears flood her eyes, overwhelmed and clearly in love with my brother. I can't deny that fact.

I only have an awesome view of cameramen with gnarly beards. I sigh heavily, wishing they'd hurry up. I almost stick my head through the middle of the seat, just to look, but my joints are welded together in agitation.

And then, the front door swings open. "Ryke, did you sleep with Daisy when you were on the reality show?! Are you going to trial?!" But Ryke doesn't climb in.

My father takes the front seat next to Anderson. Before he slams the door, he shouts back, "There is no trial because he hasn't been charged. Write that up in your goddamn papers." He shuts them out, drowning the noise for point two seconds.

Because the backdoor, nearest Daisy, opens. The cameras go wild behind Ryke. Yelling so many things at once and trying to edge closer to catch a picture of Daisy. She kneels on the seat while Ryke stands right outside the car.

"Ryke, I'm so sor—"

He leans down and kisses her, with the door purposefully ajar so the cameras can capture the moment. No shame. *Good for him.* Though their embrace is a little *much* for me. I have to look away when it's clear his tongue slips into her mouth.

My father is really quiet in the front seat. He keeps clearing his throat like he's choked up. I frown, what happened in the jail?

After another second, Ryke slips in the car and slams the door closed. Daisy is about to slide in the middle seat between me and my brother, but Ryke pulls her onto his lap. He whispers in her ear, and then she nods and rests her head on his shoulder.

"You okay?" I ask Ryke as Anderson speeds off towards his apartment complex or maybe my dad's house. One of the two. The paparazzi pile into their cars quickly, but we have distance on them.

"I'll be fine," he says, hugging Daisy closer to his chest. I notice that one of his hands rubs her lower back in a circular motion. He finally looks at me. "Dad has something to tell you."

My brows furrow, and I just wait for my father to speak.

He audibly coughs into his hand, definitely choked up now.

Ryke glowers at the headrest. "Dad," he says through gritted teeth.

And then my father rotates in his seat to face me. His dark brown hair seems grayer by his temples, his face more severe and forehead more wrinkled.

In one breath, he says, "I'm going to get sober."

My mouth slowly falls. I had to hear him wrong. "What was that?" My pulse kicks up a notch. *What was that?*

He rolls his eyes. "You're really going to make me say it again?"

I freeze in shock. I contemplate what happened, how he refused to mumble the words aloud with this back turned to me. My dad isn't a coward, but this is a proclamation so weighted that I can't accept it fully. "Yeah," I snap. "Say it again."

He sighs heavily. "I'm not going to drink anymore, son."

I scrutinize him for a long moment. And come to one conclusion. "I'll believe it when I see it."

"You and me both," he mutters but determination creases his brow.

Our father wouldn't do this out of the kindness of his black fucking heart. So I look to Ryke. "What'd you do?" I ask.

Jonathan answers first. "He's going to be a part of this family." He turns back around and I hear him say under his breath, "Like he was always supposed to be."

I read between the lines.

To have his son back in his life, my dad is willing to be sober.

It's a hell of a declaration, and I don't even mind that he wasn't willing to do that for me all these years. I just mull over the possibility that I may one day see the impossible. My dad without his whiskey.

Chapter 62

2 Years : 03 Months

November

LILY CALLOWAY

I have been included into the boy club by accident. No one noticed me except Lo, but he's not about to kick me out of my father's den. This has to mean that my invisibility powers are blooming. Maybe my baby is magical. The thought almost makes the pregnancy not so bad.

"What are you wearing?" Lo asks his brother with a frown. Connor, Lo, and Sam dragged Ryke into the den the moment he parked his Ducati in my parent's driveway, Daisy with him. The Sunday luncheon starts in thirty minutes, so I thought it was a success that he showed up on time or even at all, clearly putting effort into his relationship with my little sister. He accepted my dad's invitation even after my mom had Ryke thrown in jail. This was my father's version of waving a white flag.

Ryke making peace and putting the issue behind him actually eases a lot of tension. And I know he's doing this to try to repair the bridge between Daisy and my parents, the one that's been crumbling.

"It's lunch," Ryke says like they're crazy. "I'm wearing a fucking shirt and pants."

All of the other guys are dressed in button-downs and black slacks. "It's formal," Lo tells his brother. "I thought you realized that."

Ryke glares at the ceiling and then checks his watch. "I don't have time to go back."

"You can switch with me," Lo says, already unbuttoning his shirt. I sit on the armrest of the couch, watching my boyfriend shed his clothes. I cross my ankles, and Lo glances back at me knowingly. The corner of his lips rise.

Yes. I am very, very attracted to you. But my traitorous-self stops fawning over his defined muscles and sculpted chest. My smile fades. Lo frowns at me, but he's distracted by his brother, who anxiously runs his hands through his hair. He really needs to stop messing with the strands. My parents don't like the whole disheveled, I-just-rolled-out-of-bed look.

"Aren't you going to get in trouble for wearing a regular T-shirt?" he asks Lo like *what the fuck?* Seemingly, there is a flaw in this plan.

But Sam clears it up. "He's Loren Hale." Yep, that about describes the difference nicely.

Ryke's face hardens. He touches his chest. "And I'm Ryke Meadows. What the fuck are you getting at?"

Sam whistles. "You don't know Greg Calloway that well, do you?"

Lo passes Ryke the shirt. "What Sammy is trying to say is that I'm going to get special treatment. You're not." He clarifies, "Dad raised me and he's Greg's best friend. Plus, I'm not dating the youngest Calloway girl." Lo faces Sam Stokes, who stands rigid, a string of animosity between them. Faint but visible in their closed-off postures. "I got the best free pass while you had to jump through ten-thousand hoops. Poppy's money must have meant *so much* to you."

"No amount of money is worth the tests that Greg put me through," Sam says, his back arched in defense. "If you don't believe that I love Lily's sister—"

"I'm just messing with you," Lo says sharply.

Ryke holds the button-down, solidified to stone as he processes what this means. I have a good feeling that Ryke will be tested just like Sam. The question is: will he last to the very end or just give up on the idea? "And Connor got a free pass too?" he asks.

"I was trusted from the start," Connor says, busy texting, only half in on this conversation. "Not shocking to anyone." He grins.

"Maybe if I punched you, you'd be a little fucking shocked," Ryke says.

"Only because you always talk about it but never actually do it," Connor says. "What's surprising is that I haven't returned you to the pound. I prefer my animals with a bigger bite."

Ryke flips him off.

I spring to my feet and sidle next to Lo, my arm curving around his bare waist. I feel his fingers brush the nape of my neck. Lily 1.0 would have turned this scenario into a very, very sexual fantasy. Lily 3.0 has snuffed most of them out, but I stand on the tips of my toes to kiss his cheek.

That felt good. Even better when Lo wears a genuinely happy smile.

My body warms. Maybe I can tell him today. After lunch. He seems to be in a much better place.

"I know Greg doesn't like me, but I'm *trying*. Isn't being here enough?" Ryke asks.

"No," Sam says. "It's a small start, but it's definitely not enough. I spent *years* trying to gain his trust and his acceptance into the Calloway family. Since Jonathan is your dad, it shouldn't take you as long, but no offense, you're notorious for being with many women. I even questioned what you're doing with Daisy."

Ryke rolls his eyes, agitated, but has no reply. He takes off his dark green tee, and I train my eyes to stay on Loren Hale for a prolonged second.

"You have a tattoo?" Sam asks with a mixed expression like: *you're screwed, buddy* and *I feel sorry for you.*

I pipe in, "Didn't you watch *Princesses of Philly?*" During the show, Ryke spent many weeks filling in the tattoo along his shoulder and chest: a phoenix with some red and orange coloring. A black chain is tied around the ankles of the bird and extends along his ribcage, ending with an anchor by his hip. That anchor is in a naughty place, and he knows it.

Sam just realizes that I've crept into the room. Invisibility gone. "I never watched the show, no."

Oh.

Ryke puts on Lo's nice shirt and starts buttoning it. "So what if I have a tattoo?"

"Greg hates tattoos," he says.

"That's too bad," Ryke says flatly, "because his daughter has one."

Whaaa. "Which sister?" I ask.

Ryke gives me a look like I'm being dumb.

Oh. Right. Daisy.

Sam scratches the back of his head. "Word of advice, don't mention it now, or really ever. He'll think you're a bad influence on her."

"He already thinks that," Ryke retorts. "Just say it: *I'm fucked.*"

"Maybe you should fix your hair," I suggest.

He lets out a frustrated growl and tries to comb his fingers through the thick, messy strands. He's making it worse. "Stop looking at me with that face, Lily," he retorts, more nervous than I've ever seen him.

"What face?"

"Your constipated face."

I gape. "That is just mean."

"That was pretty mean," Lo says.

"It's the fucking truth."

I cross my arms. "You know what, I was going to help fix your hair, but I'm retracting my offer." I raise my chin in confidence. *Take that.*

Connor finds a hole in my declaration. "You can't retract an offer that was never stated."

I look at Ryke. "Would you like me to fix your hair?" He opens his mouth, but I cut him off. "I retract my offer. Ha!" I raise my fist to Lo, and he knuckle-bumps me. And then he kisses my temple. I got a kiss out of that. I try not to smile too hard.

"As fun as this is," Sam says with his phone in hand, not sounding as amused as the rest of us, "we better head into the dining room. Poppy just texted me. Jonathan is here, and apparently Samantha's not coming."

"She's embarrassed about what happened," Connor clarifies. "Good thing for you, Ryke, you may not have to deal with her for a while."

"Fucking fantastic," he says, heading to the door. I'm not sure my mom's silent treatment is any better than her constant, nagging presence. At least, for me the quiet moments have granted more nausea than the early weeks of my pregnancy.

Lo slips the green shirt over his head. "Ready?" he asks me. Lo and I don't attend luncheons all that much, but we decided to come to this one in support of Ryke and his relationship with Daisy. It won't be as hard with my mom here, but I still have a huge baby bomb to drop today.

I'm praying he'll withstand the blow.

LILY CALLOWAY

"Let's talk about the future little Calloway," Jonathan says at the dining room table, Sunday family luncheon in session.

"Cobalt," Connor corrects him, sipping his wine.

Jonathan's eyes flicker to the liquor briefly, but he makes no motion to switch his coffee for alcohol. I can barely believe he's sober. I don't even think *Jonathan* believes it, but three twenty-four-seven sober coaches sit on chairs by the door, proving that he's dedicated to his rehabilitation.

"Right," Jonathan says. "Whatever you need for your baby, Hale Co. will provide: toys, cribs, diapers."

After Connor learned about Rose's pregnancy on the road trip, my sister announced the news to the family and subsequently the world.

Television networks have been proposing a new reality show that focuses on the days leading up to the birth. They've turned them down, but the excitement from fans, family and friends is palpable.

I just have a strong feeling my news will have the exact opposite effect.

"I'm *barely* warming to the idea that I'm breeding," Rose says, pinching the stem of a wine glass, water only, "so can you please not talk about baby toys? The last thing I need to think about is a toddler smacking me with a rattle."

"The best part," Lo says, "those toys have my last name scribbled on the side." He gives her a signature half-smile. Rose's baby playing with a Hale-monogramed toy—that's a picture she would not accept in any universe.

Rose's eyes narrow icily. "I'd like to see the reviews on those plastic rattles. I bet twenty kids have choked on them already."

"That insult died in your womb."

Rose rolls her eyes. "Your insensitivity isn't anything new, Loren."

"I'm sorry," he says flatly, "I didn't realize that witches had feelings beyond satanic anger."

Okay, this is heading in dangerous territory. I pinch Lo's arm, and he takes the hint, grabbing his water to stop himself from going on.

"What happens if you have a boy?" Daisy asks from the other end of the table, with Ryke, Sam, Poppy and my dad. Ryke has his arm around the back of her chair, which may or may not be a good move. I can't tell where my father is concerned. He cuts his prime rib with a steak knife, looking to Ryke every so often in stiff warning.

Rose silently fumes at the question, her knife ripping into her salmon. She demolishes the tender piece of fish, and Connor rests his palm on Rose's hand. She slows down her jerky knife movements.

Rose says, "Then I'll try to get pregnant right afterwards, just so I can have a girl."

Connor grins, a blinding one. "I don't pray to anyone but myself, but I may make an exception, just so we can have a boy first." He wants lots and lots of kids, so Rose's proclamation is like his heaven right now.

"Your prayers won't work against fate," Rose retorts. "There's a fifty percent chance I'll win over you."

"It's not fate. It's science, darling."

"We'll see then," she says.

Connor's grin stretches across his face, and he says a word or two aloud in French and then stops himself. He rarely looks irritated, but on account of a certain someone *lying* about their foreign language knowledge, it has induced a Connor Cobalt scowl.

"What other languages don't you know?" Connor asks Ryke from across the table. All this time, Ryke has understood what Rose and Connor whisper about in French. So unfair. He's fluent in French and Spanish, for sure, from studying as a kid, per his mother's strict request.

"Why?" Ryke asks. "Is it that important that you talk in code with your wife?"

I raise my hand sheepishly. "I just want to add," I say to Connor and my sister, "that I don't understand some of the things you say in English. That is all." Everyone stares at me for a hot second, and I kinda slump in my seat, regretting that interjection. There are just *way* too many people at this table.

Connor tells him, "Rose only knows French, so that's really not the point." He goes off and adds a couple words in what sounds like Italian.

Ryke absentmindedly replies back in the same language, just as fluent.

Connor looks amused, like he's playing with a new toy that's built to test his wits. He switches to German, which sounds pretty on his tongue, but Ryke has enough of this game that Connor wants to start. He shuts it down with a middle finger.

My father looks ticked off, wiping his mouth with his napkin. I'm sure he wanted someone less vulgar for Daisy.

But my little sister hardly cares about my dad's feelings. She pushes her food around on her plate, more sullen since the jail incident. She just hasn't forgiven our parents yet.

Lo asks the nearest server to bring out coffee, and I realize it's for me. I've been yawning more than usual, and on the plane ride from California to Pennsylvania, I basically passed out from exhaustion. He's catching on. Yesterday he said that he'd take me to the doctor, but I mumbled a *no thanks* and distracted him with sex. Not one of my most noble moments.

After lunch, I remind myself. He'll learn that our new future will consist of an extra person. I stare at the white tablecloth. It's scarier when I think of it like that. How are we going to be responsible for another human being?

We've struggled for so long just to take care of ourselves.

"So when will you start showing?" Lo asks Rose, actually nicely. Maybe this won't be so bad.

"I already have a small bump," she says, trying to salvage the salmon she demolished on her plate.

"What happens when they find hooves on the ultrasound?" His nice streak didn't last long.

Jonathan cuts in, "Honestly, Loren, when you take over Hale Co. *you* have to be more sensitive to these things. The company has already been through hell and back. It won't survive if you don't care about the industry."

Lo grinds his teeth before saying, "Like you're so sensitive? Like *you* care about this shit?"

Jonathan devours the insult with a harsh glare. "When you're a father—"

"That's just it, I won't *ever* be a father," Lo interjects, gripping the table as he leans closer to Jonathan. My heart catapults to my throat.

I'm paralyzed from head to toe.

"You love to do the opposite of everything I say," Jonathan declares. "I tell you to run. You walk. I tell you to drink. You get sober. I tell you to lead my company. You start your own."

I remember—one time, maybe on our very first date as a real couple—Lo professed a similar acknowledgement of his teenage rebellion. But this is different.

Lo's face reddens in anger. "Get this through your head." Every word is emblazoned with power. "I will *never* subject a child to this fucking torture. I'd rather be burned alive than live knowing I put someone through this kind of hell." It's like a fist has torn out my heart, snapping each artery terrifyingly slow. And he just continues on. "So destroy all of those goddamn dreams of grandchildren." He rises to his feet. "Your Hale empire begins over there, with him." Lo points at Ryke down the table. "Not me."

He throws the cloth napkin on his seat and walks away, fuming.

I can't follow him. My haunted, petrified gaze is fixed on my half-eaten plate of food. Tears are submerged beneath the weight of his opinion. He'd rather die than embrace the thought of bringing life into the world.

"Lily," Rose whispers.

I'm okay.

I internally shake my head. I'm not.

I don't see how I can ever break this news in a good way. I don't see how *this* can ever be okay like I hoped.

Chapter 64

2 Years : 03 Months

November

LOREN HALE

"We're offering a solution," Connor tells me, sitting in the living room. For Christ sake's, every time we attempt to watch a movie, a serious conversation is somehow brought up. "It's nothing to be upset about."

I touch my chest. "I'm *not* going to live with you. You've been a great roommate for these past two years, but you're having a baby, man."

Everything has changed with Rose's pregnancy, and the topic is honestly straining my relationship with Lily. She's been distant from me since the luncheon. And I know it hurts her that we're never going to have kids, but it'll hurt even more if she's reminded of it every day with Rose and Connor's baby hanging around us.

I add, "You don't need to be dealing with our shit on top of that."

"You're not ready," Rose chimes in. "You relapsed only a few months ago—"

"I'm never going to be ready, Rose!" I yell, my pulse thrumming. "If you're waiting for me to be cured, then you might as well give up now. This is going to last forever. Not a month. Not a few years. I'm an addict. I could very well stay sober for ten years and relapse again. You gotta accept that."

Her face marbleizes. "And what about Lily?"

"I can take care of her like I always have," I say adamantly, but a pressure weighs on me. I've been doing a good job until…I don't know. Maybe when we returned back to Philly. After the road trip. She's just withdrawn from me. It's the worst goddamn feeling in the world.

"Oh," Rose says, "you mean when you spent *years* letting her have sex with different men every night." It's like a right hook in the jaw.

I can't even stomach that part of my past anymore. There is not a day that goes by that I don't wish I brought Lily into my arms sooner, that I supplied her with everything she was searching for, stopping her before she sought it with other men. That I quit drinking for her, from the start.

I channel the hurt that courses through me into something darker, but I notice the small bump through Rose's black dress. And I stifle a vindictive retort.

"That's your pregnancy pass for the fucking night. Whoever is growing in your belly is a demon. Straight up making you evil."

Rose holds her hand out like *shut up*. "I don't care about the baby. I want Lily to live with us, and if she wants to, then you shouldn't be fighting me on it."

"She doesn't," I shoot back.

"Have you asked her?"

"Yes!" I shout. *No.* I grimace internally, my hands shaking. I just haven't hand the chance, really.

"How long has she been gone?" Ryke suddenly asks.

And the bottom of my stomach drops. I check the cushion next to me, already knowing Lily isn't on it. "Shit," I curse. I shoot to my feet. Fear rattles my bones, vibrating every ounce of me until I'm filled with dread and panic. And the rawest form of adrenaline.

Just forced to act by instinct. I barely hear Connor announce how long she's been gone. I don't wait for them to follow. I run to the one place she retreats to whenever she battles her addiction.

"LILY!" I scream, jostling the doorknob to the bathroom. I pound on the wood. "LILY!" Fear has already begun to cannibalize my soul. Yesterday, she rejected me when I attempted to kiss her after the luncheon. I thought space was what she needed—I didn't think that it was this bad.

I've been so wrapped up in my own problems that I couldn't see what was happening. I cannot lose her. Not for a moment. Not for second.

She is the only reason why I'm *still* living this life.

I frantically try to enter the door, the water gurgling through the walls. The shower is on.

"Move," Ryke tells me.

I shift so he can slam his shoulder into the door. After two tries, it blows open. He barrels in before me, the shower curtain rings clinking against the rod as he yanks it back.

As soon as I see Lily, clothed, sitting in the plugged tub with the shower beating down on her thin body, I jump right in, the water freezing. I fit her between my legs while she trembles, while she clutches her knees to her chest. Water pours on us, soaking our hair, our clothes. And I hold her delicate face between my hands as she cries.

My chest collapses, every part of me screaming inside. I feel like I've broken the only girl I've ever loved. And all I want to do is rearrange the pieces and put her back together. I search her eyes that brim with tears, and even when Ryke shuts off the faucet, we both shake from more than just the cold.

"Lil, shhh," I say, her pain just tearing right through me. "You're okay." She clings to me like I may slip through her arms, pull back and leave. I wouldn't. I can't. Our love is rare. It's one I can't abandon, even if I tried. When she screams, an identical one rips through me. When she cries, my world rains with grief. When she loves, I truly, truly fly.

I have never wanted anyone else but Lily.

"I'm…sorry…" she sobs, her black, long-sleeve shirt sticking to her thin body. She buries her head into the crook of my shoulder, and I hug her close, rubbing her back. Warming her with the friction. This is catastrophic. Another Wednesday, where we both lie exhausted and fractured on the carpet. Clung to the fact that we can't live without each other, but beaten down by the roadblocks that say we should.

"Sorry for what, Lil?" I whisper.

"I meant to tell you…" Lily murmurs, coming out of her hiding place on my shoulder. Her wet hair is darker and molds her pale cheeks, sadness pouring out of her eyes. I stroke her head. *It's okay, Lil.* "Yesterday, I was going to…I got scared…"

"Lily…" I say softly. "…you can tell me anything."

"Not this." She shakes her head, crying profusely. I brush my thumb over her cold skin. "Not *this.*"

Hot tears roll down my cheeks. She could have cheated on me. The thought chokes me for a second. I can't think of anything else that would cause her this much agony and guilt. My lips are close to her forehead as she stares at her hands, like they're a gateway out of this world.

I take them in mine, lacing our fingers together. One at a time. If she wants to leave, I'm coming with her.

"You have to tell me, Lil," I whisper as more water pools in her green eyes. "I can't guess." I try to hold back more emotions, but I connect so succinctly with her that it's almost impossible not to *feel* every single thing. Like the flick of each nerve. Like fingertips to fire then snow. I am terrified of what she might tell me, but I am more scared of losing her. "Please…don't make me guess."

She nods a couple times, staying quiet. And then her lips part in shock and realization. "Do you think…you think I cheated?" Her face shatters at that possibility. *What?* I almost start crying heavily. I suck it down, my nose flaring from holding it back.

This pain. It's like someone bulldozes me flat. On the ground. "I don't know, Lil," I breathe. "You've been acting distant, and you didn't come with me to Paris, so you had that time alone…I just, I don't…I don't know."

"I *didn't* cheat," she says, her chin trembling again. She looks like she could punch me in the arm, like she usually does. But she has no energy to do so, no fight left for that blow. "You have to believe me."

"I do, Lil," I say, taking a breath, not of full relief. "But you have to fucking tell me what's going on."

"I was upset…overwhelmed." She rubs her eyes with her palm but the tears have yet to cease. "And I wanted to do things and I just thought…this would help." The shame builds as she glances between the showerhead and her knees, crumpled into herself.

"Just spit it out," I urge. "Whatever it is. Just get it off your chest right now, love." I just want her to feel okay again.

She focuses on our laced hands. "I didn't know how to tell you…I thought while you were in Paris, I'd figure out a good way to say it, but I don't…I don't think there's a good way. And I just kept putting it off, thinking *tomorrow will be the day*." She keeps rubbing her eyes.

Then finally, she drops her hands.

And she says with a big inhale, "I'm eight weeks pregnant."

I go cold, like a car impacts me on the right side. Glass shattering. The car swerving. Spinning. The airbag popping into my chest, knocking the wind right out of me. The shock and fear pummels me into a state without thoughts.

"You can't be..." Blood rushes to my head. My eyes fall to her stomach, the black shirt that suctions to her belly. I roll the fabric to her ribs. I mistook the faint bump as weight gain. Nothing detrimental to our lives. Nothing that could overturn us.

I finally look to the other people who've been standing in the bathroom. Ryke. Connor. Rose. *Rose.* "*You're* pregnant," I say to her.

"We both are," Rose says in a quiet voice, scared of me. Everyone is frightened of me.

Of how I'll react.

I have never once wanted a child. Never even considered it for a moment's time. I'm selfish, damaged and spiteful. No matter how much I love Lily, there are things about me that will never change. "That's not possible," I say. Though it is. With the amount of sex we have—too much and too careless—*this* could've always been an end result.

"The probability is slim but it's not impossible," Connor answers, his hands casually pocketed in his slacks. He's known this for a while. "Their cycles had synced up after living together. I don't use protection with Rose, and I'm sure you didn't with Lily."

"I forgot to take my birth control a few days," Lily whispers, not able to meet my eyes, staring only at her hands, the ones I've abandoned. "I didn't realize it..."

I pick up both of her hands again, and her tears fall harder. I squeeze them. "You could've told me sooner." My mind reverses back to yesterday, and I frown. What I admitted out loud about kids—I had crushed her and I didn't even fucking realize it. I go further back. Paris. I still feel that night like a deep scar beneath my skin. I was lost, and no part of me would've functioned the right way with this news.

She had eight weeks, maybe less, to tell me the truth. And all of them, I wasn't strong enough to handle it. I can sit here soaked in freezing water, clutching her in my arms, and admit that.

"I know you don't want kids," she sniffs, restraining the tears as much as possible. "And I didn't want to stress you out with this…I'm sorry."

The guilt slams into me. "Shhh." I press her harder to my chest, her legs clenching back around my waist. "It's okay, Lil." I never meant for her to bear a burden *this heavy* alone. Not one we should've carried together.

"It's not," she says, wiping her cheeks and then staring up into my eyes. Her big round green ones are glassy and reddened. "You don't want a baby."

No. I have never wanted a baby. But met with this reality, I only want to do right by Lily. I just want to fix every wrong that I have ever made. I am ready, so fucking ready, to defeat this.

To never face these demons again.

I am done feeling sorry for myself.

My fingers tangle in her damp hair. "That doesn't matter anymore." I put my hand to my chest. "We're addicts. You and me." I motion between us. That fact won't change, no matter how much we wish it into oblivion. "Maybe we shouldn't have kids, but we have the means to raise him or her well."

"And you have us," Rose proclaims.

Lily and I look back at the three people who've been the foundation of our healthy lives. Rose raises her chin with a determined expression like *you both can do this.*

And then Connor. He stands poised, with more confidence than either of us has ever acquired. I can almost feel it radiate off his body and flow through mine. His lips begin to rise, knowing the effect he has on me, and most people.

My brother. Ryke has his arms crossed over his chest. I think he knows, as well as I do, that I am nowhere near ready to have a kid. But the negativity has been swept from his hard, dark features. He has that same sturdy, unbending will in his eyes as the rest of them.

The perseverance to do anything, to be anything. To thrive.

Someday, that word will belong to us too. After years of coming up short, it's all I've ever wanted.

Chapter 65

2 Years : 03 Months

November

LILY CALLOWAY

The steaming shower fogs the glass door. We're in our bathroom upstairs, where privacy exists, and Loren Hale towers above me, the water blanketing us in hot sheets. We thaw ourselves after the icy bath, his intense gaze never shifting off mine.

Out of all the reactions I imagined he'd have, this was the one I least expected. But the one that I love the most. It's the one where he is indisputably committed to us, as a team. I wouldn't ask anything more from him.

My hands crawl up his toned back, and his palm falls to my bottom, the other cupping my face. His amber eyes fill me whole. He leans so close, his mouth pausing an inch from my neck. A cry escapes before he even presses his lips against me.

But when they close over the tender skin, I buck into him, my leg rising around his hip. The thick fog makes it hard to breathe, my body heating with the water and his touch, sensual and slow.

His lips meet mine, his tongue parting them, sliding in a hypnotic movement. I dizzy in his hold, and he raises my other thigh over his waist, lifting me off the tiles. My heat pulses like blood pumping in my veins.

He kicks open the shower door while we kiss deeply, my hands snug around his neck. He carries me back into the room, not caring that water drips off our wet bodies and onto the floor. All of a sudden, he sets me flat on my back, our soft, warm comforter beneath me. We barely part long enough to stop kissing. Every nerve melts, my heart oozing with this pace.

My legs are already split open around him, and he breathes heavily the longer he draws out the inevitable. And his hand disappears between our pelvises, my lips swelling against his. I can feel how wet I am before his fingers do.

I moan, my head tilting back. He kisses my jaw, and then he slowly, slowly slides his erection deep, deep inside of me. As his other hand returns, I grip both of his forearms, his palms on either side of my head. He rocks against mine in a melodic rhythm, and a groan breaches his lips. He rests his forehead against mine, his hot breath entering my lungs.

"Lily," he chokes as he thrusts forward. Again and again.

My eyes roll back the longer we continue, the higher we go. It feels like eternity, like hours upon hours and years upon years. An embrace that lasts lifetimes.

When we slow down, when I arch against him and our lips part in a bright, overwhelming climax, we lie on the bed, our legs tangled together. My head rests on his chest, listening to the steady beat of his heart.

"I love you," he whispers, combing my damp hair off my forehead.

I lift my chin to look at him, about to say *I love you too* but it sounds too practiced, not encompassing even half of my sentiments.

He sees it in my eyes. "I know," he says, lifting me higher on his body so he doesn't have to stare down. We're eye-level, our heads on the same pillow, turned towards each other. My ankle rubs against his leg, and his hand strokes my arm.

"Lil..." he says softly, but it's my turn to read the answers behind his gaze.

"I'm scared too," I admit. "We've never even been able to keep a goldfish alive. Do you remember BJ?" I ask. He begins to smile at the memory. I add, "He didn't even last a week before he floated to the top of the tank. I think I overfed him."

"He probably died in realization that you named him Blow Job," he says, his eyes light. "Though you definitely overfed him."

"We don't have the best track record," I conclude, "but this time can be different." We couldn't keep a goldfish healthy because we were too consumed with our addictions. We've done a one-eighty, so what's to say that this won't fall into place?

He stares deeply into me and says, "I just don't want our kid to be damaged like us."

My breath catches and it takes me a minute to collect the right words. "We can't live in fear of that. It'll cripple us."

He pulls me closer, and he kisses me so strongly that the air is vacuumed from my lungs. A head rush of epic proportions.

When we break apart, his forehead on mine, he whispers, "You and me."

I smile against his lips. "Lily and Lo."

"And someone else," he says.

And someone else.

I have many more months before I meet that someone, but we're beginning to accept this new world, a new reality where we're no longer allowed to be selfish. It's our greatest test yet.

Chapter 66

2 Years : 03 Months

November

LOREN HALE

I draw circles on a paper napkin at the kitchen bar, Ryke on the stool next to me. The girls are huddled in the living room, tension stretching the air. But it has nothing to do with me. Or Lily. Daisy has finally let her sisters focus on her for once.

Something happened. Months ago. A year, maybe with Daisy. It's bad. I can see it written all over my brother's face. Connor watches us from across the counter, drinking coffee from a Styrofoam cup.

The mugs are packed in cardboard boxes, all the cupboards bare. Everyone is moving back to Philly when Lily graduates, but we have no idea if we'll be splitting apart from Connor and Rose.

Ryke rests a hand on my shoulder. "How are you holding up?"

"Ask me again when it fucking sinks in," I say.

"That you're going to have a kid?"

"Yeah," I nod. "And I already feel fucking awful for the thing."

Ryke pauses. "He may not have addiction problems, Lo."

"No, it's not that." I stop drawing and point my pen at Connor. "Our kid is going to have to compete with theirs. It's already fucked and it's not even born yet." I selfishly wish they weren't having a baby. Then I'd know, for certain, that we'd have their undivided attention, their help with every misstep we make. It's going to be a bigger challenge without that. It's going to force Lily and me to take full responsibility. Maybe it's better this way, even if it's harder.

Instead of being sympathetic, Connor grins into the rim of his cup and Ryke is *smiling*. My brother says, "Connor's kid is also going to be a snot, so you can rest assured that yours won't be totally fucked."

I begin to smile too.

Connor is about to reply, but a painful sob emanates from the living room. We all stiffen, our shoulders pulled back in alarm.

"Should we go in there?" I ask, picturing Lily and her sisters in tears. But I remember how Lily hugged Daisy in Utah when her little sister was bawling, how she's been the shoulder to cry on. My muscles loosen.

"Five more minutes," Connor says.

Maybe that'll give my brother enough time to share the cliff notes version of what happened. I resume drawing boxes around my squares, the pen bleeding through the napkin. "It has to do with her sleep issues, right?" I ask, remembering in Paris how Daisy had a night terror. She slapped Ryke in the face without realizing it. I didn't even deduce that she might be having them every time she slept.

"Yeah," Ryke says softly. He shifts on the stool so we're angled towards each other. "It hasn't been just one major event that triggered her problems. Most nights, she can't even fall asleep at all."

I frown. "Has she seen—"

"Yeah, she's seen doctors for her sleep disorder, and she's been going to therapy for post-traumatic stress."

I go rigid. "Post-traumatic stress?" I'm beginning to realize that we only see fragments of people, and the pieces that I've been given create one of the most incomplete pictures of my brother, of Daisy and their relationship.

In the background, we can hear the faint sounds of Daisy crying as she talks. Ryke looks so torn up that he has trouble concentrating on our conversation and not the girls.

"Ryke," I whisper. I have to know what happened.

He takes a deep breath. "I guess it started after Lily's sex addiction became public." My brows pull together, recognizing how long ago that actually was. "Daisy was teased a lot by stupid fucking teenagers from her prep school. On New Year's Eve, she said some fucking guy kept throwing condoms at her."

I glare. "What?"

Ryke's eyes narrow. "They kept making fucking remarks about Lily..."

"Because she's a sex addict?" My voice shakes.

"Yeah," Ryke says. "Everyone wanted to believe that Daisy was one, would become one, whatever would fucking create a good story." Veins ripple in his forearms, his muscles tense. "And then during the reality show, a camera guy, not part of production, broke into the townhouse one night, and he went into her room and started taking pictures."

I pale. "Where was I?"

"Asleep," Ryke says.

I glower. "Why did *no one* tell me about any of this? It's been over a year."

Connor interjects, "It all started because of Lily's addiction." Guilt. They were afraid of saddling Lily with more and more guilt.

I recall all the articles that speculated how Daisy would turn into a little Lily, a future sex addict, but I never saw how it affected her. She hid it too well from us. "She seemed happy." I cringe. *Not happy exactly.* Daisy has always been sad, in a way. Depressed. I've known it like everyone else.

"She was miserable," Ryke confirms. "She had trouble sleeping almost every night after the fucking guy broke into her room."

"What about after the show?" I ask, staring off, dazed by the reality of how much our addictions have truly affected those around us. It's a double-edged sword. We need their support, but in being closer to them, we've only made their lives harder.

They probably thought we'd rationalize Daisy's issues as a reason to step away from them, to distance ourselves from the people that have lifted us every time we've fallen. Maybe we would have.

"Daisy had to move back home after the show, remember?" Ryke says, shaking his head at the thought. "I hated it because I saw how bad she was during *Princesses of Philly*, and I couldn't go into that house when her mom was home. So she was largely dealing with the ridicule by herself." He pauses. "And then something worse happened before she graduated."

Connor sets down his cup, and the confusion on his face takes me aback. "You don't know either?" I wonder.

"No," Connor says, his eyes like pinpoints on Ryke. "You never told me."

"It wasn't my story to tell," Ryke retorts. He's been waiting for Daisy to rehash everything to her sisters. He looks physically ill. "I hate even thinking about it."

Connor pours more coffee into his cup, listening intently with me. I have no clue what *more* could've happened to her. It already feels like too much.

"She had a couple prep school friends named Harper and Cleo," Ryke says. I try to prepare for the worst. "On their way back from shopping with Daisy, the girls stopped the elevator." He hesitates for a second. "Some guys had told Harper and Cleo that they wondered how many inches could fit inside Daisy."

I flinch back. "*What?*" I snap angrily.

Connor keeps his expression blank on purpose, which just irritates me more.

"They had bought a couple dildos," Ryke continues.

"No." I shake my head repeatedly, imagining just how this ends. I have met kids as bored, as cruel and as fucking stupid as ones like that. I have been the subject of harassment all throughout my adolescence, some justified, others without reason. I can taste the fear and the hatred that swallows my youth.

I would never wish that on someone like Daisy.

"She fought them off," Ryke says, anger swarming his eyes like he wishes he had been there to stop it all himself. "But only after they gave her an ultimatum. She could either put it in or they'd torment her until graduation. She chose the latter."

No.

I shake my head. No. "She lived in fear for how many fucking months?" Scared to walk the hallways, afraid that something equally terrible would occur at any single moment.

"She had six months left," he says.

I crash forward this time, my elbows on the counter. I bury my face in my hands. Six months. Post-traumatic stress. "I'm sorry," I immediately say. That's why he wanted Daisy to live in the same apartment complex as him. That's why he spent so many days and hours with her.

That's how they began to fall in love.

"I'm really sorry," I say again. "I should've known that you were only trying to help her."

"I could've given you something though," he says. "I was an ass about it, and I could've given you *one* thing to make it seem like my intentions were good. But I didn't think it mattered." He meets my eyes. "It's not all on you, Lo."

He rises to his feet at this. The truth carries a lighter silence, unburdened. I watch him pace in the kitchen, focusing on the girls through the archway. The pen busts as I draw another circle, staining my palm black.

That's about the same time Lily passes through the archway, the tracks of her tears visible along her cheeks.

I stand up, and she fits in my arms while I lean my back against the kitchen counter. Her faraway gaze haunts me, the guilt and remorse flooding through. Her addiction is the source of Daisy's pain. There is no other way around that, and it's a fault that Lily will bear the rest of her life.

"You okay, love?" I whisper.

Very softly, she says, "I wish that had been me."

I know. I kiss her temple and draw her even closer, her heart pounding against my chest. I notice each box in the kitchen, the bare counters and the emptiness of each room. We've lived here for a long time, and it's strange shutting another chapter of our lives together. It's even stranger thinking that chapter may not include each other.

And it just hits me, right here, the decision to our future. I look to Connor about ten feet from me. "Does your offer still stand?"

"Which offer?"

"The one where we move in with you guys," I say. "I was thinking…" And this just pours through me right now. I let the moment guide me. "…that we could buy a house with a lot of security. More than this place. And Daisy could live with all of us. I think she might feel safer than living alone with Ryke. And when the babies are born, we'll just… we'll figure it out then."

No one affirms aloud—but the look in their eyes say *yes*, a million times over.

Chapter 67

2 Years : 04 Months

December

LOREN HALE

I sit up on the weight bench and Ryke grabs the bar out of my hands, setting it back. He tosses me my towel, and he takes a seat on the end of the bench. We've been at the gym for thirty minutes already, no one here this early in the morning but us. Connor would've joined, but Rose had a doctor's appointment.

I watch Ryke stare at the towel in his hands. He's barely spoken since we started lifting weights.

"What is it?" I ask sharply, picking up my water bottle off the floor.

He opens his mouth, but he shuts it when the words don't come to him.

"Is it Daisy?" I wonder, my back straightening. I comb the damp strands of hair out of my face.

"No," he says quickly. "She's been better since we moved."

"How much sleep does she get a night?" I ask.

"Five hours most nights, less on bad ones." He balls his towel, distant. It takes him a long moment before he blurts it out. "I'm doing it."

I frown. "Doing what?" I rest my elbows back on the metal bar, my legs on either side of the bench.

"I'm going to make a statement to the press." He can't look at me. He just stares up at the fluorescent lights hung across the gym ceiling.

Still, it jolts me back. "About the rumors…" I trail off. I didn't expect him to make a statement about the molestation rumors, not even after we cleared the air in Utah. I could see that he had made a promise to himself, to never protect our father again, and I didn't want to force him to break it. "You don't have to—"

"I do," he says, nodding. "I should've done it months ago. The hardest things in life are usually the right things. I just hated Dad too much to do the right thing." He throws the towel on his gym bag. "When I clear his name of the allegations, I want you to know that it's not for him, okay?" He turns to me. "I'm doing this for *you*, and for me."

I pat his back, choked up for a second. I rub my lips as I process these feelings. It takes me a minute to finally say what's been inside of me for years. "Thank you."

Without my brother, I wouldn't be sober. I'm not even sure I'd be alive. His decision to enter my life and never let go was one that saved me. No *thank you* will repay what he's given me. But it's all I have. And by the smile that begins to lighten his normally darkened face—something tells me that it's enough for him.

Chapter 68

2 Years : 04 Months

December

LILY CALLOWAY

I hug my chunky knit sweater tight around my body, the wind whipping my hair as I step outside. No vans parked on the street. No one snaps pictures of me. The gated neighborhood reminds me of our childhood, not all of it good, but the unease sits beneath these temperate feelings.

It's a shelter from the media storm.

I pass a fir tree on the lawn, walking down the driveway towards the mailbox with quick steps. My cheeks rose in the cold, but nothing stops me from checking the mail every morning. I open the lid with giddy anticipation, and I spot the long tube and my excitement explodes into fireworks.

I pull it out like it's a dream.

"You did it, Lil," Lo says, heading down the driveway with a cardboard box labeled *Christmas.* One of my puffy winter jackets rests on top of it. He sets the box down and joins me.

"I can't believe that I didn't even cheat," I say, waving the tube around like a lightsaber. "Towards the end, at least." Although Connor caught me scribbling a cheat sheet on my water bottle label my very last semester. He gave me a lecture about not needing a crutch, and I tossed the bottle away before the exam. Without his tutoring skills and ethics, I would've never made it this far.

"Open it," Lo smiles.

I pop the lid off the tube and delicately remove the thin paper that contains my certificate.

"Now you're an *official* college graduate, Lily Calloway. How does it feel?" he asks, pride overtaking his features.

"Good," I say. *Really, really good.* It took me a long time to graduate from Princeton, especially after transferring there. I passed with a very low GPA, but I passed. That's all that matters to me. I look up at him. "But it's not as good as other accomplishments." Going through recovery, taking the steps to be a better me, that achievement surpasses all others.

He tugs my Wampa cap on my head, pulling the flaps over my ears for warmth. "Are you too good to hang out with me now?" he asks, propping an arm on the mailbox.

I lose myself to his amber eyes for a moment, and then I say, "We're the same."

His lips slowly rise, dimpling his cheeks. He nods to the box, telling me to follow him up the driveway. "I got us out of furniture shopping with Connor and Rose." He collects my puffy winter jacket and helps me put it on through each arm.

"How'd you do that?" I ask, watching him lift the cardboard box, the handwriting looks childish. Like...one of ours when we were little.

"We have to decorate that tree." He nods to the big ass Christmas tree in the middle of the yard. I told Rose it was going to look weird off season, but she shooed me and said that *this* was the house. She stood outside of it, hands on hips, like she once did with our sisterhood house. The Princeton one where our boyfriends subsequently joined us.

"Good thinking," I tell him. I'd much rather decorate a tree than spend hours listening to Rose and Connor digress from furniture to Faulkner to Shakespeare and scientific things that hurt my head.

"Want a ride?" he asks me, bending down. I jump on his back a little haphazardly, Wampa almost flying off.

"Careful, Lil," he tells me. He has to hold onto the box, but I have no trouble wrapping my legs around his waist and holding onto his biceps like a monkey. "Can you feel it?" he asks on the short trek to the tree. I feel him roll his eyes. "Not *it* but I mean him or her or whatever."

It's weird for me too. "Not really, not yet at least." The bump on my belly is a little bigger but not by much. He sets me on my feet, the giant brick and stone house looming behind us. Eight rooms. Even more bathrooms.

It reminds me, every day, that we can afford our mistakes. Sometimes I wonder if that's why we end up making more.

He squats and opens the flaps of the box. "So I was thinking," he says, while I try to peer into it. "If we have a boy, I know what we should name him."

My lips part a little in surprise. "You've been thinking about names?"

"I mean, yeah," he says. His brows crinkle as he looks back at me. "Haven't you?"

"Once, maybe twice." I haven't let myself revel in the good parts of being pregnant. But now that Lo has, I think I can begin to.

He rises from the box, holding a bundle of ornaments, plastic toy action figures with strings on their heads. From our childhood. We used to play with them during the holidays, plucking them off the Hale family Christmas tree in the den.

My heart speeds as he sorts through the collection in his hand and picks out a certain one. He passes it to me, the blue paint chipped on the X-Men's costume. This was his favorite superhero when we were little. Not Hellion, who appeared in comics in our adolescence. And not Scott Summers, who slowly grew into a man that he admired.

In the beginning of everything, he empathized most with Quicksilver. For being the son of an undesirable man. For being rebellious and wishing that life would just hurry up already. He's not perfect by any means, but that's why Lo loves him: every imperfection, every flaw. He is a hero in my eyes because of each one.

"Maximoff," he says. My tears brim. I flip the ornament over and see Lo's name etched into the back. He draws me closer and rubs his sleeve below my eyes. "Say something."

"I love it," I say with a laugh the produces more tears. *Maximoff. Quicksilver's last name.* And then it clicks. "Remember when we said that the best Ravenclaws are the ones who can cheer for the Gryffindors and the Hufflepuffs?"

Lo nods.

"Luna," I say. "For a girl…"

He smiles. "It's perfect…just don't tell Rose and Connor that it's because of them." He knows that Luna makes me think of my sister and his best friend. "It'll go to their heads." Very true.

If we have a girl, the origin of her name is a secret that stays between us.

I stare back at the ornament in my hand. "This isn't pretend anymore, is it?" We spent three years playing house together before we became an official couple. Lines between our relationship and our worlds have always blurred. Like one foot in an alternate reality and one in Earth-616.

"No, love." Lo tilts my chin up so I meet his swirling amber eyes. "This is real."

Epilogue

2 Years : 05 Months

January

LILY CALLOWAY

"House meeting is in order," Rose announces. I think she wishes that she had a gavel to bang on the table, but she has to settle for the less dramatic route. Silence.

She sits poised on a Queen Anne chair in front of the fireplace. With Connor in the adjacent chair beside her, they look like royalty presiding over us common folk. I think they know that, which is why they both seem a little too excited.

"Did you guys have house meetings back in Princeton?" Daisy asks Lo and me. Even though we all roomed together in the townhouse during *Princesses of Philly*, this is different. That situation was temporary and our setting was strict and guided by production. Here we have more freedoms, and that means learning to deal with each other on a new level.

Daisy curls up with Ryke on the suede couch, adjacent to the one Lo and I sit on.

"Yeah, but King Connor and Queen Rose never had their own throne," Lo says, his arm around my waist and fingers tucked in the band of my leggings. At least I wasn't the only one thinking they looked like royalty.

Rose narrows her yellow-green eyes. "When you detail everyone's complaints and suggestions and announcements, then you can sit in my chair," she says, waving a piece of printer paper, signifying all the work she's done.

"Or you can just sit on my lap, darling," Connor offers to Lo, the corners of his lips curving in a grin.

Lo laughs, "Tempting."

"Can we just fucking start?" Ryke asks, running a hand through his damp hair from his shower. Daisy's is equally as wet, tangled in a messy bun on her head.

All three guys went to the gym this morning, and Daisy joined them at Ryke's request. My little sister and Lo's older brother are flying out to Costa Rica tomorrow, and Ryke needed to assess her skill level at the gym wall. She told me with a mischievous smile that he wanted to "bust her ass on real rock" which sounded so dirty in my mind, and I'm *still* slightly unsure whether that was a hidden innuendo for anal sex.

I should have just asked because it's been plaguing me every time I see them together. Like dirty pop-ups. Right now, I keep my focus on Rose and her supreme posture.

"First, and most importantly," she says, "there's the issue about cleanliness."

Oh yeah, I knew Ryke would be burned by Rose for the mess he leaves around. And by the disarray of Daisy's room during the reality show—clothes *everywhere*—I know she prefers living in disorderly chaos too.

"Daisy and Ryke," Rose says. "You both need to wash your dishes or put them in the dishwasher. The sink is not a trashcan. Neither is the coffee table or the garage or the den."

"Fucking A," Ryke groans and leans back into the couch like he can't believe this. "We're not twelve, Rose."

I can feel Lo's grin behind me, and I elbow him to wipe it clean. But Ryke catches sight of it. "What's so fucking funny?"

"I've had to live with Rose for almost three years. It's nice to see someone else suffering under her reign."

Daisy chimes in, "Rose, I like being able to have this kind of freedom. Mom always got onto me about my room—"

"I will not be manipulated about this. Nice try," she says, "but *no*."

Connor looks impressed by Rose outsmarting Daisy, which really is a higher compliment to my little sister.

Daisy shrugs like *had to give it a shot.*

Rose snaps her fingers, regaining everyone's attention. "It's not a hard concept. If we're living together, clean up after yourself."

"What if I don't fucking want to," Ryke refutes.

"What?" Rose glares like he's offering another choice to a true and false test.

He kicks his feet up on the table to further infuriate her. Connor says something in Italian, and since Rose only knows French, I realize quickly that he's secretly speaking to Ryke.

"Whoa!" I hold up my hands. The room silences on impact, all eyes turning to me. Wow, that worked better than I thought. "Can I make a rule about no secrets in foreign languages?"

"Learn the foreign language and there won't be any secrets," Connor says swiftly.

Easier said than done. But I see the power in Rose's eyes, like she's accepting a new breed of challenge.

Ryke nods to my older sister. "Let Daisy and I hire a maid like we wanted."

"No," Lo and I say together.

Ryke groans again. Lo and I have already voiced our opinions on servers and staff, maids and butlers. We grew up with them, and this house, humongous as it is, already reminds us of the places we were raised.

Neither of us wants to return to that. To walk through the hallways, reminded of times that were darker and more sinister. Fresh starts and new beginnings mean changes, and I want to change how I live. Plus, we've been backstabbed and screwed over far too many times. I can't imagine trusting someone enough to allow them free rule of our house.

"You have a warning," Rose tells him before moving on. "Second order of business. The hot tub is not a place to fuck." Crudeness, but she barely even falters or blushes.

And then the realness of that accusation sinks in. "Who had sex in the hot tub?" I didn't.

"Well it wasn't us," Lo starts, raising his eyes at me, and he's having a hard time looking at the adjacent couch.

Oh. Ohhhhh. I grimace as a pop-up image of Ryke and Daisy screwing in the bubbly hot waters fills my brain. Erase! Delete! Ahhhhh.

Daisy's eyes are giant saucers, and I'm more aware that she's much younger than all of us. She's probably feeling that age gap right about now too. Something about us knowing that she's having sex with *Ryke* makes a layer of awkwardness sweep the room. Or at least, it's sweeping big fat gusts towards me, completely missing Rose and Connor.

Maybe their throne-like chairs have magical, immunity properties.

"Is this meeting just a way to bust my balls?" Ryke asks angrily, his hand on Daisy's head as she slouches. His fingers are lost in her hair, and I wonder if he's giving her a head massage or something.

"You're not broken in yet," Connor says. "It'll take you a couple of months, or a year since you always refuse to be trained."

"Fantastic," Ryke replies.

"Not *fucking* fantastic?" Daisy whispers to him with a bright smile.

He actually smiles back, and his eyes graze her intimately, reserved for bedrooms and foreplay.

Connor clears his throat. "The last thing…" His eyes land on Lo, but Connor's deep blues are filled with only seriousness. All the humor and banter dies right there. I don't think this is about dirty dishes and screwing in hot tubs anymore. "It's something that affects the four of you." He scoots to the edge of his chair so that he's a little closer to us. My heart skips a beat. "As you know, the Calloway's publicist is revealing Lily's pregnancy to the media tomorrow."

All day, I've been bracing myself for the firestorm. If the reaction is anything like my parent's, I'll be facing discontent and disapproval. Lo and I aren't married. He relapsed only a few months ago. We're not the bright and shining couple like Rose and Connor.

But I think I'm ready to bear the judgment. I've been through so much of it already that I can't see a future where ridicule tears me apart anymore.

The only snag in Connor's statement is the beginning: *It's something that affects the four of you.* If this is about my pregnancy, then why does it affect Ryke and Daisy too?

"I don't understand," Lo says first, his voice full of annoyance. Like the world is clawing at him before he has a chance to raise his guards.

"I spoke with a contact that I have from GBA News," Connor says. He collects many people, so it's not surprising that he'd know someone on the inside. "They have the exclusive rights to break the story about Lily's pregnancy. I called him to ask what kind of backlash there would be. I wanted to prepare you two." His eyes flit from Lo to me.

So maybe we do have time to put on armor.

"What he told me," Connor continues, "was something I didn't expect."

I wait for someone to crack a joke about Connor not knowing everything, but Ryke and Lo stay eerily quiet, their silence only intensifying the moment.

"He said that people will debate whether the child is really Loren's. Or if it's Ryke's."

His announcement drops an indescribable weight in the room. No one mentions a paternity test. How if I took one, the argument would be put to rest. That's not the point.

The point is that this is wrong. That I've finally trampled over the three-way rumors. I've finally moved on.

It's something that affects the four of you.

Ryke is whispering in Daisy's ear, his eyes hardened to stone. She stares faraway at the rug and shakes her head. "We're together," she says under her breath.

The muscles in his jaw tighten, and he rises to his feet. "Can we have like ten fucking minutes to talk about this alone?" Ryke asks us. "It's a big deal."

I'm frightened to make eye contact with Lo or to even move. My little sister is dating Ryke, and now people will believe that I'm having *his* baby. How many times will my addiction hurt her?

Rose stands. "That's probably a good idea."

In a quick second, Ryke holds Daisy's hand and they retreat up to their room. Both Connor and Rose exit into the kitchen, giving us privacy too.

I want to believe that these rumors aren't different. But they're ones that may actually sting both Ryke and Lo more than any others. They could affect all of us in new ways, challenge us again.

"Lil..." His voice isn't as edged as I predicted. In a deep breath, he says, "Look at me."

I turn my head to stare up at him. I read his features, the creases of his forehead, the flicker of hurt, but it's not as dark as it could be.

"Is this the right thing, being here?" I ask him. I don't want to cause Daisy anymore suffering, and if we distanced ourselves from them, then maybe—

"If I've learned anything in the past two years," Lo says, "it's that we need to be surrounded by people we love. And honestly, I don't think they'd even let us have it any other way."

I try to smile, but it's a weak one. I agree though. No pushing family and friends aside. We've grown closer to them through every struggle, and we shouldn't abandon that over a theory or a what if. We're all united together by these events, a team that I don't want to disband. Not now.

He cups my face, his thumb stroking my cheek. "One day at a time," he says, his amber eyes boring powerfully into mine, "that's how we're going to take this."

One day at a time. "Isn't that too slow for you?" I ask. The Loren Hale that I'm used to wants no delay on life, no drawing out the agony. He hates the wait.

I watch his gaze fall to my belly. And then they flicker to my features. He searches them like he's engraining each freckle, each piece of me. "Life moves too quickly," he says. "I don't want to speed through a single moment. Not anymore."

I cry into a laugh because I never thought I'd hear him talk this way. He brushes my tears for me, our lips only a breath apart.

And I whisper, "One day at a time then."

Acknowledgements

We are almost to the close of Lily and Lo's story. If you believe that we would've reached this point without you, you're so mistaken. You helped shape these people. Every day you supported Lily and Lo and wished for their happy ending—it was another day that made it easier for us to bring these flawed characters to life. Thank you: for sticking with us, for standing beside them, for taking this long, emotional journey. It's not over yet. Hold on tight, okay?

Thanks to our family. Through this past year, we've recognized how grateful we are to have you all in our lives. You don't have to read a single page to shout about our books, to praise them and praise us, and that means so much—that you all would be willing to love us unconditionally like that. Thank you a million times over.

Big thanks to Aestas at Aestas Book Blog. We can't begin to describe the impact your support for the series has had on us. You're a huge reason why so many people initially read our books, why we're able to continue writing, and why we are now living our dream. This is our promise to repay you with great books...or at least ones that don't suck.

Tackle hugs Siiri at Little Pieces of Imagination. Our friendship with you has made this experience so worthwhile. Whether it's discussing television shows, talking Coballoway (a ship name that you most definitely created), or flipping through Addicted series inspirational pics—you're someone we just truly love.

Other bloggers and friends we absolutely love and admire: Sue at YA Hollywood and Sil—you girls always dazzle us with your graphics talent and flatter us with your kind words. Sue, you have some serious superpowers, and it's making the world a better, brighter, more fandom-loving place. Sil, every taco reference and Cancun shout-out is dedicated to you. Jenn and Lanie—giant hugs are in order when we meet you two. Writing wouldn't be nearly as fun without having you both in our world. Here with you, we feel like we're always flying, Peter Pan style. Amy Fox and Bella Love—thank you girls for loving our books enough to gather people to talk about them. That is simply one of the best gifts we've ever been given. Ashley and Erica at Back Porch Romance, Perla at IB Teen, Michelle at Four Chicks Flipping Pages, and Amber at For Your Literary Pleasure—thank you for your amazing words after we publish each book. They not only put tears in our eyes but they've given us more confidence in our writing than you will ever realize. You've empowered us, and for that, we thank you so, so much. We're blessed to have all of you as readers and fans.

We can never name every person that has impacted us over the course of the series. The list would be pages and pages long. We hate excluding anyone, more than anything, so if you didn't see your name, know that you mean so much to us. Every time we begin a new book, we think about all of you, about which teams you're on, who *you'd* like to see as you flip the page and the best story we can ever give you.

You are in our hearts and in our minds. As Lily would say, *thankyouthankyouthankyou!*

Continue Reading...

LILY & LO'S ROMANCE

DOESN'T END HERE!

THE ADDICTED SERIES

CONCLUDES WITH

ADDICTED AFTER ALL

Connect with Krista & Becca

WWW.KBRITCHIE.COM

WWW.FACEBOOK.COM/KBRITCHIE

WWW.INSTAGRAM.COM/KBMRITCHIE

WWW.PINTEREST.COM/KBMRITCHIE

Join Krista & Becca's reader group

WWW.FACEBOOK.COM/GROUPS/FIZZLEFORCE

CPSIA information can be obtained
at www.ICGtesting.com
Printed in the USA
LVHW041140110522
718484LV00001B/9

9 781950 165988